A NIGHT OF REDEMPTION

THE REDEMPTION SAGA

KRISTEN BANET

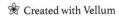

Overcome those who would see you fail.
Those who don't know you.
Those who do.
Even yourself.
Don't give up hope.
You are brave.
You are strong.
You are not alone.

GLOSSARY

GENERAL TERMS

- **Ability Rankings** - Common, Uncommon, Rare, Mythic. A simple system created to judge how rare abilities are among the Magi.
- **Burnout** - When a Magi uses all their magical energy and must consume life force to continue.
- **Doppelganger** - Magi with the sole ability to shape-shift into other human beings. (Legend)
- **Doppler** – Slang for Doppelganger
- **Druids** - Female Magi with a plethora of natural abilities. They take over large areas of uninhabited land as caretakers. (Legend)
- **Imp** - Derogatory term for agents with the IMPO.
- **International Magi Armed Services (*IMAS*)** – The Magi's military in case of war against non-Magi or an uprising against the WMC.
- **International Magi Police Organization (*IMPO*)** – The Magi's organization for tracking down Magi criminals across the globe.
- **Legend** – A unique groupings of Magi. They are of equal power and have the same abilities per

group. Incredibly rare. Many non-Magi legends have their roots in these Magi.

- **Magi** - Humans with magic. They have anywhere from 1 to 5 abilities and a magical Source.
- **Reading** - A ceremony after a Magi comes into their magic, where a Magi who can 'read' (see Ability Glossary), discovers all the Magi's abilities. This information is then recorded for the Registrar.
- **Registrar** - A documentation system for recording all Magi and their powers during their teenage years. Viewing a Registrar entry requires approval by the WMC. Magi are required to submit to having a Registrar entry made via a Reading. There are lists Magi can join for public use, such as lists of healers in case of a global crisis, also kept with the Registrar.
- **Source** - The well of magical power inside a Magi. It's two-fold in how it can be measured—strength and depth. How powerful a Magi is versus how much magic they can do before running out of energy.
- **Vampyr** - Magi with the sole ability "borrow" abilities from others. They can also become immortal by "feeding" off a non-Magi's life force. (Legend)
- **The World Magi Council (*WMC*)** – The governing body over Magi. A group of 15 individuals voted into power every ten years.

1

SAWYER

I t was sunny that day. At odds with the mood, the sun made people squint as it tried to warm up the cold December day and glared off the fresh snow. It made Christmas decorations around the city seem to shine and glow.

It made the city seem beautiful.

She would have enjoyed it if it weren't the day it was. If there wasn't a shadow over her heart. If it didn't feel like somehow she'd gotten dragged into an eternal night with no chance for a dawn.

"Sawyer, we need to get inside." A steady palm ran over her back, but the voice was shaking. Just a little. Just a tiny bit that made it obvious the man wasn't ready for this.

Sawyer nodded. It was time.

As she walked into the chapel, she felt a bead of unease form in her chest. She'd never been to a funeral before. She certainly hadn't thought there would be one she had to attend this trip to New York.

Assassins, corrupt politicians, fire, and blood. Those, she

expected. She hadn't expected to be saying goodbye to a man who gave her a chance. Not once, but twice.

"I barely knew him," she mumbled to herself, hoping it would help deaden the grief.

"It's okay," Jasper told her softly, leading her further down the center aisle.

They found the rest of the team in the front row, reserved for family. Apparently James didn't have any, so his will had said the team was his family. She was positive he wrote it long before she joined, but it still touched her.

She had barely ever seen him, hardly knew him, but she could feel how deeply and genuinely he cared for the guys. And that's what made it all hurt so bad. They were reeling, cracking under the weight of not having him anymore.

She sat down next to Zander, Jasper taking the spot on her other side. At the end of their row, Quinn was with Elijah, who was still wheelchair-bound from his injuries. He could use crutches for short times, but none of them wanted to take the chance with how long this would be. Vincent sat next to Thompson, towards the main aisle. He was expected to get up and say a few words during the affair.

It was quiet. Considering the hundreds of people in the chapel, it was so quiet. Not even the sound of anyone crying. No, the chapel was full of hardened IMPO agents, politicians, and soldiers.

It broke her heart a little more.

She had barely known him, but he'd only had his work. He'd only had the guys and Thompson, who she'd learned was an old teammate of his. He'd only had her, too, in a strange way. Her interactions with the men who answered to him peppered their history, giving them an invisible connection.

Sawyer would have thought it was her fault. Again, a

game, assassins, and somewhere in the background, Axel. Again, a dead body. But this time, blame was the furthest thing from her mind. As music began to play, serene and gentle, something angry curled in her chest. No, this wasn't her fault. This wasn't Vincent's fault, or Thompson's. It wasn't D'Angelo's. It wasn't even Naseem's, though Sawyer considered making it his fault several times over the last few days.

This was Axel's fault.

Just his name brought a rush of extreme hate that she hadn't known she was capable of. It happened every time his name came up. A rage that boiled and bubbled and festered would rise in her chest, as if it had always been there.

"Sawyer," Jasper whispered harshly in her ear.

She pushed it down, the rage and hate. Now wasn't the time for her fury. She hadn't noticed how cold it had gotten around her until it began to warm up again. Whispers were breaking out around her. The men of her team, the ones who filled her heart with every breath they took, were staring at her patiently. They knew. They had dealt with this for a few days now.

Ever since the WMC laid down their last order to her, the rage would boil up to the surface. Kill Axel. Become the executioner and deliver the justice the WMC had sentenced. There was no reason to catch him again. His life was forfeit.

Be the assassin they all knew she was. Assassinate the man who made her what she was.

She had known it was coming the moment she'd come to terms with him having escaped. Nothing prepared her for the feelings the order had given her.

"Sorry." She looked down at her hands, tucked in her

lap, hoping she didn't lose it again. Not today. Not during this. Her rage could come tomorrow.

"It's okay," Zander mumbled, taking her hand and holding it tightly. Jasper took her other arm, tucking it into his. Lifelines, grounding her, bringing her back to the present.

They understood.

A priest began to talk shortly after that, silencing everyone's whispers. They hadn't been all about her. Some whispered how much they wished they knew James better. Some had whispered about the placement of the team and Thompson, wondering where James' family was. Some just missed him.

The priest quoted scripture of a dozen religions, even some things not from any religion. Just well-written passages from books that moved people, probably ones chosen by Vincent or Thompson. Magi weren't a religious group. With magic, they all found it somewhat difficult to fall into one belief or faith like non-Magi. Because of that, she knew the funeral was probably strange to any non-Magi in the room. She'd never been to a funeral, but she knew this was normal for her people.

The priest, thankfully, didn't act uncomfortable with the strange reading he'd probably been asked to do. She stared at him in deep thought, trying to ignore the lamenting words of grief. The longer she stared, the more she realized he was probably a Magi as well. It would make sense.

She didn't know why she was even thinking about that. Maybe it was avoidance of why they were there, why she was sitting in the front row for a funeral.

Finally, Director Thompson was called up. She nearly jumped, not expecting him to stand up. Everything had been so still until that moment.

He wasn't crying. Stony-faced, he stared down at the paper he put on the podium, and she had a feeling he'd grieved privately. Now he just needed to get through this.

"James was my oldest friend. He was a passionate soul that dedicated himself wholeheartedly to a goal. The goal was always the same, tied to the one thing he wanted to defeat more than anything else: injustice. He couldn't tolerate it. He'd never been able to. The first moment we met in the IMPO Academy, I could tell he would either be the best agent in the world or the worst, and I told him as much. We were sitting next to each other for an Internal Affairs and Investigations class, the perfect place to talk about how he was going to treat everyone equal, from criminals to his fellow future coworkers. Let's just say he didn't make a good impression on many with that speech."

A round of chuckles. Even Sawyer couldn't resist snorting, covering her mouth to stop from getting too loud.

"But it struck a chord with me, and it turned into one of the most important things I'll remember about the man. Everyone deserves a chance, a fair shake. Everyone deserved to meet justice on a level playing field. No one got special privileges with him. We're all Magi, and therefore equal. I would always remind him it's much more complicated than that. Politics, power, lifestyles, and so many other things contribute to the world we live in, but none of that ever colored the way he approached the world and the people in it. If he met two wildly different people on the same day, he met them both with the same open mind, ready to hear their side and draw his own conclusions."

The Director closed his eyes for a moment. She watched him tap fingers on the podium, his knuckles going white as he stopped and just clutched it. Signs he was breaking down.

Then they were gone. She watched Thompson collect himself and continue as if that moment never happened.

"And he passed it on to anyone he could. Two men were offered the position of Director: him and me. After all the things our own team had gone through, and as the last two members of it remaining in the IMPO, everyone thought he would take the job. When he passed and I stepped into the role, I asked him why. He said he wanted the chance to truly teach the next generation the ideals he and I hoped to instill in the IMPO, ones that had been lacking. He did that with the same wholehearted dedication he did everything else. And I would say he succeeded."

She couldn't listen anymore, tears flooding her eyes. She leaned over, knowing the next part of the speech was going to continue with the impact James left on the people around him, and particularly, the two teams he'd been handler for. The two teams that gave her chances. One team that stole her heart.

Oh, she knew the impact James had on the world. She knew better than most, even though she had never gotten to know the man well enough.

Sawyer regretted it. She should have spent more time with him. Talked to him on the phone about anything. Maybe even told him about the guys and her earlier. Something.

Sooner than she anticipated, Thompson was done and Vincent was given the podium. Jasper clutched her hand as he walked up.

Her heart broke with the first words out of his mouth.

"He was the father I never thought I would have."

Next to her, Zander's shoulders began to shake and she squeezed his hand tightly. Jasper's fingers began to dig into her hand.

"He never forced himself into my life. I could rely on him without expectations, much like a son could blindly believe in a father in their youth. I know..." Vincent trailed off. Unlike Thompson, he wasn't keeping himself under control as well. Vincent always had control – but not today. Not now. She knew it was eating him, tearing him apart. "I know my brothers..." He gestured to the team. "I know they feel the same." Vincent took a deep breath before continuing. "I...James was a man who believed in people. He always saw the good, always saw how we could impact the world around us in a positive light, and guided us to do that. He always thought that the good a person could do would always outweigh the bad, if they put the effort into it. He knew what sort of team he had in me and these guys." He waved back at the team. Elijah and Zander, the known worst troublemakers in the group, both chuckled. "He knew we'd break the rules to do what we thought was right. I would say he was proud of us for that, but we gave him a lot of paperwork in the process."

More chuckles filled the room, a bright spot in the pain.

"And he let us make our own decisions and stood behind us." Vincent's dark, olive-green eyes fell on her and she couldn't break the eye contact. "Even if those decisions would upset everyone around us. If we thought we could make the world better in the end, he followed us. A father supporting his sons in their endeavors, only offering a kind word and a warning. He let us take the risks and see what happened. He picked us up if we failed and he praised us when we succeeded. He was just that type of man.

"His impact will continue to be felt. He'll forever be a guiding light in our lives, and, I hope, in the IMPO. I hope we can aspire to be him, to be like him. I hope we can continue to take everything he taught us and continue to make the world a better, more just place. A fairer place. A more equal place. A place where we can come from anything and try to do more, be more. He gave me the chance to fight against the family and life I had growing up. He gave my teammates, my brothers, chances to prove themselves in the world. I hope we continue to take that into the future. I know I will. I know my teammates will."

Vincent's eyes stayed on her. She didn't think he would say anything about her, but the message was clear. Not to her. She already knew. No, the message was to the onlookers, the grievers.

He continued for longer, but she was overloaded with it all. This was his last chance to say something about a man who had changed his life. It was too much for her. It was all too much.

The music came back as she and most of the guys stood up. Elijah rolled on his own, following them. She had offered to be pallbearer for him and he'd graciously accepted. It shocked several people to see her there, but she didn't mind helping James and the guys with this. No, she could pull her weight. Thompson was the sixth person, and they walked it down the center aisle, ignoring the staring eyes and keeping the march to the beat of the somber music.

The coffin was loaded carefully. While the funeral was smack dab in the middle of the city, James was going to be buried in upstate New York. They had a drive ahead of them and they loaded into a limo for the second half of this sad journey.

There was a heavy silence when the trip started, but it didn't last long.

"I'm upset James never had the chance to tell us a ton of

outrageous stories about you," Elijah said softly, looking at Thompson expectantly.

"Yeah, he knew some things," Thompson mumbled. "I wish our last teammate could be here, but not even I could convince him. He doesn't do the IMPO scene anymore. If it were smaller, maybe."

"Last?" She couldn't stop the question.

"Well, we have two other old teammates still alive, but..." Thompson sighed heavily. "One left the IMPO, permanently disabled after the other betrayed the team. Our Judas is still in prison. I haven't told him yet. I'm not sure I want to."

"Yeah, you never know what you'll find on those trips," Vincent commented, looking away from all of them. Trips to the prison. She knew she hadn't expected what they would find on their own visit to the Magi prison.

"I'll tell you one anyway." Thompson smiled wearily at them. "The time I caught James with another man."

It was Zander who began to sputter. Elijah laughed, the wonderful sound filling the space.

"There's not really much to the story. He hadn't known the fellow was a man until it was too late. There was a lot of alcohol involved. It was a Halloween party while we were in the Academy." Thompson was now snickering. "Now, this is where James would always cut in and try to tell me to be kind. The guy was nice and I liked him. He was a really decent fellow, but there was some cross-dressing involved that night. I still knew he was a guy. Not sure how James missed it. I think he was lying."

"Did he freak out?" Zander asked, looking at the Director with wide-eyed fascination.

"No. James always slid around on what he was interested in. He was vocally into women, but I had caught him behaving strangely on more than one occasion with another man. From my understanding, once it started that night, it didn't stop." Thompson just kept chuckling. Sawyer snorted into her palm, leaning on Quinn. They quieted down, something uncomfortable falling over the group.

"Who's going to be our new handler?" Vincent asked, still staring out his window.

Sawyer made a noise. Now wasn't the time for that question. From the look on the rest of the guys' faces, they agreed. What could he possibly be thinking?

"Thanks to the...nature of your current investigation..." Thompson shifted around, like he was suddenly in pain. He purposefully didn't look in her direction. "I'm not going to assign you one."

"Why?" Vin finally turned away from the window. Sawyer wanted to hold him. He looked beaten down and abused, with dark circles and redness around his eyes. His skin was too pale and washed out. He wasn't getting enough sleep. She could swear he had dropped ten pounds in the last few days.

"Because you were important to him, so you're going to be important to me. You're going to report directly to me until the time you all leave the IMPO, whenever that may be. You'll be the first team with the Director of the IMPO as your handler." Thompson sighed. "It's the only thing I could think of. There's no one I would want to place you with. James handled you solo. He had no other active teams. I don't want to put you with a handler that has another team. Plus, I can get you whatever you need. I have the weight of my position to help you. I think you'll need it."

"Thank you," Vincent whispered, turning back out his window.

"Tomorrow, I need you all at my office for one last thing:

his will. The lawyers are ready to get through the reading and sign everything to where it needs to go."

"Fuck." Elijah groaned. "Between that and getting a new place that's secure, we're going to be in red tape for weeks before we can get anything done about the case."

"Don't worry about that," Vincent said sternly. "You just need to worry about healing."

"Yes." Quinn patted Elijah's leg, the big cowboy on his other side. Sawyer wanted to curl up in a ball, remembering how she'd seen him on the pavement. There had been no reason for her to believe he was alive, much less able to heal. He'd been bent and broken, twisted like one of the pieces of metal from the SUV.

It haunted her. Thanks to that, her mind kept going back to Quinn in the Amazon, and Jasper without his leg for the first time.

They had all been so broken and hurt, and it wasn't over. They were still trying to put it all back together, and yet their future hung over their heads. A job.

A hit.

She needed to get through this without thinking about it more. She knew she couldn't let the rage come back up, not yet.

The talking died off and they arrived at the cemetery in dead silence. They helped get the casket over the grave and onto the crazy lift used to lower it down into the freshly dug hole.

The priest said a few more words and they began putting flowers on it.

And sooner than she expected, it was over. They watched the casket being lowered, and it was done.

The other mourners began to leave until it was just Thompson and the team. She started to get uncomfortable once more. Again, she was hit with the fact that she had never gone to a funeral before. How did someone leave without feeling like they were leaving someone important behind? How did someone tell others it was time to go?

Thompson left first, without a word. She knew he wasn't going to go far. They all had to go back to the city together. She couldn't stay longer. She was amazed she'd stayed as long as she had.

"Take your time," she mumbled to them. She touched the closest one to her on the arm - Quinn. He'd been amazingly silent through it all. Since the moment she broke the news, since his initial breakdown. There had never been any tears, but she knew it hurt him.

"Stay close to Thompson," he ordered softly, glancing at her. She nodded in agreement. For her safety. The team had guards, a protection detail, thanks to Thompson, just for this. They were discreet, thankfully, had done well to disappear during the service, but there was reason to believe things could get ugly again at any moment. With Axel out, the team's safety wasn't secure. She knew from experience that the man was good at surprises.

She walked away quickly, trying not to look at the other gravestones. The moment she could see Thompson and one of the guards talking in the parking lot, she blinked the rest of the way. It made the guard jump, since she appeared right in his line of sight. Thompson didn't spook, though. He turned to see what had freaked out the IMAS soldier and waved a hand for her to come closer.

It was odd. She did step closer and he grabbed her, an arm over her shoulder in a somewhat possessive manner. In some ways, she knew Thompson better than she ever knew James. She spent more time with the Director, and even that was only a few short encounters.

But she had saved his life. That was something they both knew. He was the first person who spoke to her when the WMC gave her their decision. He'd been furious. They hadn't told him what was going to happen. She had already guessed. Even if they hadn't set her to the task, she had been preparing for it the moment she knew he was out.

"You seem more put together than them," he noted softly. "How are you, really?"

"I've never been to a funeral, but I've lost people. It's okay. It's not, but…I have personal experience knowing that it will be." She didn't try to pull away.

He nodded slowly. "If you need anything, any help with them or on your own, let me know."

"How are you?" She needed the attention off of her.

"My oldest friend was just laid to rest, but I also have an organization to run. Just like you have a…"

"Yeah."

The IMAS soldier stared at them strangely. Thompson waved him away and just kept holding her as they watched the guys stand next to James' grave.

"When do we tell them it's time to go?" she asked softly.

"When they're ready. Though if we need to drag one or two away, I'll need your help. It's possible."

It felt like an eternity before Quinn took the back of Elijah's wheelchair and began to leave.

"I never read the report on his injuries," Thompson said, and she knew he was fishing.

"The accident broke his back in two places," she answered. She hadn't yet vocalized the words. Saying it made it seem so real, even though nothing got more real than seeing it, being there. She couldn't even bring herself to say all of it. "The internal damage is just bruises now, but that's the reason he's still in the wheelchair."

"Is he doing physical therapy?"

"Yeah. Once a day, along with Zander pumping a little more magic into the healing. The problem is, so much magic has already been used that his body needs to make the last couple of steps itself. Just time and rebuilding the strength at this point."

"Of course. I'm glad he's healing. James was so worried-"

"I know." Her throat tightened.

"About both of you," he finished, tightening his hold on her. "Sawyer, if you need anything, please tell me. Please. I know they are all grieving and need time, and that leaves you in a strange place."

"I'm grieving too," she reminded him.

"You are, but you're a lot like me. And Vincent. I'll help you stop him from working himself to death." He eyed her, not continuing as Quinn and Elijah got closer. Neither of that pair said anything as they slowed and stopped next to her and Thompson. Elijah grabbed her hand and squeezed.

And slowly, the group continued to grow until it was only Vincent standing out there, staring at the grave. None of them said anything, or made any move to go get him until Thompson tried.

She grabbed him. "I got it," she whispered.

This was something she needed to do. She walked back out to Vincent, who didn't turn to look at her. She reached out and touched his shoulder as gently as she could.

Even that made him jump and spin. His eyes looked wild. It was the most startling thing. How wild and angry his eyes looked. "What?" he demanded.

"It's time to go, Vincent."

He looked stricken and turned back to the grave without saying anything. He wrapped his arms around himself.

She stepped closer, wrapping her arm around his waist.

"It's time to go," she repeated in a murmur, trying not to be forceful.

"I'm not ready."

"You never will be." It was a simple truth. No one was ever ready to say goodbye like this. The person just had to be strong enough to keep moving forward.

"This is Axel's fault," he growled.

"Abstractly, yes. He wasn't the one who did it, though." Right now, that distinction seemed important. "The woman who killed him is dead as well. He went down a hero, Vincent. He saved a lot of people."

"You don't need to tell me that," he snapped, glaring back at her like she offended him. "This is his fault, abstractly or not. Whether James is a hero or not. My brother-"

"Is going to die very soon, too," she snapped back. "Don't forget that." She never would, since she was the one tasked with the job. Since she was the one who fully intended to deliver that final blow.

Scars. Every kill was a scar on her soul, but she was willing to take them now more than ever. She would take all those scars on her soul to keep the people she loved alive. Her approach to death-dealing, her mindset about it, had changed over the last months.

That wiped all the emotion off his face. Then it began to turn green. She pulled him close, his head slamming into her shoulder. She felt guilty for reminding him of it at that moment, but knew it had to be done.

And finally, the tears came.

He was grieving a father figure. He was scared and running on fumes. He was in so much pain; she knew he didn't know how to cope with it.

She could feel his fingers digging into her back. She had

known this was going to come. It was bound to happen eventually. "I love you," she whispered. "We can do this. One step at a time, Vincent."

"And what's the first step?" he asked, groggy and depressed.

"Leaving," she answered.

He pulled back and glanced once more at James' grave. Then he nodded, holding out an arm. She smiled weakly, taking it. They hooked elbows and took the first step.

"What's the next step?" he asked softly, his emotion level dropping.

"We go back to the condo. We eat something and get some deep sleep."

"And tomorrow is the will reading." He sighed. "When in there do I start helping you hunt Axel?"

"After we know our family has a place to live." She kept moving them forward. He nodded again for her. "We can't rush this. Not now. We have to make sure Elijah is okay. We need a new home. We can't keep Sombra and the wolves cooped up in the condo. We have a lot of work to do."

"Of course."

"You did really well today." She tried to make it sound casual.

He leaned and she felt his lips press against her cheek. "What's after that?"

She considered that. There were some things they could get started now that would only help them in the future. She needed to give him goals to reach. "We need to set up alerts on the Dark Web. Anything relating to Axel or anyone close to him. It's something I can work with Jasper and Zander on. I know it like the back of my hand, though they might go through new channels since my identity is outed and the world knows I'm on the other team now."

"And?"

"We need a list of all properties he's ever used. I know several. You probably know all of the places that mean something to him on a personal level."

"Yes. Good thinking."

He sounded so professional. They drew closer to the group and Zander opened the door to the limo. Quinn helped Elijah in first and they all piled in after. She stayed glued to Vincent's side. She had a sneaking suspicion she was needed there.

She had to hold these grieving men together. The pain wasn't over yet. She glanced at Elijah. He knew. He knew how to keep moving forward. So did Quinn. And Jasper, someone she knew better than to forget. He started moving forward the moment the news hit, trying to help the rest of them.

Her men were so strong, but she still felt the indescribable need to hold them.

Something about all of this felt like it could break them apart, and that was something she would not tolerate.

2

ELIJAH

Elijah stayed quiet on the trip back into the city. The funeral was now behind them. He hated funerals, but he understood the need for them. A chance to put someone to rest, a chance to openly grieve and let loose the pain of losing them. He'd needed it, even though he hated it.

He'd needed it, since he didn't have what his teammates had. He had been in a stupor, drugged and hazy when the news came. He'd had no chance to process it until everyone else was well into their own grief. Quinn had noticed and helped him, explaining that Zander had knocked him out so he could come to the grief with a clear head.

He'd understood the reasoning, but it hadn't helped him with dealing with the pain. James was gone.

"Do you want to walk inside?" Quinn asked him carefully, eyeing him as the limo came to a stop in front of the building. Elijah looked up and nodded. He was tired of the wheelchair but he knew why he had to use it. In a few more weeks, he would be free to work out like he normally did again. He just needed to play it carefully as Zander walked him through physical therapy.

"Yeah, I can manage getting to the elevator and into the condo." He got out on his own, trying to ignore the stiffness in his back. There was no more nerve damage and the vertebrae were fully healed, but his muscles needed more time.

None of them really spoke as they huddled in the elevator together. Sawyer was the only one who took the time to say goodbye to the Director. Elijah wanted to feel bad for not saying anything, but he couldn't bring his mouth to open anymore. Not for platitudes and social courtesies, anyway. He'd leave that to her.

Vincent unlocked the door and held it open so they could all shuffle in.

And it hit Elijah again.

The tightening of his chest. The pain.

There were too many memories in the condo. Too much of James and the years he'd obviously lived in the place.

"Did something happen in here while we were gone?" Zander demanded, looking around ahead of the rest of them. "Did someone break in? Get that fucking security team-"

"The lawyers came while we were at the funeral to take anything important to the will," Jasper reminded him. "Nothing was stolen, Zander."

"Yeah, Sombra just hid out in the guest bedroom with the wolves during their visit. They didn't let them touch our stuff." Sawyer went into the living room and sat down on the couch. "Quinn, did you warn them?"

"I warned the animals. I got to meet the lawyers beforehand so I could judge their threat level and let them know our bonds would be staying here. Vincent, where's Kaar?"

"Outside flying. He can't handle the feelings in the condo anymore," Vincent answered softly, walking into the kitchen.

Elijah sat down slowly next to Sawyer, wrapping an arm around her. He was immensely pleased when she leaned into him, her head going onto his shoulder. It felt good.

"Say it again," he whispered to her. He was put out that the first time he'd heard the words was on the edge of dying. He had really thought he was dead and so was she. So he kept asking her, pretending that he needed the reminder. That he couldn't remember it, clear as day, even though he could.

"I love you," she murmured.

"Just checking," he teased gently.

"I'm going to give you real memory loss if you keep treating it like a joke," she ribbed back.

He chuckled, glad for the threat. It was normal. It was so wonderfully them, and it showed him everything could go back to the perfect they had before. The only thing that would be missing was the man they had relied on without ever telling him how much he meant. The only thing they couldn't get back was James.

His chest tightened again. He willed it to relax. He willed himself to keep breathing. He knew this pain. He could get through it. He knew Quinn was doing the same thing. He had a feeling they all were.

Sawyer began to play with her cellphone, pulling away from him. A moment later, she stood up and went out on the patio. He could see her on the phone now. He wondered who she could possibly be calling. He could count the people she knew well enough to call on both hands.

"I mean, they didn't need to take his stuff," Zander complained, looking distraught. "It's not theirs. It belongs here. In his space. And I..."

"Zander, it's okay. You know that it's probably all going to go to Thompson. They're just doing legally what they have to. It's okay." Jasper raised his hands, trying to calm Zander down. Elijah knew what his problem was.

"He knows we won't steal it!" Zander pointed at the now blank spots where pictures used to hang. "Why would they take those down? This is his space..."

He wanted the condo to be just like James had left it. A psychological way to keep the person in their lives forever. Maybe he would walk through that door one day and everything would be just how he left it.

Elijah groaned, closing his eyes and leaning back on the couch. Someone turned the TV on and sat next to him. He peeked warily.

"I can't deal with Zander right now," Jasper mumbled.

"Yeah," Elijah sighed in sympathy. "He'll be okay. He doesn't handle this level of change well."

"Don't I know it," Jasper muttered with a bite Elijah hadn't expected.

A fracture was appearing between them. They were the two oldest friends on the team, and their different ways of grieving were causing a rift.

Elijah frowned and placed a hand on Jasper's shoulder. "I'll talk to him later, but don't hold this against him. He's like the rest of us, not thinking clearly." He knew Zander could be annoying, immature, and a downright pain in the ass, but this? This was abnormal, and caused from a pain so deep none of them could make it through alone. This wasn't something he should be judged for. This was something they needed each other for. They couldn't start falling apart now.

Sawyer walked back in quickly, shoving her phone in her pocket. He watched her make a straight shot for Zander, grabbing him when he was in arm's reach.

Elijah watched the temperamental redhead fall apart the moment her arms were around him. "This is his space," Zander cried softly.

"Was, Zander. He's gone, baby. He doesn't care anymore about the pictures on the wall. It's okay." She said it quickly, just holding him. Elijah felt tears flood from the back of his eyes, that pressure he knew they were all trying to push back constantly. "It's okay. Just breathe. Zander, just breathe for me."

And he did. Elijah could hear Zander's gut-wrenching attempts to do that. Breathe. Every single one became a sob.

Zander had a lot of problems, but there was one thing they all knew and even respected about him. He felt deeply. He felt fully and without reservation. It led to recklessness and rash behavior, but the man was honest about everything going on with his heart and it was admirable.

"That's it," she murmured. "It's going to be okay. We're all here with you. I'm here with you. He's not hurting. He's not in pain. He doesn't care about the pictures anymore. You don't need to worry about that. It's okay."

None of them could do anything except watch the scene unfold. Sombra belly-crawled slowly closer to her Magi and the man. Finally, she bumped her head to Zander's leg. Zander pulled away and looked down, giving a very weak and shaky smile. His eyes were red and tear-swollen.

And for a moment, things looked better. He scratched the big cat on the top of her head, kneeling down for her to rub her head against his chest.

"The animals are good at comfort without being annoyingly human," Quinn commented, walking in with his wolves trailing him. The wolves joined Sombra and eventually, the three of them knocked Zander over, who gave up. He just let the animals lick his face and try to rub on him. Elijah chuckled at the scene, his heart feeling lighter again.

Quinn moved to sit on his other side while Sawyer disappeared. It was at that moment when he realized Vincent was no longer in the room. He had no idea where their leader had wandered off to.

"Is she looking for Vin?" Elijah asked his closest friend.

"He's sitting in James' office," the feral Magi told him.

They all settled down, aimlessly watching the TV. Zander got up, the animals following him, and reclined in front of the couch, his head between Elijah and Jasper's thighs. The pack of animals sprawled out around him, almost making a conscious effort to keep touching the redhead. Silent comfort. "Sorry about that," he mumbled.

"You're fine, Zander." Elijah ruffled his hair, making him jerk away. He laughed louder at that response. After messing with Zander a little more and the laughter died, he went back to watching the television.

There were shots of the funeral. They had all known it wasn't a closed affair. The timing of James' death, and the reason, had made it a WMC state affair. He'd been a hero, truly. The world had been watching. People talked about what was said. Clips of Thompson and Vincent flashed before them. Excerpts of what was said.

Someone even commented about how Sawyer was a pallbearer while he wheeled behind the group, out of place in a way, but part of the group anyway. He'd wanted to do it himself, but he felt Sawyer was the only replacement he could accept. He was glad someone he loved stood in for him.

And she deserved it, too.

There she was, in the front with Jasper as the two shortest members. Marching to the slow beat of the music. A commenter made the astute statement that if anyone knew how much James believed in second, and even third, chances, it was her.

She belonged there.

Elijah couldn't think of a better replacement for himself. "VINCENT, STOP!"

Speaking of his replacement. Sawyer's roared order echoed in the living room. Jasper quickly turned off the television and jumped up. Elijah and Quinn were the next up and moving. Zander untangled himself from the animals, following behind them.

Elijah heard more as he entered the back hallway.

"I'm not stopping until he's dead. Don't try to make me." Vincent sounded pained, like a wounded animal.

"We fucking talked about this. We have other things to get done first. You can't-" Sawyer was angry. He considered that. No, not angry, just frustrated. Tired.

"I WANT HIM DEAD!" Vincent roared. Things clattered in the room, like they were shoved off something, probably the desk. "HE DESERVES IT! I'M NOT GOING TO REST UNTIL HE IS!"

Elijah slammed to a stop, grabbing who he could to stop them. Quinn and Zander. He had his hands on Quinn and Zander. He watched Jasper stop, paralyzed, in front of the office door.

This was about Axel, which meant it wasn't their place.

Elijah would follow orders. He would work his hardest to help Sawyer in her task. But it wasn't his place to get between those two when it came to that man. It wasn't any of their places. This was a wound between them.

The silence was deafening. He wondered what Sawyer could be thinking, what could be racing through her mind. Surely she felt the same. He figured she was more than ready to drive a blade into the man's chest.

But he also knew she wanted them to be better, to be more ready. To rest and heal and grieve. He knew that she was patient and would want them hunting at their best. They weren't close to that.

"And I'll do that for you," she said evenly, finally breaking the sick silence. Elijah's gut churned. Emotions were too high, and yet she said that so evenly. "For you. For me. Fuck, for the WMC. For Henry and James, absolutely I'll do that. But you need to do this for *me*. You need to stop for right now. You need to step back. Just for a moment."

He couldn't miss how her voice broke right there at the end.

"Sawyer…"

"No, Vincent." She shut him down swiftly. "You need to rest. You haven't in days. You can't tell me it's helping, either. You've lost weight and look like hell. You can't do this to yourself."

"Why not?" he demanded angrily. Angry enough that Elijah winced.

"Because he doesn't deserve it."

"He doesn't deserve this?" Vincent's voice was rising again, back into an angry yell.

"He doesn't deserve *you*. He doesn't deserve knowing he put you in this place. He doesn't deserve the *victory* of it, knowing he's made *you* destroy *yourself* without needing to even lift a finger in the effort."

Elijah slumped against a wall. Zander joined him, wide-eyed, and Jasper backed away from the door slowly. He wasn't sure why any of them had jumped up, hearing Sawyer yell like that. The idea that she needed them to help with their leader? Either way, it had given them front row seats to Vincent imploding and Sawyer trying to hold him together. Elijah had already tried more than once to get the man to sleep. They all had, but none of them touched the Axel subject.

Sawyer jumped into it with both feet.

Then she stormed out of the office, nearly running into Jasper.

"Fuck!" she snapped, startling. "Shit. Sorry, guys. Let's go watch a movie. I'll come back here to check on him if I need to."

"I can," Elijah offered.

"No. I will." She sounded certain and looked unmovable on the topic. "It's for me to do."

They shuffled back into the living room, and she chose some really bad comedy that did get them laughing. Weakly, but laughing.

Halfway through the movie, Vincent walked out, looking broken and lost. She just waved a hand and he sank in front of her, his head between her legs as he sat on the floor. He watched the movie with the rest of them. He didn't laugh, but Elijah was just glad to see him there.

Their Italian fell asleep in less than ten minutes. Sawyer played with his hair with one hand, and held Quinn's hand with her spare one. Elijah stretched an arm over Quinn's shoulders and played with her hair. Zander and Jasper enclosed Vincent on the floor, leaning on the outside of her thighs. Animals sprawled all over the room. Elijah glanced at the glass door to the patio. Kaar sat on the rail, looking inside, his head tilted to the side. It was as if he'd come back just to watch Vincent sleep.

And they all watched the dumbest movie they had probably ever seen. It wasn't any good, but for the first time since James died, they all sat in the same room and spent the moment together.

Elijah closed his eyes and leaned on Quinn more. Tomorrow they had more work to do. Today, he could just enjoy this and pretend like nothing was wrong.

3

SAWYER

S awyer put herself in charge the next day, making sure the guys all woke up and got showered and bathed for the meeting. She cooked breakfast, Jasper jumping in to help her when he realized.

For a weird moment, life felt so normal, even though they weren't home and everything was wrong. They were never going home. That was something she hated, and now it was time to start worrying about it.

"After the meeting," she mumbled. Everything was steps.

"What?" Jasper frowned as he flipped bacon.

"I was thinking about everything we need to do. New place, getting the animals adjusted. Our stuff back home. We can't stay in this condo forever." She snapped her fingers, remembering something else. "I promised Vincent yesterday that me, you, and Zander would jump on the Dark Web and dig around for Axel stuff. If either of you know how, we can set up alerts on certain sites if he's mentioned or anything. Could give us a lead on something, and it's something Vincent doesn't have to think about."

"Yeah, we have a lot to do. We can set that up after this

meeting. Thompson wants to talk to us today about the living situation too."

"Yeah, I know." She sighed. It was time to get them all out of James' space. Zander's outburst made that apparent the day before. They were already rattled by the funeral. She'd thought she'd gotten Vincent to a good place, but he'd broken the moment they walked back into the condo. The space had driven him back over the edge again and she had to fight with him to get back into the world around him.

She was thankful the guys hadn't stormed in for that argument. It was for her to deal with. Axel was a subject only she could safely push Vincent's buttons with. He wouldn't listen to anyone else.

And Zander? She was the best one to say what needed to be said. She wasn't going to leave it up to one of the other guys, not while they hurt so much.

She felt the weight on her chest. It had started before the funeral and it seemed to be growing. She would carry them. She could do that. She was strong enough. She would jump between them when they needed it, making sure each was okay. They deserved that from her, for giving her all the hope and joy and love they had offered her in the short six months they'd had together.

As she thought about that, the rest of the team wandered in. Zander walked to her and kissed her cheek, with a groggy good morning. Elijah and Vincent just fell into their spots. Quinn checked the fridge for their animals' breakfasts and she smiled.

"I got it," she told him, picking up two of the three full bowls on the counter. Huge servings of raw beef, unseasoned. A meal that would get them through the day, in case things got too busy to feed them dinner. "I think we should take them today."

29

"Me too. I wish they could have gone yesterday, but..."

"Funerals aren't a good place for animals," she agreed. It had been hard, leaving her girl in the condo again, but it had been necessary.

"We'll get them out and moving around today." He smiled at her, taking the bowls. She grabbed the last one, Sombra's, and put it down by itself in the kitchen. The wolves were fed in the dining area with everyone else, but Sombra was food possessive.

Breakfast was quiet and finished quickly. Then everyone came alive, finished getting dressed, and they loaded up.

She hated that the day felt nearly normal.

She wanted to go home. This wasn't supposed to be normal. Normal was their remodeled plantation house. Normal was an early morning run through the woods with wolves on their heels. Normal was the gym and the garage.

New York, James' condo, and the IMPO headquarters weren't supposed to be normal.

"Where's this meeting?" Zander asked.

"In Thompson's office. He and I agreed doing it at the firm wasn't going to work. We'd rather be in a place we all know," Vincent answered patiently. She eyed him. He looked healthier already. The night of sleep had done him good and she knew he'd slept through the night. She'd fallen asleep right next to him in bed to make sure.

She tried not to think about how he moved away from her the moment he realized they were cuddling. She had slid in to give him a more pleasant wake up. She hadn't been thinking sexually, just easy. Soft. Careful.

And he'd jumped away from her like she was on fire.

She sublimated to get out of the SUV before it stopped, reforming to breathe in the crisp winter air. It wasn't normal either. It used to be, but she missed the clean air of Georgia.

There had been no touch of city smog at their plantation home.

"Y'all have a good meeting," she told them as they unloaded. Vincent glared at her, probably for her stunt to get out of the vehicle.

"And where will you be?" he asked sharply.

"Getting stuff done for you," she answered. Things she could do without him. She'd texted and talked to Thompson about it the night before. He'd checked the will. She wasn't addressed in it and there were things she could start for the team that they didn't need to worry about. Not yet, anyway.

They just had to make it through this meeting on their own.

"That doesn't answer the question," he retorted. The entire group was just waiting for the Vincent and Sawyer stand off to end.

"I don't answer to you." She crossed her arms. "I'll be safe and you can know all about it afterwards. When you are done with this. This is more important to all of you right now and it's going to stay that way."

"Of course you don't answer to me," he mumbled, looking away.

She reached out and poked his chest. "Don't be an ass. Let me do this, Vincent. You go with the guys and get through this, and I'll be waiting on the other side. I'm not going anywhere or doing anything dangerous."

He met her eyes again and nodded slowly. She moved to touch his face and he stepped away, walking swiftly away from the group. She hadn't been able to say the words on the tip of her tongue. She had wanted to tell him that she loved him.

She watched his back with wide eyes. While she wasn't

paying attention, someone touched her back.

"Give him time. He's not in a good place," Quinn whispered to her.

"I know." She knew better than most. She collected her feelings and put them all away except one. She smiled to the rest of her men. "Love you guys. You can do this. I'll see you later."

Quinn smiled kindly at her, kissing her cheek. Then he followed Vincent. Elijah followed suit, then Zander and Jasper.

She waited for them all to enter the building, then pulled a set of keys from her pocket. She turned them over in her hand. They would be mad at her for this, but this was for her to do. She hadn't lied to them, though. It wasn't dangerous.

She went to James' car, left there since the morning after he died. It was being turned over to Thompson and he already had custody of it. He was letting her drive it for the day. He'd had someone drop the keys off at the condo building and she picked them up before she woke up any of the guys.

The drive was quiet, with Sombra sitting in the passenger's seat, just watching the world pass by, not giving Sawyer anything about how the big cat felt. She kept the radio off, her thoughts focused on her task. She had interviews to get through. When she parked at the prison, she knew the first one was already prepared.

"I'm here for Missy," she told the guard at the reception desk. "The doppelganger."

"Of course, Miss..."

"Matthews. Director Thompson should have called ahead for me."

"Oh." The guard looked up from his calendar and

realized who she was. She patiently smiled as he jumped up and made a call.

Only a moment later, another Magi guard walked out of a door and waved her to follow. She did, knowing he was leading her to one of the visitation rooms. He unlocked the door and moved aside.

She didn't enter immediately, listening. Missy wasn't making a sound.

"Did you get a real inhibitor on her?" she asked the guard.

"Yes, ma'am. We've never had a doppelganger in here before, but we managed."

"What form is she in?"

"Uh. The one from that day. She never changed into anything else."

Sawyer wondered if it was her original form. She had no idea how old Missy was, or what she truly looked like. It was always something she had wondered. Those curious questions would probably never be answered, and they weren't the topic of the day.

She walked in, phasing through the door, leaving Sombra in the hall. The cat didn't like it, but didn't make too much of an emotional fuss over it. Sawyer didn't want to expose her beautiful animal bond to Missy when it wasn't necessary.

Missy wore orange and sat chained to the table. The inhibitor also cut off her inhuman strength and speed, something Sawyer was thankful for. The woman before her might as well have been human.

"Look who it is," Missy greeted her in a sing song tune. "No little Castello this time? He's cute. No Axel, but probably enough like him to make you feel like it is. Sadly, he's just the younger, cheap imitation in the end, isn't he?"

"No, this is between me and you." She slowly sat down in front of the psychotic bitch. "Vincent isn't the Castello I want to talk about. Actually, I don't want to talk about either of them."

Missy jerked back, startled by her. Sawyer rested her elbows on the table between them and spread her hands in a small shrug. It made Missy narrow her eyes.

"What do you want?" the doppelganger demanded.

"I want to know how you're still alive, actually." Sawyer leaned back, getting comfortable. "I saw the life fade from your eyes. I saw everything end in you. I sent you to hell, or whatever afterlife is out there, if there is one. I put a dagger in your heart. You shouldn't be here."

"I see no reason why I should tell you that." Missy shrugged this time. "Though you should have cut my head off. Would have worked better for you. Maybe."

"I'll remind you that Axel switched with you knowing his execution was fast approaching." Sawyer was about to drive her sharpest knife in Missy's heart. While the doppelganger was absolutely off her rocker, she was passionately in love with Axel. "He probably never thought you would lose your temper and reveal the ruse. He left you here to die, Missy. Expendable, replaceable, worthl-"

"Stop."

"Worthless past this. He never did want you the way you wanted him. And now he found the perfect way for you to prove your undying love. By dying for him. Expendable. No longer his-"

"Stop!"

"He's never cared about anyone past how he could use them," she continued, the words a bitterness flowing off her tongue. Her rage was only matched by the rage radiating off the doppelganger. "He won't come save you, Missy. It's too inconvenient."

"STOP! STOP, STOP, STOP!" Missy banged her hands on the table. Sawyer did. She slammed her mouth shut as the doppelganger unraveled, like she knew the woman would. "You don't know! You don't know the way he feels! You were just a tool! I've been there since the beginning. Since he was a boy! I knew Vincent too! You'll never understand!"

That made Sawyer raise an eyebrow. "What-"

"I saw his potential before any of you. I helped him build who he is. He cares for me!" Missy was shrill and awful towards the end of that. "I found him Felix! I found him Talyn and the rest. I had those connections, being what I am. You gave him nothing. I gave him *everything*."

Sawyer tilted her head to the side slowly. There was a lot to process with that outburst, which was what she wanted. She hadn't expected the information she received from it, but it had gotten her something.

Missy had always been around. That was just a curious thing. She would need to ask Vincent if he remembered anyone from his childhood and the time when Axel was beginning to rise that would fit Missy's supposed role in their lives.

The second thing that stuck out was Felix. The Ghost she never knew much about, Sawyer was always bewildered by his place in the group. He was cowardly and strange. He was anxious. He was a weak Magi with very little in terms of abilities.

Yet Missy mentioned him first.

That was something she would need to dig into further, if Missy didn't tell her anything more.

"Felix?"

"Ha. No. I'm not telling you anything."

"A pity," she mumbled at the crazy woman in front of her. Missy's eyes danced with a dangerous light. She knew so much and Sawyer could feel there was nothing else to gain. "I think I heard what I need to, though. I needed a lead and you just gave it to me. Thanks. For once, you've actually helped me."

The shock that took over Missy's face was something Sawyer wished she could get a picture of.

"Excuse me?" Missy practically squeaked out those words.

"I've never thought to look into Felix. I even let him go when we captured Axel back in August. I didn't think he was anything special. Obviously he is. I'm amazed I never thought to look into him deeper."

"No. NO!" Missy tried to stand, but the chains held her to her chair.

"I pity you, Missy. I know what order he gave you, and I thought you would do it before now. He gave that order to everyone in case we were caught." Sawyer kept all her emotions locked away as she spoke. She couldn't give away anything. "You haven't gone through with it, though. Do you honestly think he'll come to save you? Really? He's never saved anyone but himself, don't you know that? He's not coming. You're trapped here and you just..." She shook her head slowly. "No...I think you get the point."

"I hate you," Missy snarled. "You'll never catch him again. He won't make the same mistakes."

"I was never trying to catch him the first time. Just imagine what I can do with a little bit of elbow grease and all the dark lessons he taught me." Sawyer kept her eyes locked with Missy's. "Just imagine what I can do with the full weight of the IMPO, the WMC, and the IMAS behind me. Just imagine that for a moment. I have one goal in my life right now, Missy, and it's not to catch him. It's to kill him. Imagine what I can do with that."

Missy broke out into a sob and Sawyer realized it was over. She kept her emotions locked tightly away. She had to get out of the room now.

She left quickly, looking back just once. She wanted to remember this.

Missy would probably be dead tomorrow.

It wasn't Sawyer's fault, by any means. It was the truth - and a harsh one. Axel had one order for any of his own that were captured: kill yourself before you give away anything. Missy had failed. The doppelganger wouldn't allow herself to fail her master a second time.

The door was closed and locked. She kept walking to the far wall and leaned on it as the first sob welled up in her chest. Sombra rubbed on her legs, sending waves of comfort and safety at her.

There was a time, so long ago, when that could have been her. It could have been Sawyer sitting there, screaming and wailing for him to save her, knowing he wouldn't. Knowing it was over. Knowing he would never come.

If it wasn't Sawyer, it would have been someone else having that conversation with Missy. They wouldn't have known what Missy would do. She did.

"Have someone watching her at all times," she ordered the guard closest to her. "She's going to try and kill herself. Axel would want her to so she doesn't end up giving away any information. Make sure it doesn't happen."

It was all she could do to make sure she wasn't the thing that made Missy kill herself. She hoped it worked.

This was why she had wanted to do this without the guys. Knowing this. She could knowingly push Missy to say something, so someone else didn't do it accidentally and get hit with the shock.

"Yes ma'am," the guard responded sharply, and began saying something into a walkie on his chest. She didn't listen anymore. She needed to collect herself and get ready for the next interview.

She waited another ten minutes, composing herself, and then began to move to another room. "Bring me Naseem."

"It will take a moment." The guard seemed startled she said anything. She hadn't told them she intended to talk to the assassin.

"That's fine."

She could be patient. Patience was something she was good at. It gave her more time to prepare herself for what she was about to do.

Her guys would be so mad at her, but she couldn't fail this time. She needed to use every resource to make sure she could do the job given to her.

In the back of her mind, the fear scratched. She was going to lose them like they lost James. Like James lost his last team.

And it would be her fault, like it always was when Axel had anything to do with it.

So she steeled herself and walked in the moment the guard gave her the go-ahead. Sombra didn't make nearly the same fuss this time, knowing this was just how it had to be. There would come a point where her cat was going to get back in the action, but this wasn't it. She was there to give her Magi support and strength.

Naseem, like Missy, sat handcuffed and chained on the other side of a steel table. The inhibitor he wore was apparent. It should have put her at ease. He wasn't a danger to her.

But then, she wasn't scared of him, but what she was about to ask.

He raised his eyebrows at the sight of her. She sat down silently and for a moment, they just stared at each other.

"So you know," he finally murmured, no emotion in his voice. Nothing gave away what was running through his head.

"I do," she answered softly. "I just spoke to Missy. You ever meet her?"

"She's missing a few screws," he said, as if they were just passing gossip around.

"Yeah, she is. She always had been missing something important. I think it's the ability to think for herself past..." She trailed off as another wave of guilt ran through her.

"I never understood," Naseem commented mildly, "the fear people had for him. Not really. He was politically very powerful. As a Magi, he's godlike in his abilities and his strength. But I never understood the fear that made people stop talking."

"And now?"

"Excuse me?" He frowned, causing age lines to appear on his forehead. She realized he was a bit older than her in that moment. Probably in his forties. He'd been in their world for much longer than her. She was the young upstart in comparison.

"You said you never understood. Do you understand now?"

A beat of silence. One that was quick, but for a millisecond, it felt like an eternity.

"I do." He nodded slowly. "Why are you here?"

"Teach me."

Those words hung on the air as she watched the realization dawn in his eyes. For just a second, his eyebrows went up, then he narrowed his eyes at her, an anger coming from him that she had expected.

"Why should I ever teach you anything, *Sawyer*?" He sneered her name at the end.

"Because when you and your remaining friend die, there will be no one else who knows. Pass along the skill. Professionally, it's a legacy." She needed it. She couldn't fail, and if he could teach her this, then she would have an advantage she never had on Axel before.

Naseem opened his mouth and she cut him off before he got a word in. "We don't like each other, you and I. A good man died because of you. Thankfully, he took out one of yours. He died a hero to your villain and yes, Naseem, you are a villain. You are not just the blade others wield. You aren't a tool. You enjoy the job and that's the biggest difference between us." She shrugged after that. "But who else would you teach, if not me? Why not teach the person who took you down?"

"And what does it get you? Hell, little girl, what does it get me other than a sentimental feeling that doesn't help me when I'm dead?"

"It gets me another skill I could use to deal with Axel Castello. It gets you life in prison instead of a death sentence."

She could make that happen. Free rein, that's what the team had been given. It wasn't like Naseem was going to get out. Security was heightened. The prison was impenetrable now. With Axel out, everyone was tested to make sure they weren't a doppelganger like Missy. That was a play Axel could only use once and then no one else would be able to pull it off.

"Parole?" he asked softly.

"Sorry, but I can't get anyone to agree to that - and I wouldn't try." She was willing to give him a life.

She wasn't willing to give him the chance to get back to work.

"Then no."

And that was it. She had expected the answer but needed to try anyway.

"Fine." She stood back up. "I don't know your execution date, so I'll apologize for missing it now. I'm a bit busy." She turned and walked to the door, stopping to listen to him talk. She would give him the chance to finish his sentence, at least.

"I didn't expect you to. You are now just another IMPO agent, not an assassin who needs to see your kills. Plus, trying to catch Axel again will keep you busy."

She tightened her hand on the doorknob.

"You've made the same mistake as Missy," she murmured, meeting his emotionless eyes again. "I'm not out to catch Axel Castello. I'm out to kill him."

His eyebrows shot up again and she just left, leaving him in the silence of that.

It wasn't public knowledge. Very few people knew Axel was free. Everyone who did was under a magical non-disclosure agreement. They knew Sawyer and the guys were getting sent after him. But only the Council, her team, and Thompson knew the end goal.

Sawyer was a hero to the public now. They couldn't know that she was being sent out for the very thing they were all afraid of. An execution. An assassination.

She kept walking quickly all the way to the car in the parking lot, unable to stop.

As she slid in, she knew that was the most probable outcome she could have gotten from the trip.

Now she had to get back to the guys and act like everything was normal. That she wasn't falling apart as she did all this. In the end, she was fine. She knew she would be.

If all of this paid off for her and they lived, even if they hated her for it, it would be worth it.

4

JASPER

Jasper tried to get comfortable in the large executive chair, one of several brought into Thompson's office for this meeting. He didn't want to be here, but it was needed. While they were all still reeling, they had to get these things done. They couldn't just stop and fall into despair. There was too much to do.

And so Jasper knew there was no avoiding the lawyers or the will. No avoiding another piece of James being gone.

At least going through this would keep them busy. It would give them just a little more time before they began to deal with the massive, Castello-shaped elephant in their lives. The one that had Vincent unable to sleep and had Sawyer looking like she was going to kill everyone who walked within a few feet of her.

Oh, the pain and rage in those two. It suffocated him while he slept, as their dreams pounded his mind and magic. It echoed his own rage and pain. It echoed in Zander, Elijah, and Quinn.

While those two felt it acutely, they all knew it was

eating the group. Not just Axel, but all of it. The loss of their home, the loss of their comfort and peace, and *James*.

"Jasper, did you hear that?" Zander asked, snapping a finger in his face.

"Hear what?" he snapped, glaring.

"They got started. James left you his library."

"He has a library?" The glare morphed into a frown as he looked around the table. "There's not one in the condo."

"No, the library - rather, you received the books in it - is located at his residence in upstate New York," one of the lawyers explained. "A residence that..." He shuffled through papers. "Yes, here it is. Thompson, it says here that if they refuse it, it goes to you, but as it stands, you all will inherit a large property-" He kept reading.

"It's our old team house," Thompson interjected calmly. "He knew I never wanted to go back." The Director chuckled humorlessly. "That bastard."

"We're missing something. Please, continue to explain," Vincent ordered, waving his hand and frowning at the papers. Jasper agreed; they were missing something.

"I thought he would have deeded it to me on his death, but he deeded the old team house to you guys. It's a big place, a lot like your plantation down in Georgia." Thompson waved a hand absentmindedly. "I was planning on giving it to your team once this was over, since I have no need, or want, to return to it. It will be easy enough to secure. Only a few people, these lawyers included, know it's still there. I'll have the address wiped from their memories."

"That works, sir," the lawyer agreed. "Is it in need of any repairs? We can go ahead and set-"

"The IMPO handles that internally. You can continue," Thompson commanded, leaning back.

"Well, to you, Director, he left his collection of photos. We took everything from the condo and he had many placed in safe-keeping or in storage. We'll provide you the access to that."

"Is that all?" Thompson raised an eyebrow.

"He wrote a note here..." The lawyer fumbled around. "Here it is. Yes..." He handed it warily to the Director, who moved faster to grab it than Jasper would have expected.

It took only a few seconds, but then Thompson began to laugh. He laughed harder than any of them were comfortable with. It boomed and echoed around the room.

"That fucking prick." He wiped tears from his eyes, and took a moment to collect himself. Jasper had never felt so curious. What had James put in there? It was obviously meant to get his old friend laughing and explain why nothing was going to him. "I had guessed but oh, James had a way with words."

"What?" Vincent demanded. Jasper was glad the Italian was doing most of the talking. It was decided before they came in, so that they weren't all talking over each other the entire meeting. He represented the team and they could all just listen.

"He's left everything else to you guys. I'm only getting his most sentimental things, like pictures of our old team and other related objects. That way we're not... 'burdening the youth with our old man shit,' as he so eloquently put it."

Jasper snorted. Then his shoulders began to shake. Next to him, Zander threw his head back, his laugh clear. Elijah howled. Quinn shook his head, looking confused.

Jasper glanced at Vincent as he tried to hold back the laughter. A small smile began to form on the rough, haunted face, just for a second.

Then it was gone and the Italian got up abruptly from the table and began to stalk around the room.

He figured it was enough that it nearly formed at all. It was some progress. He knew Vincent just needed a bit more time to find balance again. He'd been rocked to the core, more so than most of the team.

"So, we're getting a house?" Elijah asked, out of turn. "Seriously? And...everything else?"

"The condo, the house, all of his financial assets. He didn't leave a note. I'm sorry."

Jasper's heart, though full of humor for a moment, still felt the weight of that. They would never have precious last words from him like Thompson got.

"He thought of you boys as the team he and I never had. One we failed to achieve because of mistakes. He... thought of you as the sons he would never have." Thompson tapped a hand on the table, as if the movement would distract from the grief. "Know that. That's why he left all of this to you. You're our future. He and I were the past. There's no reason for old men to need any of that. I don't need any of this. You all do. Just accept it."

Jasper took several deep breaths as Vincent walked back to the table. Zander leaned on him. Just a simple movement, and Jasper felt less alone for a moment. Vincent began taking the papers from the lawyers.

"Let's just sign all of this and get out of here," he mumbled.

"Wait," Thompson said, stopping him. "We need to talk about moving all your things from Georgia to the new house. We need to talk about you moving in. What you need, when you need it by."

"You can handle all of that," Vincent snapped. "Just do it.

We don't care. We can...personalize it later, or something. I don't have time for interior decorating."

"Yes, we do," Quinn said softly.

Everyone turned to stare at him.

"No, we don't," Vincent growled.

"We've hunted him for a long time, Vincent. We took the time to make sure our home was what we wanted it to be. We can take today to make sure our new one will be too.

Vincent glared at the feral Magi, who wasn't intimidated.

Jasper stood up slowly, putting a hand between them to break the stare-down. "Vincent, you and I can do something else while these guys handle this. We can divide and conquer like Sawyer did."

"No," Elijah disagreed quickly. "We're doing this as a team. James left this for us, gifts from him. We're not going to disrespect that and ignore it. Vincent is going to sit down and sign the paperwork and we're going to make plans to move. We can't go on a mission without a home base, without a place where we're all able to get our work done."

Jasper glanced back at Zander. The redhead shrugged. "I'm with Elijah and Quinn on this one."

"You've been outvoted, Vincent. Sit down. We're doing this. Today. Hell, even tomorrow. Even a week from now. I'm still healing. You know Sawyer and the rest of us are right."

"Every moment you all tell me to rest, the further he gets, the colder the trail goes."

Jasper didn't have an answer for that. He knew Vincent was right about that, but the team just wasn't ready to jump in on catching Axel. Not yet. They had to move fast, but they couldn't go so quickly that they weren't prepared.

"You were still outvoted," Elijah whispered.

Vincent slammed his hand on the table.

No one on the team attempted to calm him down. Jasper

had seen Vincent in a lot of bad places in his life, but he had never seen this all-consuming fury. He'd never seen Vincent so full of rage, pain, and hate. Not for anyone in the room, but for Axel.

Yeah, Jasper also hated the man. Hated him for everything he had done to Sawyer, and to the world they lived in. But he couldn't muster the power of the emotion that Vincent had. It made Vincent the scariest man he'd ever seen.

It took several long moments. The lawyers and Thompson just waited, watching Vin with wide, surprised eyes. The team was patient though. They could be patient for him. They knew all the things he was working through, and they knew he would come out on the other side.

Well, Jasper hoped they were right about that. He hoped he was right about it.

Finally, Vincent slid into his chair, nodding, accepting defeat. The battle was over, but the war wasn't, and Jasper knew it. It was okay. Soon, they would need to let themselves off their own leashes and get to work.

"We're already practically a month behind him, Vincent," Elijah whispered. "It's already cold. We can take a week to do this, then we get to work."

"It's so hard," the Italian whispered. "Eli, it's so hard."

"I know," the cowboy murmured. "Oh, my friend, I know."

Smartly, no one said anything else, and the paperwork was dealt with. They signed the deed together. Each of them would own the home James left them. Thompson began calls for the inhouse contractors to deal with the property.

Jasper didn't let it worry him that strangers would be wandering around the new house he hadn't even seen yet. It was standard procedure. Every day, while work was going on, those people would go to the property on an IMPO bus. The driver had memory manipulation and would wipe their memories of the address when he loaded them up at the end of the work day.

Since too much of that would lead to complications, the work had to be done quickly. Their last house was done in only four days. He bet this one would be faster since it was already an older secure team home.

"How are you?" Zander asked him softly.

"I'm fine," he answered, shrugging as he looked out the massive windows of Thompson's office. He could see the place on the street where he'd followed as they loaded Vincent into the ambulance. This had been her angle to it. Right here, she'd seen that nothing in the seemingly easy night went according to plan. Right here, she'd found out James was gone and had run for him and Vincent.

He felt like he was connected to that night because of it. A connection he didn't want. A night that should have finished their problems, not given them a hundred more.

"What are you thinking about?" his friend wisely asked.

Jasper ignored the question for a minute, letting his thoughts continue. A hundred problems. James' death. No home. None of their things. Axel out. Woefully unprepared for the task presented to them.

And yet, Jasper knew his team would succeed. He didn't know at what cost, but he knew they would make it through. Would they still be a team at the end? Could Sawyer and Vincent hold together when all was said and done, or would this be the thing that broke them?

What came after this?

He didn't know and he wasn't sure he knew how to figure it out.

"I hope this doesn't ruin us," he whispered, hoping only

Zander could hear him. "I don't want this to ruin Vincent, and I think it can."

"We can keep him," Zander promised. "We can keep him with us. We'll come out on the other side."

"I hope so." Jasper knew Zander would blindly push towards the goal, and something about it was admirable. He let nothing convince him that failure was an option.

"Believe me. And Sawyer too. We're not going to let this...you know what I mean."

"I do." Jasper huffed. Zander wasn't one for poetry.

"Guys," Elijah called out to them. "You two want anything new in particular at the new place?"

"A big bed in Sawyer's room," Zander answered. Jasper groaned, but the ridiculous statement had gotten laughter out of *everyone* on the team. Even Vincent. "I'm being serious!"

"Of course he is," Thompson muttered. "You all...You know what? No. I'm not asking questions."

"Better that way," Vincent agreed softly.

"Do you know where she is right now?" Elijah said it in an accusing way, narrowing his eyes. Jasper had turned all the way around by then, watching everyone move around, look over documents.

"I do. It's nothing dangerous."

"Why does everyone need to say it's not dangerous?" Zander shook his head. "We're not asking if it's safe. She can take care of herself. I trust her to do that."

"Because we tend to assume everything she does is dangerous." Quinn mumbled that explanation, but smiled.

"What's she doing?" Vincent asked again.

"She went to the prison for an interview. I figured it was something she could handle on her own. She knows what questions to ask-"

"She went to talk to Missy without us?" Vincent's head snapped up from whatever he was reading. "She went to interrogate her about Axel without *me*?"

Jasper didn't like the sound of that either. Of all the things. He could see why she would do it, but he didn't like it. They should be there with her as she confronted the doppelganger.

Yet she purposefully sent them to deal with this and went alone.

"Damn her," Vincent muttered, dropping the papers. He started for the door.

"You'll finish this," Elijah ordered. "Then we can all yell at her."

Vincent stopped, turned on his heel, and got back to work. Jasper was impressed that Elijah had thrown himself into the position of keeping Vincent in the right place. He wanted to run after her too, but this all really did need to get done.

He glanced back at the window, thinking about it.

Axel had gotten out a month before they even knew. The trail was already cold. It hadn't even been a week since James died.

When he looked back to the table, and noticed Vincent waving him over, he hoped in another week everyone was in a better place.

He signed whatever form was put in front of him.

He snuck a peek at Vincent's face while he did. It was closed off, like it used to be. Before Sawyer, before it all broke and she changed them. Changed them for the better. Brought them closer. Made the team feel whole in a way it never had before.

Jasper considered what the next week would hold for them. And the week after that. And a decade from now.

He didn't want to lose his brothers to this, didn't want to lose Sawyer. Vincent looked like he was already lost. Sawyer was off dealing with things from her past without them, like she didn't need them.

He could already feel them fracturing.

5

SAWYER

Sawyer walked off the elevator with Sombra next to her and saw the guys and the wolves leaving Thompson's office. She was right on time.

"Hey guys!" She smiled at them, covering all the strange hurt in her from the trip she'd just made.

"You..." Vincent was already glaring at her.

"Thompson said something, huh?" She sighed, reaching out to grab the elevator door to keep it from closing. She held it while the guys walked on and slid in last. "Yeah, I went to visit Missy." Not even Thompson knew she had wanted to talk to Naseem, so she wouldn't mention it now. He'd denied her request so there was no reason to say anything, not in her mind.

"Why did you go without us?" Jasper asked, looking hurt. She had expected it from Zander, but her redhead just moved himself closer to her. She met the green eyes of her temperamental one.

"I know if I yell at you, I'll be in trouble, so I'm going to let them do it. You're not hurt, so I'll be quiet."

She would have laughed if it weren't for the fact that Vincent looked like he would yell. He looked livid with her.

"I went without you all because that's the deal I'm going to make with you guys. You are all going to get this other shit handled. I can't do anything about our living situation, or the will, or James' things. I wish I could, but I can't. I can only help you grieve. I know we're all being pulled in two different directions. But I can look into the...case while you handle this. Once everything is settled, we'll all sit down together-"

"And what if you get a big break before we're done?" Elijah cut her off. He didn't look upset. Well, not nearly as upset as Vincent.

"Then I get you, we drop everything, and we go for it. But the likelihood of that happening is small. He's gone. We're starting from square one. I would rather be the one getting our pieces moving. Vincent, this is what I tried to tell you yesterday. You guys need to focus on this. When I need one of you, like Jasper and Zander to help me set up alerts, I'll divert you for a moment, but that's it."

Vincent slowly nodded, as if he understood her reasoning but was still angry. She knew the anger wasn't truly because of her. He was hurting and lashing out. She knew his logical mind would win out in the end, even if they had to remind him at every turn to remember himself and what was needed.

And she was willing to keep doing it.

"Fine," he finally muttered, looking away from her.

She didn't have the urge to reach for him and say she loved him this time. She knew when she would be unwelcome. It hurt, but she couldn't force him to accept her comfort.

She reminded herself of her promise. She would do

anything for them, even if they hated her by the end of this. She didn't need the pardon; she didn't need any of it. She just needed all of them, herself included, to live through this.

And Vincent seemed like he was already beginning to hate her, even though she hadn't yet done the deed. She hadn't yet killed his brother, and it was already forcing a wedge between them she couldn't fathom. She thought they were okay at the end of the funeral, but that moment was long gone and the hurting, angry Vincent was back.

The elevator dinged at the bottom. The walk out was silent and as always, it was being watched. Like every time she walked through this building, eyes found her. She kept her chin up and led the guys out, taking charge and setting the pace. She was never a natural leader, but she would be while Vincent got his head together, if he ever did. She didn't let them drag their feet, and once she was behind the wheel of the SUV they had used that morning, she looked at her passengers.

"What happened today?" she asked Elijah.

"We have a house. James left us a fucking house. The one his and Thompson's team used back in the day. All our shit will probably be in it before the end of the week." He gave her a tired smile. "I'm worried about you doing the prison thing alone, but...thank you. The team needs this time to handle this sort of stuff and I'm...really happy you care enough about us to deal with the other thing for a moment by yourself."

"Care enough? Elijah, I love you. I love all of you. I'd do anything for y'all." She reached out and took his hand. He kissed her knuckles, holding it.

"I love you too, little lady."

Those were words she'd never thought they would

share. She had nearly missed her chance. He was such a wonderful man, Elijah Grant. They weren't perfect together, just like they weren't perfect individuals. He was scared of telling her how he felt because of his past. She had avoided getting to know him past flirtation and friendship.

No, none of them were perfect, but she liked to think their team was perfect. The five of them, all together, were perfect for her, and that was why she needed to protect them. That was why she was willing to do what she'd done earlier. Elijah just reminded her of that.

Back at the condo, the guys dispersed and she meandered into the kitchen. Then she saw Elijah's medications on the counter.

"Quinn?" she called softly, knowing he was the closest. He was hanging in the living room with the animals.

"Yes?"

"Can you take Elijah his medication? And do you know if he took it this morning?"

Quinn was suddenly next to her. She didn't get spooked. The feral Magi was feeling protective over their cowboy and his injuries. They all were.

"I don't know, but I'll ask."

"I mean, they're just muscle relaxers, so he might not have wanted to get doped up before the meeting, but he might like them while we're relaxing around the condo for the rest of the day."

"He says they make him feel...fuzzy. I've never taken anything like them, so I don't understand. He hates taking them though, even if they help him stretch and rebuild the muscles in his back."

"They cloud his thoughts and make him tired. Just see if he would like one or two now?" She handed him the bottle and he nodded, even getting a glass of water. To her, that meant Elijah was going to take the medications, even if Quinn had to force them down his throat.

She pulled a premade salad from the fridge and had just sat down on the couch to eat it when Quinn came back in.

"He's taken them and is lying down for a short nap. What are you planning for the rest of the day?"

"I'm going to eat this salad and then look over some things. Might as well get to work, ya know?"

"Of course." He sat next to her, casually putting an arm over her shoulder. He kissed the side of her head, something normal and tender. He was becoming more normal every day.

"You haven't talked about any of it," she finally said, her eyes on the television. She wanted this to be casual.

"I know."

"Would you like to?" she asked gently.

"I'll miss him. He fought hard. He is the hero they all keep calling him. It hurts, but…that's life. I'm not the type to fall to my knees over death. It hurts, but I can keep surviving. I said goodbye yesterday. I've never been to a funeral before. It was strange, but it felt…final. I see why we humans do it."

She considered that and nodded slowly. He had a point. He was pragmatic about these circle of life things.

"As for the other thing…" He trailed off for a second before picking back up. "As for Axel, I'll be the male I've always been. We've defeated him before. We will do it again. Together, as a pack, we're stronger and smarter than he will ever hope to be."

"You're right," she agreed, kissing him slowly. "Thank you for that." She finished off her salad and stood up. "I'm going to get to work. Oh, no one told me where this new house is."

"North of here. Upstate New York. None of us have seen it yet. I think we're going to make a trip out there tomorrow. You should come."

"I will, promise." She had nothing else to do that required her to be away from the team.

She threw out the salad container then went into the back of the condo. She didn't look for any of the guys, instead ducking into James' office where she knew Vincent moved all his work about Axel to.

She sat down behind the desk and just looked at it all for a long time. Pictures of him, his Ghosts, his old properties. All of this was defunct now. They didn't even have an up to date picture of him. She knew, based on Missy's performance in the prison, that he would be scarred now.

"He's probably furious about it," she murmured. "His precious, perfect face." She ran a thumb over the scar on her bottom lip, where it had been busted open one too many times. Well, really a thousand times too many.

As she kept looking at the pictures, the invisible itch of the scar between her breasts came back, for the first time in a very long time. She rubbed it absentmindedly, the old habit returning in a second. It felt like the old bullet holes were burning. It felt like her missing finger became more apparent by the second, as she touched the picture of Axel.

Every second dragged on as it all rushed back.

She had gotten so far away from it, so far removed from the trauma. It had always haunted her, but this...this was like before he'd been originally captured. Just seeing him in an old picture, just hearing his name, made her itch and become uncomfortable.

She pulled away from the picture like it was on fire and stood up.

"No," she growled to herself. "I'm stronger than this. He can't haunt me anymore."

She took several deep breaths, collecting herself. She ignored the itch of her scar. She looked down at it, pulling her shirt down enough to see it. Thanks to Tez in the rainforest, it was faded, like the scars on Quinn's back. It was like decades had passed.

And she used that to anchor the distance she had from Axel, from the dark history between them. It was a long time ago. She had more power now than ever. She had changed since he'd given her the scar.

When she sat back down, she began to review everything. Every criminal that was captured thanks to Axel. Every minion. Every operation that was shut down. She wondered what Vincent had been looking for in the information. She wondered if it was the same thing she was finding.

She knew these names and faces. Meetings and parties. Rivalries and bad business. These were people that Axel had to deal with but didn't like to. He often said they were who he would replace with his own men if he had the chance. He'd hated that they thought they were his equals, or even close to his organization. He needed one to help him with his human trafficking operation. Another to help with his dealings in Colombia for drugs. Another for the sex trade he had going in some Pacific Island countries.

And now they were all in prison themselves and Axel was wandering around.

"You son of a bitch," she mumbled. He'd given himself everything he'd ever wanted and he'd used the good guys to do it. "These men had no idea the games they played with you. They had no idea that you could use your own arrest against them like this, to finally give you everything you ever dreamed of."

She knew the power vacuum he was stepping into now. The seedy criminal world of the Magi, the wild west of their world, only had one real bad guy in power now.

And she had to kill him.

"First, I have to find him," she reminded herself, looking back at his picture.

As the day continued, she went over old properties. She knew several, but she could also tell none of them were his treasured sanctuaries. None of them were places she had once lived. She wrote those down as well, turning on James' computer to dive into realty and discover what might have sold or just changed hands.

She drew on everything she used to. She dove into the Dark Web and began to dig. She was once a master at this hunt. Her years as a solo thief had honed these skills. She loved the ground work. She found that he didn't legally own any of the homes she once occupied. She had never thought he did. He didn't put his real name on anything. He hid them through fake shell companies and others who would take the fall long before he would if the information was dug up by the wrong people.

Sawyer knew he probably never expected to be captured while trying to kill her.

It felt like hours later when she came up for air, having learned a lot - but none of it immediately helpful. She could ask the IMPO to raid all of these places, but she didn't think it would help anyone, or hurt Axel.

Her eyes fell to the chess board she knew Vincent had set up.

Chess. Pieces moving on the field. Right now, on Vincent's board, the white side was winning. Appropriate.

Axel was winning. He'd had months to secretly move the pieces around while the two people who knew him best had no idea. She and Vincent hadn't been paying attention. They had gotten ahead, put him in check, and then they walked away, thinking the WMC would put him in checkmate.

"Idiots," she mumbled, standing up to look closer at the board, just to think.

There was no reason to raid all the locations she knew because Axel would already know those were her ins. He would have walked away from those places and found new secret hideaways first, actually. He would know that she wouldn't rest.

"I wonder," she murmured, touching the black queen. "Are you going to come after me, Axel? Or will you make me work for this? Have you let go of the obsession with killing me?" She pushed the black queen up to the white king. "Because I haven't let this go. I tried and you dragged me back in when I just wanted to hide out and forget all of this. So when I take you back to check and secure a checkmate, I hope you know it's your fault."

She didn't know why she needed to say the words. He couldn't hear her. She constantly checked the condo for bugs. She didn't take chances with him being out. Their location wasn't secure. The only things she had going for her was that they were in New York, security was still heightened, and Axel wasn't that bold.

"Well, he is, but he's not an idiot. If he comes at me head on, he loses. I have too much backing behind me now for that sort of war. He could just treat me like Vincent now. Always a step or ten ahead, always gaining power." She felt a wave of frustration. "I'm going to catch you. You brought me back in and now you get to suffer the consequences of it.

Last time, I just wanted to hide out and run the moment I got the chance. Make a new name and disappear." She wrapped her fingers around the black queen. "Not this time."

She stood there, thinking about it for a long time. She didn't have what she needed in this office, so instead she considered the future of the board. Pawns who were possibly in play and who he would rely on as a knight or bishop. And what could Felix have possibly done? How was Missy alive?

Questions that needed answers. She needed to treat every fragment of information as important. If she didn't, one could slip by her and disappear, when it would be important later.

"Sawyer?" a rough, tired voice called softly outside the door. She looked for the time and caught the clock on the wall. When had it become nearly midnight?

"Yeah, Elijah?" she called back. "You can come in."

He walked in slowly, Quinn following him. They ignored the state of the room around them. She hadn't even noticed the mess herself while she'd been alone. It looked like a tornado had gone through it.

"Come to bed," Quinn ordered softly. "Everyone else ate dinner. We convinced Vincent to just read a book and relax for the evening since you were in here."

"I'm..." She wasn't ready to leave this space yet. She was so patient with Vincent, normally, since she understood. Once someone waded into the world of playing games with Axel, it was hard to pull away. It consumed your thoughts as you tried to figure out every move he could make and what moves you could make that would surprise him.

It was so hard to pull away.

"I'm not going back to sleep until you come to bed too.

I'm grateful for you diving into this while we deal with the mundane crap, but you need to sleep too. You can't become...well, you can't be like Vin."

She met the hazel eyes of the patient, loving cowboy.

"And if I don't want to go to sleep?" she asked softly.

"I didn't say you need to sleep. I said you need to come to bed," he fired back, a smile beginning to form. "Whether bed puts you to sleep or not is up to you."

"Pervert," she teased, a small smirk taking over.

"Yes, well, you both need to lie down and rest," Quinn cut in. He reached out to her. "We're staying in the master bedroom right now. Come on."

She let him pull her out of the office. She didn't want to leave, but she knew she had to, and his physicality, his realness, making sure she moved, helped her take those steps. Elijah closed the office door behind them when they were in the hallway.

Together, they slid into the giant back bedroom and she pulled off her shirt, enjoying the sight of the big, comfortable bed.

Then she realized the situation she was in.

"Are we all sleeping in here?" she asked, looking at them as they stripped down.

"Of course we are," Elijah answered nonchalantly. "I mean, you've cuddled with Quinn and Zander before. No different."

He had a point. She wasn't sure why she brought it up. Shrugging, she pushed down her jeans and slid in bed wearing only her underwear. She'd forgotten a bra all day, not really caring about it. She just hadn't cared when she woke up that day. Missy and Naseem didn't care enough to point it out. The guys were distracted. She'd gotten away with it.

She pulled a pillow to her face and nuzzled into it, taking a deep breath and trying to relax. They got into bed on either side of her, but didn't touch her. They wouldn't unless she asked, or made a move to show them it was okay. She figured neither of them were in that mood either.

Elijah began to snore quickly, and Quinn followed him shortly after.

She just laid awake, considering her future, considering the pieces of the board. Her mind wouldn't rest.

She couldn't handle it anymore and tried to get out of bed, kicking blankets away from her. She didn't use her magic, and she quickly realized she should have as Quinn's arm wrapped around her waist.

"Stay," he ordered, his eyes still closed.

"Sorry, but I can't just lie here," she answered softly, kissing his forehead. "I didn't mean to wake you."

"Do you need help?" he asked, his ice blue eyes opening and practically shining in the dark. She always felt trapped under his stare and he said nothing, sitting up just enough to kiss her collarbone. "Because we can do that for you."

"We?" Frowning, she just let him continue to kiss her, trying to not get pulled under by his spell.

A large palm ran up her back and that made her pause. That was too big for Quinn - because it was Elijah. "Stay in bed, little lady," he murmured. She felt the bed dip more as he drew closer and kissed her shoulder. "Stay with us for the night, please."

She turned to him and only met a serious face. There was no playfulness, no teasing. They were serious.

"We can help you sleep," Quinn offered again, the arm around her waist pulling her tighter against his body. "Let us."

"I've never done this."

"Well, we almost lost Elijah without having the chance. Let's do it now. If you never want it again, then fine, but let us do this with you tonight. Just tonight." Quinn captured her lips at the end of that, while her mind reeled. He had a good point. They had almost lost their cowboy and she knew they had both teased about wanting this.

"We've wanted to have you with us for a long time now," Elijah continued where Quinn left off. "It started out as a pipe dream, an idea. It became a teasing joke. We'd never thought you would actually love us. We never thought..." He kissed her shoulder from behind her. "And now, with everything going on, let us help you sleep."

She closed her eyes, trying to hold back tears. As she nodded, Quinn growled in pleasure and kissed her again. He fell full on his back and pulled her over him, hands roaming and exploring. Elijah's hands didn't stop either.

"Wait," she gasped. "Elijah, you have to be careful."

"Yes, that's right," Quinn agreed. He sat up, pushing her up with him. "Elijah..."

"I'll lie on my back and...relax," he agreed with a devious grin. "Only if someone here lets me eat her out."

"Excuse me?" Her eyebrows flew up.

"Why don't you come sit on my face and force me to relax?"

She wanted to smack him. It was the dirtiest question she'd ever heard. He fell back, spreading out, his dick hard. She hadn't really considered that they were already nude. Of course they were. They slept that way.

"Do it," Quinn whispered in her ear.

"Why?" She was flabbergasted.

"Because Alpha females take what they want from their males." Now Quinn's grin was just as devious as Elijah's. She had a sneaking suspicion they had talked this entire fantasy of theirs through.

She was nervous as she crawled across the bed, Quinn breaking the side of her thong before she could get too far. It was tossed away.

"Uh..." She was on her knees next to her cowboy's head. He kept grinning and grabbed her, forcing her to swing a thigh over his head. He pointed her towards the headboard, so she stared at the wall. His mouth closed on her and his massive arms held her thighs in place so she couldn't try to get off him.

As his tongue lazily swiped over her entry, Quinn moved to kiss her again, also on his knees. One of his hands traveled down her back and he pushed a wet finger in her ass. That brought a shocked gasp from her. Elijah forced her to move her hips as he fucked her with his tongue, his nose rubbing against her clit in the best way she could imagine. He knew what he was doing. Of course he did.

Quinn's finger continued to pump, as the feral Magi also nibbled on her neck. She moaned with every movement of the two men.

And she shattered quickly, her orgasm crashing into her. Based on the supremely satisfied noise from the mouth beneath her, it was exactly what the cowboy had wanted. Only when she was finished riding out the sensations did he let her go enough so she wasn't forced on his face. Quinn slowly pulled his finger out, kissing her hard.

"Now for the best part," he murmured. Elijah just chuckled underneath her. She looked over her shoulder and saw the hard dick waiting for someone to ride it. Elijah's cock was always a sight and it was hard to miss. "If you think you can handle it. Because I love this." His hand continued to rub on the curve of her ass. Oh, she knew he did. They didn't do it very often, but Quinn enjoyed being able to bury himself in her tightest hole when she was willing.

"So..." She knew where this was going. They wanted to have her together all right.

Of course they did.

"You can say no, little lady, and we'll find other ways to blow your mind."

No. This seemed like just the thing that would leave her boneless and thoughtless enough to sleep. It wasn't something she had ever done before, but she would do it with these two men. She trusted them to not hurt her.

And she loved them.

She moved back and sank on Elijah's cock first, moaning at the full sensation he gave her. He was a massive man and a cocky one...literally. He grabbed her hips and thrust into her once for effect, just because he knew she would whimper and moan for him.

Quinn moved behind her and she could feel the coolness of lube as he pressed his dick against her.

And then they broke her all over again. He entered slowly, like he always did, but nothing between these two men was ever slow one on one. They definitely wouldn't be easy on her together.

Elijah pulled her down, kissing her hard as he stayed buried in her and Quinn fucked her. She was thankful they weren't moving together, giving her body a chance to figure out whatever these sensations were.

Quinn snarled, leaning over them both. He thrust into her at a reckless and frantic pace, as if they would never again get the chance to have her together. As if he had to make up for lost time. And there was lost time. None of them had been together since before they came to this city, before Naseem attacked her that first night.

He panted over her as she screamed against Elijah's broad chest. The cowboy was nice enough to hold on to her.

Finally, Quinn gave out first. Several, fast, erratic pumps and he came deep inside, giving her a moment to enjoy the feeling of being pressed between them.

"Now it's my turn," Elijah murmured with a hot need that gave her a round of shivers. She was primed. Quinn hadn't pushed her over the edge, but Elijah fully intended to. As the feral Magi pulled out, the cowboy got started, grabbed her hips with a nearly bruising pressure. He thrust up into her at a more even, measured speed.

Quinn collapsed to the side, but didn't stop being involved in the action. As Elijah sent her into the heavens, Quinn kissed her, passionate and loving, taking every noise she made and muffling it with his lips.

Then stars entered her vision as she couldn't hold on anymore and they sent her to another place. A place where she was blissful. Elijah didn't stop as she rode out the orgasm. He didn't even slow down. Right as hers ended, he slammed into her once more, groaning as he spilled inside her.

The moment he was soft and slid out of her, she fell off him, landing between her men. Quinn wrapped his arms around her waist, curled around her back. Elijah wedged an arm under both their heads as she nuzzled into his chest.

And she knew she couldn't let Axel take this away from her.

But sleep didn't hurt either. She could get back to work tomorrow.

6

SAWYER

They loaded up the next day, feeling just a little bit lighter than they had in days. It was a fraction of how they once were, but Sawyer was glad to see that all of them seemed even just a tiny bit closer to normal.

And it felt right that it would be on a trip to their new normal. This new home James had left them. She would be shocked, but James had made it clear he'd cared so much for the team. The guys. They meant everything to him. This felt right.

And it was his old team house. That was something. She was curious because of it.

She knew the guys were shocked. They covered it well, but this man had left them everything. The only things Thompson got were sentimental items between the both of them, but everything else, all of James' assets, went to the guys. She couldn't even feel neglected by not receiving anything. She had no claim there, she thought. She and James had that awkward history, but they were never close. It was something she always reminded herself of.

She hurt because the guys lost someone important to them.

But today, everyone was a little lighter.

"I want the room closest to Sawyer's, whatever she picks," Zander said loudly in the back. She sighed, keeping her eyes on the road. She'd become chauffeur for the group, but they didn't all fit into the SUV this time. Quinn and Elijah were following her with the wolves.

"We'll see," Vincent mumbled back from the passenger's seat. She glanced at him, daring to take her eyes off the road for only a second. He was reading a book and ignoring all of them effectively.

With another sigh, she pulled off the freeway, careful of the ice and snow on the side, and went out into the sticks of New York. This was going to be their new home, their new area. She needed to get used to it.

The driveway was long and gated. The house, while not a classic plantation house, was absolutely a mansion that would fit them. She didn't like the red brick, or the dark windows. She missed the pretty white historic home down south.

But this was going to be home now. Thanks to everything that had happened, she didn't have a choice but to settle in this new place.

She parked and silently waited for the guys to get out. Sombra jumped out as well, but, unlike her men, didn't wander off to go look at things. She waited for Sawyer on the perfect concrete driveway.

"Yeah, I'm coming," she muttered when impatience began to flow through the bond. She cut the engine and slid out, looking around. They were secluded and far from the city, but still within a day's drive. It made sense, since who knew when they would need the airport.

She walked in last, the guys having already disappeared inside. She looked around, able to see a large living room with a huge TV on the wall and other furniture. It looked like James had kept the place up to date and cleaned. She could see the entryway to the kitchen and dining room. She walked deeper in, careful and hesitant of the new location. She could hear footsteps upstairs. It was big, but it didn't feel like it, unlike the plantation house.

"Sawyer, come pick a room!" Zander called. She sighed and found the stairs, walking up. The moment he saw her, he gave her the brightest smile she had seen in days. "There's not enough bedrooms up here for all of us, but there are a couple downstairs too. Quinn and Elijah are going to take those. Me, you, Jasper, and Vincent are up here. There's space in the attic for the gym."

"And offices?" she asked, considering what they once had.

"Two other rooms on the first floor. Like we used to have. Me and Jasper, Vincent and Elijah. Quinn doesn't need one, not here in the house anyway." He wrapped an arm around her waist. "Come choose a room. I think I know which one you should get. There's a master suite."

"Of course," she mumbled, letting him lead her. Sure enough, while most rooms were a standard bedroom, ten by twelve or similar, the master suite wasn't. It had a private bathroom and was twice the size of the other bedrooms. "Cool. I get the biggest bedroom and my own place to bathe, away from your balls."

He just stared at her for that comment. She couldn't resist a smirk. Yeah, if they wanted her to have the big room, she wouldn't deny them. It made some sense. She wanted a place to bathe and was always fighting with the guys. She also had the most company.

"We're going to get you a huge bed," he murmured. "To fill up the room."

"Let's not. A king would be fine." She did miss having a semi-large and expansive bed.

"Fine," he huffed, still smiling. She kissed him gently, enjoying that he was enjoying this. She was happy that this was making them feel better about James. And once this was all over, they had so much work to do.

"So what's next?" she asked, holding on to him.

"All of our things are being transported from Georgia. That includes your stuff. They'll finish moving it all by the end of the week. We can get some renovations done if it's needed, but James took care of this place, since we're the third team to be living in it."

"Third?" She frowned. James and Thompson. Her and the guys. Who...

"His first team. The ones..."

Zander realized the implication at the same time she did.

The men who lived here after James, and before them, were dead because they played a game with her and Axel.

"It's fine," she whispered. "I'm fine. This place is nice and we'll make it our team's home now."

"Okay." He seemed uncomfortable now. He was looking around the room, considering it. "One of them was married, but they had no kids."

Hence a master suite. So he and his wife had an apartment together, in a sense. Of course.

"We'll renovate the house so it's ours. Someone was going to live here eventually." She didn't want his mood to sour.

He nodded, kissed her cheek again, then pulled away. "I'm going to tell them to remodel this room right now."

She let him leave, watching him walk out and find one of the contractors roaming around.

Of all the things that James could leave them.

She left the room when she felt a bit better. She wanted to get out of the beautiful home. She went out the back, knowing this would be something she did often. The woods were closer to the house than they were in Georgia, and she saw Quinn standing at the edge of them, staring into the deep, dense forest.

"It's pretty out here and the boys like how cold it is," he told her as she stopped beside him. "We can have some fun games out there."

She saw his eyes twinkle a little. She knew what games he wanted to play. Their Halloween this year had included a very fun game out in the woods back in Georgia.

"How much land?" she asked.

"Two-thirds of what we had in Georgia, but enough for me and the boys. It's better than a yard and I don't need miles and miles of space like the Druids do."

"So you like this place?"

"I really do. I'm honored he left it for us. That he kept it so long, thinking to give it to us."

She was glad. This was healing, in a way. She missed the plantation house but she was happy they were already finding things they wanted in this new home. It was just like moving. It happened in life. Plus, their old home wasn't safe anymore and she didn't know if she could sleep in the bedroom where an assassin tried to stab her in her sleep.

That's what she would get out of this new place. A new piece of security, privacy.

With that, she kissed him and let him go wandering in the woods with his wolves. She knew Sombra was hanging out inside, exploring the warm interior and not wanting to

73

go out in the chill. The cat sent her flashes of where she'd seen the guys. Elijah and Zander were now in the attic where they wanted to put the gym. Jasper was just wandering around aimlessly, ducking his head in rooms. Vincent was standing in a room she didn't recognize.

She had a guess, so when she walked back in, she stayed on the first floor and found the bedrooms. Four on the first floor and she knew two would be turned into offices.

She got it on the first try. In the middle of the room, Vincent was just taking in the space, seemingly lost in thought.

"Vincent," she said quietly, stepping closer as she closed the door behind her.

He turned to her, those dark olive-green eyes haunted. "Sawyer."

"I love you." The words came easy and she finally had a chance to say them again.

"I love you too," he responded gently, a small smile forming on his lips. Lips she hadn't kissed in what felt like an eternity.

"I would ask you if you were okay, but I already know the answer." She didn't beat around the bush.

"I know." He looked away at that, turning to the window. "I'm trying."

"I know," she promised, repeating what he'd said. She slowly walked closer and wrapped her arms around his waist from behind. He didn't move to touch her back, but he didn't pull away either. She leaned so her head was resting on the back of his, pressing her entire body to his. It was the sort of touch that had nothing sexual about it. She just wanted to hold him for a moment. Hold this man that knew everything she was covering up.

"I used to be better at hiding it. Not letting anyone know just how..."

"It's okay," she whispered. He used to be better at dissembling his emotions and putting them away. Somewhere, he'd lost the ability to do it so well and she'd grown better at it.

"Don't be mad, but I'm desperate to know what Missy said." There was something humorous and joking in the way he said it.

She nearly chuckled. Of course. It reminded her of what Missy had said specifically about him and Axel.

"You once knew her. Apparently, she was in Axel's life for a long time. Yours too. Anyone you think that might be?"

"That's insane," he mumbled, shaking his head. "No, I have no idea who Missy was, if she wasn't lying."

"Vincent, you need to understand that Missy is psychotic and obsessive. She loves Axel with everything in her." With a deep breath, she finished it. "But she's not a liar."

He turned around, and they stood chest to chest now. "I'll remember that. I'm sure there's a few options from my childhood and teen years that she might fit."

"She would have been closer to Axel, always. She said she could 'always see his potential.'" It sounded disturbing in hindsight. This Magi, who might not always be a woman, was grooming Axel, following him, even when he was a boy. Missy was certifiable. "Remember, she could have also been playing a male friend. Axel was always weirdly uncomfortable when she tried to be loving with him. I never knew if it was because of just the idea that she could become a man or if they had any history before me."

Vincent nodded slowly, his expression thoughtful. "Thank you for dealing with that. Seeing her, and handling what we know until..."

"Yeah, it's fine. Plus, this should be done quickly and..." She had a small thought. One she wasn't sure would even work.

"And?"

"An idea, but one I can do without you. Keep focusing on this. It's nothing." She kissed his cheek.

He looked distant for a second, his eyes unfocused. When they found her face again, she knew he was back. "I told the guys to come back down. By now, they should know what they want and where. We can do major renovating later on, but we need to move in quickly."

"Where are we meeting them?" she asked as he wrapped an arm over her shoulders.

"Outside. Let's get back to the condo. You and Jasper can work on the Dark Web stuff like you promised me."

"Yeah, we really need to get that moving," she agreed. "And what will you do?"

"Keep reading my favorites. It's taking my mind off it for a moment."

It was better than nothing.

They loaded back into their rides and Sawyer felt like they were a little lighter as she drove away from the house. It wouldn't last, but it was something.

7

ZANDER

Zander settled in behind the desk with Jasper, looking at what Sawyer wanted from them. She left them a list of more than a dozen secret addresses, all hidden from general searches on the web. These were places where someone had to tell you they existed. You needed a backdoor to get into them. They were exclusive.

And they were the places where criminals talked online. Where gossip spread and bounced around. They had caught her in one or two of them during her time with the team.

"This should be interesting," Jasper mumbled, opening his laptop.

Zander could only nod, opening his own. He wished for a minute he was the meathead he let everyone think he was, so that he wouldn't need to help with this tedious shit. He and Jasper were the best two with computers on the entire team. Together, they could get something working for this case.

"Axel," he sighed out. "I can't believe we're doing this."

This time, Jasper could only nod. They had a program based on the same principles of the IMPO's facial recognition software they used on Sawyer. It had a search parameter, like names and locations, and would ping and collect all of those references, wherever they were made. It was a ghost program. Nearly undetectable, since it wasn't actively infecting places. It just monitored from the outside, waiting for things to pop up.

He frowned. "Are we running the facial recognition software at headquarters with Axel's picture? Or Felix, that one Sawyer let walk since she had bigger shit to deal with?"

"Felix, yes. Not for Axel. It wouldn't recognize him based on photos of him without scars and he is definitely scarred, but we don't know how bad. The program likes exact matches and we wouldn't be able to get that. We'd have to loosen up the parameters."

"And then we would end up with ten thousand false ones." Zander saw the issue.

He tried not to be angry about what had happened. He remembered his blow up in the Council Chamber. He'd nearly jumped the Councilman that passed the order to Sawyer. He'd wanted to explode. He'd wanted to hurt people for it.

How could they do this to her? How could they do this to the team? It was their fault he was out and yet, she was being punished. They kept finding ways to punish her.

Even over a week later, he was dealing with the anger and the grief. James, Axel, Sawyer, Vincent. Their lives were a mess. He felt like a child for breaking down the way he did after the funeral. He'd never thought he was weak.

"Zander, get started," Jasper ordered. Zander blinked and saw that Jasper had already begun on his laptop.

"Sorry, was thinking." About how weak he'd been. He needed to be strong for Vincent and Sawyer. He hated Axel, but they were his victims. They were the people nearly broken by the man. He couldn't let this all destroy him when he needed to help them.

"About? We'll talk while we work."

"I need to be strong for Sawyer and Vincent. I can't lose my temper like I did with the WMC or break down like I did after the funeral. They don't need to deal with that. They don't need me weak and childish. They need me to buck up and deal with shit."

Jasper sighed and kept typing. Zander started on his half of the list, hoping to fill the silence he received from Jasper.

They were nearly halfway done when Jasper looked at him again.

"Me too."

"What?" Zander frowned deeper.

"I want to be able to help them. Everyone on this team needs help and to help each other. But just because you want to help them doesn't mean you don't also deserve help." Jasper elbowed him. "I lost my patience after the funeral, and for that, I'm sorry. You should have been able to talk to me. Sawyer shouldn't have needed to come in and deal with me, or you, or anyone else. She deserves her chance to get her head around this too."

"I think her head is around it," he mumbled, typing in the next address. "She's so...focused, Jasper."

"I've noticed."

They all had. The night before, they had all noticed that she locked herself away in that office and never came out. He was glad to hear her well past midnight with Quinn and Elijah, since that at least meant someone had the balls to convince her to sleep. Like how she'd stepped in and forced Vincent to stop and rest.

It all made what he was doing more important. This was them trying to focus on the case without letting it consume them and stop them from having real lives. It could be years before they caught Axel again. They couldn't let it paralyze them. It never had before. They had worked on it between cases, any time he was seen moving, shaking hands, or anything like that.

This was just another case. This was what they always did.

And Sawyer knew all of that, she had to. She knew how to make sure to have a life while doing all of these things. She knew how to hunt and to live. She knew how to balance everything.

"She's a great agent." Zander said it randomly as he finished.

"She's a great assassin. Being an agent is probably easier," his best friend corrected softly.

"No, I meant agent," he snapped back. It made his friend pause. When Jasper's stormy eyes looked back at him, he explained. "She's treating this like a job. Not a vendetta. She's making sure that we remember that we're still homeless agents. We need a base of operations..."

Now he saw his friend's point.

"The two worlds aren't so different," Jasper reminded him. "Agent, assassin, good guy, bad. The only difference is the line and even then, there's a thousand shades of grey." He snorted. "We all just have people telling us to be their dogs, be their weapons, and enforcers. Just depends on who, doesn't it?"

Zander's eyes went wide. A year ago - no, just six months ago, it would have been Vincent saying that. Jasper had never seen the law in greys. He'd believed the worlds couldn't be more different.

Until her.

"And all of that is okay, as long as we do all of this for the right reason," Jasper finished, something wild in his eyes. Something that had never been there before. "But you know, they might think they're justified and right too. Crazy, right?"

"You want out, don't you?" Zander asked softly, noticing how pained Jasper looked.

"I do. I don't want to do this anymore. No matter when it ends, when Sawyer is pardoned, I'm getting out. I can't...be someone else's bulldog. Not after the shit we've been through thanks to the people we're supposed to look up to. I just can't anymore. I can't just be the other side of the coin. I thought I was upholding the idea of a better world, better for all Magi, but..."

He reached out and hugged Jasper with one arm. "I'll support you with anything you decide to do," he promised his oldest male friend. "Anything. I swear it right here, right now."

"I'm not going to ask you to leave with me. That's my promise to you. You do what makes you happy, too, Zander."

He thought about it. The IMPO, after this? He could totally see Jasper's point. They had only joined the IMAS for the money and work, to make a better future. They had jumped into the IMPO because Vincent, James, and Elijah had given them something that seemed better for them. Then they stuck around since it gave them the resources to find Sawyer.

But the IMPO wasn't his dream job. He didn't have one. Hell, even as he thought about it, he considered what he did on the team. He helped with martial arts and self defense. Maybe he could take a page out of Sawyer's book and become a teacher.

Then he immediately scoffed at the idea. He didn't have the temperament for that. He'd hurt all his students.

They didn't say anything else, though. Zander kept his thoughts about it to himself. He didn't have anything to ease how Jasper felt about the IMPO and, in turn, the WMC. He couldn't wipe away their problems from when they were with the IMAS. None of these organizations had been good to them, even when they had been at their best.

He let Jasper leave to go get Sawyer without following . When she walked in, she didn't say anything either. Zander had a feeling Jasper didn't tell her anything except that they were done. Now wasn't the time to think so far into the future.

Sure, it came from her being a great assassin, but her focus and determination were some of her strongest traits. She couldn't be distracted by the existential crisis they were going through.

"It's all ready. You don't need to do anything. Just leave the program running and it'll tell you when something comes up." He waved at the screen in front of him.

"I know, thank you. You can go hang out with the guys. I'll be in here, reviewing and organizing this mess so it's easier to work with." She ran a hand over his shoulder and he grabbed it, giving a small squeeze in appreciation and love. As he stood up, he made sure to wrap an arm around her waist and hold her for a moment.

"I heard you last night. Have a good time?" He was genuinely curious if she did what he figured she did. It gave him ideas.

"I did." With a knowing smile, she didn't confirm or deny what he was really asking.

"I bet they did too," he murmured, kissing her lips, nipping the scar.

"You'll need to ask them."

He chuckled as she pulled away and motioned for the

door. He took the hint. He couldn't stay if he wanted to tease and talk about sex. He knew Jasper would never be into that, but he was curious. Curious how it would be with another guy helping him blow her mind. Seemed like just another team assignment, in a perverse way.

He winked as he closed the door, making her laugh. He found Elijah in the living room, and motioned for the big cowboy to stand up.

"Time for your physical therapy."

Elijah groaned, but got up without any further complaint. It was a simple regimen of stretching, and muscle-strengthening exercises.

And it continued to push Zander closer to the edge of leaving the IMPO. No, the idea was never going to leave. As a healer, Zander had to step back and look at what their jobs had done to their bodies. Magic could only go so far. Their luck was going to run out, and one day, no one would be there in time to save someone.

Like James.

It could have been any of them, if they had thought to leave someone else with the Councilwoman. D'Angelo had sent them gifts and notes, hoping to apologize for everything. They just put it all to the side. For once, Zander couldn't even blame her. Shit happened, and they just needed to clean up the mess and get on with the next mission.

So he thought about Elijah's accident. Quinn being torn up in the jungle and Sawyer going missing out there as well. Jasper losing a leg.

They had been broken by the IMPO and the WMC. By their own people, by friends and enemies.

It wasn't healthy. At the rate they were going, none of them would make it to forty. It was a chilling realization.

Zander was reckless, and he knew that. He made decisions based on how to help someone else, forgoing his own safety, but he didn't want to die young and still lose everyone anyway.

And here he was, doing physical therapy with Elijah, who was as put together as magic could make him. Now they just needed to rebuild his muscles. He was lucky.

Many knew about the badly-broken back, but Zander didn't even tell Elijah what his insides had looked like. Or his head and the nasty, awful crack it had. They had put the man back together. They had held him in the world of the living and forced his body to fix itself as they tried to gather pieces and hold them in place so that they weren't regrowing half a kidney, or lung, which had been shredded and torn up by broken ribs.

It had been a rough time.

They had been so lucky.

Zander knew the luck would run out. The luck always ran out.

8

SAWYER

Two weeks flew by Sawyer, and she didn't know where they went. She stood looking at the new big house, the guys all heading inside with the animals, but she couldn't pick up her feet.

"You know," Thompson said mildly. "I always disliked this house for some reason."

"I'm not sure how I feel about it yet," she said softly. "But we'll be close to New York, I guess. That helps with the case. We'll be able to come in and get things done at headquarters if it's needed. Since James isn't here to do that stuff for us anymore."

"Of course. I'm there, but you don't want me doing much of his old work. I don't know the first thing about it except he made my life a pain in the ass for you all. Just let me know when I can throw my position behind something you need."

"Thanks," she sighed, nodding.

"How's it coming?" he asked, obviously interested, but trying not to act like it.

She growled. It wasn't. Nothing was moving. The

mentions she got about anything to do with Axel were just references to him, but nothing that led to a lead. Nothing that helped her. And once the move-in was finished, she had to bring the guys back into the fold on the case. Sadly, there was barely any case. They were quickly approaching January and she had nothing.

"Take until New Year's Day off and settle in. The case will still be there in January."

She narrowed her eyes on the Director. It was like he read her mind. She didn't know his abilities, but she hoped that wasn't one of them.

She didn't have a way to argue either. Continue monitoring, continue going over old locations. She had already contacted him to have that done. Without telling teams why, other agents all over the world were sent to see and secure a building, a warehouse, or a condo. A farm here and there. Anything she knew from before. Anything Vincent had already known about Axel's organization.

None of them had given her any leads, but they told Axel she was coming. They were at least a warning.

"Fine," she muttered. "The added buildings are still being done, right?"

"Yeah. Elijah's workshop. The garage is finished being expanded as much as we could as well. We also upgraded the old outdoor shooting range."

"Amazing." It was like this was home.

"Go. I need to get back to New York."

"Have a safe drive, Thompson," she called as he got in his car. She waved politely as he drove away, then walked into the house. She tugged on her bond with Sombra and discovered the cat was in her room. She went up, knowing the first thing she needed to do was get used to her space.

Her new, big space, where a woman once lived with a

man who had tried to play games with her and Axel. The thought refused to leave, but she ignored it as she stepped into the room. It looked completely different than the one she had seen only a couple of weeks before.

As she sat on the edge of her king, she realized it was barely her room. Sure, it was deep blue tones with greys like her attic room in Georgia, but it didn't feel like her.

That would just take time.

All in all, she did like the look of the room. She felt like she could be comfortable in it. It was spacious and bright, with two large windows that looked over the backyard. Her private bathroom matched the room.

If she could design a room for herself, it would have been this. Zander had done well, if he was the one who did it. She even had a giant walk-in closet where a massive safe sat in the back. She reminded herself that she still needed to secure her weapons and got to it. She couldn't leave them in a bag forever.

She wasn't paying attention, so when someone cleared his throat, she nearly jumped. Spinning, she saw Vincent standing in the closet doorway.

"When do we get to work?" he asked.

"Whenever you want," she said carefully. The fact that he didn't walk out and start immediately shocked her.

"I've been thinking about who Missy could possibly be from my past, but I'm not drawing any conclusions. There were always a few people who preferred Axel to me and vice versa. We didn't have a rivalry back then, but people tried to play us against each other, especially when I came into my powers first, the younger son." He leaned on the frame. "She could have literally been anyone, right?"

"Yeah." Sawyer didn't know how to help him. It was something they had worked on since Missy had said that to her. "Thompson told me we should take until New Year's Day off and then jump back into it."

Vincent was quiet, looking at her hanging clothes, until he sighed heavily. "I'm inclined to agree with him. We missed Christmas." There was something guilty about the words.

"It's okay," she said softly.

"No. We promised you that we would do something. How are you? None of us...ask enough."

"I'm fine, Vincent. I just stay focused on the task and I'm fine." It was all she had and it was somewhat of a lie. She couldn't bring herself to drown in grief anymore. She had to focus on this. When it was all over, she didn't know where she would be or what she would do, but she could focus on this.

"Well, I'm going to tell the guys the plan. They're all pretty anxious, because we've moved in now and they probably expect me to whip them like a slavedriver."

She had expected it too, honestly, but she was thankful he wasn't going to. It meant he wasn't letting it consume him anymore. She wasn't going to let it consume her either, even though they were both threatened by it at every moment. She had to approach this like every hit, every job, every mission, and every case. Clear-headed and ready for any sign that things would take a step in the direction they needed them to.

She was better at her work now than she was when she tried to leave him and nearly died. She was even stronger than she had been in August. She wasn't scared of Axel Castello anymore. She was angry, and viciously so, but not scared.

She didn't say it to Vincent, but she thought it.

"Go on. I'm sure they'll be excited." She smiled brightly

and waved him along. "I need to organize this mess."

"Of course," he agreed, looking around at the things that hadn't been unpacked for her. "I have to do the same to the office. Jasper is buried neck-deep in the other one. I'll give you one guess where Quinn is."

She chuckled, glad this new home was working out for everyone. That was good. It seemed to be helping them heal from the loss of James, and that was so important.

"What's going to happen to the plantation house?" she asked.

"It'll be put up for sale on the market. I'll miss it, but only because it was our first big house together. We'd finally been set up somewhere nice."

"But?" She knew there was one.

"It was too far from the closest city. It was in the middle of a backwoods area. It was just a pain. It was old, too. Things breaking all the time. You know."

She did. The AC loved to go out in the summer. She waved a hand, gesturing for him to leave so she could get settled in. He kissed her forehead before going and she breathed a sigh of relief. He was doing so much better. She knew forcing him to distance himself from trying to catch Axel would help. They couldn't rush this job or he would always be ahead of them. She knew the rules. They had to be patient, play the board right, send the right signals. They had to tell the man they were coming for him without making it easy for him to side-step if they pushed too hard.

And she could be patient. It was frustrating, but she could do it. She'd hoped to get even an inkling of what he was doing and where, but everything she heard was that he was directing orders from somewhere. He wasn't moving around; he was hiding somewhere, planning something.

And while he'd once obsessed over killing her, none of

the moves she'd heard about had anything to do with her. He hadn't made any public statement about the woman working with the IMPO that used to be his assassin.

Other people were. The public was quiet due to the recent events of New York, but criminals were getting louder. Everyone wanted Axel to say something about her. Everyone wanted her to be dealt with, as all his old places were raided and claimed in the name of the IMPO and the WMC.

And he was eerily silent.

She almost wondered if he was running scared. She didn't think it was the case, but it was a possibility.

"I should get this done," she said to herself, looking at the mess in her room from the closet. It would give her a much-needed distraction from Axel and the case, the job she had to do if she ever wanted to be free to choose her own life again. She had a feeling riding out the next four and a half years wasn't going to cut it anymore. She wouldn't want to, anyway. If they pardoned her in four and a half years and Axel was out there, powerful and dangerous, she would never be safe. Her men would never be safe. Charlie and the kids would never be safe.

"Oh shit!" she exclaimed. "I live in New York!" She grinned. She didn't know why she hadn't thought of it yet. It would be easy to drive into the city once a week and spend the night at the gym.

She could go see them. She had to tell the guys. She wanted to make the trip. She didn't know why she hadn't while staying in the condo, and Charlie had kept his distance after James died, letting them grieve. He'd only stopped by once to check on Elijah, to see how he was healing.

She was still grinning as she left her room and went

downstairs, phasing into Jasper and Zander's new office. It, like always, spooked both men inside.

"SAWYER!" Zander cried out, angry with her.

"I want to find a day before New Year's to go see Charlie and the gym. Visit for the holidays."

They blinked at her until Jasper finally shrugged. "I don't see why not."

"I mean, I just haven't been thinking. We live in the same state now. I can go see them and...after everything, I would really like to."

"Yeah, we'll make a trip before the end of the week. We'll take the entire team, if Vincent was serious about letting us finish enjoying the holidays." Jasper smiled as he kept placing books on his new shelves in the office. "You'll be able to see them more often, if we're going to be living up here for a long time."

She didn't respond to that, only smiled, showing him that she already figured that out.

"Maybe we could do a class with the kids," Zander suggested, grinning now as well. "That would be fun. Someone a bit more up to your speed for them to watch with you."

"Oh yeah, they would love that," she agreed. "We'll make the plans. Maybe I can convince the entire team to join in on it. Not all of you have gotten to meet them."

"CHARLIE, IT'LL BE FUN," she promised again on the phone, three days after she had come up with the idea of a visit. The guys had agreed instantly to her request to go visit Charlie. For some reason, having the new home made things seem almost normal again. Now they could settle.

"All six of you, after everything that's happened. In my gym. Fun. Sure. We'll go with that."

Even though he said it gruffly and somewhat sarcastic, she knew he was teasing.

"Going to be jealous of all the cool young Magi with the kids? No one is going to want the old man teaching them anymore?" She resisted laughing. Barely.

"No." It was such a pouty word.

Then she laughed, pulling the phone away from her face as the unstoppable, belly-shaking laughter hit her.

"Sawyer, you could have visited earlier. I've been telling the kids you need time to grieve and..." He turned serious on her, which killed her laughter effectively. She was glad he couldn't see her fidget, growing uncomfortable.

"I need the distraction," she said softly. "I...Charlie, my entire life for the last few weeks has been grief and trouble. Plus... you don't know yet and we need to talk."

"All right. You all can come down whenever you want. My gym is always open to you, Sawyer. Haven't changed your room at all."

She smiled. She was going to hurt him with her news. She hadn't told him yet about Axel. Very few people knew. He deserved to know, though, in case she showed back up on his doorstep, broken and needing help. The possibility was real. Plus, he was publicly her friend. The world knew about Doctor Charles Malcolm and the girl named Sawyer Matthews, once known as Shadow. He could be a target.

She decided she would text Thompson next and have security put on him. Charlie would hate it, but she wasn't going to let him be vulnerable once the action picked up. And it would. The quiet part of this game was going to end eventually and then everyone would be in danger. This was just another piece of prep for her final game with the older Castello brother.

"We're planning on leaving in the morning. It's why I'm calling, you know. I'm going to let you go, though. Stay safe, Charlie."

"Get some sleep." He hung up on her and she sighed.

Every time she turned around, it was another thing to do with Axel. She hadn't even considered that this trip would remind her to keep Charlie safe. She should have thought of it earlier, she really should have. Feeling stupid, she dropped her phone on the bed next to her. Sombra jumped up onto the bed and curled into her side, a warm comfort.

"I didn't put you at risk with the Triad," she murmured to her jaguar, "because I was worried you would get hurt. I'm going to need you for this, though. Are you ready?"

Nothing but confidence in her hunting skills came through the bond. A pure, animalistic confidence, knowing that she once ruled the jungle, sitting at the top of her food chain.

Sombra was ready.

An hour later, there was a knock at her door. Without waiting for her to respond, Jasper walked in. "What did Charlie have to say?" he asked casually, walking towards her bed.

"He says we can visit whenever, so we're still on for tomorrow." She didn't need to move to make space for him on the bed. He stretched out on her other side.

"I've been thinking more about it. I'm glad we're so close. You've missed Charlie and those kids a lot since we took you away in July."

"I have," she agreed. "It's going to be so good to see them. I should have visited them while we were in the condo, but...something about having a new home again makes it feel easier to relax and make those visits, ya know?"

He nodded. "I think you'll be happier in the long run."

"Me too."

Happiness was something she needed, even just a little of it. There were so many good reasons for her to be unhappy.

She wasn't going to let Axel take away the reasons she had to live and smile. Not this time.

9

QUINN

Q uinn watched his wolves carefully approach the small children, who cautiously reached out to touch big wet noses. Sniffing was happening on both sides of the stand-off. Sombra was even more careful, belly-crawling to a tiny one that couldn't have been much more than a few inches taller than her and weighed much less than her two hundred pounds.

"You didn't say you were bringing wild animals!" Charlie complained, waving a hand at the scene as Sawyer laughed.

"They're our animal bonds! We couldn't leave them. They'll be good with the kids, promise."

Quinn just nodded. From the bond, he could pick up the curiosity and protectiveness of his wolves. These were Sawyer's kids. Not her pups, but hers. Therefore, they were pack pups. Pack pups deserved to feel safe and have play time.

Quinn chuckled as Scout's need to play began to escalate into some bouncing around like he always did as a pup himself.

"What's he doing?" Charlie demanded, stepping closer. No one else was even concerned, but he knew Charlie was protective over the little non-Magi children, even though he knew animal bonds were safe. He'd met Scout, Shade, and Sombra before, but he never thought they would be around a bunch of four to seven year olds. He'd already made that very clear to them when he saw the jaguar and wolves jump out of their vehicles.

"He wants one to play tag. Or all of them. None of the children will be hurt," Quinn answered, smiling back at the big male. "It's okay."

"Do they know they have to be soft?" Charlie asked, calming down as Shade was finally being hugged by one little girl. Sombra was on her back for a belly rub by her tiny new friend. Two kids began to chase Scout, giggling. Anyone watching the scene couldn't resist a smile either.

"Yeah, they do. They helped raise pack pups and they know humans are more fragile."

Quinn's heart squeezed painfully. There was a time when his wolves were excited to play hunting games with the pup they knew Quinn was going to have someday. They had never had the chance.

They had the chance with Sawyer's strays, so they were going to take it. They made it very clear to him that he would need to fight to get them to stop playing before they dropped from exhaustion.

"Okay..." Charlie backed off after that.

Sawyer was still laughing as the big man walked away. She leaned her shoulder against his. "Sombra loves this. All these unsuspecting people to steal from." She was chuckling as she said every word, a wide smile on her face.

It was the first one like it he'd seen in a few weeks. She seemed at peace for a moment, even while he knew the idea of Axel being out there was eating her apart. She didn't let it show. She lived in the moment and only for the moment.

"Yes, I bet she does," he replied. "Where did the guys wander off to?" He hadn't been paying attention, because while he trusted their animals, he did want to keep an eye on them. Sombra was still new to being around so many people, and Scout could get too excited if he wasn't careful. He knew that was why he still had Sawyer next to him as well.

"Zander is teaching a class for the teenagers. Elijah is with Jasper, and they want to talk to Charlie about how they could change up their respective physical therapies. Neither of them really need it anymore. Elijah's back up to speed, but better safe than sorry."

"And Vincent?" he asked, glancing at her. A heavy sigh was his reply and she pulled away, nodding towards the front door.

His eyes followed the direction of hers. Vincent hadn't come in yet. He was smoking outside, staring away from the building. It was almost like he was scared, glancing towards them, looking inside every so often then turning away again.

"What's wrong?" he asked.

"I have a guess, but I don't want to push it." She crossed her arms. "I was hoping this would be some healing for him. A few weeks ago, I considered asking him if he'd want to make a trip with me, but never got the chance. I think it has to do with..."

A nephew. A boy with dark curly hair and olive-green eyes like the rest of the men in his family.

Quinn could understand Vincent's pain. He'd never even had the chance to meet Henry, and now they were on the case to catch the man who killed him. A brother. A father.

He eyed Sawyer again as she watched Vincent. An old lover.

An enemy.

Axel held many places in the lives of those around him. Quinn only really knew of the man. Sure, they had hunted him. He'd only been in the same space with the evil Magi once, when they fought in that hangar bay and arrested him. Other than that, Quinn was on the outside.

"I can go talk to him," he offered. He had yet to tell his brothers about his own boy. Maybe then Vincent would find the strength to come inside.

"No-"

"I can do it," he repeated. Vincent deserved to know his pain and what healing he received from this visit, so that maybe he would be strong enough to confront his own. He left Sawyer there and headed for the door. He saw Vincent's eyes go wide as he approached.

Once outside, he saw Vincent light another cigarette.

"I'm not in the mood for the kids right now," he said quickly, looking away from Quinn.

"You're thinking about Henry, and it's okay to admit that."

Vincent flinched at the statement but didn't say anything.

"You should come in. These kids and people are important to Sawyer. She wants us to do gifts with them later." He tried to soften it, change it to the present.

"Of course she does," he said softly. "I thought I could, but I can't, Quinn."

"If I can, so can you." He wasn't going to let his pack leader hide from his pain any longer. Weeks of this. Lashing out and back-tracking, like there was a festering wound somewhere that couldn't be treated or healed. He needed

Vincent to lance it and let the infection out or the festering was going to destroy everything that meant something to him. He just couldn't let Vincent do that to himself.

"What do you have to do-"

"My son was killed," he answered, not letting Vincent finish the question. "And if I can go in there and let my wolves play with young ones, so can you. If I can constantly meet children and enjoy their company, knowing my son should be their age... then so can you."

Vincent dropped his cigarette and cursed as he picked it back up. "Why didn't you ever tell me you had a son, Quinn?"

"I only told Sawyer while we were in the Amazon. I've never even truly told Elijah. Hinted a little, but never said the words. I understand, Vincent. If there's one thing I get, it's that."

"I never even got to know him." The Italian sighed, flicking his cigarette. "I never got to know him..."

"But you know Sawyer, and she's told you a lot about him. And she loves these strays like she loved him."

He saw Vincent's Adam's apple bob from a thick swallow. Then he nodded. "Thank you for saying that," he whispered.

"You won't feel comfortable the first time, or the second, but one day you'll look at this as a chance to have the friendships and experiences you should have had with him." That's how Quinn and his wolves were going about it. This was another chance, and Sawyer was giving it to them. That made it special.

These children were her second chance, and she was sharing them. With people like him and Vincent.

He wondered what Vincent thought about that as the male looked into the window. Quinn looked as well. Sawyer was watching them and smiled, then a teenager ran up to her, throwing some play punches. She responded in kind, landing a soft blow on the boy's stomach. Both were laughing as she hugged him close and it was returned.

"Come inside," Quinn ordered. "Enjoy it, heal, or don't, but don't darken this for her. She's been working hard for you and all of us so we could take the time to get a new home and James settled."

"That makes it worse," Vincent said. "I thought I was okay for so long now. Axel was behind bars. I grieved Henry and the missed chance. And now…"

Ah. Quinn could see. Axel being free didn't just tear open one wound. He tore open all of Vincent's wounds. He reopened scars and flayed Vincent by just breathing.

And for that, Quinn felt the rage he knew was building in Sawyer, deep in her heart. He'd caught glimpses of it. Now he truly understood. How dare *this Magi* do this to his pack's leader, his friend, his brother. Vincent belonged to *him*, not this other Castello. Vincent belonged to her.

No. He wasn't okay with all the pain Vincent felt just because his littermate walked free. Being born of the same bitch didn't mean he should be allowed to have so much power.

And Quinn was tired of having to tell Vincent that Axel didn't matter. He had brothers. He didn't need Axel.

"You have a pack. Put that male out of your head before I start getting pissed off. I'm tired of him hurting you, Vincent." The words were growled out and angry. "I told you. He isn't your brother. I am. Jasper, Zander, and Elijah. We're your family. Sawyer is your mate. Forget that male. He's just the enemy."

And he's a dead one. If Sawyer didn't get the chance, Quinn decided he would. No male deserved the right to live if he could continuously inflict this sort of pain on those he was supposed to be in a pack with. No male deserved to have a brother or a son if this was what he did to them.

"One day, I'll get annoyed with you for giving me that speech," Vincent responded softly. "But I'm always grateful for it."

"I just don't understand why you hold on to him and you let him cause you so much pain," Quinn said with exasperation. "I don't understand, Vincent."

"I know."

Quinn frowned at Vincent's simple answer, something about it annoying him. He reached out, took his cigarette and threw it. There was nothing it could set on fire. Then he took a handful of Vincent's shirt and pulled, forcing the man to follow him inside, ignoring how the Italian demanded that he stop. He noticed that Vincent didn't sublimate and get away, though.

He dragged Vincent inside and straight to Sawyer.

"This is yours," he said. "You can deal with it." Then he left Vincent with her and went to find Elijah, or anyone else. He heard her clear laugh as he walked away. His wolves wondered where he was going. He didn't have an answer.

He didn't stop until he was in the back classroom. There was no Elijah, but Zander was there, grinning as he taught youths only a decade younger than the team.

"And everyone, meet Quinn. He's the one who brought the wolves." Zander pointed him out. "What are you doing back here? Figured you'd play with the little ones all day since they want to play with the *puppers*."

Quinn managed an uncomfortable smile as everyone turned to him. "I got annoyed with Vincent so I left him with Sawyer. I was hoping to find Elijah, actually, so I'll-"

"Stay! You can help me." Zander jogged to him at the

door from the front of the classroom. He threw an easy arm over his shoulder. "They've been asking me about things, like what sort of shit we do with the IMPO."

"Oh. We catch murderers, and bust...white-collar crime, like fraud and things like that." Five years before, he wouldn't have even known what white-collar crime was. "Well, most of the IMPO does that. We're Special Agents. We deal with serial killers and larger crime organizations. Sometimes a legend."

"See, Zander said the same thing, but you guys work with Sawyer!" one young female said, her eyes bright with curiosity. "She's always been, like, a major badass but she never told us that she, like...killed people. That's fucking wild."

He looked at his redheaded friend and raised an eyebrow. He only received a sigh in response. He focused back on the young adults. At their age, he was a father, or about to be. A few were his age when he'd walked away from his old life. They were so different from him. It was why he preferred the much younger children. He could relate to them, in a way. There was an innocence in the children that wasn't in these older ones.

"She's a predator," he started, hoping he could relate how it was working with Sawyer. "She's focused on the hunt, whether it comes with a kill at the end or not. She's intelligent and knows how to use every available resource for the task, including those around her. She's dangerous, but she's not. She knows when it's called for. You all know she's capable of violence. I've heard stories about what she's done to protect you. So has Zander. Working with her is like watching it in action." He saw the oldest look away, like he was remembering something. "You've seen it, haven't you?"

"She dealt with some problems for me. More than once," the young man answered.

"She's dealt with some problems for me too. More than once." There was no shame in it.

Zander nodded next to him, agreeing, but not jumping in.

"She killed my father the night we met. He was beating me, I thought I was going to die, and she was suddenly there. In a matter of moments, I wasn't being kicked into the ground and my father was...screaming for help. I didn't get up for him. It all happened so fast. There's no describing it, so I never tried."

Everyone turned to look at the oldest boy in the group now.

"Liam, are you serious?" the young woman asked, her mouth gaping.

"How do you think I ended up living with her and Charlie until I went to college?" he asked back. "I have a brother, but he's not stupid enough to come back and bother me. She saved my life that night. I'll never forget it."

Quinn smiled as the kids started talking about how they each met Sawyer. That was better. He didn't think she wanted them to be talking about the darker spots of her life. She might have hurt a lot of people bringing this pack together, but in the end, this was her bright. This was her good half. The passionate, the fearsome, the protective.

"Thanks," Zander whispered to him. "They've been bothering the shit out of me, but I haven't found a way to get them diverted off of knowing more about how she was Shadow."

"I wasn't planning on diverting them. I was going to tell them until they were scared as shit of her, and make them regret it. And Sawyer would probably have been upset with me, but a healthy dose of fear is sometimes good." He shrugged. "This was luck."

Zander began to chuckle, leaning into him to hide it from the teenagers.

"Are you okay?" He didn't like how Zander's shoulders were shaking as hard as they were.

"Oh, man, if only they knew what case we were on right now," he finally said, gasping for air. "I shouldn't be laughing, but it's the only proper response to how fucked up it is."

Quinn looked around again. At Zander, at the teenagers, at Sawyer in the main room with Vincent. The Italian was finally on the ground, with a kid on his lap, smiling as the child appeared to be telling him something. Shade and Scout were keeping a close eye on their leader. Elijah and Jasper finally walked out of the back with Charlie, laughing about something.

Sawyer's new world. The one she made for herself.

And they had to put the old one to rest. These kids wanted to know Shadow and they didn't know she was in the building, right behind those dark eyes. Always just beneath the surface. Sawyer was hunting. When she looked up and noticed him, he caught just a flash of it, that focus, then she smiled and waved, the feeling disappearing.

First they had to let Shadow rest. They had to make sure that persona wasn't always haunting them in the back of her eyes.

10

SAWYER

"Charlie, I need to talk to you privately," she said quickly, grabbing him before he went anywhere else. Now that Vincent was settled, enjoying the company of a six-year-old on his lap, she could handle this. He needed to know that she was going to put protection on him. Just in case everything went sideways.

"All right," he responded, waving a hand. She thought they would go to his office, but instead, he led them all the way up to the old apartment. He locked the door behind them and pointed to the dining room table. It felt like old times, like she was about to be checked over and berated for getting as hurt as she did. It felt like the last time they had a private talk about Axel.

She sat down obediently. There were times she just wanted a father like Charlie, and she figured he knew that. She just wanted to be the young one, the one who needed some advice, some guidance, and even a telling off. She hadn't realized how much she genuinely missed sitting at this table, knowing she was about to divulge a secret she could only tell him.

He didn't sit with her immediately. He wandered into the kitchen and got them each a glass of water. He pulled out two of her favorite premade salads, which surprised her, and brought everything over to the table.

"We'll feed your men and the children junk food," he said casually, putting a salad in front of her. "But I'm trying to bring my weight back down and I know you don't like eating trash."

"Worried about your health, finally?" she asked softly, watching him pop open the salad.

"It's about time. With you dealing with the IMPO, there's only me and Liam here with all of these kids. He's too young to be on his own, I think. I never had kids. You and he are all I have left of me when I go. I want to stick around until I think you're both ready." He smiled sadly at her. "James was my age."

She nodded slowly. "Yeah…"

"He loved your men like sons. He wasn't ready to leave them here, I think."

"I know."

"You and Liam are the children my wife and I always would have wanted."

"Damn it, Charlie." She couldn't touch the glass of water. Her hands were shaking too badly for a moment as tears flooded her eyes.

"What's so important that you needed to tell me alone?"

"We discovered Axel escaped from prison," she whispered, hoping there weren't already bugs in his home. She hadn't checked. She should have. "I…"

"They want you to catch him again." His voice was strained, his face tight with an emotion she couldn't yet identify.

"They want me to kill him, and I'm going to. They'll

pardon me if I do it. They were going to pardon me for the Triad situation, but then we found out that Axel was free and..." She finally grabbed her glass and took a long swallow of water. "I've spent the last few weeks digging into everything I can about him. No leads yet, but when they come, I have a feeling things are going to get wild."

"And what does that mean?"

"I'm going to put protection on you. Don't argue with it, please." She knew there was a possibility. "Please, Charlie. I can't let him come after you. I couldn't handle that."

"Why would he?"

"To hurt me. To knock me off my game. Maybe even just to get revenge against you. You publicly admitted you're the reason I'm alive after..."

"Okay. I'll accept the protection. I'm going to keep Liam here too, so he's protected."

"I'll have one of our agents follow him to class and shit," she promised.

"I wish I could say I can't believe or understand it. Why would our government do this? Why would they ask this of you?" Charlie leaned back, dropping his plastic fork, shaking his head. Anger, that was the emotion on his face. He looked so upset for her.

"But you do understand, don't you?"

"I do," he admitted softly. "And when it's all over?"

"I don't know. I plan on living through this, Charlie. I plan on them living through this. I don't care what I have to do to succeed, but no one is going to die for this. Not you, not them. Not me." She gave an aimless shrug. "But I don't know about when it's all over. Where I'll be, what I'll do. I can't think about that yet. First I need to do this, ya know?"

He frowned, going back to his salad. She started eating her own, letting the silence grow longer. She didn't think about after. She couldn't. She needed to stay focused on the task. She needed that. She had so much to do and things would get missed if she wasn't completely dedicated to them right now. The future was just that. The future. She wouldn't worry about it, not yet.

When they were both done, she played dutiful daughter figure and took all of the trash, tossing it out for him. She noticed his trash can was nearly full and pulled out the bag, tying it off. She placed a fresh one in. Tossing the old one over her shoulder, she stopped next to him before leaving.

"Thank you for listening to me. Charlie, you are the first important thing I ever had after him. The first person I trusted, the first person I knew would never hurt me. The first person who taught me that sometimes we all fall and it's okay to get back up, fighting back stronger and faster." She swallowed the lump in her throat. "You've defended me and I hope-"

He stood up and wrapped beefy arms around her shoulders. She needed it. Of all the people who knew how Axel had left her, only Charlie got to see. Only he got to see for years the nightmares and the pain, and yet he loved her anyway. He was always there, watching out for her, dealing with her.

"You can do this, Sawyer. I hate that you have to, but you can do it. I'll be here on the other side of it, and will be for a long time after it. I promise I'll always be in your corner, whether it's Fight Night, or the IMPO, or the press. I've got you. Just promise an old man you really will do this and it'll be the end. That I'm never going to have to worry about whether you come home alive or not."

"It'll be the end," she promised. She knew that much.

"Take the trash out," he ordered, trying to lighten the mood.

He pointed to the door and she chuckled as she made the short walk back down the stairs and left through the back of the gym. She tossed her bag in the dumpster and stayed there for a moment. Damn that old man for breaking her heart and still being everything she ever needed from him. She could only wish she helped people as much as he helped her. He never had to hurt people. As a healer and a doctor, he knew how to do everything else. He put people back together. He put her back together.

She went back inside and saw him finishing the climb down the stairs.

"Let's go order these boys some junk food," he said, smiling.

"Yeah." She was smiling as they went back into the main section of the gym. She saw Vincent and frowned. He wasn't as content as when she'd left him. He was pale and sickly as he walked away from the younger children towards her. "What's wrong?" she asked quickly.

"I think I have guesses as to who Missy was," he answered.

"And?"

"Too many people," he said ominously. "I want to go see her."

"Vincent..." She didn't think that was the best idea. "We promised to take the holidays off. This is work. She's not going anywhere." If anything, she felt Vincent visiting might just escalate Missy. So far, the prison had been doing really well at keeping Missy from harming herself. It helped that Missy hadn't tried either, which boggled Sawyer's mind. She would have thought Missy was loyal enough to her master.

"I want to go see her, Sawyer. I'll leave it to you to schedule. Not right now, but tomorrow. Make it happen."

She recoiled slightly at the order as Vincent turned on

his heel and walked out the front of the gym. She watched him light a cigarette and enter his own world again.

Pulling out her phone, she sent the text to Thompson. He would make sure Missy was ready for whatever Vincent had planned for her.

SAWYER DROVE SILENTLY the next day. She was taking only Vincent to the prison, leaving the team to enjoy another full day with Charlie and the kids. Sombra would have the company of the wolves. She wasn't going to put her big feline through another visit.

She didn't want to admit she was pissed off at the man next to her. He knew she had wanted some holiday time, but apparently that didn't matter. Apparently, they had to catch Axel right now, or bother Missy or something. She didn't know what he was going to get out of this right now that he couldn't deal with in a week.

Was catching Axel a priority? Yeah, it was.

But she didn't want it to overtake her life. She was done with losing everything for that man. She wanted this to be another case, which was going to take time since Axel was already ten steps ahead of them.

She had just wanted some peace for the last week of the holidays. The team had done nothing for Christmas. Couldn't they at least have the week between that and New Years? Even just the last few days of the year?

Apparently not.

"Stop sulking," he said softly, looking away from her like he had the entire drive. "We'll do this, then get back to the guys."

Gritting her teeth, she resisted a very Quinn-like snarl. Sulking? Her? She wasn't sulking.

"Fine," she snapped. She turned into the parking lot too fast, knowing Vincent wasn't going to be ready for it. He swayed and hit the door, turning to glare at her when he regained his balance from it. She slammed the brakes a little too hard when they were in the parking spot, causing him to jerk forward.

Sulking.

"Someone's in a bad mood," he muttered, getting out of the car, her car, as fast as possible.

She ran her hands over the steering wheel, considering the last time she and Vincent had been in it together. He'd been drunk and upset. She'd been exasperated.

But she hadn't been furious with him and he hadn't been... whatever he was now. She knew what his problem was that night. She had no idea what was going on with him now. He would give her the same small, loving smile sometimes and others he would be completely closed off to her. This wasn't Elijah, or any other time she had an issue with one of the guys.

This was Vincent Castello, and she knew he was being torn up inside but she had no idea how to get him to tell her. She had no idea how to tell him to open up so she could help or find someone who could. She didn't even know the source of his issue yet. Was it that Axel was free? Was it the fact that she had to execute him? Was he reeling that hard over James still? All of the above? None of it?

She just felt the gap between them widen with every time he shut her down, and it was barely fixed when he finally offered her a normal smile or comment.

She got out of her car, watching him walk inside. He hadn't waited on her. This was what she kept thinking about. They didn't spend time together anymore and...he was treating her like one of the guys, or like he had when they met. Not one of his closest friends, not his lover.

Just the criminal he needed to deal with.

That thought ran through her mind like a hot poker, more painful than she considered it could be. No, she only caught glimpses of the Vincent she had come to know and love. This man was the one she'd had issues with when they met.

She walked in and saw him waiting at the front desk, the guard not there. He kept tapping a knuckle on the plexiglass, hoping to catch someone's attention.

"You were so excited to get us moving this morning that we're early. Sit down. They'll have her ready when they come to get us." She pointed at the waiting area. He frowned, apparently not liking her order.

"This was supposed to be-"

"I told you the meeting would be at ten a.m. You decided we should be here at nine thirty. This is on you. Sit. Down."

He groaned, pushing away from the guard window, and went over to the waiting area.

She waited another two minutes and smiled as the guard walked into the back room where she could see him.

"Hey. I'm going to pretend you aren't here for a little while longer."

"Oh, okay," the Magi mumbled, sitting down in his spot in the window. She just kept smiling.

"Is she ready?"

"Yes, she is. Why are you...?"

"Teaching a friend some patience," she answered. He was forgetting the world didn't run on his schedule or hers. Hell, it didn't even run on Axel's. It ran the way it ran and nothing, no amount of being an ass, was going to speed it up or slow it down for any of them.

So, she waited with the guard for another ten minutes, until she felt like that was good enough. Being early wasn't a bad thing, but rushing was. She hoped Vincent spent the few moments of silence in the waiting area thinking about how to approach this calmly and not whatever he was now, whatever was wrong with him since James died.

She went and waved at him to follow her. He sublimated and crossed the distance in half the time of just walking. She frowned as he reformed next to her. She decided he must be feeling anxious. She narrowed her eyes on his hands, noticing how they stayed curled up until he shoved them into his coat pockets. A guard led them back to the same interrogation room she met Missy in the last time.

Before he walked in, she grabbed Vincent, knowing she needed to give him one last warning.

"Vincent, I did this without you or the rest of the team last time so you didn't have to know this part." She took a deep breath. "Axel had a standing order for his Ghosts and me that if we got arrested, we needed to...handle it before we gave up any information."

He turned slowly, looking over her face. She waited for the judgement.

"He wanted you to kill yourself," he whispered, devoid of emotion.

"Yes."

He nodded, looking away again. "And you came here since you knew..."

"I knew seeing her and saying what needed to be said could push her over the edge. The fact that she hadn't tried yet meant she was still hoping he would come save her. He won't, and I needed her to tell me anything I could get. So we had a conversation between two people. Two people who used to work for him." She swallowed.

"You were willing to be the push over the edge." He narrowed his eyes at her.

"Yeah, because I wasn't willing for you to be that push. Or any of the team, really. So, whatever happens in there, I need you to understand it's not you. She's not...the way she is because of you. Hell, while I accept some responsibility, it's not my fault either." She wouldn't carry Missy around like that.

"How has she not gotten away with it yet? Suicide."

"I've had the guards on watch for it. I warned them before I left last time. Just in case."

"That's nice of you," he murmured. "Okay. Thank you for that." He turned back to the door, but she didn't let go of his forearm. "Sawyer..."

"I'm coming in with you."

"I wasn't going to leave you out here," he responded, looking back at her over his shoulder. "I'm not dealing with any of these people without you."

That relieved her in ways she couldn't describe. At least she had that. He wasn't going to pass over her to deal with people he didn't know, when she had a wealth of knowledge and experience with them. That meant he still trusted her.

They walked in together, like they had when they visited Axel earlier in the month.

No...when they had inadvertently visited Missy, thinking she was Axel.

They sat across from her. She didn't look as pleasant as she had the last time Sawyer saw her. Her hair was wild and so were her eyes. She glanced between them furiously, baring her teeth in an anger Sawyer knew had no end. Missy hated them. They were her enemy and she was theirs.

"You were my tutor. And one of my father's advisors."

Sawyer didn't react, but she wanted to. Internally, she was gasping in shock. Her eyebrows would have climbed up her forehead like they were trying to escape.

But she showed nothing, just like Vincent as he said those words.

"I know this since there was a tutor who always knew certain things about my father's business I never could quite explain. And she kept saying she was just preparing us for the future when Axel and I asked. The advisor, a man, would always make sure to spend time with me and Axel when he visited, where all the others, including our father, would ignore us. You made sure to keep interacting with us."

Missy finally changed from anger to a smile. "You were always intelligent. Took you a decade longer than Axel to figure it out, but then, I gave him the hint a decade ago." Missy leaned back in her chair, relaxed finally. "What does it change, Vincent?"

"I just want to know your story, really."

Missy laughed. It was a laugh that made Sawyer uncomfortable. "My story? I could tell you my story over the last three hundred years. Did you know that we doppelgangers won't die of old age unless we accidentally take on an old form? As long as I find a new, appealing, younger form to take every few decades, nothing can stop me from living for eternity. No, you want my story with Axel, and in a way, you. I can tell you that. It won't help you, but maybe if I satisfy your curiosity, you'll leave me alone.

"I was working for your father as an advisor. I've always positioned myself in criminal families. Government isn't my thing and they would look too closely for me to get away with it. Becoming your father's advisor was easy, honestly. He wasn't the worst Castello, but the family was slowly, very slowly, losing power. Then I met you and Axel. Like everyone else, I thought you would be great at first. Then your mother died.

"Then I saw it. I saw what sort of potential Axel had and cultivated it. I knew you could be useful. I never thought you would ever want out, so I positioned him to make you his second in command, along with me. Along with the hand-picked loyal people I've met over the years. Talyn is still in this prison somewhere. I've known him for over a century. One day I went to him and said I found the Magi that could make us everything we'd ever wanted to be. Rich, powerful, immortal. With Axel, nothing would ever stop us, and when he passed away of old age, we would have a trained and hand-picked successor, one Axel taught to live on for him."

Missy shrugged, still smiling. "It's not a complicated story."

"But it ends here. He's not coming to break you out." Vincent was staying nonchalant as well.

Sawyer was trying to comprehend how old Missy was. And she was in love with Axel, it was clear every time she said his name. She fell in love with a boy and helped raise him into the man he became. Something about it made Sawyer a little sick to her stomach. It could have been Vincent.

"Yes..." Missy's face turned sour and bitter, like suddenly she had a bad taste in her mouth. "I never thought he would leave me and Talyn here. I never..."

"He thought you were freaks," Sawyer mumbled.

"Oh, I thought he would leave you in a prison to die. And there was a time I thought you were loyal enough to kill yourself. Loyalty. That's what I think was always missing from you. Sure, you had that teenage girl love for him, but you will never know the depth of Talyn's and my need for him. Our hopes for his future. Our future." Missy had ignored what she said and continued to drive that painful nail into Sawyer's mental coffin containing her feelings for Axel.

"Yet you're still here and haven't proven that loyalty," Vincent noted softly. "He's left you, Missy. And Talyn. Maybe we can talk to him next. From what I know, he's been locked away in a lonely cell since the moment we caught him. We want to learn more about his kind and so we're not bothering him about Axel. Maybe I should start."

"Or maybe we can use Missy for the science experiments and learn more about doppelgangers," Sawyer muttered, knowing everyone in the room was ignoring her now.

"He'll come for me!" Missy screeched. "He has to! I made him what he is."

"Then you should know," Sawyer snapped. "We've had this conversation. If you know Axel as well as you think you do, then you should know he's never coming for you. You are officially dead weight, damn it. Your loyalty to him might be that deep, but it doesn't go the other way, Missy. We're tools. You, Talyn, me. We're all just pawns in his fucking game, damn it. Stop thinking you're more important to him than you are. He could have tried to get Talyn out when you switched places with him. He left Talyn once already. He's. Not. Coming."

"Sawyer." Vincent's tone was patient but strong. He wanted her to stop. "Missy, we'll stop bothering you."

Missy had tears in her eyes and crossed her arms over her chest. Sawyer had thought Missy would go down by now. Thought she would have finally followed the last order. Now Sawyer knew why it hadn't happened. Missy wasn't allowing herself to believe it. She refused to think, for all her centuries, that a man she helped make would leave her here to rot and die.

The power in that, Sawyer didn't understand. Or maybe she did. She refused to die because she hated the man that much. Missy was refusing to because of how much she loved him.

Two sides of the same coin, in a really sick and fucked-up way.

"Let's go, Sawyer. She's not going to say anything."

"I could have told you that," she replied, following Vincent out of the room. "Did you get what you wanted?"

"I think? I'm not sure. I just needed to hear that. I never... She made him. She and Talyn, and my family."

"It could have been you." Sawyer's mind kept going back to that. The Castello brothers were very different men, but in some ways, they were very similar. Vincent and Axel shared a cunning mind, though Vincent's was tempered and controlled by his emotions, even when he wanted to lock them away. Axel was unbridled intelligence and cruelty and normally had no emotions. When he did, he had no control over them, unlike Vincent.

Two sides of the same coin,

"It could have been me - you're not wrong. Weird to think about."

"Do you really want to talk to Talyn?" she asked softly. She was willing, but by now, she figured there wasn't anything they could learn from him. Missy was free more recently and would know recent changes to Axel's organization where Talyn wouldn't.

"No. He's fine where he is. We made that deal with him. He's on his best behavior, teaching us about his kind. One day, since he can't change forms, we'll parole him."

"Why didn't I know that?" she demanded in a hiss.

"Because he won't be paroled until we're all dead. He's immortal. He's biding his time. He knows he's not in danger if he doesn't give up anything on Axel, and in the long run, this helps him more and us more as a people. Funny, isn't it? He became neutral. Why is that?"

"I would guess it's because Axel didn't save him from me that day in the hangar bay," she answered, considering it. "He was using a portion of Axel's magic and Axel hung him out to dry when he ran out. Axel always thought it was gross for Talyn to be what he was."

"Exactly."

"You should have told me sooner," she said with a bite.

"I learned last night, actually. I had been hoping to play Missy and Talyn against each other and called Thompson myself about it. He let me know. He actually gave Talyn over to research teams and such. He's technically no longer in the custody of the IMPO. Why didn't you ever try talking to Talyn?"

"He's been in prison too long. He wouldn't know any relevant information." It seemed simple to her. Vincent went through a lot to get to a conclusion she had already found. Talyn wasn't going to be helpful.

"That's also a valid point."

Yeah, she knew that, so she didn't respond.

They walked out of the prison together, Sawyer waving at the guard at the desk. When they were back in her car, she sighed, not starting it up immediately.

"We need to talk," she admitted to him.

"About?" He frowned, his dark olive-green eyes becoming hard.

"Us."

That got his jaw to drop. "Do you...want to...end it?"

"You've been pushing me away," she whispered. "This?

Vincent, you barked an order at me, even when we had made a deal to let it rest, just until after the New Year. You can't...treat me like that." She shook her head. "No, I don't want to end it, but I need..."

"You need me to be...normal, and I haven't been." He looked away from her again. "I'm sorry. There's been a lot on my mind."

"I know, but I need you to not let this keep getting to you. Vincent, you're erratic, and that could get one of us hurt. And that's not something I'm willing to allow."

"I understand. I'm trying."

"You're getting better every day, but then something comes up and you fall back into it, this obsession. This need to do everything right now, even when you don't have to."

"And you don't want to get him? Right now?"

She thought about that. Her immediate answer was yes. If he were easy to get to, she would do everything in her power to finish it. But that wasn't the answer she could give him. It was more complicated than that.

"I would rather do this right, and make sure we all get out of it on the other side, than rush it because of my personal feelings and get someone hurt." She met his gaze and they sat there for a minute.

"Nothing I've done could hurt anyone else."

"Except yourself," she corrected.

"Sawyer..." He sounded annoyed and exasperated with her.

"I'm tired of this argument. Let's just get back to the guys," she said quickly, not wanting to do this *again*. She was tired of telling him to back off, calm down, focus.

She was just scared to see what happened when she let him off the leash. She was so scared.

11

VINCENT

Vincent's heart pounded as he sat next to her. Fuck. He'd really thought there for a moment that she was going to say she couldn't be with him anymore. That she didn't *want* to be with him anymore.

It had been the most terrifying second he'd ever experienced. He couldn't do this without her. He would have fallen apart weeks ago. He thought he was holding himself together all right. He didn't think it was so bad that she was that frustrated. Sure, she'd gotten hot with him once or twice, but today had been different. She'd been furious with him for needing to do this right now.

Glancing at her in the driver's seat, he swallowed a lump in his throat as they pulled up to the gym. He should tell her why this was driving him mad. It was everything. All of it. He didn't just need to catch his brother. No, the team had to kill him. They were never supposed to be the executioners. This wasn't the role of the IMPO. It had been a mess in the Amazon, assisting the IMAS because Quinn was being forced to go. They weren't supposed to be the hand that delivered judgement.

Not him. Not his team.

Not her. He'd never wanted this for her.

They had done so well, that first case. They had caught the killer, and he was getting help. They had opened up the ability for others to come in and clean the area up. Then, it all went to hell.

He was tired and mad. Not just at his brother, but his bosses. Vincent had to run to them because they were the good guys.

Now, he wasn't sure. What sort of good guys told a woman she had to kill and keep killing to earn her freedom? And what kind of man was he that he wanted his brother's head? That he'd screamed for it, in retribution for James.

What kind of man did that make him?

And yet, when Vincent opened his mouth, he couldn't get the words out. There was more, and yet he couldn't even say a tiny bit of it. He was a ball of conflict and pain, and he wasn't sure where to go with any of it.

Quinn kept telling him that he should let Axel go and that Axel wasn't his brother. Not in his heart. Vincent knew that. He'd let go of that part a long time ago.

No, Axel was just a cruel man who kept hurting him and the people he cared about.

"I..." Again the words failed him.

"Yeah?" She frowned, her eyes still on the road.

"I'm sorry for my behavior," he finally whispered.

"You're hurting. It's obvious to everyone, and we'll make it through it," she promised. "This is the hardest thing you and I will ever deal with. The guys know it. We're not going to just abandon each other now."

He nodded. Well, at least she understood that part. He knew she understood that part, but no matter how many times someone said it to him, he had a hard time thinking he could make it through and not hate himself for it in the end.

He wanted his brother dead and he was sitting next to the woman who had to do it. He had two conflicting feelings about that. One, he was furious with the WMC. He hated them with every fiber of his being for what they had said to her in their Chamber. They had given her this awful task to take on her soul. This was only going to add to every scar she'd already gotten.

But another part of him was glad it was her. He and the team could help her and if anyone else knew failure wasn't an option, it was her.

They stopped in front of the gym and he slid out first, knowing he still couldn't find the words. He went inside instead, looking for the clean, innocent company of the kids inside. They didn't know the things haunting his every step, making him feel like his world was upside down.

Quinn had been right about that too. They were healing, Sawyer's 'strays.' He could think he was their uncle too, in a way. He was Sawyer's friend, and Sawyer was in charge. And that meant he could get away with anything to make them smile, since he was the adult that didn't need to follow her rules.

He wasn't going to tell the guys how much he was enjoying playing with toddlers, though. If that got out, he would never hear the end of it.

Kaar landed on his shoulder right before he walked inside, wanting to experience the kids as well this time. He'd let Vincent learn about them the day before, and now he wanted to be cool and special like the big animals.

Vincent chuckled. Yeah, he wanted to be big and cool

like Sawyer and Quinn too. Like his raven, he was too stand-offish for most of the kids. But a few wanted to talk to him and let him read a story.

It gave him just a moment of peace. He was almost a little mad at himself for realizing who Missy was when he was playing with them the day before. He hadn't wanted to deal with any of it, but he knew it would be on his mind for days if he didn't confront it.

"Vincent!" one of the young girls said loudly, running for him. "Who is that?" she pointed to Kaar, who fluffed up, trying to seem impressive.

"Well, yesterday I said I also have an animal bond, remember? Kaar is my raven. He's nervous and doesn't like crowds or people too much. He likes to be alone, but he wanted to come meet you and everyone else today." He lifted an arm for Kaar to jump on and he lowered down onto one knee so the girl could gently touch Kaar's head. "Now, he's a bit more fragile than those three." He nodded for the two wolves and jaguar, all rolling around as kids laughed and watched them wrestle. "But I know he loves snacks." He looked over his shoulder and saw Quinn, focusing to send a message.

"Quinn, do you have anything for Kaar to eat from the kids? And maybe bring a small fold out table or something he can stand on?"

The girl cooed things to his raven, making the bird feel showered in affection that never usually happened. In only a couple of minutes, Quinn and Zander were there, setting up a place where kids could sit in the gym with Kaar so no one had to carry the big bird around and he didn't need to waddle around on the floor.

"How's that, boy?" he asked, giving Kaar a seed to nibble on. He only received pleasure from the bond in return.

Perfect. If Kaar was coming out of his dense and distant shell, that was good. He stood up and backed away as the kids ran for the bird, being very gentle when they got close.

"I'll watch them all," Quinn told him. "They've been very good with the animals."

"Is it always like this?" He didn't think Quinn knew, but he was confused by why all the kids and students were there again on a second day.

"They come for days over the holidays when their parents are at work, if their parents can't afford daycare. We keep them busy and other...activities are normally slow during this season." Sawyer walked up, wrapping an arm around Quinn's waist. "No Fight Nights. Plus, they learned we were going to be here at the gym for a couple of days, which meant they all had to be here. They weren't going to miss it."

"Of course not," Vincent said, chuckling. Already, back at this gym, he felt lighter. He could absolutely see why Sawyer had found her secret refuge here with them and Charlie. Why she had lived the life she had. It all made sense to see smiling faces and hear innocent questions. And no judgement. None of these children were judging him, or the team. Not like the people in the WMC did, or the IMPO.

Not like he judged himself or people judged Sawyer.

"I like it here," he finally admitted. "Thank you for making us do this trip."

"Of course," she murmured, leaning over to kiss his cheek. He wanted to melt from the touch. How long had it been since he and Sawyer were together? Before this entire thing set off, certainly. Back in Georgia. Too long. He wanted her. He wanted to be with her again before everything went back to hell.

They spent the rest of the day with her students.

Teaching them, playing with them. They ate bad pizza while Charlie and Sawyer had salads, trying to be healthy. But, for a moment, Vincent just let this take him away from the rest of it. He laughed with Elijah as one teenager tried to pick a play fight with the big cowboy, not realizing Elijah could just pick the kid up and render him helpless.

"I've had calves weigh more than you, kiddo!" Elijah teased, the rowdy youth thrown over his shoulder.

Vincent lost it, laughing harder than he had in weeks. Quinn was next to him, snickering. "I'm glad to see everyone having a good time," the feral Magi said to him, smiling.

"Me too," he agreed. "It won't last."

"No, but we needed this. A reminder that the rest of the world is alive and there's more people that need us. James wouldn't want us wallowing."

Quinn's wise words hit him in the chest. Zander and Jasper wandered over as he considered them. No, James wouldn't want them wallowing. He'd want them at their best. He'd want them to get the job done, be safe, and get home. He'd want them to keep smiling and having these moments.

"So we head back to our new place tonight, right?" Zander asked, looking exhausted.

"Zander is officially tired of children," Jasper informed them, smiling. "They've been beating him up for two days now."

"I mean, you could have tried to help me out!" Zander groaned, throwing his head back in exasperation. Jasper only laughed without sympathy.

Vincent was glad to see that the weight of their case wasn't breaking those around him. No, it was only him. They were all taking Sawyer's advice. This was just another case to them, and it wasn't moving. He wondered if, to them, this was just like before they met Sawyer. Back to the slow hunt.

No. He couldn't do this slowly this time. He couldn't let his brother gain power and wander around the globe like he owned it.

The need to catch Axel gripped him again. The anger, the exhaustion, the pain. He couldn't do this again. This had to end.

"We should load up so we can get home before night falls," he said, not quite an order. A strong suggestion. And tomorrow they were going to sit down and focus on the case. They had to.

"Good idea," Jasper agreed, still smiling.

"And tomorrow we're going to talk about the future of our case against Axel. We can't put this off," he added softer.

"Of course," Zander mumbled, kicking his feet around.

VINCENT LOOKED over his team in the new meeting room at their new home. It was familiar, but different. He felt familiar, but different. He was the same leader of the same team, but in the time they had Sawyer with them, it had all changed. This was finally a physical representation of it.

"We've had time to heal and grieve over James. Now we need to get started on this case with Axel," he started, firm and unmovable, his eyes falling on Sawyer, who just gave him a small shrug. He figured she would fight to the bitter end over getting them off until the New Year. It was still a few days away.

"I don't disagree, but finding where to start isn't exactly

easy, Vincent." She sighed. "I've been over everything with a fine tooth comb. No one is chatting about Axel right now. They're all keeping low profiles. They *know* we're hunting. It might not be public knowledge, but word travels. Paid off staff of the WMC probably let it slip to one of their contacts, who spread it far and wide."

"I know all of this." He knew where she was coming from. She had spent weeks digging through the same things he had and found the same thing. Nothing. Evidence of what Axel had done but not what he was doing now.

"What would change the game?" Jasper asked, looking up from his laptop.

"Getting someone to flip," she answered instantly. "Missy, Talyn, anyone. If we can get a flip, we rattle him. He's used to complete loyalty. The problem? None of them will think we can win, so they will make deals to save themselves but not help us or hurt Axel. Because if Axel wins..."

"They're dead." Vincent finished that. "Yeah, that's been the status quo for a long time. It's just something we need to tolerate."

"I've looked over everything I knew about his old organizations. I have nothing. Everything I ever touched, everywhere I visited or lived that had to do with his dealings, is no longer connected to him in even the smallest of ways. He's wiped me clean out of the game." Sawyer groaned. "This is why I was hoping for the holidays. I wanted more time to try and find a place for us to start."

By the way she said it, he believed her. This was big for her. She had to succeed if she wanted a future. A normal, bright future.

"What about raiding his old places?" Zander asked, frowning. "Why can't we just stir up trouble?"

"I'm already having other teams in the IMPO do that,"

she said, smiling. "Sorry. If Axel is ten steps ahead of Vincent and I, we're ten steps ahead of the rest of you."

"You couldn't tell us that?" Elijah grumbled and groaned.

"I wanted you to focus on this," she reminded him. "Big baby. I would have told you when we had this meeting. Like I just did."

Everyone except Vincent began to chuckle. None of them were mad at her for doing these things and keeping them from the team. She wasn't putting herself at risk. She wasn't out trying to finish the job without them. She just handled some legwork. It took a good teammate to do that while the rest were being pulled in different directions, cleaning up messes and putting out fires.

Vincent took a deep breath. He was annoyed with their attitude already. His team was scattered all over the room, nonchalant and relaxed. Jasper had his leg off, cleaning it. Elijah and Quinn were leaning on each other in their seats. Sawyer had her legs kicked up, right next to Zander's. That pushed his last button.

This was supposed to be serious.

"You two, get your damned feet off the desk," he ordered with a bite. This was not play time at the gym anymore.

Zander's feet fell immediately. Sawyer's were slower as her eyes narrowed on him. She didn't say anything, though, and he took that as a bad sign. He was already regretting snapping at them.

"We can try to root out the contacts he has in the WMC, but that could take months," Elijah said, obviously uncomfortable now. "And I don't think it's a viable plan. Find one, there's five more, and Axel handles the problem."

"So that takes it out of the equation." Jasper sighed.

"What about digging up all his shell companies? We can track him through the money."

"Would take longer than finding a pawn." Sawyer shook her head. "No, we need a break. We need something big to start with. He's got miles on us now. He knows the entire board and where the pieces are. We're playing blind."

Vincent frowned. "Excuse me?"

"Think of the board, Vincent," she whispered. "You can't beat Axel at his own game. It's never going to happen, but you can imagine his side of things. Then you start breaking the rules of the game. You need to surprise him. It's the only way to knock him off his game and regain the ground we're missing."

"What do you mean?" one of the team asked, confused.

Vincent got it. Know the board. Play the game. Then break the rules by making moves that he could never expect. They needed to know the board. But how were they going to learn it?

He kept the eye contact with her.

"How would Shadow hunt him?" he asked softly. "How do you want to do this?"

Pain lanced him with every word. He wanted to do this as an IMPO team. He wanted to do this right. He didn't want to ask this of her.

But, through the pain, he was still grateful it was her.

She didn't answer immediately, concentrating. He knew she was lost in thought at his question. It took several long silent moments for her to say anything.

"I knew everything. It's how I did my job. I knew every movement they made, I knew where they slept. I knew what meetings they had coming up. The problem is, this isn't any old hit. This is much bigger. I've never done big like this. I've also never had to hunt quite like this. I was always at least pointed in the direction of my target. I don't know where Axel is and no one here will ever be able to get close to him without him knowing. He probably knows everything about each of us. He knows the board and I don't."

"So, with everything we know, we're starting from scratch." Zander groaned. "We could be hunting him for another four years."

"We'll leave it there for the night. Tomorrow morning, we'll meet back down here and put our heads together. Think of ideas. List pros and cons. We can work this out." Vincent was mad that this was where he had to stop the meeting, but there was nothing else any of them could do. But now they all knew that Axel was their focus and needed to stay their focus.

He turned to leave the room, ignoring how Sawyer jumped up to follow him, but stopped, suddenly hesitant. He knew he was a mess. There was no doubt about it. He wanted blood, and yet, he also wanted to finally get a good night's sleep.

Having neither was killing him.

He went up into his room and began to pace. He needed a break. Sawyer said flipping someone could do it. She was right.

But could he do it?

And who?

"Missy..." he whispered into the dark.

It was ballsy. He wouldn't be able to take Sawyer, not this time. He would need to be his brother. He would need to manipulate her into falling for him and leaving Axel's suicidal idea of loyalty behind.

He checked the time, looking at his phone. It was nearly midnight. He couldn't do this with the team, but they would never let him leave the house without them. Not with everything going on.

He dressed for the bitter cold and checked the hallway. Quinn would realize he was gone first, if he was awake. That meant he would need to move fast.

He pulled on his boots.

He could do this.

He was in his car without anyone trying to stop him. He was off the property when he dared to light a cigarette. He dialed the prison, hoping one of the guards on graveyard would pick up. The moment he heard the other line pick up, he started.

"I'm Special Agent Vincent Castello. I'm heading to the prison. I need to speak with Missy immediately."

"Yes sir - though, come in through the East lot."

"Why?" He frowned at the directions. That wasn't the normal parking lot for visitors.

"Missy was taken to medical earlier. We sent word to Director Thompson and he said that he would let you know what happened when her condition was stable."

Vincent ground his teeth. "What happened?"

"From my understanding? The meeting with you and, uh...Agent Matthews upset her."

Of course it had. He hadn't been particularly kind. Now he was going to need to repair the damage of that. This was his fault.

"I'll be there shortly." He hung up with one hand and tossed his phone across the car into the passenger's seat. Damn. Sawyer had warned him, but he couldn't stop the guilt that threatened to crush him.

He'd seen one man kill himself. Now he and Sawyer had nearly driven another to it.

And that thought stayed with him until he pulled up

and parked in front of the East entrance to the prison. His phone was going off and he ignored it, leaving it there.

He was just like Axel. Willing to push people to the breaking point to get the answers he wanted. He'd done it to Jon when they first had Sawyer in their custody. That man had blown his brains out in a hospital room.

He wondered what he would find with Missy. Would she even be healthy enough to talk?

It didn't matter. If he could do this, then he could have an in on catching his brother.

"I'm looking for Missy," he told the first guard he saw. The guard just pointed down the hall to a sign for the medical wing. Vincent didn't even lose a step, storming into the medical wing and seeing her immediately.

The massive head wound, the bruising over her face. They were so prominent that he finally stumbled on his entire plan, his focus breaking.

"What..." He slowed down, looking for a nurse. "What did she do?"

"She started bashing her head against the wall, screaming he had to come for her. That she loved him and he had to come." The nurse shook her head. "It was crazy. She nearly spread her brain matter all over the wall."

Vincent swallowed bitterness as he walked closer. He sat down next to her quietly. When he touched her hand, it jumped and she grabbed his. Held it tightly. Her eyes cracked open, barely.

"Axel? You came for me?" Every word was hoarse and a struggle for her. He knew with healers she would live, but the recovery would be a mess. There was a small smile on her face that made him confused.

And then he registered what she said.

"No. I'm Vincent," he whispered. He wouldn't pretend to

be his brother. He couldn't allow her that illusion. The small smile died. She tried to pull her hand away and he let her.

"Why?"

"I heard what happened and I wanted to see you. You don't need to do this for him, Missy."

"He'll come," she said stubbornly. "I've been hurt. He'll come."

"You know better, Missy." He had to break her belief in him. It hurt him to do it. It hurt him to use her own pain against her. He hated this, but he needed to catch his brother.

"He said I was his best friend."

"He said I was his brother," he murmured.

That made Missy go still, a small gasp leaving her lips.

They sat in silence as the realization settled in on Missy. Axel would kill his father, his brother, his son, his best friend, and his most loyal to get what he wanted. Any loyalty to him was never returned.

"Pawns. That's what she called us," Missy whispered. "I never thought I would go from trusted confidant to pawn."

"I never thought I would go from brother to pawn."

She lifted a hand and hit her forehead right in the middle of the mess. He grabbed her wrist and pulled it away, stopping her from trying again. He was thankful she didn't have all her unnatural strength.

"Missy, stop. Stop."

"I loved him," she cried. "And he never loved me!"

"Don't hurt yourself, please," he whispered. He couldn't manipulate her anymore. He couldn't even try. The idea of trying to get information from her disgusted him. Everything he said now was from the heart. "It's going to be okay. He hurts people, Missy. That's what he's always done.

It's what he'll always do. You're just another victim, but you don't need to hurt for him."

"I gave him everything. I gave him Felix and Talyn, and connections, and everything I had spent centuries building up for the perfect man. And he's thrown me away like a PAWN!" The last word was a screech. "Like HER!"

Vincent winced at her pain and anger, but he just kept saying what he would tell anyone in this position. He didn't think about what Missy had ever done for Axel. He didn't think about any of her past or her behavior.

"Don't hurt yourself." He slid on the bed next to her. "He manipulated me into killing my father, remember? Then he and I fought, and he tried to kill me. Remember? And you know what? I didn't let him defeat me. And you hate her, but Sawyer didn't let him defeat her either. If you do this, he wins. He gets away with hurting you this bad."

He slid an arm carefully over Missy's shoulder as the half-baked crazy doppelganger began to bawl and curled up in the fetal position. He just held on to her. He hadn't expected this. He hadn't expected this to be what he walked into.

Missy had really wanted him to be Axel there to take her away and be with her. She had been loyal...to a point. She had loved Axel more.

His heart couldn't handle how his brother drove people to this. Vincent couldn't do it, couldn't use this in his favor. He just held a woman who had been his enemy for so long, fed by his brother into the crazed monster she could be. He thought of Sawyer too.

Axel had a way with women, that was obvious.

The bitter, sarcastic humor was the only thing in that moment that kept Vincent from falling down a dark hole of despair. This wasn't how he planned on the night going.

Missy finally cried herself into a deep sleep. Vincent untangled himself from her, feeling weak. What had he been thinking, coming here and trying to use her? Why had he done this?

"How long until she's healthy?" he asked the nurse, keeping his voice down so he didn't wake her.

"She's not going to heal quickly," the nurse said quietly, walking closer.

"Why not? There are healers here."

"The tissue...It's not responding to healers." The nurse sounded disturbed and Vincent looked away from Missy to find the nurse.

"Excuse me?"

"The reason we told Thompson is because she wasn't healing. It's like someone had just pumped so much magic into her that her body can't accept any more to use for healing. Which doesn't make any sense. She hasn't been healed that extremely any time she's been in our care."

Vincent's heart began to race. Elijah had a similar problem. There came a point where magic couldn't do anything else and the body just needed to work it out on its own since there could only be so much magic in the vessel.

But what had done it to Missy?

As he was lost in thought, Sawyer walked through the door with Sombra, glaring at him, pain in her eyes, like she was a wounded animal looking to lash out. The pain in her eyes echoed what he'd just seen in Missy. This was the sort of pain Axel loved to inflict on people. He'd seen it in those dark eyes before. He knew it was always there with her, even while he and the guys tried to heal it, love her, care for her. The pain had been dragged back up from where she had laid it to rest because of the WMC and Axel. Because his brother had decided he wouldn't be defeated yet.

In that moment, he knew what he needed to do, and everything settled into place.

He had promised her anything. He'd meant it.

Now he had even more people to fight for. Missy in the hospital bed. The woman he loved standing in the doorway, reasonably angry with him. Both women, like so many other people, who had once cared for a man who only left them for dead.

12

SAWYER

"It's hard enough dealing with this case," Sawyer hissed as she walked in, "without you wandering off without telling anyone."

Sombra had yanked her awake. The wolves were scampering around. Quinn had looked frenzied and upset. It had only taken seconds for the entire team to be awake, trying to find him. She had never felt more terrified. Had he been taken? Had he been hurt? Was he running? Did he have a break and decide to go deal with it himself?

"I had several moments wondering if you were driving into a trap set up by your brother. That you were out there, about to die." She was over the fear already. She had gotten over it the moment she called the prison and found out he had already contacted them and was on his way.

Now she was just angry.

"I'm sorry. I had wanted to talk to Missy alone, but-"

"But you knew none of us would ever allow you to go out and do this by yourself!" She wanted to strangle him. "Because it's not safe, Vincent! Because we don't know if he's going to target us or when!" She glanced at Missy, trying to not wince at the state of the doppelganger. "You could have been anywhere and we would have never known." She looked back at him, trying to find anything on his face that could tell her why he did this and if he understood the pain he'd caused her. She'd left the team outside, saying she would deal with this.

"I'm sorry," he mumbled. She saw that he was pale. He was tired. He hadn't yet slept at all.

"Why did you come here?" she asked.

"I wanted to see if she would...flip. Help us. I didn't think she would be..." He waved a hand at her. "He did this."

"I know he did. I tried to tell her that he wasn't going to come, but she's loyal-"

"She's not loyal," he said, cutting her off. "She's madly in love with him."

Sawyer just nodded. She knew that. Loyal, in love, it didn't matter. Missy wasn't going to flip for them.

"It could have been you," he whispered, still looking at Missy.

"Yeah, it could have been," she agreed softly. "Let's get out of here, Vincent."

"No, I want to stay," he murmured. "I want to be here when she wakes up. They say she's not healing as quickly as she could be. Something about how her body is already too full of magic. Like what happened with Elijah when he was healed. This is going to have to heal the normal way."

"Okay, we'll stay. Let me tell the guys. They can go to the condo for the night and we can stay here." She wasn't sure why he wanted to stay, but she would stay and let him. She could be here for him to keep seeing the aftermath of his brother.

It took a moment, but she ran back out and sent the rest of the team on their way. She and Vincent would meet them later. It was all safe. Everyone would be okay. When she was back inside, Vincent was sitting at the bedside again and the quiet nurse was gone.

"I came here to try and manipulate her onto our side," he admitted. "I came here to try and play the same games he does. I couldn't. Seeing her like that, Sawyer, all I could think about was you and what he'd done to you."

"Missy and I are like Axel and you. Two sides of the same coin. Do you know what you and I have that they never will?" She pulled a chair beside his.

"A moral compass?" he asked.

She nearly laughed by the sarcastic way he'd said it. "No." She leaned into him. "Though...yes. Actually. We do have that on them. I was thinking more that we have each other. Axel and Missy, and the rest of them? They might be a tight-knit inner circle, but they still hold each other at arm's length. They never truly liked each other. They crumble under the pressure, alone and without anyone they're supposed to trust to back them up."

"We could pick them off one by one..." Vincent gasped.

Sawyer felt it hit at the same time. "We could..."

Vincent's eyes were wide and she knew her expression mirrored it. "His inner circle would know everything."

"I know." She took a deep breath. "We have two here. A lot of them died that day in the hangar bay, but Felix is still out there. Whatever he means or does, I don't know, but..."

"We need Missy's help." Like that, Vincent was deflated again. "I'll stay here with her, but I don't think I could ask her for...her help. I mean, look at her, Sawyer."

Sawyer had been trying not to look too hard. She was of the same mind as Vincent, though. The doppelganger had paid enough, doing this to herself.

"What did she say when you got here?" she asked softly. "Do you need to talk about it?"

"She finally realized he's not coming for her."

"Well, damn," she mumbled. "That could kill her in its own right. I never thought she would...be this way. I thought she would die to prove herself to him. I never..." She felt awful. She had never realized Missy loved this deeply. "I'll stay here with you and we can wait for her to wake up."

"Thank you," he whispered. "I don't...want her to be alone."

"I understand."

And so, she waited with him, reaching out to take his hand. She squeezed it gently and he responded in kind, letting her know he was still with her.

DAWN WAS BREAKING through a window when Sawyer saw Missy's eyes begin to open. A soft groan left her mouth. For once, Sawyer didn't dread having to deal with someone she used to work with. She genuinely hated that Missy was in this state. She had given so much to Axel, just like Sawyer had, and for what? For him to want her dead. The only difference was that Axel expected Missy to do it herself while he'd tried to kill Sawyer repeatedly.

"Good morning, Missy," Vincent greeted her kindly. "How are you?"

"Upset," she snapped, reaching to gently touch the broken bones of her face.

"Why?" he continued calmly.

Sawyer remained quiet. She didn't know what she could possibly say to the doppelganger.

"I was really hoping..." Missy shook her head as rage

came over her face. "I was hoping you were him for a moment. He's never going to come."

"I'm sorry. I really am, Missy. I know what you're going through."

She knew Vincent meant every word of that. Sawyer knew what she was going through too. She was glad, and yet she hated, that Missy was finally dealing with the harsh reality.

"I want him dead," Missy growled. "You're going after him. You'll do it." Those last lines were said to Sawyer.

"I will," she agreed. "Now you understand why."

"He...It was okay for him to treat other people this way. I never thought..." Her sentences became broken and fragile. Oh, Sawyer knew this so well. She knew how bad it hurt to realize nothing ever mattered. Nothing was ever good enough to truly make Axel care.

"I know." Sawyer looked away, down at her hands, leaning over on her knees. She didn't want to look at the doppelganger anymore.

"I thought I was important to him. Even when I made mistakes, I thought he would never..."

"Yeah."

"Kill him, Shadow." Missy's voice went angry again, hard and vicious.

"Can't. Need to find him first." Sawyer had found her in.

Vincent coughed, realizing she was going to do this. She wasn't going to allow Vincent to become his brother, to use people. But Sawyer was willing to cross those lines to make sure she could keep the people she loved safe and their souls clean. She was going to cross all of them if it meant she saved them in the end. She hadn't thought this would be Missy's attitude when she woke up, but she was going to use it.

"I..." Missy trailed off as she must have realized what Sawyer wanted.

Looking up, meeting the other woman's eyes, Sawyer didn't back down. Silence descended over them, this time heavy and agitated. It was nothing peaceful like it had been while Missy slept.

"What would you like to know?" Missy asked, raising her chin in the same way Sawyer always did when she was willing to die for what she wanted. Sawyer had more respect for her in that moment than years of being colleagues.

"I need to know who's a Ghost right now. I need to know where they are. I need to know everything."

"I can tell you that," Missy agreed. "On one condition."

"You want to live through this," Vincent finished for her. "We'll protect you. For this, we'll make sure you live for centuries more."

"Good. That man doesn't get to toss me aside like I'm nothing. I've seen times he could barely comprehend. I taught him everything I know. I cultivated his greatness. He doesn't get to do this to me." Every word was bitter and biting. Every word held all of the pain Missy felt.

Sawyer could relate. Deep in her soul, she knew exactly what Missy was going through.

"And for all of this, I'm also going to ask you and the WMC to work together for the betterment of our longer-lived Magi, like yourself and Talyn. Would you be willing to work with Talyn and the research team? It would give you a good life, secure."

"I would. More than Axel ever promised us." Missy began to laugh. "Looking back, it's so obvious that he played me."

"Yeah," Sawyer mumbled again. That she understood well, too. Every word out of the doppleganger's mouth reminded Sawyer of a time when she had been the same way. All the pain, the betrayal, the hurt. But there was a shred of hope in her too. Missy had flipped.

"I can get the team. We can bring in our information and start collecting everything we need. If we move fast…"

"I don't know where Axel is hiding right now. He jumps between the homes of the Ghosts, as we would each look over his different organizations. I was normally involved with his non-Magi arms dealings." Missy smiled. "I can give you where all the Ghosts like to hang out, those traitorous assholes."

"That's enough. That's more than enough."

Sawyer didn't have words. She got up and went out to make the call to the team.

"Sawyer?" Jasper answered, groggy.

"Missy's flipped. Get here."

"Seriously?" His voice was suddenly sharp as if she took a cattle prod to him.

"Yeah. We're going to pick Axel's organization apart, piece by fucking piece." She was grinning as she ended that. "We're going to get this son of a bitch."

"I wouldn't call him that," Jasper chuckled. "That's also Vincent's mom."

"He's a son of a bitch too for disappearing last night." She looked back into the hospital room. "I'll forgive him for it, though."

"All right. We'll be there as soon as possible."

"Tell. No. One."

"Of course. We can't have this leaking." Jasper hung up on her then.

Her heart raced. Axel's own detached, monstrous ways would finally be his downfall. She could feel it, and it felt good.

She walked back into the spacious medical wing, glad Missy was the only patient there and the single nurse was gone.

"Missy, before we continue, how are you alive?" she asked, sitting back down.

"You mean, how did I live through the day at the hangar bay in Atlanta? I didn't. You killed me." Missy snorted. "Felix. Necromancy. It's rough. He had to get a group of healers to fix the body while he brought me back to life or I would have died again immediately. We have some on standby, Magi we have blackmail on. Every bit of magic I have right now is his while my body tries to expend it and replace it with my own. We were warned that if it ever had to be done, it could take up to a year for it to resolve. I'm not the first he's had to bring back. If you want to finish Axel's organization, you need to finish him."

Sawyer nearly dropped her phone. Vincent was just speechless, his jaw even dropping open as he stared. Just gaping, they considered what Missy had just told them.

"No fucking way..." she mumbled finally, shaking her head. "I always thought he was just a pet. He never...He's such a coward."

"Of course he is!" Missy laughed. "He can't bring *himself* back. We brought him that day just in case one of us went down dealing with you. We never expected to *lose*. We had never really lost. He told me the rest of what happened that day. I died. They showed up." She nodded to Vincent, implying the team. "Everything went to hell. When Felix realized it was a losing game and Axel would be captured, he grabbed my body, setting in motion an emergency plan. Bring me back first. I can get in and out of anywhere. A simple kill, replace a guy. Easy. I never thought..."

"That Axel would then just leave you here."

"I figured he would get out and come back for me when he stabilized. I didn't think he expected me to go all the way through with his execution." Missy looked away. "Bring me back just to let me die after all I've done for him."

"Have you heard from him?" Vincent asked.

"Once. Orders passed. Follow the plan. I didn't want to think he..."

"So you didn't follow the plan or go through with it. You just waited and realized he's really expecting you to end it." Sawyer sat back down. "Yeah."

"Kill him," she snarled. "Show him what it means to betray me. To leave me to hang for him. I was loyal, and I loved him, and he..."

The anger was back. Sawyer knew it so well. She'd loved him and he'd brutalized her. He had killed the few things that had mattered to her at that time in her life.

Sawyer needed Missy angry. Angry meant she would want her piece of the man and would give up anything. She couldn't let Missy fall to the broken heart.

For once, seeing the anger and the crazy in Missy's eyes was a blessing. Sure, the woman had tried to beat herself to death on a wall, but the nurses and guards stopped her. Now they needed to keep her alive while that rage continued to temper and grow, until she gave them everything.

"So we need to get our hands on Felix..." Sawyer frowned. She didn't remember what Felix managed for Axel.

"He'll probably be the last you get to. Axel started keeping him very close once we got rid of you. We might have thought you were dead, meaning you weren't a threat, but Axel lost his best killer when he lost you. He grew a little paranoid. That only got worse when we discovered you were alive. Felix does everything for Axel, with Axel. There's no separation between the two now." Missy began to giggle. "Felix is in love with him. It'll never happen."

"Apparently it'll never happen for anyone," Sawyer mumbled. That made Missy sober up too. How many fell for the charismatic man, only for him to lead them to their destruction? Sawyer and Missy. Felix was next. How many did she not know about? Henry's mother, the prostitute who Sawyer never knew? Was she even a prostitute, or had she been someone who played the game and lost, and that was just the story he gave?

"So, Axel made Felix so loyal to him that when he could have gotten out, he dove right back in. Brought you back to life, got Axel out, and continued on with business..." Vincent stood up now and began to pace.

"Of course. Have you met your brother?" Missy's comment was snide, but they all knew Vincent's question was rhetorical. They all knew Axel was good at getting people to draw close to him by dazzling them, giving them things and attention.

Then he was good at slowly taking it all away until the person was so dependent on him that they had nothing else, no one else. Nowhere to turn for help. Nowhere to hide.

That's the reason everyone died when they tried to get away from him. Sawyer had been lucky. She had fought hard to survive that night when she realized her plans had all gone to hell, even after the doppelganger had put two bullets in her. After they had tortured her. After they had dumped her in the ocean.

The hazy and awful memories came back like the tide. Choking on water and blood. Pain consuming her body, she swam for the shore, desperate. She called on her magic, even though it could have killed her too, which helped close the distance. She dragged herself out, coughing and weak.

She stole car after car. She could get to New York, certainly. Someone there would help her. Someone had to stop him. She couldn't die until someone avenged Henry and Midnight.

"Sawyer?" Vincent was suddenly in front of her. "You okay?"

"I'm fine," she whispered, stepping back as she pushed the memories back down. "Got lost for a minute."

"I never understood what broke you and him," Missy commented.

"He killed my animal bond and then his own son," she answered. "After years of him beating and blackmailing me, he killed the only things that could keep me in line."

"I didn't know he even had one until recently. Felix told me after he revived me that Axel had failed once in getting someone revived by him and that Felix would never fail him again. Which is why he saved me."

Sawyer's throat threatened to close up.

"He tried to bring back a boy?" Vincent asked, incredulous and upset.

"Necromancy isn't some dark art. It's just difficult and rare and needs to be done within hours after the death, where the damage to the body isn't so bad that it can't be repaired. Axel didn't get whoever it was to Felix in time."

"That would explain why Felix is now always with Axel," Vincent said, nodding. Sawyer curled her arms around herself as he stared at her. She didn't want to think about that. She didn't want to think or even consider the possibility that Henry could have still been in the world with them. If he was, maybe she would still be Axel's monster. Or maybe she would have had the courage to run for it with him.

The 'what ifs' would kill her if she followed them too far, so she stopped thinking about them.

"Start giving us names and addresses, Missy. All of them you know." It was a command and one that didn't allow for disobedience. If the doppelganger wanted to betray her former master, then she needed to prove it.

Right on cue, the rest of the team walked in, looking between Sawyer, Missy, and Vincent. Jasper was at her side immediately, wrapping an arm around her waist. Zander glued himself to her other side. Elijah and Quinn went to Vincent, flanking him. It was as if the team knew their leaders would need the physical comfort. That they would be raw from dealing with Missy alone for this long.

They were right. She was feeling raw. She was also feeling ready. She was so ready for this.

13

SAWYER

Sawyer stood in the front of the room, in front of a projection of their targets' profiles. Missy gave them so much, Sawyer had nearly felt lost at where to start. One team to take out eight of Axel's inner circle? It was impossible.

Then Vincent had mentioned something about having every available resource, they could pull it off. And he'd been right. She felt the annoyance of having to trust other teams, but it was something she could deal with.

Which is what had led to this. Only a day after Missy had broken wide open for them, pissed off at Axel, and Sawyer now had two extra teams to help in the case.

"Are you sure I can trust them, Thompson?" she asked softly, not taking her eyes off the profiles in front of her.

"I'm positive. They're strong teams and will take orders." The Director stepped around her and blocked her view. "Is this it? Three raids in a single night."

"The first night, yes. Then one team is going to take a break while two teams do a raid. Then we all go back in for the last round. Three rounds. I want it done in less than a week."

"That's..."

"We can do it," she promised. "It's why I have you keeping any local IMPO agents on standby, to clean up our messes so we can move quickly to the next. Our only objective right now is fast strikes and clean captures. The rest, you can sort through."

"Was this part Vincent's plan or yours?"

"His. I just agree with it. If we move fast enough, we'll knock Axel off balance. We'll ruin his side of the board and he'll be left scrambling. It's our best bet." She knew Thompson was concerned about the pace. If someone was injured, they were out until it was over and then teams would be working a man or more down. If one escaped, the others would be alerted too quickly for the IMPO to continue the raids.

Which is why she didn't mention anything about knowing where the safehouses were. Missy had given those up too, but unless they were needed, she wasn't going to send people to them. They were the perfect corner to back her enemies into. If that leaked, then it was over. She was back to square one without anyone to give up anything. Only her team knew those addresses and hideaways, and it was going to stay that way.

"They're all ready to come in," Vincent called. She looked over her shoulder and nodded. He pulled the door open. Zander pulled his feet off the center table. Jasper took his leg off the table and began to put it back on, Elijah helping, since they had been checking the enchantments on it, to make sure they were strong. Quinn left his wolves with a bone in the corner, which made Sawyer look down at Sombra.

Through the bond, Sawyer pushed the idea of partnership and family. Together, she and Sombra were going to go hunting. It was time for her to let the jaguar off her leash. They had to trust each other, work together. Sombra, the massive jaguar, wasn't Midnight, the vulnerable housecat. This time, Sawyer wasn't the target, which meant Sombra wasn't one.

No, this time, they were the predators and they had the first play.

The only thing Sawyer got back was the solid acceptance and eagerness for the hunt. It was exactly what she needed to feel from her feline.

The two supplementary teams entered the room, taking places in the back. They were all professional. No comments were made. The COs positioned themselves at the front, much like she knew Vincent would have done if it was their team.

"You all know why you're here?" she asked loudly, letting it carry over the room. She knew they hadn't been told, but they might have heard a whisper. She had to make sure they hadn't heard too much or there was a bigger leak she would need to worry about.

"Special Agent Castello and Director Thompson only said we were needed. So we came. What's the case?" One of the COs decided to take a seat as he spoke. The other followed suit. Sawyer continued to eye the other teams. She was the only woman in the room. These teams were all just a bit older than her guys, probably in their thirties. They were broad-shouldered men, intimidating and ready for action.

They would work.

"Vincent and I, along with our team, are running a case that isn't public. Not officially."

"My brother escaped from prison. We've been tasked to track him down." Vincent met her gaze from across the room. They didn't add that the team, specifically her, was supposed to execute him when they found him. That wasn't the priority. Not yet.

A few of the IMPO agents covered up gasps with coughs. A couple others didn't bother, just lighting up the room with a string of curse words that she was nearly impressed by.

"How?" one demanded.

"A member of his organization is a doppelganger. She switched places with him when he made an extended trip to the medical wing after he got jumped by other inmates. That's what we know. The problem is, we learned that nearly a month after the incident." She shoved her hands in her coat pockets. New York was so cold that even the meeting room inside the IMPO headquarters was freezing. "We all got brought into the Triad and Councilman Suarez's mess, which meant Axel went unnoticed for a long time. We're behind."

"What changed? Do you need manpower?" One of the other agents was practically tilting his head like a curious dog.

"We've gotten the doppelganger to flip, when she realized Axel wasn't going to break her out, no matter how close she was to the top of his organization, or him. She's been giving us information about how and where to find his inner circle." Vincent walked up next to Sawyer. "These are the people we're after. We needed more hands to help grab them. Director Thompson recommended your teams."

"Yeah, we can help with this. I didn't know Steel was a Ghost. Would explain how fast he climbed up and took over South America's drug world. We've been hunting him for a year."

"We know where he lives, where he sleeps. His other properties. You're going to get him." Sawyer smiled as the other agent did as well. She liked these guys a lot more than other agents she had met.

"And when we get him?" the other CO asked, leaning back in his seat.

"We're going to get all of them. Night one, we're going to execute three different raids on them, taking who we can. From there, we're going to hit another two."

"They'll figure it out and dig in deeper," one complained.

"Yeah, they might." Sawyer looked back up to the faces in the projection. "The problem with Axel's men and women is that they don't back each other up. They're all self-serving. If one of their colleagues was caught, they have no reason to believe they will be. That person failed. That area of Axel's organization will need to be rearranged and new management will need to be found. That's why he runs this the way he does. They don't all sit around him, all the time. They are off handling business, with nothing on them that could lead back to their boss...or each other."

"Which means they have no reason to think they'll be at risk if we take out two or three." The CO was nodding now, accepting the logic.

"I figure, we'll get round one off cleanly. Round two might be a little more difficult. We're planning on hitting all of these in a week. By the third, there's a chance they've finally ducked for cover. A chance. And this isn't everyone. These are just the main members. Axel has others."

"And when he gets worried, he'll call all of them to him, to protect himself," Vincent continued. She'd never felt more in sync with him than in that moment.

"It's like fox hunting," one of the new agents snorted.

"We're flushing them out of their tunnels, making them go to ground, and we're the hounds."

"Exactly."

She wanted Axel to be alone. She needed it. If he still had places to hide, people to duck behind and distract her, she would never get him. This was too perfect to pass up, and it made sure none of his current most loyal people would come back to break him out or take his place.

The anger she had felt since his escape was now side by side with a violent happiness.

"We'll readjourn in an hour. I think my team is hungry and you all need time to think about whether you want in on this." Vincent waved a hand, dismissing everyone casually. Sawyer tapped Zander's shoulder to get him to follow the team when he didn't move like the rest of them.

They walked out the back of the IMPO building on the ground floor, Vincent lighting a cigarette the moment he had the chance.

"They'll say yes," he said, before anyone else could even consider starting up a conversation. "Sawyer?"

"They look like they can handle it. I didn't feel like any were out to get me either. Not a single one of them threw me a side-eye or snide comment. That could change, but it would be nice for it not to happen ever again. We have enough to worry about without drama concerning me."

"Agreed." Elijah nodded her way. "They don't seem all that bad. When do we want to start strikes? You and Sawyer hadn't decided yet by breakfast, and I would like to know before you two go in there and tell them."

"Tomorrow night." Vincent answered. "Everyone okay with that?" Nods all around. "Perfect. Missy is secured, and we increased protection on Talyn as well. It shames me to say, but Missy has given us everything she can. Now we need to not fail in protecting her."

"Yup." Sawyer hated the woman, that hadn't changed, but they'd made her a promise. They would keep her alive, let her live a decent life away from crime for the information. Not a free life, but better than just being in a prison cell. Now they just needed to succeed in the task, which meant it couldn't get back to Axel until it was too late for him to do anything about it. "We can do this, Vincent."

"What do you want to do if one of the other teams captures Axel, on the off chance it happens, or he happens to be there?" Vincent was watching her carefully now.

She didn't have an answer, not a good one.

"Let's cross that bridge when we come to it," Elijah instead spoke up. "If they can secure Axel, perfect. We win. If they have to kill him, even better. It was still our case, our break, that led to it. She goes free."

"We can't give him back to the WMC alive. They've proven they can't be trusted to keep him," she whispered. "I'll execute him if any of the teams capture him. I promised the WMC I would deliver that blow. They'll see his body in the end, no matter how it comes."

Vincent was watching her carefully and she looked away, unable to handle the stare. She wanted it. She wanted to kill Axel, bleed him out. She wanted to watch the life fade from his eyes and drop to the ground. For everyone. It was better she did it. She could kill and her guys would never have to. She could take out this evil in their lives so they didn't get hurt. She wanted to take it from them, so they didn't have to worry about it.

"Okay." Jasper stepped next to her, kissing her cheek. "We'll be there with you for it."

She nodded, closing her eyes. They weren't going to turn

away from her when she did it. That was important. She had worried. She still did. She knew if she had to cross another line, betray a trust to do this, to make them *all* safe, she would.

She hoped they wouldn't turn away from her when she did that. She had run from Axel before, thinking she would always fail. Been a coward. Not this time.

She reminded herself she wasn't going to lose another one. Not like she had lost Henry or Midnight. She and Sombra were going to avenge them and protect their new family.

"We can do this. Just another case. If you have to kill, then that's how it goes," Quinn said patiently. "Sometimes, it's the only way to stop evil. And it's the best way to protect the world around us. Kill the thing ruining the ecosystem."

"Always with the nature metaphors," Zander teased. "Is there a nature metaphor for threesomes?"

Elijah snorted. Sawyer rolled her eyes. Jasper began to chuckle. And suddenly, the world felt less heavy. She playfully glared at Zander, trying to ignore the small amount of embarrassment she felt. She wasn't going to hide anything she did with the guys, but she couldn't stop the small, very small, blush threatening to expose her.

He just grinned in response and she knew he'd said something to make everyone laugh a little. He'd grown up so much.

"Is there a nature metaphor for jealous?" Elijah asked, wiggling his eyebrows. "If you ask nicely, maybe Quinn and I will play with you too."

Quinn growled, and it was one of those growls she only ever heard in the bedroom. There was even a teasing touch to it.

That made everyone laugh as Zander sputtered and turned red.

"*Save me.*" Zander's voice entered her head. She just shook her own in response. He was on his own.

"I'm not into other guys!" he exclaimed. "Sorry, Elijah, but this redhead only gets on his knees for his lady."

"All right," Vincent cut in, smiling. She was glad that no matter how far he went, the team could still pull him back to happiness. "Everyone focus. We need to find something to eat before this meeting continues."

"And tomorrow, we're hunting. We should be focused for that too." Quinn leaned down and scratched the head of Shade as Scout turned in circles, obviously excited for a hunt.

"Yes, and tomorrow we're hunting," she agreed. They began to file back into the building, but Sawyer was stopped by a hand on her elbow. She turned to see Jasper and Zander hadn't moved yet. "You guys need something?"

"Vincent, y'all go on. We'll catch up," Zander said, waving the rest of the team inside.

"Okay. Come in soon, though. I don't want us separated for too long." Vincent's eyes fell on her when he said it. The door closed and she looked at her two oldest friends.

"What's going on?" She leaned against the wall, looking at both of them.

"I wanted to talk to you about something..." Jasper was shifting around, nervous. She waited patiently. "I'm going to leave the team after this is all said and done. I can't...keep being an agent after everything."

"And I'm leaving with him," Zander added softly.

She let that sink in. Leave the team? They couldn't...do that to her. This was their family. She had thought it was. She was doing everything so they could all stay together.

"Leave?" The word escaped her, falling out of her mouth with a vulnerability she couldn't contain.

"Not you, just the job!" Jasper corrected. "Not the guys. We just...I can't do this anymore, Sawyer. These people have blurred the line between everything I was taught about right and wrong, and you haven't helped. My government. Our government, our bosses, are asking you to be the assassin Axel made you, to kill him. What if they decide not to give you the pardon after this? What if they tell you to go out again? I can't support them. I can't be their dog that sits on command and kills too. I joined because I thought I was upholding the law, but..."

She looked away from him and his blasted stormy blue eyes. Zander just filled her vision instead, all flaming red hair and green eyes, with those freckles she could count and remember from their youth.

"And I'm not going to stay without him. The IMPO was never the career we wanted. After this, I think it's time for me to really find what I should be doing with my life. Like Jasper, I don't think this is a good place for me because of what they've shown me. How they've treated me and the team. I can't do it."

"And what about the rest of us?" she asked softly.

"We're not leaving you or them," Zander said stubbornly. He grabbed her shoulders. "We'll keep living with you all, and...being with you. I would never let you go. This isn't like when we were teens. This isn't like when Jasper and I aged out and had to find work fast so we enlisted. This is just a career change. That's all."

"Me neither. Just the IMPO." Jasper reached out and touched her cheek. "We wanted to tell you before the rest of the team. This seemed like a good time to do it, before we jump deeper into this case and things get dangerous. We're not going to tell them for a little while, though. We really wanted you to understand first."

"Okay..." She nodded, accepting that for a moment. "Okay. We'll come back to this conversation later." She couldn't let this happen. She couldn't let the team fall apart. She had to do something about it, she just didn't know what.

"Sawyer..." Jasper murmured. He wrapped his arms around her. "I'm happy right here with you and Zander. I'm just not happy with the job anymore. That's all."

They were breaking the family. She held onto him with one arm and reached out to grab Zander's shirt with the other. Sombra pressed against her legs, trying to keep them all together since she sensed Sawyer felt lost. Like she was losing her males forever.

"We'll come back to this later," she promised. She couldn't focus on it yet, but she was going to find a way to keep her team together. She needed them, all of them. "Don't do anything rash yet."

"Of course," Jasper agreed. "Zander?"

"It's not like we were going to quit tomorrow." Zander shrugged. "Like we said. We're going to see this case through, then figure it all out. Just wanted you to know now. Didn't want to drop it on your head when it was over."

She hadn't even begun thinking about after and here they were, planning on leaving when it was done. She shook her head, pulling away. She walked back inside, unable to find anything else to say. She marched back to the meeting room, Sombra, Zander, and Jasper trying to keep up.

She sat down silently at the large table and grabbed the salad she knew someone put there for her. The other teams were gone, off to think and talk about their own deal in this large case. They weren't being let out of the building, and she knew Thompson was also having them monitored so no leaks happened.

For a moment, she just ate lunch and ignored the world. Looking around, she saw Zander still teasing Elijah and being teased back. Jasper sat quietly reading, shoulder to shoulder with Vincent.

She now had more work than she figured. Leave the team? No, she couldn't allow that to happen.

She finished her lunch and threw out the trash. Then she went back to the files. She knew these names and faces. While she had been in, they had been seconds to other inner circle members. They were replacements, like their seconds would be their replacements and so on.

She refocused from her man trouble to the case as she stared and memorized every detail she could. She had an idea. Axel knew she was coming. He knew Sawyer Cambrie Matthews was coming for him, but he'd never been scared of her. He wasn't scared of some Magi girl.

But he was scared of Shadow. That's why he always wore a shield when he was in the same room with her when things had turned ugly.

14

SAWYER

S awyer settled into the small room with two beds. They had to do this fast, so they were able to secure a portal to make it to California without losing time. That meant they only had two rooms at the shabby hotel no one would think to look for them in. The hotel hadn't had space to give them the three minimum the team normally needed.

And since no one wanted all three big animals in one room, she couldn't room with Elijah and Quinn. She was with Zander and Jasper instead.

She was still cranky with them.

"Going to ignore us this entire case now?" Zander asked, dropping his suitcase next to hers.

"Considering it," she replied. She had too much to worry about, and now them? Leaving the fucking team? She was stewing and she knew better than to stew. They had shit to do. She couldn't be wrapped up in this. This was something they needed to deal with after the case.

And yet, she wanted to rail at them. Leave the team, over her dead body. They needed to keep the team together.

What would the rest of them do without Zander and Jasper? Zander was their healer. Jasper was one of their most intelligent and reliable.

"Let's get some sleep," Jasper said with a sigh.

She glared between the two beds as each guy claimed one. "Why don't you two share?" she asked.

"How about we don't?" Zander fired back, pulling a blanket over his head. "Come to bed, Sawyer. We can argue about it tomorrow. Or weeks from now. There's no reason to be pissed off at this exact moment."

No reason? She wanted to agree, but her heart wasn't accepting it. They were at least here for now. That was something, right?

"You've left me before and now you want to leave again. I thought this was supposed to be our second chance and now-"

"I'll repeat this again, then," Zander snapped, sitting back up. "We're not leaving you. If we can't live with you, we'll buy a house down the street if we have to. We'll build something right on the edge of the damned property. We'll always be with you. We're just looking to change careers."

"And what about us?" she demanded. "What if we have a case and you two aren't there and we need you? What if Elijah gets hurt again? Or Quinn, or Vincent, or *me*?" She had to know what they were going to say to that. She relied on them. She didn't know what was going to come after Axel, but she had never figured it wouldn't include some of them. She always figured she would keep them all or lose them all. Not bits and pieces falling away from her, slipping through her fingers like sand. That's what this felt like. That Jasper and Zander were slipping away and she couldn't catch them and hold them close. "We need you."

"We'll work it out when it's time, Sawyer." That was all Jasper had to say.

She shook her head, finding a chair near a small table. She would sleep later, after they woke up. She didn't want to deal with them.

One of them turned off the lights and she reviewed her files in the dark. So many things to worry about now. They were going after a man named Alfie. Powers were fire manipulation and illusions. Some said he tortured prostitutes he brought in illegally by actually burning them a few times, then making a strong enough illusion to make them think they were burning alive. It was a psychological torture that made Sawyer sick to her stomach.

Between Alfie and the problems behind her in bed, she wasn't much looking forward to the next few days. Tomorrow, they would raid Alfie's San Diego home, while the other teams went after someone in London and another down in Brazil. And Alfie wasn't even the worst. Just one of a group of men and women that thought they could do as they pleased with Axel's backing and a little magic to help them subjugate and control everyone around them.

"Sawyer," Jasper called softly. "Come to bed."

"I'll need to sleep in tomorrow if I want to be fresh for a raid at night," she reminded him. "I'll come lay down in a few hours." She knew she wouldn't be able to sleep.

And she never did. The guys woke up in the morning, hurrying to go about their business, and she just waited, staring at files as the sun began to leak in from the window.

"Take a nap today," Jasper suggested gently when he kissed her forehead after he got out of the shower and Zander went into their bathroom.

"I will," she promised. "The plan is simple. We know

where he lives. I've been reviewing his blueprints all night. If-"

"I know the plan, Sawyer. We talked about it all day yesterday. We know. We're just spending today to make sure everyone has what they need."

He was right. They had planned these raids in only a few days, and the idea was solid and simple. The guys would approach the front, a standard arrest. They would make it known they were coming in and anyone who didn't surrender would be considered enemies of the WMC. Sombra would run with Quinn and the wolves, patrolling the property around the compound in case they had to stop any runners.

They were a distraction. Sawyer would already be on the property and she was gunning for Alfie. Her main objective was to bring him down and put handcuffs on him without any casualties and before he could deliver orders. If she took control of him and the compound's speakers, it would make it clear to anyone else that they should just surrender. They had already lost.

"I'll get some sleep," she promised again.

Eventually, with both the men out of the room, she did. Not a lot, but enough.

Sawyer slid into black leather pants and a fitted black turtleneck. Next, thick black socks and her best boots, with steel toes, just in case. She walked to her bathroom mirror while she slid on her gloves. In the mirror, she tamed her hair, making sure it was straightened and in a slick bun, out of her way. It couldn't be in her way tonight.

Alone in the small hotel room, she took her time to

prepare for the raid, continuing to wander around as she worked. It was a ritual. It always had been and always would be. There were some changes, though. While she had slept, Elijah snuck in and took care of her blades. She knew they would be sharp and ready thanks to him.

She slid a belt through her leather pants' hoops. She attached her daggers' sheathes and then made sure it was all secure. Next, her shoulder holster, for the sidearm. She never wanted to be the type to carry a gun, but she had relented finally and added it to her ritual. On the same thick leather band going over her chest, she carefully placed her throwing knives. Testing the position, she pulled one out and threw it across the room. It hit the target, landing in the center of a reproduction canvas. The IMPO could replace the cheap art.

She didn't bring her kukri. It seemed excessive at that point. She opted instead for a third dagger on her thigh and a thin one for a boot sheathe, a place she could pull it out in case something sent her to the ground or to her knees.

Then she opened her bag, staring at the last piece. Picking it up with care, she walked back into the bathroom.

To an average viewer, it looked like a black ceramic mask with eyeholes and small nose holes. They had no idea.

She looked at her own face one last time, took a deep breath and put the mask on. Activating it was simple enough. It recognized that she could sublimate and something in it, an enchantment she didn't understand, pulled on that. It became nearly fluid as it wrapped over her face, covering and darkening her features to the point where they were indistinguishable. It slid underneath her jaw and down her neck just enough that there was no gap between the turtleneck and the mask. Paired with her dark eyes and hair, the dark outfit, and her general visage, she was exactly what everyone had always called her.

A shadow.

Apt.

She stared for a long time at her own reflection. This was how she had done it all without anyone knowing who she was or what she looked like. There was no way to discern what sort of face lay under the mask, since it was just that deep of an inky black.

With another deep breath, glad she could still use it after so long, she touched it and pushed outwards with her magic, practically forcing it off. She didn't need to wear it yet; it would scare people. While that was the intention, she didn't need it *yet*.

A knock at the door meant her time was up. She had to be ready.

She was.

"Coming," she called, walking out of the bathroom. She pulled open the room door and Vincent stood silently waiting on her. "I'm ready. Let's go."

He didn't move, his eyes falling to the mask. "Why?" he asked softly. Why was she bringing the mask?

"I want them to know," she answered honestly. "I *need* them to know and I need them to be *scared* of me."

He didn't reply, just backing out of her way. She had no idea how he felt about it, but that wasn't going to change her mind.

They walked out the hotel through the staircase and out the backdoor. She looked over the team, nodding at them in appreciation. All black. IMPO official uniforms. Handcuffs and weapons ready for anything.

"We're ready, then?" Elijah looked between her and Vincent.

"We're ready. Sawyer, we're going to drop you and Quinn a mile from the property. You can make that distance in..." Vincent trailed off. She knew he didn't forget, but wanted her to clarify again, so they all knew the time limit.

"Seven minutes," she answered. "Without magic. It won't even wind me. I'll be fine."

"Which means we won't go in for twenty-seven minutes. Twenty minutes. That's what we'll give you to get to him and begin securing him. If you run over a little, we're going to think you found more trouble than expected and it's going to get personal."

"It's not already personal?" she asked, managing a small smirk.

"I'll rephrase," Vincent murmured, leaning close to her. "If you get hurt or don't report in on time, the team and I are going to get pissed off and I'm not going to particularly care if Quinn sinks the entire damned compound under the earth."

"That type of personal," she whispered back, nodding. "Okay. I'll make sure to get it done."

She hadn't expected him to answer back with 'I would kill everyone there.' It was sexy and she was shocked it came from him. Vincent, who was so moody and all over the place recently, would kill everyone in that compound, not caring if they needed information. He would do it, and so would the guys, if she got hurt.

Talk about crossing lines. Here she was, worried about what the case would lead her to do to succeed.

"Let's get moving," he ordered, finally breaking eye contact with her.

This was the first mission where they were letting her off the proverbial leash and sending her out to do what she did best. Infiltrate and eliminate on a solo mission. She hoped it didn't come to what Vincent was talking about. She was rusty, but she wasn't that rusty.

They loaded into the two dark SUVs. The local IMPO agents were on standby, but they didn't know why. They wouldn't until Vincent made the call for the team to go into the compound. Which meant only the team knew she was going to be going into that compound before anyone else.

It was the safest way, but as they drove, she could feel how uncomfortable the team was. She rode with Vincent and Jasper and neither spoke until they hit the drop off spot.

"Be safe," Jasper told her. "Please."

"I can do this," she promised, leaning to kiss him in the front seat. It was sweet, a reminder of the wonderful things he gave her. Normal and loving. A piece of a real life, like the ones everyone else had. She turned to Vincent next in the driver's seat. He kissed her next and she wanted to melt from it. She hadn't touched him in so long and the kiss held all the secret emotion Vincent never showed anyone but her. And even then, sometimes she couldn't see it either. "Quinn is watching my back out here."

"We're not worried about your trip to the compound," Jasper reminded her.

"Yeah, I know." She jumped out then, not wanting to get sucked into the worry. She had this. She could do this. This was her life. It was her career. Thief to assassin back to thief. Until the guys caught her, this was the only thing she ever knew how to do and she had the magic and skill to be the best at it.

"We're going to do perimeter runs," Quinn said as they began to walk into the wildness towards the compound. "Sombra is on a capture, don't kill order until the wolves and I get to her. It's the best I can do."

"She needs the work and she'll do it well. I believe in

her. I just can't take her into the compound. She won't be able to follow me the entire time and disappear like me." Sawyer rubbed her jaguar's head. "Happy hunting, girl."

The jaguar made a noise and Sawyer almost thought it was the same sentiment back at her. Happy hunting, Magi.

She took off, running towards the compound, leaving Quinn and the wolves by themselves. Sombra ran beside her for a moment then tore off down a different trail. Sawyer heard her for just a second as the cat climbed into a tree and disappeared into the night.

She felt bad for any fool that came in contact with that cat. There weren't many trees in the arid land of Southern California, but it was dark enough that Sombra could hide in any of them and no one would know.

And it was dark enough for Sawyer to put on her mask as she ran and disappear herself. She shifted into smoke over a long stretch of barren land and slid between shrubs, dodging the flood lights as she grew closer and closer to the concrete wall of the compound. It was actually just a mansion with a high security fence. There were several things like it peppering California, which meant no one really paid it any mind. Several rich people loved to live in such seclusion.

She was at the bottom of the eight-foot concrete fence when she stopped for the first time. A mile. She didn't have a watch but she knew she made great time. The adrenaline of the hunt was coursing through her, focusing her. It was almost supernatural. She felt like a predator in that moment, a beast, as Quinn always used to describe her. Something about this made her feel alive in a way being an agent never had. She had loved this. The mental and physical work. She had hated the killing at the end of it.

Looking up, she blinked to the top of the fence. She

knew other Magi would feel her, but they would never find her. That's what had made her so deadly. They could only catch the aftermath of her, but never pinpoint her location. She moved too fast for people to nail down. Very few Magi even paid attention to the magical feel of others the way she did, and almost none were tuned to it like her.

She dropped down on the other side of the fence, landing as smoke so she didn't risk any injury or sound. Reforming, she began to creep. She could feel them, though. Her Source reached out and found them, letting her magic know they were there. There were ten Magi guards roaming the yards around the mansion. She was at the vent she wanted before any of them knew she had snuck through without an issue.

Sublimating, she slid in and followed the path the blueprints told her would be best to get to Alfie's office.

She slid in, knowing he was there doing paperwork on the other side of the room.

As she reformed, he looked up with a frown that quickly morphed into a wide-eyed look of terror.

"We never met, but I'm sure you know who I am," she greeted him.

He nodded slowly, standing up. She stepped closer, pulling out not a dagger, but her handcuffs. They had never let her carry them before, but those rules had been tossed out the window.

"And why are you here?" he demanded.

"I work for the IMPO. Why do you think I'm here?" She glanced quickly at the clock on the wall. She still had twelve minutes. "Obviously *he* didn't send me, not like the old days. No, I'm here for my own reasons. You know where he is?"

"I don't." Fire formed in the palm of his hand. She didn't feel too threatened by it. In such a small room, full of paper, he would cause himself more trouble than her. "I never did anything to you. My part of the organization doesn't matter. I'm sure we can cut a deal."

She blinked in close, snapping one of the handcuff sides on his extended wrist. The flame died out, no longer fueled by his magic. He was still stunned by her sudden move as she connected an elbow to his jaw and sent him into the wall. Before he could find his own balance, she used the handcuffed wrist to twist the arm behind his back, forcing his face into the wall next. In a second, she had his other hand and cuffed it as well. Then she dropped him on the floor, knowing he was too shocked to stand on his own.

"I'll give you whatever you want," he said frantically. "Please. I have money. You and I could rule this place. We can take him down together. I know you want Axel. I know you do. Please don't take me down with him."

"There's nothing I want," she informed him patiently. "In fact, I already have everything I need or want. The only thing between me and that life is Axel."

"Why not just go after him?" Alfie stared at her incredulously.

"Because he took everything from me, and it's time I finally returned the favor," she whispered, squatting in front of the drug lord menacingly. "I'm going to take his pawns, bishops, and knights and then I'm going to take his king." Him.

"He says the queen is the most powerful piece on the board," Alfie mumbled, understanding her reference. Anyone who ran with Axel knew his obsession with the game.

"I am."

There was a confidence oozing from her that she couldn't hold back. Alfie had been easy. She didn't think they would all be this way. Once news was whispered in the morning that this happened, their security would ramp up. She didn't mind. She had dealt with tough security before.

"My men are going to come in here and get me."

"No, they won't. In ten minutes, the IMPO is going to flood this nice little piece of land you have. They're going to free the poor women you have in the basement. They're going to arrest everyone here. Anyone who tries to run is going to meet a pack of wolves outside your fence, ready to take them down." She smiled. "And your closest guard is..." She felt for it, closing her eyes for just a moment to focus. "Ten yards away and below us. The floor below us, probably at the bottom of the stairs."

"How..."

"I was Axel's best killer for a reason," she reminded him. "Settle in. We're going to be here for a moment. And when the IMPO shows up, I'm going to jump on your comms and let your boys know to just put their weapons down. We don't want anyone dying unnecessarily here." That wasn't the point of the mission. They wanted to capture all of these rats and fleas without killing any of them. She had a point to prove. She could be an agent. Capture, detain, and win the right way.

Up until the last target. Axel was already sentenced and slated for execution.

And when she delivered that execution, there would be no one to save him.

15

JASPER

He rode quietly in the passenger's seat as they made the trip to the mansion compound. Elijah and Zander were now in the backseat of the SUV. After dropping Sawyer and Quinn off, they went to the meeting place they had designated for the regional IMPO detectives and officers to meet them.

None of them had been happy that the team had started an entire operation without bringing them in, but at the end of the night, their team - Special Agents - outranked everyone else. The chain of command was respected, and now they needed to go in and create a huge mess for the locals.

Sawyer had once told the team that Special Agents were known to criminals as guys who ran in, stirred up all the shit and then disappeared. Now he could really see it. That's exactly what they were doing to the locals.

"I was thinking," Elijah said from the back. "The other targets might think we're too busy cleaning up the three we hit to even consider we're coming for them any time soon."

"Exactly. They won't think we're leaving others to deal

with our cases," Vincent said nonchalantly, secure in his plan.

"Which is exactly what we're doing." Jasper sighed. "So, Zander and I, since we have a few moments, want to say something. We told Sawyer and she's been pretty angry with us since."

"Yeah, all of thirty-six hours," Zander mumbled angrily in the back.

"What is it?" Vincent asked, seeming genuinely concerned.

"Zander and I are going to leave the IMPO after this case."

"What?" Elijah exclaimed in the back.

"We're tired of this," Zander said. Jasper couldn't see it, but he could imagine and hear Zander's arms fly up and land back on the seat in a childish gesture of exhaustion. "We're always getting hurt. The WMC fucks us over at every turn. We're going to finish this, then get the fuck out before they kill us."

"And what are your plans?" Vincent asked carefully.

"We think we'll just get new jobs, try to find something we'll each enjoy. We'll keep living with the team, if we're allowed to, or move close by. We're not leaving her, just the work."

"But she flipped, since leaving is leaving." Elijah hummed thoughtfully. "Yeah, I can imagine she needs a little reassurance. You two bounced on her before and it wasn't supposed to go as wrong as it did."

"But you still left and it still went wrong," Vincent finished, also thoughtful. "You've spooked her."

"We noticed. But yeah, that's what we wanted to say before all of this went down."

"Waited until the last minute, didn't you?" Elijah's tone

was teasing and also somewhat hurt. Like he was trying to hide that he was upset. Jasper closed his eyes, feeling bad, but he couldn't do this anymore.

"We've been...busy. We spent all day doing things while she slept. This is the first quiet moment, and...I was worried everyone would want us off the case before we finished it." Jasper found it hard to admit that. "But we're in this together. This means Sawyer is free to make her own decisions. We have to see this through."

"Exactly. We couldn't leave before this was done, but we can't keep going, after this. Jasper's lost a leg. Elijah, you nearly died. Quinn and Sawyer got lost in the jungle. We're all going to die before we're forty if this keeps up." Zander groaned. "I can't keep...barely being on time. One day, I won't be lucky. One day, someone is going to die, and I can't..."

Jasper knew how hard it was for Zander to admit any of that. The reckless man had never thought five minutes into the future or past his own immediate wants and needs. And here he was, admitting that he wanted to live longer than this job would ever let them.

"I understand," Vincent whispered, nodding. He kept his eyes on the road. "Of course you'll both still live with the team. We're family."

"Amen," Elijah hooted in the back. "You can support from home, ya know?"

"Thanks, guys. Elijah, you'll...talk to Quinn, right?" Jasper didn't want to hurt the feral Magi who believed in pack above all else.

"Yeah, he and I can talk, no worries." Elijah smiled at him. "I'll be sad to see you both off the team, I won't lie, but your reasons are sound and it's not like you're leaving us. I know we'll never be rid of you."

"As long as Sawyer is with us, I think none of us will ever want to leave completely," Zander reminded the big cowboy.

Elijah laughed. "Yes, you're probably right about that. Just make sure to shower that woman in some love. She's probably going off the deep end. With her background, I can see it."

The SUV slowed a few minutes later, after they let the conversation drop. Jasper felt a bit better as he saw the main gate come into view. They were there. He checked the time. A couple minutes late. She would have been in just over twenty minutes by now, which worried him.

When they stopped completely, it was Vincent who got out of the SUV.

"Let us in. We have permission from the WMC and the Director of the IMPO to search the premises. It's over. We're taking Alfie in. You can do this the hard way, but I wouldn't recommend it."

"And who thinks he can just drive up here and say he can do whatever he wants?" one of the thugs yelled back.

"Special Agent Vincent Castello." Vincent didn't back down, his chin held high. Jasper knew it was picked up from Sawyer. There was something superior and confident, to a frightening level, when it came from either of them. Sawyer had done it her entire life and, well, they were all spending so much time with her that they were bound to pick up her habits.

There was a moment of silence as that last name settled in over the thugs at the gate. Jasper heard other SUVs pulling up behind them. They were rolling in with over thirty Magi who worked for the IMPO. They didn't get IMAS involved, not this raid. It was too close to the city for that.

One of Alfie's guys raised his gun towards Vincent. A

shot rang out and the guard dropped. Wolves began to howl. A screeching, awful sound came over the emergency speakers. Jasper watched as some of the guards also clutched their ears as their headpieces screamed in their ears.

"Is this thing on?" Sawyer's voice came over the speakers. "Yeah, perfect. I have Alfie in custody, everyone. Put your weapons down. You lost this fight before it ever happened. It's over, and the only thing you can do now is plead out or get killed. Your choice."

Jasper nearly chuckled. Trust Sawyer to say that so nonchalantly to the criminals in front of them.

It happened quickly. Some of them started running, while others began firing. Some did drop their weapons and went down, looking for protection. Bullets hit the windshield, but Jasper didn't blink. They were trained to trust the bulletproof glass. Pushing his magic out, he created a gust of air that knocked several of them down.

"Most of the general thugs are non-Magi," Jasper reminded the guys in the back. "Be careful with them."

"Yeah, we know," Elijah said, getting out of the SUV. Zander went next, looking for any injured. Jasper sighed, leaving and pushing back more as Zander dropped a shield between the IMPO forces and the gate. It freaked the employees out. Non-Magi knew about magic, but they never truly integrated that well with it. A thug with a gun in a neighborhood, which is where most of these men came from, was normally the most powerful guy in the neighborhood. But no one could ever expect the magic shield, or the guy who could hit them with air. Or Elijah, making their weapons too hot to hold.

Or Quinn, as the earth shook and wolves howled and a couple of screams came from the nearby hills.

"Handcuffs on all of them," Vincent ordered loudly, walking forward. "We're not leaving anyone. They probably have hostages and prisoners in the basement. We need healing services to check on them."

The real work began as the Magi pushed their way through the gate, walking as Zander and others kept shields up. They handcuffed those on the ground that they passed. Vincent sublimated and went after a Magi who was about to call on whatever magic he had, disarming him before the man knew how close he was.

The raid was going exactly how they thought it would. While they were giving all the lower-ranking fools a problem, Sawyer dragged Alfie out the front door, snarling at one of the thugs who tried to stop her. She dropped Alfie unceremoniously and kicked the non-Magi thug in the gut, sending him back into the dirt as well.

What bothered Jasper a bit was that she still wore her mask. It was eerie, not really seeing her, just a black emotionless face of sorts. He also hadn't known she would be wearing it. He had no idea what to think of the assassin in front of him.

This was what the WMC had wanted: Shadow doing their dirty work.

Because of that, he felt disgusted. Not with her, *never* with her, but them. The people who were supposed to be leading the Magi into better futures. The WMC was rotten and he hated it. He hated that they had pulled her into this, pushed her this far.

"How was your part?" Elijah asked, grinning.

"Good," she answered.

And when she spoke, people began to realize who was walking among them. The local IMPO officers stared at her, wide-eyed. The thugs were confused as it began to dawn on them that they were in the middle of a grudge match. Vincent Castello against Axel. Shadow coming after her master.

This wasn't about Alfie, the thugs, and whatever business they were a part of. They were just another piece.

"How are you, Alfie?" Vincent asked, walking closer. "Enjoy working for my brother for as long as you have?"

"Fuck me," Alfie groaned. "I'll tell you anything."

"You will," Vincent whispered.

"He's like a leaky faucet," Sawyer commented, shoving Alfie to Zander. "Hold him, please."

"Of course, love." Zander grinned. "Well, actually. Elijah, here. I'm taking a unit down into the basement. Time to see if the rumors are true. We might actually help someone tonight."

"Good idea," Sawyer agreed, nodding. "Vincent?"

"Just as planned. Good job."

And with chaos around them, Jasper knew everyone on the team was feeling supremely satisfied. Raid night one went according to plan. They needed to check in with the other teams once they had a moment.

He felt good and a little sick, an odd sensation. She wasn't taking off her mask and he really wished she would. It would have made him feel easier about the entire thing, certainly. More like a normal raid and another day on the job. Her standing there with that black void for a face made him feel like they weren't the good guys.

Then again, he hadn't truly felt like a good guy for a while. He'd tried, but this was the straw breaking the camel's back. He wasn't completely sure when the change had started, he just knew there was no turning back now.

"It was easy," she replied shrugging. "It won't stay this

way. They had no idea we were coming. The others will become more paranoid every day."

Jasper stepped closer to her and she eyed him. "We told Vincent and Elijah. They understand."

"Oh, not right now, please," she snapped, walking away from him. He winced at the tone of her voice. He should have known better, but he also wanted her to know as soon as he could tell her. If the other guys weren't hurt, then she might let go of her anger sooner.

"Maybe you should corner her when we make it to the next hotel," Elijah suggested. "Just...uh...be ready to protect yourself."

"She wouldn't hurt me," he growled at the cowboy. Mask or not, Sawyer wouldn't hurt him or Zander. He knew that. He trusted her with his life. "She's just mad, but..."

"You should be focused on Axel, not what comes after him," Elijah reminded him.

"She and Vincent are focused enough on Axel for the rest of us." Jasper resisted rolling his eyes. He had never done that to anyone and didn't want to start. "Plus, I've done really well not touching on my feelings about him, and I don't want to start."

"Ah, covering it all?" Elijah asked, shoving Alfie to another agent to take away. "So you aren't feeling the boiling rage that we're going after the man that brutalized her? Or made Vincent's life hell before we met him?"

Jasper clenched his jaw. Oh, of course he felt it. Of course he wanted blood and gore from Axel, for all of that and more. For every stain he left on their life. Every haunted, twisted, awful nightmare she had marked Jasper with. He wanted retribution for all of it.

"If I give in to that, Elijah, I'll never be allowed to look myself in the mirror ever again," he whispered harshly, looking away from the cowboy. He realized they were alone now. Sawyer was off doing something. Vincent was talking to other agents. He knew Quinn was still in the hills, taking down anyone trying to run, because there were always runners. Zander was helping any prisoners of Alfie's. His team was doing what they always did.

Elijah hummed for a moment before stepping back in front of him. "Is it that bad?" he asked softly.

"Our government has sent out an assassin to kill her creator. Our military tried to get all of us killed through ignorance and stupidity in the Amazon. Our organization had someone in it willing to kill you and Sawyer, not to mention a lot of other people, to install a new regime in place of the WMC." The anger built up in him. His faith in everyone was shattered, completely gone, not even the smallest thing remained. "The only thing I have any sort of respect for anymore is this team, Elijah. And we're going after the man who has made hell on earth for some of our family. Those two bear the scars from him. Fuck, Sawyer now also bears the scars of what *our* side has done to her." Jasper took a deep breath, trying to contain it. "That bad? It's so much worse." Jasper stepped around the cowboy and headed back for their SUV.

He had to get out of the IMPO before it broke him. Before all of this broke him and took away everything he loved, not just about others, but about himself. He needed Sawyer to understand that he was absolutely okay with this mission, and that was part of the problem. He wanted her to kill Axel and cut him open. He wanted her to kill him in every nightmare and then kill him in the real world. He wanted her to run over to the WMC and tell them to shove it.

He didn't feel good, and that was exactly the issue. He

couldn't live like this. They would deal with Axel, and then he had to get out before it completely ruined him, if this job hadn't already.

He leaned against the hood, trying to push it all down. As grief faded from James' death, he was being consumed by this. He hadn't even told Zander the whole of it. The whole of everything going on in his head and the feelings in his heart. He wasn't willing to admit out loud that he was okay with them going out and killing a man. He deserved it, Axel Castello.

But Jasper felt sick that he was fine being an executioner. He wasn't fine with being fine. He wanted to hide behind his shield. All the things his parents taught him, everything he had left of them. The world's a good place, they would always say to him. Their people were good people. Their government loved them and Magi around the world could rely on them.

Now Jasper felt like it was all a lie and he couldn't handle it. He needed to tell Sawyer all of this. She would understand if he just explained all of it.

Not knowing how long he stayed there, he jumped when someone touched his shoulder. Looking up, he found a concerned Zander.

"Hey, man..." Zander murmured, rubbing his back gently.

"How were the prisoners?" he asked, needing something else to think about.

"Good. Or they will be. You don't want to hear about all of that. We're going to load up soon, I think."

"Great." Jasper shoved his hands in his pockets, nodding. Sure enough, they got word as soon as Vincent's voice echoed in their heads.

"We're leaving. Travis is waiting for us at the hotel to portal

us to the next location. Plus I still need to get on a secure line and find out how the other raids went."

Jasper didn't wait. He jumped into the SUV and turned it on. Zander jumped into the passenger's seat. Elijah didn't come back to their ride, leaving Sawyer and Vincent with them.

"He's going out to get Quinn and the animals to meet us," Vincent explained.

"Sombra is having too much fun tormenting one guy. Quinn should be stopping her and securing him soon," Sawyer added.

"What is she doing?" Zander sounded a little more excited than he should. Jasper caught a grin out of the corner of his eye.

"Just chasing him around, terrorizing him. You know her. She loves a good game. I've told her to just take him down, but she knows he's the last one." Sawyer was chuckling now. Jasper looked into the rearview mirror and caught her removing her mask. He watched it move off her face like a smoky ink and become the emotionless, porcelain-looking mask he'd seen before.

"That was cool," Zander commented. "Can I try?"

"No," she answered, chuckling. Jasper turned to see out the back window as he backed out. He caught a glimpse of her running her fingers over the mask. "It takes sublimation to use and practice to make sure it doesn't kill you."

"Well, damn," Zander mumbled petulantly. "It's hot, I'll give you that."

Jasper could barely restrain a cough of shock. Vincent raised an eyebrow. Jasper swiftly moved them out of the other agents' way and got them moving. He didn't want to touch that statement with a ten foot pole.

They made it back to the hotel in record time and

Vincent disappeared to talk to the other teams. Elijah and Quinn were there only minutes later and Travis shuffled and tried to get comfortable, waiting on the team to give him the go ahead for the next portal.

"You doing all right, Travis?" Sawyer asked. She must have noticed he wasn't totally comfortable.

"Too many portals. You know, it gets exhausting. I'm just hoping I can make all of them. I don't want to have to pass this off to another Magi." Travis smiled. "Seriously, that's all. I've been the Magi for your portals for a long time, Sawyer. I don't want that to change."

"I'll be stranded before I take someone else's portal," she promised softly.

Vincent was back only moments later. "We're good, and they're moving now to the next locations. Everything hit perfectly. We've got Alfie, Janie, and Martinez in custody."

"Who's next?" Elijah asked from his spot, leaning on a wall.

"We're going after Leonard. Fergus and his team are going to get Gerald. Travis?"

"I'm on it!" Travis jumped up and the magic began.

One raid down. One night to sleep, then another. Jasper knew this was going to be a gauntlet.

16

SAWYER

Sawyer found herself in another quickly-booked, cheap hotel, rooming with the same two men and Sombra, who was already curling up for a cat nap in the corner. She still didn't know how to feel about them, so she stayed focused on the mission. Leonard, living in the Congo and selling arms to any backwoods dictator that wanted them. He made Axel a fuck-ton of money. That prick, of course he would set himself up to take over for Karen and Missy when they were out. What had Sawyer said about that group once? The best of the best at being the absolute worst.

He'd found some to match up to the old ones.

Axel sure knew how to pick them.

"Sawyer, are you going to sleep today?" Zander asked, shouldering her as he stopped to drop his bag.

"What time is it?" she asked. She didn't have a watch or see a working clock in the room.

"Already five in the morning. We need to hunker down and then get to work tonight."

"This is going to run the fucking team ragged," Jasper

muttered, shaking his head as he tossed his things on the other bed.

"It's what we have to do," she reminded him.

"I know. I'll be in the shower." Jasper stormed out. The room practically shook with how hard he slammed the bathroom door. Sawyer didn't know how to react to any of that.

Zander was innocently stripping and laid down on the bed, as if it never happened. "Come on. We can watch a movie while we all take turns getting clean."

She sighed. So fucking normal in the middle of one of the most important weeks of her life.

"Yeah, we can watch a movie," she agreed, pulling off her sweaty work clothes. She didn't like the idea of getting in bed like this, but Jasper had just claimed the shower first and she wanted off her feet. In her sports bra and black cotton underwear, she spread out next to Zander but didn't touch him.

He flipped a movie on and threw an arm over her shoulder. As the movie got started, she relaxed in a way she hadn't for days, begrudgingly admitting to herself that Zander was right there with her. They weren't leaving her...yet.

He must have noticed her jaw clench or heard her teeth grind. "Calm down, Sawyer. I'm right here."

"You won't be for long," she reminded him.

"Please stop pushing me. I don't want this to be a fight. Of all the things, not this." He leaned closer, kissing her neck. She tried to pull away as his long, lean body pressed against her side. "We're leaving the IMPO. We're not leaving you."

"You're leaving the team," she repeated.

"After this case. But we're not leaving you."

She didn't see the distinction. To leave the IMPO was to leave her. She was bound to them. She was their fucking predator. It was her life. This case...

"And she finally stopped to think about it," Zander murmured, figuring that's what her silence was about. He kept kissing her neck. "Sawyer, after this case, you don't need to stay with the IMPO either. They'll pardon you. They'll have to, if they don't want us taking this all public. And I will. If they play you again, I'm letting the world know everything and you'll be free anyway. We're leaving the IMPO, not you, because you'll be able to come with us."

She was somewhat speechless. Was that really their plan?

"What about the other guys?" she finally asked. She would never leave any of them. She couldn't. That wasn't an option. She was too happy with this, the team. She couldn't toss aside Quinn and Elijah for Zander and Jasper or the other way around. And then there was Vincent. They had so much together, all of them. They had been through so much. Leaving them wasn't an option.

"We'll stay with them no matter what any of us choose. We talked to Vincent and Elijah. We'll find places to help them or do what we want. We're not going to break this up, promise." That eased some of her fears immediately. Zander's face was open and honest, telling her he couldn't lie. "And you can do whatever you want, Sawyer. Anything you want."

"I'm not sure what I want after this," she admitted. "The IMPO at least knows how to use my skills. Where else would I go?"

"We'll think about it when we get there," he promised.

"Why couldn't you just fight with me like I wanted?" She had been hoping for yelling and screaming so she could tell them again how she hated the idea of them leaving. Then Zander decided to play her with some logic. Damn him.

"Because I'm learning when not to get pissy with you. Plus, this is more serious than a screaming match. This is just the way it is. Jasper and I are leaving the IMPO, and an argument between you and me? I guess it feels like that cheapens the discussion."

She swallowed a lump in her throat, choking on her emotion. Good gods, he was different. He was moving faster than her, faster than she was ready for, that was certain. And when he looked up, there was such an honest love in his green eyes that she knew he wouldn't leave her.

"I'm sorry I freaked," she mumbled. He gave a satisfied chuckle, leaning in to kiss her. She sank back instinctively and he took that as the opportunity to crawl over her. She made him work for it, dodging his attempts until he finally caught her in a kiss that sent all sorts of signals to her mind, heart, and body. She pushed him away, realizing where this was going to go. "We can't. Jasper could walk in."

"I don't particularly care," he whispered, kissing her again. "And neither should you."

She glanced at the bathroom door then back into green eyes. "How fast can we do this?" she asked with a small smile. She needed it. She wanted to touch him and remind herself that he wasn't going to leave her, not ever. He belonged to her and he wasn't going to walk away, not from her. "You really mean all this, don't you?"

"Every fucking word, Sawyer. You can be anywhere, doing anything. As long as you come back and I have a piece of you. Just as long as you let me stay in your life."

"Always," she promised, touching his cheeks. She pulled him back down for another kiss. He groaned. She reached down and shoved his boxer briefs past his hips, freeing him for her. She ran a hand along the underside of his shaft. He was trying to push a hand under her sports bra to push it up.

They were still trying to finish getting naked when the shower cut off. They were naked when the door opened, completely oblivious to Jasper walking out.

"Are you two fucking serious?" he asked.

Sawyer felt like she jumped out of her skin for a moment.

"Ignore us," Zander said with a groan. He kept kissing her neck, even after Sawyer stopped responding. She was caught staring at Jasper in the bathroom door, a towel hanging low on his waist.

And Jasper's appearance did nothing to stop how much she loved what Zander was doing to her body as a hand slid over her ribs and belly to between her legs. Jasper's eyes narrowed at the same location.

"Really?" he asked, a guttural sound. She could see his chest moving from how hard he was breathing. He was like a storm tied to a post, and the post was about break. Along with everything around him.

"Come on!" Zander finally stopped kissing her and looked back at his best friend. Sawyer didn't say anything. "We're caught up in some shit. We were trying to have a moment."

"Yeah, I see that," Jasper said, snapping like a rabid animal.

And Sawyer knew something was wrong. This wasn't embarrassed Jasper. This was hurting Jasper.

"What's wrong?" she asked softly, pushing Zander away as she swung her legs off the bed. He groaned again, falling on his back. They all ignored the erection standing tall for everyone to see, and the redhead did nothing to cover it.

"We're not leaving you," Jasper muttered.

"Zander and I just talked, I'm sorry for-"

"I'm leaving the IMPO before I become an awful person like all of them. That's why I need to get out, and you need to know that. I heard what you and Zander were talking about. I heard all of that."

She stopped walking to her Golden Boy. Oh. Oh, that changed everything.

"I hate that they can send you to do their dirty work. They fucked this up. They should have done it months ago, and yet they gave him time to play his fucking games. I hate that I want you to do it for everything he's ever done to you and so many other people. I hate that I'm part of an execution squad and part of me is *okay* with that. It's not my place to say who should live and die, and yet..." He touched his chest, trailing off. "I killed a man and I don't feel a shred of guilt for it...I'm saving myself. Before I'm...one of *them*. All I have left of my parents is their sense of right, and I'm losing that, Sawyer. This job is taking it away from me and I just can't do it anymore."

She took one stumbling step at his admission. Her Golden Boy was broken. She saw the storm in his eyes, could feel it in his heart. This was his problem. This had been his problem since she had shown up. She knew it.

"Why didn't you say anything sooner?" she asked softly. "About how bad it was?" She knew he had tried and she had flipped out, but this seemed so much more than he let on. This was eating him alive.

"I was already feeling shitty about the IMPO and the WMC when we came to New York, I think, but James...The grief helped cover it up. Now we're on this case and this is it. This is the last I can do, especially with the way I feel right now. I'm going to support you one hundred percent to finish this, but then I *need* to get out." Jasper looked away from her.

She reached for him and pulled him into a kiss. "I love you," she murmured against his lips. She felt selfish for her previous behavior. She hadn't known just how deeply this was tearing her gorgeous man up. She should have. She should have realized how deeply this was affecting him. "I'm sorry. I'm so sorry I didn't listen when you first tried to tell me."

He kissed her back, then pulled away. "I'll go on a walk while you two-"

"Stay!" Zander ordered, sitting up. "We can..." She looked back at him, frowning. "I mean...Uh..."

"Oh." She realized why his face was getting red. He was still hard. She knew Jasper was too, since he was hiding it from Zander with her now. "You want to try that?"

"I mean...uh, it would be nice for all of us to have some time." Zander ran a hand through his hair. "I'd like to try, and what better time than the present?"

"No." Jasper pulled away from her. "Oh no. I get it now. Zander, sorry, find another guy for that."

"You don't need to participate!" Zander was frantic now.

"You want me to watch?"

"You want him to watch?"

She and Jasper looked at each other.

Zander was redder than his hair. "I think now isn't the best time for anyone to get thrown out of the room. I think we need to...do something together."

"Like watch a movie, then," Jasper answered, pointing at the small TV. He dropped on his own bed. "If you two get busy during it, then keep it quiet. I'll listen to music and read."

Sure enough, Jasper had headphones on and a book in front of him faster than she and Zander could react.

"Zander," she hissed. "Why would you put him on the spot like that?"

"I think he needs some love," Zander answered. "And I think it's the only way you're going to get him to accept it right now."

She narrowed her eyes on him.

"And I want some love too. Quinn and Elijah could do it...why can't we?"

"Quinn and Elijah also sleep together," she reminded him. "They're comfortable being naked together." She had never wanted to push any of them further than they were willing to go. They had a strange relationship, one she still refused to question. She was going with it, wherever they wanted to take it. She still wasn't sure how she ended up having a threesome with Elijah and Quinn, much less these two.

"Let's just watch our movie," Zander said, sighing in defeat. He pulled her back to him and they slid into bed. She laid her head on his chest. Zander eventually went to shower, then her. The bathroom was too small for both of them, so nothing happened as they both just tried to get clean.

It was the second movie before Zander's hands began to roam again. This time, she felt a lot more awkward, but nothing could stop how she moaned softly as he brushed a finger over her nipple. Nothing could stop how good it felt when he ducked down and took it into his mouth, rolling a tongue over it. She didn't want to say no, but she tried.

"Zander, we've got someone else in the room."

"You need some love," he murmured against her skin. "I'm going to give it to you. I need some love, too, babe, remember? Please. We're busy, and one of us could get hurt, and you've been mad at me."

"Okay," she whispered, unable to find that 'no' she had wanted to tell him. He was right. She did need some love, and so did he. She didn't know what this relationship was, but even the suggestion of it ending had sent her off into pissed-off mode. The fear of losing them had almost made her shove them away without even listening and hearing what they were saying.

They would make it work, no matter how it played out.

He continued to lavish her with licks and kisses, moving down between her legs. They weren't under the blankets. She could see every muscle in his shoulders and back, all perfectly maintained and formed. She gasped, trying to stay quiet as he licked her clit. Her head fell back as two fingers slid inside of her.

She wasn't thinking of anything except Zander as her head rolled to the side and she found Jasper staring at her, breathing hard again. Those stormy blue eyes. She just stared into them, moaning as Zander enjoyed her and she enjoyed what he was doing to her.

The book went down first. She wrapped a hand in red hair to hold him there as he pushed her towards the edge.

The headphones came off next. She moaned louder, her back arching as the fingers picked up speed.

He was off the bed as her orgasm came closer.

Jasper kissed her right as she wanted to scream Zander's name. He grabbed her roughly, smothering the scream with his lips, forceful and passionate. Demanding in a way she never knew of her Golden Boy.

Zander pulled away, but she didn't know where he went as Jasper moved to get on the bed with them. He broke the kiss, and she couldn't find any resistance in her as he rolled her onto her belly. Jasper lifted her hips and pushed into her without pause, leaving her a puddle of confusion and pleasure.

Zander showed up again, kissing her. He wasn't questioning it either. Thank god. She felt like if either of them said anything, Jasper would pull out and run for the hills and never come back.

But wasn't this what she always wanted? He was thrusting harder than she figured she would ever get from him. It was rough and out of place, but it fit at the same time. It was possessive and claiming, even a touch angry. His hands held onto her too hard, probably making bruises on her hips. A hand wrapped in her hair and Zander held her lips to his as Jasper took out his emotions on her body. There was love in there too, like the way he caressed her ass at one point.

"Sawyer, I love you," he groaned. She couldn't respond thanks to Zander, only hit her peak on him, gripping him, holding him. He couldn't keep going either, coming deep inside her. He was panting as he pulled out and fell down.

She didn't have the chance to say anything, as Zander forced her to roll onto her back and entered her before her orgasm was even done.

"Oh fuck!" she gasped, shocked.

Jasper groaned. "I know why you wanted this now." There was something dirty about the words, like he was about to really enjoy the show, now that he was done.

She wrapped her arms around Zander, then her legs, biting into his shoulder as he pounded into her without any semblance of mercy that she had already had two orgasms. He was relentless, like he always was. They rocked hard, and she found herself bumping into Jasper. Zander panted over her as Jasper shifted and moved to kiss her shoulder and neck.

"You're beautiful," he murmured. "It's so gorgeous to watch you come."

She had never expected to hear dirty talk from Jasper, but from the roughness of his voice, she figured that he had finally broken and the storm was free. She knew there was something wild in there, she always had.

And now it was hers too. She turned her head to kiss him as Zander pulled up to sit on his feet, holding her hips as he thrust deeper inside her.

"Oh, fuck, that's what I want to see." He groaned, his fingers biting into her flesh harder. She was going to have a ton of tiny fingerprint bruises at this rate, maybe even a handprint or two. Not like she cared at that moment. With Jasper showering her lips and breasts with attention and Zander between her legs, she was going to have a final orgasm. The idea of bruises almost seemed good. They would remind her of this night for a few days, at least. And what a night it was.

She came hard, screaming for them, her legs shaking as she couldn't hold on anymore. Zander didn't last a second beyond her, following her into bliss and happiness.

She had both of them pressed against her when her eyes closed. They would deal with the weirdness when they woke up. There would be some. Jasper had been a virgin only a few weeks ago. She could blame all of this on Zander and then disappear for the raid while Jasper was forced to get mad at his best friend for whatever just happened.

That seemed like a good idea.

17

ELIJAH

Elijah stared at the wall, a grin on his face, like the fool he was. Hell, they were all staring at the wall, listening in some degree of abject shock and amusement.

"Well, I wasn't expecting that," Elijah said, unable to wipe the grin off his face.

"You did tell them, and I quote, 'shower that woman in some love.'" Vincent put his book down, probably tired of trying to pretend to read.

"Yeah, but I thought that sort of love was up to Quinn and I." Elijah began to chuckle. Quinn joined him, unable to contain the weird sort of elation at the sound.

"I think they needed that," the feral Magi said softly, his wolves lying around him. "They needed to show her they aren't leaving. That's good. She was skittish of them the last couple of days, and now we know why, and now she won't be. It's good."

"But *Jasper*?" Elijah looked between his friends, hoping he wasn't the only one who thought this was completely out of the blue and madness.

"Maybe he's drugged," Vincent said, shrugging. "And before you get the idea one day there will be more of us together like that, absolutely not. I'm not into it."

"Why not?" Elijah's mind had been going places. It always went places.

Vincent raised an eyebrow at him. "I'm a private person. I like intimacy and quiet. The idea of sharing a bed with a rough and ready man and her absolutely doesn't appeal to me." Vincent shrugged. "Why are we talking about this? We should be working."

"I mean, we have our plan. We're setting her up with an earpiece and microphone for this one, but not much else changes." Elijah eyed their leader. "Why are we setting her up with electronics?"

"I didn't like not having contact with her." Vincent sighed, moving his book around like a bored boy. "I didn't like not knowing where she was or what she was doing. She could have been captured by the time we got there. I was bluffing outside the compound. I had no idea if she was successful."

"But we trusted her to do it." Elijah crossed his arms, leaning on the wall as Sawyer was still with her boys, filling the room with sounds they all knew well by now. He couldn't bring himself to feel jealous. He wasn't a jealous man; he never had been. Instead, he was just happy someone was getting some love while they were on this grind to capture several high-ranking members of Axel's organization.

"I still do. I just want to be able to get in contact with her or vice versa. I was uncomfortable. She agreed to it. It's not up for debate." Vincent narrowed his eyes and Elijah groaned.

"I wasn't trying to debate, just trying to find out where

your head is. You worry about her, thank god. I was worried for a moment."

"Why?"

"She's going to kill him and I don't know how you're taking that," Elijah whispered, studying Vincent carefully. Quinn smartly stayed quiet, reading whatever he had. Elijah hadn't asked yet and probably wouldn't. The feral Magi was now diving into scientific Magi journals, particularly about naturalism and how it was helping non-Magi scientists.

Vincent's face went from curious and confused to shut down in an instant as Elijah's question hung in the air.

"I'm fine," he answered. "It is what it is."

"Are you sure?" Elijah stepped closer.

"Elijah, I don't know what to tell you. The WMC passed down the mission to her. She accepted. We're helping. He deserves it. It's time to end this. I'll be okay."

"Okay...and will you and Sawyer be...okay?" Elijah could see it. The two of them were dancing around each other. They were like magnets that kept changing their damned charge. Sometimes he could see them drawing closer to each other, like there was nothing stopping them. Then there were moments they pushed and distanced themselves. It was unstable. Eventually, he figured they would crash together and it would either make them stronger or break them completely.

And that didn't bode well for the entire team.

"Uh...I think when we get through this, we'll be okay." Vincent went back to looking at the wall. "I think I just need to get through this, Elijah. I have to get this done."

"Well, if you need to talk, I'm always going to be here for you," Elijah reminded him. "I'm going to step out and get some fresh air."

"Leave them alone." Vincent didn't glance at him as he

said it. Elijah got the message loud and clear though. "Quinn, go with him. Stay out of sight, as well. If anyone sees you-"

"I know, Vin." Elijah nodded towards his wolf Magi, who was looking up now. Together, they slid out of the room and wandered through the hotel, somewhat aimlessly.

"What's on your mind?" his friend asked him when they went out the back together.

"What Zander said. About me nearly dying. About you nearly dying. About how many times Sawyer has been hurt. Vincent doesn't mention it, but he was stabbed in New York. Since he was healed, we all just moved on, but..."

"You're feeling mortal," Quinn correctly guessed.

Elijah was feeling mortal. Too mortal.

"He's right, I think." He kicked a stone, looking out into the dark jungle of the Congo around them. It was humid and sweltering, like the Amazon had been. It made it all too real, remembering the Amazon. He wondered if Quinn felt the same. He knew the feral Magi could probably point out the closest Druid within a hundred miles. There had to be one out there, maybe even one like that bitch had been. "I've been injured on the last two cases."

It had been Zander's fast thinking to get them out and leave Sawyer and Quinn that had saved his life in the jungle. He'd been so mad at the time.

"I know." Quinn wrapped an arm around his waist. Elijah slid his own over the feral Magi's shoulders. They had gotten more touchy-feely since Sawyer got involved, not less. Once he'd worked his shit out, they felt even more at ease, not driven apart.

"I don't want to lose anyone too young," he admitted. "And Zander, gods save us all, is right. One day, our luck will run out."

"I know."

He didn't like that Quinn was agreeing with him. He looked down at the darker skinned, earthy beauty with those ice blue eyes. He had always thought Quinn was attractive, but now? He seemed so much more comfortable in his skin that it was becoming unavoidable to acknowledge. Like Sawyer, there was something other about him that drew Elijah in. A strength and yet a strangeness.

"But first we need to make sure the pack is safe," Quinn continued, meeting his gaze. There was a feral anger in the ice that nearly made Elijah step back. There was a roll of power through the air and earth, a bitten, angry, cornered animal that promised danger.

"Quinn?" He wasn't sure how to proceed.

"Axel can't hurt them anymore. I was okay when James died. I'll miss him and I'll honor him. Life and death is a cycle and I can live with that. He saved so many, and that's honorable and he deserves every ounce of our grief and praise." Quinn bared his teeth. "But Axel hurts the pack and if no one else here can do it, I'll be the strongest. I'll do it. I'll kill him, because he's not allowed to hurt the pack anymore."

Elijah did move away at that point. "You're angry." It was a statement of fact. He had known Quinn was angry, but this...this was beyond what he had considered.

"I am. Are you?"

"Of course I'm angry!" Elijah sputtered, incredulous his best friend would even ask that. What he hadn't expected was so much rage in Quinn's eyes.

"Good. Then we're going to do this, and forget the rest. We can deal with everything else when the pack is safe."

Elijah took a deep breath. He had never seen Quinn like this, not this angry.

"I've held back for so long," Quinn whispered. "I could have killed him months ago when we captured him. I've nearly lost so many of you since then. My family. My only family. We're going to get him this time, Elijah. We have to. We have to succeed in this hunt."

"You want us to stop talking about the future." Elijah felt it hit him like a train. Quinn was in the same place as Sawyer and Vincent, he just had never admitted it. He was like them. There was only this and nothing past this.

Elijah was angry, but he wasn't short-sighted like this. He couldn't be. He had done this once before when Blair was killed. He knew the repercussions of decisions made in rage without thinking of the future. This wasn't healthy.

But he could only really say one thing.

"Whatever you need, Quinn, I'll do." He meant every word, because at least he would be by Quinn's side to keep him safe. Even if it meant protecting Quinn from himself. Jasper and Zander would be there for Sawyer and hopefully she would keep Vincent in line. She was doing a decent job of it so far, even if they both had slip-ups.

Quinn nodded, then fell silent. He had apparently appeased the wolf, thank god. Elijah wasn't sure what to do. Vincent was upstairs reading chess manuals, sharpening his mind to handle Axel. Sawyer was pulling out her mask to go after these people. Quinn was next to him, barely restrained violence with very few outlets until the next raid. Upstairs, Zander and Jasper already had one foot out the door because they were breaking under the pressure of what the job had done to them.

Elijah went back to looking out into the jungle. He wasn't sure he could take much more of this. They were only on the second raid, and people were still interviewing Alfie,

Janie, and Martinez, hoping to get any information from them that would lead the team to Axel.

He wasn't even sure the entire team was on the same page anymore. They were all going through these motions, but it felt like everyone had different goals. He wanted this over and done with, but he didn't even know why. To keep Sawyer safe, to keep Vincent safe. The team. That worked for him. Jasper and Zander wanted to complete the unfinished business so they could get out, complete the only mission the team was ever really made for. Quinn was raging next to him, viciously protective of his people. To him, this was taking out a rival that was threatening the people he cared for.

Sawyer and Vincent just wanted to bury their pasts once and for all.

But they weren't on the same page, not emotionally.

And he understood Quinn's question better. He knew Elijah was angry at all of this. The entire situation was driving the whole team nearly mad.

He was asking if Elijah was angry *enough*.

Cases weren't supposed to be this personal. Elijah couldn't shake the fear that someone dear to him was going to slip up and get hurt. He just couldn't shake it.

And he was feeling so terribly mortal.

ELIJAH WAS SUITED up and ready as Zander and Jasper walked in with Sawyer for the last meeting. He wondered, trying to shake his fears, how it was for them, waking up. When it had been him, Quinn, and Sawyer, it had felt like a normal day. It had been easy to fall into the three of them waking up together, since they were so comfortable with the idea. He was glad she enjoyed it; that had worried him for a small moment.

But Zander and Jasper? Zander was down for anything, but pulling Jasper into those sorts of things...Jasper wasn't known for being the adventurous one of the team, that was certain.

They were slightly uncomfortable. He could see it a few steps into the room. Jasper shuffled around, working, not looking at Zander. Sawyer was looking down, turning her mask over in her hands, thoughtful. Zander seemed to look guilty.

He would need to talk to all three of them if this was going to linger, if they didn't work through what they had done together. Elijah wasn't sure if he should make light of it or ignore it for the time being. It was Quinn who made the decision, actually.

"It's good, to do things that strengthen the bonds between a pack," he mentioned lightly. "Are you feeling better?" he asked Sawyer specifically.

"How do you feel about it?" she asked back.

"They aren't leaving the pack. If you had talked to me, I would have told you the truth of the matter."

"You didn't know yet," she reminded him. Elijah resisted a chuckle. He knew what Quinn was about to say.

"You could have come to me, instead of being angry with them."

"And what would you have said?"

"They won't leave the pack, since I wouldn't let them. They know that too, which is probably why they didn't tell me earlier."

She began to chuckle. Zander did as well. Jasper groaned, holding his face as he sat down on the edge of one of the beds.

"He's right," Zander mumbled. "We knew he would just shrug and dare us to try to truly leave. Quinn is possessive like that."

"Oh, I know." Sawyer was smiling now.

"How are you, Jasper?" Elijah asked softly.

"I'll talk about it later. I just need to stay focused on this right now." Jasper smiled wearily up to him, both tired and apprehensive. Elijah nodded. "Where's Vincent?"

"On the phone with the other team running tonight. They're in Spain, and we're going at the same time."

"Good to know they're in position. The timeline of this is the worst."

"Happy New Year's Eve, everyone," Sawyer announced, ignoring the work conversation. "Are we ready to kick off the new year?"

"Oh shit, that is right now." Zander huffed. "We'll finish the raid and have a drink together. Happy New Year, everyone!"

"Woo!" Elijah played excited. Just another new year and the IMPO. He wasn't sure he was really looking forward to it.

"They're ready," Vincent said immediately as he walked in. "Put the holiday talk away, we're working. Once this is over..." He trailed off, shaking his head. Elijah knew he didn't even want to consider the after. Vin would need to eventually, but he wasn't ready for it.

"Let's move, then. Are you going to wear that again?" Elijah pointed at her mask, meeting her dark eyes.

"Of course."

"Why?" Zander asked. "Why? It's hot and it's cool as shit, but why?"

"Because I want them to be scared," she murmured,

running a thumb over one of the cheeks. "I need them to be scared."

"You think the mask makes you scary?" Quinn was frowning.

"They're scared of Shadow, the assassin. Sawyer, my face...I was just Axel's whore. I'm not a threat - but I am with this mask on." She looked up at them again. "Plus, it makes me disappear in the dark easier. It's just a good mask."

"Sure," Elijah muttered. He wasn't sure how to feel about the mask. There was a line he couldn't see, but for some reason he felt like that mask was crossing it. It stank of enchantments he found disgusting. The mask had...hooks he could sense. It drained a Magi of their power every second it was worn. It bled them out. She must know and not care or had taken it into account.

The Magi didn't believe in dark magic. The Source and its abilities, whatever a Magi got were all equal. But the enchantments on that mask were one of the closest things he would have considered as dark magic. Like the healer in Texas, twisting his ability to kill with a touch instead of heal.

And he watched her push the mask to her face and it went from solid to inky and covered her face. She changed. The moment it was on, he knew the difference between Sawyer and the enigmatic concept of Shadow. Her alternate personality. A shield between her heart and what she was doing.

She wasn't stepping over whatever line he couldn't see. She was running over it with disregard. She was being everything Axel made her, and Elijah physically felt the pain of it in his chest. This was the sort of thing Axel drove his team to do. He drove them to their worst, not their best.

And the nagging sensation in the back of his mind refused to abate.

18

SAWYER

awyer waited next to the SUV as the team talked about what the plan was one more time before they split up.

"IMAS is coming in with us here. They report directly to any of us and every decision must come to me." Vincent's tone didn't allow any argument. "Unlike California, we're treating this more like the Amazon. They will see us coming and be prepared for a fight. We're talking arms dealers, paramilitary, and the rest of their ilk. Mercenaries, not thugs. They will put up a fight, even if Sawyer secures Leonard. We need to be prepared to take people down."

"Of course we will be. Quinn's coming in with the team this time, right?" Jasper asked, looking over the map on the SUV hood.

"Yes. The wolves and Sombra will stay with him as well. Unless...Sawyer, you sure you don't want her with you?"

She looked up from the blade that she had been flipping around in her hand. "I'm sure. She knows what to do. She'll be a good assist to you all. If I need her, she knows how to get to me. This is close to her home range. Just a different type of jungle. I just can't take her in with me. She won't be able to follow me well enough."

A sense of pride came from her cat though. She didn't agree, but she accepted her Magi's decision again. She would protect the males unless Sawyer needed her. The pride in the cat came from the fact that Sawyer trusted her absolutely to keep the males alive. Sawyer would trust no one else to the task, especially not a bunch of fucking IMAS soldiers.

"Okay." Vincent nodded once and went back to it. "Sawyer, if you want to get in there before us, you need to take off."

"I know," she murmured. "I wanted you alone for a moment." There was something bugging her just a little. She had thought about it earlier in the day, but had waited for a good moment. She wasn't willing to wait until after this raid, though. She had a strange feeling. She didn't like the jungle. Then again, none of them did, not really, not after the last time they were in one.

"Okay. I'll come talk to you. Guys, review your parts." Vincent walked to her, and they ducked further behind the SUV. Not too far from the team, but far enough where they could talk privately. "What's wrong?"

"Where is he?" she asked softly.

"If I knew, I would tell you," Vincent answered, frowning. "You know I would."

"That's not what I mean. Five months ago - hell, six or seven - he wanted my head and was willing to do anything to get it. Where is he?"

She watched Vincent realize what she meant. Axel hadn't come after her or the team yet, even though they had defeated him once before. She hadn't realized how strange it was, not fully, until after the first raid. It felt like they were the only ones fighting the war. Where was Axel?

"He doesn't do revenge, for one. It's not his MO." Vincent sighed. "Not like he did with you..."

"Exactly. This is me we're talking about. So where is he?" She felt like she was asking for trouble, but the question was beginning to eat at her. Why hadn't he come after her? It would have made this so much easier.

"Axel doesn't make the same mistakes twice, Sawyer. He's not going to come back after you like that. Not this time. For one, when he tried last time, you were just running from him, hiding. You were willing to exist in the same world as him and he didn't find that acceptable. Then he came after you and in the process, the team...then he lost." Vincent ran a hand through his curls. "I've thought about it too. I knew he wouldn't play that game again. Not the vendetta. Sawyer, what's more dangerous? An Axel that wants you to die, consequences be damned, or one that will do anything to win, including ignore you?"

She let her jaw drop. Ignore her? "He wouldn't ignore me."

"He ignored me for years and it won him the game. He stayed ten steps ahead, and he was winning and I was falling behind until he got sloppy. That tactic wins him this. We'll run ourselves into the ground and if we never catch up, he wins. He won't be stupid again." Vincent took a deep breath. "You know that."

"I just figured when he realized we were on the case and actually working on it, he would take the challenge. He would react and come after us."

"He doesn't even know where we are. Think about it, Sawyer. He was out for roughly a month before we even found out and he never tried to kill you. He played other people to try. Hell, his connection to what happened in New York is vague at best. He's playing this very smart and very privately. He's not going to be in the same room with us until he has to be, and then it's going to be his last ditch effort."

"And we're hoping this drives him to it." Yeah, she remembered that was the idea behind all of this. But she wanted to hunt him. She wanted Axel. She wanted to envision his face and know he was the target, not his pawns. She had, somewhere deep, hoped he came after her again like he once had. "So we're playing against a..."

"A ghost," Vincent finished, nodding. "He's not going to show himself or his hand. I know my brother, Sawyer, and so do you. Did you really think he would come out fighting like he had in Atlanta when that lost him the war for a moment?"

"No," she agreed softly. "No, I think I knew, but..."

"But sometimes it's good for someone else to say it. What did you tell me? One step at a time?"

"Yeah," she chuckled darkly.

"Well, that's chess too. One move at a time, and all the while, you try to predict the next move and the one after that."

"And then suddenly you know the different ways the game can go and you can be ten steps ahead."

"We're flying blind, in a sense, since he's gone to ground and is leading from who knows where, but so is he. He has no idea what we have in our pocket either."

"Missy. Yeah. I'll head out now. Thanks for talking to me." She touched his shoulder and he grabbed her wrist, pulling her closer before she could walk away.

"Be safe," he whispered. "And keep those comms on."

"I will." She kissed him in return, the mask making it feel

strange. She walked away before he could hold her longer. She waved at the guys as she passed them. She had to make up ground. IMAS was already rolling up - she could hear them in the distance - and she needed to disappear into the dark jungle.

It was easy to slide into the darkness, focusing on the direction she needed to go. Deep out there was a compound where thousands of weapons were being stockpiled and sold to different groups, fueling wars all over the continent. Africa was never the most stable place, and it only gave Axel a breeding ground of funds to use. This would cut him off at the knees in another area.

Another step forward to her goal of taking him down forever, wherever he was.

She could hear the trickling of the rain, feel the humidity, and, even in the night, the heat. It was so reminiscent of her time in the jungles of South America. Fuck, if she never saw another damned jungle, it would be too soon. Sure, the Congo and the Amazon were very different places, but to Sawyer, a jungle was still a jungle, and they all sucked.

Unless she had Quinn with her. For a moment, she let her mind wander to the idea of waterfalls and a small village where she and the feral Magi found something neither of them expected. A connection fulfilled, hearts full of love. Like she had found it with her entire team. Her family.

Even the thought of them reminded her why she was doing all of this. Not the WMC, not even her own redemption, that pardon just out of reach. For them. Always for them. The world wasn't safe for anyone with Axel Castello able to walk around.

Maybe this time she would make the world safe. That's

what she wanted. To go home and never fear for their lives like she had always feared before.

The compound came into view as she continued to push through the vegetation. She pulled her magic over her, watching the world become shades of grey as the cloak made her invisible. She continued closer, careful with every step not to make too much noise. She wanted to sound like any other creature in the jungle, not some human stomping around. That would be IMAS and the team. They would get noticed long before they reached the compound, and they knew it.

No, she was going to get in completely silent again, while no one knew what was happening.

She slipped through two guards and dared to sublimate in the dark to get through the chain link fence. Reforming, she cloaked so fast she knew no one would see her. She moved swiftly towards a secondary building, one she knew would be empty. It was the home of the power generator and back up. It would give her a spot to breathe before entering the main building. She snuck inside, saw no one was there and took a deep breath, dropping her cloak for the second so it didn't drain her magic further. Part one complete.

"Vin, I'm in," she whispered, knowing the tiny mic would pick it up. "Going dark."

She knew he wouldn't respond, but she also knew the entire team would be thankful to hear at least that.

There would be no vents for AC in the building like there had been in California. She had to infiltrate the slow way. A window on the first floor would work. She just needed to pick one that didn't have too many guards around it or anyone inside.

She pulled the cloak back over herself. Leonard was

using paramilitary, mostly non-Magi like Alfie. Hell, Leonard used even fewer Magi, from her guess. She could feel maybe five through the property as she snuck around. It worked in her favor, since that meant none of them would feel her moving through them unless she physically touched them. Leonard probably did it so he had less competition in his play to stay on top of the group. Every Magi would be weaker than him.

She crept over the grounds towards the main building and looked inside a window. There were two guards in the room so she moved on. She didn't care what they were doing, she wasn't going to test trying to do a silent takedown unless it was the only option. She stopped at the next window. Three guards. Still no good.

She didn't like this. Every window that wasn't acceptable meant she had to stay cloaked for that minute or more longer. With that and the mask, her magic was slowly bleeding out. She had to keep moving.

It took five windows to find one she could work with. Only one guard, watching television with an antenna and getting frustrated. She sublimated, sliding in through the crack, and crept up behind the non-Magi as he turned off the television, probably tired of it. Reforming without a cloak on her, she wrapped an arm around his neck, forcing him into a sleeper hold before he even knew what was going on. They were both staring at the television as he struggled, pale and afraid. Not that she blamed him. From the reflection of the TV, she could tell she looked like Death itself. An emotionless obsidian face that held no pity as he went unconscious, and that refused to budge from her task.

He finally went under, not making nearly as much noise as he could have. She had purposefully spooked him in hopes of getting the shocked silence instead of a fight. She had gotten what she wanted.

Sawyer lowered him to the ground, propping him up. She didn't bother to handcuff him or anything. If he was found, he was just napping on the job like an idiot. Someone would be mad at him for this, but still never know she was there.

Countless times. She knew everything because she had done this countless times. Hunting was her specialty and she was off the leash. It made her feel alive, like it always did. It made her feel powerful, the ability to creep through these men with no one the wiser. No one had any idea she was there, about to turn their lives into hell.

She slipped out of the small room, cloaking again as she did, and into the empty hallway. Leonard's office was on the top floor. Easy enough to get to. She moved towards the stairs, careful not to touch any of the non-Magi roaming around. She blinked to the top of the first set of stairs. Then the next, and the one after that. She couldn't risk creaky stairs in the jungle-beaten building.

She could feel him clearly now, and even hear him. He was talking to someone, but she didn't know who. He must be on the phone.

Right outside his door, she heard something she hadn't expected.

"I've heightened security, but it seems it didn't work. She's here. You don't mind being on hold, do you, Axel? I'll take care of this."

Shock raced through her, freezing her for a moment. It took half a second too long for her to shake it and get moving.

She pushed his door open, letting her magic cloak drop. She caught Leonard smiling as he put the phone down. She blinked towards him and ended up by herself behind his desk. Turning quickly, she saw him standing in the doorway. She was still in shock, thinking about the man on the other end of the line, the name on hold on Leonard's cellphone. She should have gone after him faster, should have thought about his powers.

"Well, looks like we had similar ideas." The next instant, his fist connected to her jaw. She just hadn't been ready for it.

She hated fighting other people who could fucking blink. She hadn't expected him to feel her when she got close. Quickly, as he grabbed her, she tried to remember all his powers. Blinking, telekinesis, telepathy. She tried to blink across the office again to shake him but he had contact now and his fist hit her ribs. She tried to hit him back but he stopped her hands with his telekinesis, pushing back on them to slow her attacks down just enough.

She sublimated to break his hold, and in a second she realized that she had fucked up. Blinking, telepathy, telekinesis, and *air manipulation*.

She knew that trick. Naseem was just as strong a master of air manipulation.

"Bad move, Shadow!" Leonard laughed as he pushed magic into her. She tried to reform. She had fucked this up royally.

Her mind screamed in pain as Leonard began to do the one thing she always avoided so carefully. He was pulling her apart by the atom.

NO! STOP! HELP! ANYONE! PLEASE!

Her own screams just echoed back to her in the void of her mind.

Stupid. She had been thrown while she was being overconfident.

Idiotic. She had distracted herself with thoughts of the guys instead of running down everything she knew of this guy, preparing herself for every possibility.

And now she was very possibly going to die without anyone ever knowing. She was going to take Sombra with her.

She couldn't die. In the seconds of pain that Leonard had already put her through, a torture that felt like her very soul was being ripped apart, she remembered she absolutely couldn't die.

She could work through the pain. She knew she could.

Pain was nothing.

A mental deep breath. It meant nothing.

She had to literally pull herself back together while he was trying to tear her apart.

She pulled all of her magic to her, every tiny piece, hoping she could pull all of her smoke back to herself. She needed it. She needed all of it.

She kept ignoring the pain. The debilitating, unreal pain.

Unreal. She focused on that word. She was just smoke. The pain wasn't real. It couldn't be. She wasn't a body. She had no nerves or flesh. No way to break her bones, not in this form.

She held onto that belief and it happened. She pushed the pain down.

She reformed.

Leonard didn't miss a beat, slamming her cheek with a fist the moment she was able to open her eyes and truly see again. It shoved her back into a close wall.

But now she was pissed off. She grabbed his fist on the next swing and threw her head forward, slamming his nose with her forehead. He stumbled back and looked up at her, wiping blood off his face.

"Well, it's a pleasure to finally meet you, Shadow." It was sarcastic and biting. He wore a dangerous smile, ready for the challenge she was about to give him.

"Likewise." She blinked forward, throwing another swing.

It was on now.

19

QUINN

Quinn watched Sawyer leave, ignoring the men talking around him. He felt her as far as he could. Since it wasn't his territory, he couldn't know her exact place as well as he could have at home, back in Georgia. That land had been so flooded with his magic, he had been able to pinpoint her to the inch, as he proved to her time and time again.

Not out here.

It worried him more than the California raid. This one was so much like the Amazon and that had him even more pissed off about their entire mission than anything had yet. Here they were, in a place so much like that place, signing up to get hurt again.

And why?

To stop a madman that kept hurting his pack. He was so tired of it. He wanted blood. He wanted to shred the rival apart and howl in victory as his pack reigned supreme. He wanted to kill and be vicious.

It took everything he had to contain it. Since that day with Vincent and the children, he was containing it, barely.

But that pain from Vincent had marked him. It had marked him deep enough that he felt the near-constant threat of Axel around every corner. The only thing he had going for him was that others needed him calm. He could be calm. He could hunt when it was time, and it was finally time again to go hunting.

It brought out something feral in him, like a piece of a man he barely knew anymore. A man he used to be, if he could have even been considered a man at the time. The Druid in the Amazon hadn't angered him like this, but Axel brought out everything he once was, took him back to times where Quinn had to be vicious to survive.

And unfortunately for Axel, there were no Druids involved in this, which made Quinn the most powerful Magi in the entire situation.

That made him feel good.

"Quinn, we're going to start moving," Elijah told him as the cowboy patted his shoulder. "How far is she?"

"Past my range," he answered. "She's disappeared into the night."

"Of course she has." Elijah sighed. "She'll check in with us, don't worry."

"I wasn't worried." Sawyer didn't worry him. No, he had pure confidence in her skills. She was a natural predator. He knew it wasn't all her time with Axel either. It was the way she carried herself. The stories he heard of her youth even told the same tale. Her time with Axel had only sharpened and honed her skills to a deadly precision.

But she was so obviously always a predator. He wasn't worried about her.

His thoughts were interrupted by an argument unfolding near him. He and Elijah both pivoted as the commanding officer of the IMAS Spec Ops team tried to talk over Vincent. They had been granted an elite team for this particular mission, which was better than the low-ranking grunts from the Amazon.

But not much better. They were still soldiers, and the team had a bad history with them.

"Well, Special Agent Castello, I'm saying-"

"You'll follow orders or we'll go without you." Vincent's voice cracked like a whip. "I won't take any damned insubordination from a bunch of soldiers in the jungle. Not again."

There was a heavy silence after that. Quinn glanced at Jasper, who was shifting on his feet uncomfortably. Then Zander, who had paled slightly. Elijah's chest began to rise and fall faster and harder than before. All small signs that the Amazon, from only a few short months ago, had left marks on them they would never escape. He knew the other men were talking to people, doctors, the same type they wanted Sawyer to talk to. For the team, it was natural. Something happened and they worked on making sure it didn't become a permanent issue.

"Yes sir," the soldier finally mumbled, defeated.

Quinn grinned dangerously. "Good, because I'm not in the mood."

"Quinn." Elijah's tone was a warning to back off, but Quinn wasn't joking and he wasn't backing down. There was too much going on for them to deal with these soldiers. If they tried any of the tricks the last men did, he would just bury them. His magic was already whipping around, proving who the most powerful person in the group was. Elijah wanted him to calm down.

"Let's move," Vincent called, breaking the entire affair up. "Team, I would like all of you close with me."

"I'm sending the animals out. Will you send Kaar out to

scout?" Quinn asked him. Vincent only nodded, his eyes becoming unfocused as he drew closer. Pushing on his bond with the wolves, Quinn sent the orders. Look, but don't engage. Observe and be ready to launch into an attack when needed. Through the wolves, he knew Sombra got the orders, the black jaguar jumping up and melting into the night without anyone saying a word to her.

The journey would be long. As the group began to move, Quinn counted every step. They were a decent distance from the compound they were raiding tonight, which was for the best. They couldn't meet up too close or they could have been ambushed. But the long walk in the cloak of night was hard. Well, for everyone except Quinn. He didn't mind it too much. He heard Elijah curse once. He heard another person stumble - probably Jasper, since the terrain was unfamiliar. He heard whispers from Zander about venomous snakes and how he hoped they didn't run into any.

Surprisingly, the soldiers were silent and focused, their weapons drawn as they crept forward, branching out from the team on either side, hidden in the bushes and trees nearby.

"Do they ever talk?" Elijah asked, looking between the team in the dark.

"Every member of IMAS Spec Ops has telepathy. They're having conversations in their heads," Jasper reminded everyone. Quinn nodded slowly. "It's what makes them so efficient."

"Not a bad idea," Vincent murmured. "They don't announce that, do they?"

"No," Jasper confirmed.

"We'd rather if some agent didn't blast our secrets either," one of the soldiers commented. Quinn bristled at the superiority of the comment. Some agent? Jasper was a fantastic Magi and his packmate, not just *some agent*.

"Well, it's good for me to know. I have telepathy. So does our healer, Zander. If you need anything, you can get in touch with one of us. You should have made sure to tell me when we started." Vincent's words were harsh and unforgiving. Glad that someone was sticking up for the team, Quinn kept moving forward, but not before using some earth to trip up the soldier who made the comment.

It was several minutes later when Zander made the anxious comment that was weighing on everyone's mind. "We're taking so long to get there. Is Sawyer okay?"

"I can't say anything to her," Vincent reminded him. "I can't distract her. She'll get in touch when she has a safe moment."

"What if she's hurt or..." Zander's anxiety began to climb.

"I would know. Sombra would know as well. The wolves are keeping me updated on any big changes in her behavior."

"That's right." Zander sounded appeased by that. "After the last..."

"Yeah, we're all thinking about the Amazon right now," Elijah muttered. "This is just too damned similar."

The slow walk continued for five minutes when they finally got what Zander had been asking for.

"Vin, I'm in. Going dark."

Quinn stopped walking as her voice came from the tiny little earpiece. Everyone on the team had. She was going dark and was in the compound. She had them by fifteen minutes, maybe more. She wasn't being slowed down by the group.

"Glad we got that news," Vincent said with a sigh. "Keep

moving, everyone, and let's pick up the speed. We have someone in there with no backup yet."

And they started to walk faster, nearly breaking out in a jog. The soldiers picked up the new urgency quickly. And it only took ten minutes for them to reach the compound instead of fifteen.

Too bad. The moment Quinn saw the fence, gunfire lit up the night - and it wasn't from his side. Three guard towers were holding soldiers and there were more behind cover, waiting on them.

"Everyone get down!" a soldier roared. Quinn ducked as he threw a wall of earth in front of the team as they scrambled to get cover and return fire.

"How did they see us this far out?" Vincent yelled. "In the middle of the fucking night of all times!"

"We might have missed some security out in the woods! Cameras or something!" Jasper answered. "We need to get inside!"

Gunfire was chipping his earth wall, but no other Magi dared to try and bring it down. Quinn used it to push forward and raised it higher to stop anyone from seeing over it.

"Everyone, stay with me!" he called back, motioning for the team to follow him. The soldiers weren't his problem.

Vincent was at his back the fastest, sublimating to close the distance. Elijah, Zander, and Jasper were close behind him.

"What's the plan?" Vincent asked quickly.

"I'm bringing it down," he snarled and shoved against his earth wall with a force of magic that had Vincent stumbling back. Quinn hadn't held back. It caused the earth beneath them to rumble harder than any earthquake.

And the earth wall came down, collapsing onto the

fence and several enemies, many of whom screamed as it fell to crush them. It took down one of the guard towers that had been hiding others.

Without pause, and leaving his team in shock, Quinn opened the earth beneath another tower and watched it fall so deep that it disappeared. Then he closed it, killing anyone stupid enough not to run.

"We need some alive, Quinn," Vincent screamed. The IMAS team was now flooding into the compound as well.

"FIND SAWYER!" he roared back. If the soldiers had been waiting on the team, that meant they could have found her already. She was somewhere in this and he was having too much difficulty parsing between all the magical signatures around him. He was enraged that he couldn't pinpoint her exact location, only knowing she was alive and somewhere nearby.

But where?

"Sombra!" he called out. "Find her!"

Yes, her jaguar would find her.

While the feline ran in to do that, his wolves jumped into the fray, taking down a paramilitary thug between them. Quinn crushed a man raising his weapon to shoot his boys and then flung a massive rock at another running out of a smaller building. The rock slammed into something electrical and sparks flew.

And the compound's flood lights died.

Quinn grinned viciously. Now they were all fighting in the dark - and he, for one, was completely okay with that.

He focused harder on finding her. Inside the big building, along with another Magi that seemed just as strong as her. He snarled. He wanted to tear down the building to stop her enemy, but he knew it would only injure her as well. He was better in large spaces, not enclosed hallways. But she was good in the dark. He hoped she was taking advantage of it.

"Quinn, contain this!" Vincent ordered, firing on another man.

With a single nod, Quinn did just that. He summoned more of his strength and threw up earth walls following the line of the metal fence, throwing it out of the ground and replacing it with something he controlled. Now he would know if anyone tried to run from his team.

"Good! Now, capture as many as you can!" Vincent glared at him.

Quinn bared his teeth, realizing Vincent wouldn't allow him to slaughter the entire enemy pack - and if he did, it would be unforgivable. He began pulling the soldiers down into the earth, where he would leave them until the team had time to restrain each one. It was bothersome, annoying work, but he knew he couldn't just kill anyone who stood between him, his pack, and Sawyer.

He wanted to, though.

Once he was done with this, he was going to get to her. Maybe seeing her alive would make him feel less bloodthirsty.

20

SAWYER

Her elbow connected with his jaw, flinging him back. He was able to connect a punch to her ribs as he staggered. She ducked as he swung another for her head, sending two quick jabs into his gut.

He grabbed onto her shirt and blinked, taking her on a journey. She wasn't able to anticipate being swung into a wall. She looked up, blinking them over the desk and slamming him down next. She held him down for a second to slam a fist into his face, as he kneed upwards and caught her in the crotch.

That brought a groan from her. That shit was painful no matter what someone had between their legs.

The door swung open as he shoved her off and jumped up. She moved in time for the knife not to land between her eyes, instead grazing her ear. Gunfire made the world explode in sound. She figured he used his telepathy to tell his men she was there.

She took cover behind his desk as bullets rained into the room. She closed her eyes for a second to find him, and noticed he was making distance. He was running, that shit.

She could hear more gunfire outside. The guys must have shown up with backup.

A snarl and a scream. She felt Sombra brush the bond between them.

"Damned cat," Sawyer hissed. "I wanted you to stay out of the middle of this shit."

The next time a gun went off, it wasn't in her direction. That made Sawyer jump up and over the desk and rush the first guy she could get her hands on. She knocked him out efficiently as Sombra appeared and jumped on the next one. She blinked past her cat and tackled the next one, who was trying to raise his gun again to shoot her jaguar.

It took seconds and Sawyer was left standing among bodies, both dead and unconscious. Sombra licked her own jaws, and Sawyer saw the thick blood dripping down from her fur on to the floor.

"Good girl," she murmured. "Now we need to catch him. Ready to help?"

Sombra's answering growl was impressive, and the cat took off in a full run. Sawyer ran after her, blinking to close the distance as Sombra jumped out of a window. She followed out the window, running after the jaguar. Sombra was following his scent while Sawyer kept her mind focused on the Magi's Source, not letting him out of her sixth sense.

They ran out of the compound right as the floodlights died and the world became dark. Not even a tiny bit of light from the moon or stars could get through the dense vegetation.

Sawyer immediately felt more at ease. Sombra paced away. They were both solitary predators, but they had practiced hunting together. Games in the woods with Quinn and the wolves. Sombra caught the scents of two other unknowns with their target and was going to head them off while Sawyer came from behind.

Perfect.

They moved fast, ducking and dodging every single obstacle. Sawyer didn't know the Congo as well as she knew home, but she was now practiced enough to manage. It wasn't long until she could hear Leonard and his two loudly running ahead of her. Their boots crunched the earth and vegetation.

"We need to get to the helicopter," Leonard ordered. "I'm not dying tonight, do you hear me?"

Sawyer grinned. No, he wasn't. She wasn't going to kill him unless she had no choice. She wanted all of them in cells around the world, thinking about every mistake they'd ever made. Every piece of arrogance they ever showed, thinking they could hide behind Axel, thinking they could kiss his feet and hope for power. She didn't want any of them dead. If she had to live with every decision she ever made, then they did too.

She knew Sombra was already between them and their goal. Already in her spot. The two men with Leonard were non-Magi. Child's play.

Sawyer kept moving and went up into the trees. She blinked from branch to branch.

"Fuck," Leonard snapped as she watched the group slow down ahead of her. He turned slowly to her, but she knew he couldn't see her, just like his men couldn't see Sombra right in front of them. "Come out and fight me!" Leonard dared, looking towards her spot.

She blinked to another tree branch, one closer, but it left him scrambling to catch a read on her again, to find the source of her magic. She blinked again and kept it up, leaving him confused as her magical radiation was just left all around them in the dark, haunting him. She needed him confused and paranoid. She needed to be able to attack from any position without him expecting it. If she stayed still for too long, he would find her with that sixth sense Magi had for each other.

Sombra snarled as a soldier tried to move away from the group. Like her, the jaguar was circling dangerously around the group. They had cornered their prey, now they just needed to find the best way to attack.

Sawyer made the decision.

She blinked onto a branch above Leonard. She hadn't wanted to blink directly in his space since he was expecting it.

She just dropped down on him, slamming him into the earth with her weight.

Sombra took that exact moment to jump out of the night onto the back of one of the soldiers, silencing a scream before it could truly form.

Sawyer pulled her cuffs out and slammed one on Leonard's wrist while Sombra jumped off her first target and went for the second. The non-Magi fired and Sawyer snarled to cover the pain of Sombra being hit as she got her kill. Immediately, the bond was filled with assurance that Sombra was okay. Just a scratch. An image flew through Sawyer's mind of two massive cats fighting. Sombra had worse injuries before. It would be okay. Just lick it clean later.

Well, Sawyer wasn't going to lick it clean. She stared down at Leonard as Sombra stalked around, still moving fine with the graze on her side.

"Are you ready for what's next?" she asked softly, leaning down into his face.

"Yeah." Leonard sounded bitter and pissed off. She was

fine with that. At least he wasn't begging for her to come to his side like a coward trying to get out of it. He knew what he was, what he had done and what he deserved.

She moved off him and hauled him up, spinning him to finish handcuffing him. She pushed him back into the direction of the compound, where there was still fighting going on. She could hear it louder and louder with every step they took.

As the compound came into her view, she decided to use the comms. She was thankful her eyes adjusted well in the dark since she could see the IMAS soldiers coming towards her. She raised her hands in peace, shoving Leonard closer.

"Shut this down. I have Leonard. We're done here." She said it to both the soldiers and her team through the ear pieces.

"I've got Quinn on it, but a lot are still hiding in the main building."

"Bring it down," she ordered Vincent softly.

It took a split second. One moment, the building was there, standing tall in the night. The next it was a pile of rubble. It was that fast for Quinn's magic to lash out and demolish the building. She wondered if it was even a challenge for him. Probably not.

She walked closer and frowned as she walked over the rubble towards the team. She could hear something strange. Someone talking. She looked back to Leonard, who was trying to reach something while a soldier held him. She stomped back to him and reached into his pocket, pulling out a cellphone.

"You've kept him on hold this entire time and then, let me guess, it hung up on him?" she asked softly. "Stupid. No one puts him on hold, and now..." Now he was calling back to find out how his investments were doing.

She didn't finish, putting the phone up to her ear as she hit the button to answer the ringing.

"Good evening, Axel," she said softly. Her comms were still on and she knew her entire team heard her say those words. She caught Vincent's eyes across the compound and he was at her side faster than she expected. He used his sublimation to make time, of course.

"Ah. I figured if anyone could deal with you, it would be Leonard. I guess not."

"If this is increased security, you need to tell your men they should work harder. They're underestimating me. I'm not sure if that's insulting to me, or...insulting to you, since you're the one who made sure I was this good."

"Always taunting," he murmured. "Tell me, what do you get out of this?"

"A pardon," she answered. "Freedom."

"I heard rumors, but I couldn't be certain. The WMC has been very close-lipped, even with their aides, and thanks to you, I lost my only paid Councilman."

"You're welcome. He wasn't hard to deal with." Even talking with him was like a verbal chess game.

"And what will you do with this freedom? Stay with Vinny? Oh yes, I have heard all about that. The entire IMPO is abuzz with the team that's fucking their criminal. Really, Sawyer, I know everyone called you my whore, but I never expected you to spread your legs and actually be one."

Her hand tightened on the phone to the point she was worried she would break it. "Says the man who can't keep any of his whores in line."

"Missy." He got that message from her loud and clear. She had meant herself, but if he was guessing the doppelganger, she knew he already had figured it out. "Thanks to her, you've gotten your hands in all my businesses, and I don't want you there. So you should thank her when I tell you that I've left a little something for you to be distracted by. You know what's so interesting about you being outed?"

"I don't, but I have feeling you'll tell me."

"Hmm. Yes, your friends came out of the woodworks too, and none of them are nearly as threatening as you are. I was coming to visit one tonight, to leave a little gift, actually. I figured you were still in California with Alfie, but the Congo is even better."

She heard an explosion in the background.

"Cute, hiding in plain sight like this. I decided to try it myself, and funny enough, it works really well. Though I won't be in New York by the time you get back. Until next time."

He hung up on her and her world began to fall apart. Vincent took the phone from her and shouted orders as her mind raced to figure out exactly what had just happened.

Friends coming out of the woodworks. New York. *Charlie.*

"The gym!" she screamed, startling him. "Vincent, get someone in New York to the gym!"

He paled and pulled out his own satellite phone, making the call. She couldn't bring herself to listen, wandering off to find the rest of the team. She was stuck in the damned Congo. She needed to do something or she would go mad with worry.

"Sawyer, I'm sure they'll be okay," Elijah said quickly as she got closer. "I'm positive. He had agents with him every second thanks to you."

She nodded and wrapped her arms around his waist. He held her for a moment before pulling away. "Where's Sombra? She need a healing? Do you?"

"Yeah, let's find Zander." She took a deep breath as Quinn appeared at her side. Sombra wandered around the group of them with the wolves trying to look her over. It was almost cute, but she couldn't enjoy it, her heart filled with dread and worry over the gym. She just had to hope Vincent got on the phone with anyone to find out what happened.

"Hey, Jasper?" Elijah said on the comms. "You know where Zander is?"

No response.

"Jasper?" Sawyer asked this time.

"Fuck, yeah!" Jasper called, but not on the comms. "I need a medic!"

Sawyer's heart dropped into her stomach. Zander was the medic. She took off running, finding Jasper near part of a destroyed building. His comms were in, but she wondered if they might have been malfunctioning. In front of him was a grinning Zander, holding his side, Jasper helping keep pressure on the wound.

"So, I got shot and hunkered down to try and heal it," Zander mumbled, his speech slurred. "But pain and blood loss suck."

"I've been here with him since shortly after it happened, trying to maintain pressure while he heals. But I think my comms set had a wire break or something. I've been trying to get someone since he went down." Jasper's voice was frantic but his hands were steady, trying to wipe blood from the wound for a moment for everyone to see. Unfortunately, more blood just gushed out, making Zander even more pale. Jasper went back to pressing the bandages down. Sawyer eyed the torn open medical bag, Zander's.

"Shit!" Elijah snapped. "We need some help over here! Our medic is down!"

Sawyer ran a hand through her hair as she watched a

soldier run to them. Glancing back down at Zander, she realized he was right. It was in his eyes. Here he was bleeding out, the team's only healer, and they were lucky they had another healer with them. In this one case.

Vincent was next to her a moment later, hanging up the phone.

"Thompson is already all over it. There was a serious situation at the prison, which put everyone on high alert. They had already started moving people under protection to safer locations. One of Charlie's protection detail on duty tonight is dead, but everyone else made it out of the gym."

"I heard an explosion-"

"Gas, but no one was there anymore. They rushed Charlie and Liam to a safehouse. Thompson is sending out soldiers to check on all of your kids."

"We got lucky," she whispered. Vincent only nodded.

"We got lucky. He's not there now, but he must have been standing there to make sure it went down. That the gym wouldn't be there anymore."

"So I would know he can get to anything I care about."

"Exactly." Vincent didn't touch her, but she saw his hand reach out and saw the consideration of it. She grabbed his hand before he could get away.

"What else?" she asked.

"I don't know. Thompson didn't have much time to talk, and we've got a lot going on right here."

"He knows about Missy," she explained.

"I heard that. I heard all of it, Sawyer. Now, we need to tend to everyone." Vincent kept hold of her hand as he turned to look down at the healer working on Zander. "Well?"

"He needs a hospital," the healer replied. "The bullet. It's in my way. I can't get it to dislodge without him bleeding out faster than I can heal. He's stable if I keep an eye on him, but he needs a team. Someone to remove the bullet and a few healers to repair the damage before he bleeds out. I'm just not strong enough."

Sawyer felt like she couldn't breathe as the night and everything that came from it caught up to her. Pulling her hand away from Vincent, she yanked her mask off, gasping for fresh air, even though it never inhibited her ability to breathe. She staggered away, shaken by talking to Axel and the gym being blown up. She hadn't expected any of this. She knew Leonard would be a hard fight, but she hadn't expected any of this.

Quinn grabbed her, holding her as she tried to collect herself.

And Zander was hurt while they were out in the Congo.

She could hear Vincent back on the phone with people, making the plans they needed to get Zander help. None of them included getting back to New York. She heard other cities mentioned, but none of them were her gym and the rest of her family.

"We're going to get him," Quinn promised in a hushed snarl. "We're going to make him pay for every hurt, Sawyer."

"Yes," she growled back, anger flooding her next to the fear for her loved ones. "Yes, we are."

It was only ten minutes later when a portal appeared and two Magi ran through it with a stretcher. They spoke in fast French, saying something about taking the wounded to Paris. She didn't say anything. Sombra whined, but her injury wasn't severe. She just didn't like that it stung.

Vincent followed Zander and the two unknown Magi first, with Jasper close behind him. Sawyer looked at the IMAS guys and remembered this time they were going to be the ones staying behind and cleaning up the mess. She went after Elijah into the portal with all the animals behind her. Quinn went last, holding Kaar for the bird's safety.

Now she was in a hospital and kept following the closest person, grabbing the back of Elijah's shirt to make sure she didn't lose him in the madhouse. Not that it was likely. He stood out thanks to how tall he was, and she wasn't short herself. But it was comforting to have a hand on someone.

And thinking of how tall he was made her think of Zander, trying to make light of the fact he was slowly bleeding to death. Because of course the jackass couldn't take anything seriously.

"In here," Vincent ordered, holding a door open.

"I'm beginning to hate hospitals," she mumbled. When she went inside, she frowned. "Where's Jasper?"

"They need a transfusion to help pick Zander up faster, just in case. Did you know those two were a match?"

"No, but it makes sense."

"Yeah, I never knew. Good to know, by the way, you know, in case of something like this." Vincent pulled off his comms, the wires and ear piece, the tiny mic, tossing them down onto the floor and stepping on them. "We did everything right."

"We did," she agreed. And yet they still somehow had the feeling they lost. Zander had been shot and Axel had been in fucking *New York*, blowing up her gym, probably with the intention of killing Charlie.

"When Zander is stable, we're getting back to it."

"Good," she hissed. "We're doing the third raid, damn it."

"I'm there," Quinn growled in rage. "Let me know what to do and I'm there."

"Wait a fucking minute!" Elijah snapped, jumping

between the three of them. "Zander is in the fucking hospital. Even with healing, he's going to need a few days!"

"We don't have a few days to wait for him to get out of bed," she reminded him, her fury ramping up at the idea they *wait*. Axel was out there, taking them on, hitting her safest place, and innocent people.

Waiting wasn't an option.

"So we go to the next raid without a healer at all? One of our guys with telepathy?"

"Not like he ever uses the damned ability anyway!" Vincent screamed. "Or someone would have known he was shot and it wouldn't have been so long before he got help!"

"We're not-"

"No, Elijah, this time you're outvoted. Three to one."

"We're down two members and you three are mad!" Elijah roared, pulling off his own ear piece and setting it on fire as he threw it away from him. "MAD!"

Sawyer glared at him. "I'm not letting Axel get away with this."

"Fine, but rushing this more than we've already done is going to get someone killed." He pointed a finger at her. "And you might be okay with it being you, but I'm not. And in the end, it probably won't be you. It'll be one of us. Hell, this time it was nearly Zander." Elijah stomped out of the room as Sawyer reeled back, hitting a wall, her eyes wide.

She slid down the wall and hit the floor, sitting on her ass, feeling like she had nowhere else to be.

"He didn't mean that," Quinn said, rushing out of the room.

She leaned over, wrapping her arms around her head. She needed to get Axel. She had to. She wanted to wrap her hands around his goddamned throat like he'd once done to her and strangle him until the life fled his eyes.

She needed it.

She was so angry. Everything was that man's fault. All of it. Her men, broken and bleeding. James, dead and gone from their lives. Charlie's gym. Henry and Midnight.

Her peace of mind, something she felt like was never going to come back to her.

If they didn't get him, he was going to get them. Didn't Elijah see that? She wasn't trying to get any of the guys hurt. She had never wanted that.

At some point, Vincent sat next to her. Their shoulders touched. She dared to look at him, only to see he looked like she felt. Haunted and upset. Enraged? Absolutely.

"We'll send another team," she whispered, hating herself for every word. She wanted to be the person going out there and hunting him down. "It's the only way."

Something flickered in Vincent's eyes, a bit of life that hadn't been there before. "Of course," he agreed softly. "Elijah is right. We can't go with Zander healing."

"He'll be back on his feet soon, though. We can go-"

"We'll play it by ear."

"We fucked up," she murmured.

"No, but we were about to." Vincent looked away from her. "We can't just leave Zander here alone. We need him on the team. We can't run off without him. We can't push."

"He tried to hurt Charlie," she reminded him.

"He's hurt a lot of people, Sawyer, but we both know pushing on without thinking is exactly what he wants."

She closed her eyes. She had been fine with the game until this moment. She had known it would get here. She hadn't thought her own feelings would overcome her better logic, but she *needed* to kill him. She needed Axel gone from this world. "Then when Zander is up, we get back to it. We make the plan now-"

"We'll see."

She sighed as he shut down her idea to get back the moment Zander was awake.

And guilt began to settle in her. She needed to check on the redheaded nightmare.

Standing up, she didn't tell Vincent where she was going. Knowing him, he would probably guess. She left the room and ignored the distant argument that had nurses and doctors avoiding one end of the hall. She knew the voices, but she had never heard them raised to each other like this. Elijah and Quinn were normally on the same page, all the time, no matter what.

As she went to find anyone who knew what was going on with Zander, she considered what she was trying to do. She had made herself so many promises at the beginning of this case. All of them to make sure it didn't lead to people being hurt. She refused to lose anyone before the end of this. She had to be careful. That's why she had set up Charlie and the gym with protection.

She had to not let Axel rattle her. That's what he was doing. He was trying to shake her up with the best thing he could, going after those she loved and cared about.

In the end, he knew it was always the easiest way to get her to fall in line. Emotional blackmail.

She found the floor's main station, several nurses wandering around it. She needed to refocus on what was important. She couldn't let Axel break her and lead to stupidity. Silently, she thanked Elijah. She would need to apologize to him later.

"I'm looking for information on the IMPO Special Agent Zander Wade."

"He's in surgery, and a young man is lined up to give him blood as well. We won't have any information for you for probably another hour. Maybe more." The nurse smiled kindly at her. Sawyer enjoyed the French accent. It was different from what she normally heard, hard New Yorkers or Southerners. The French was soothing. "Is he a friend?"

"More than that," she answered, stepping back. "He's family." She turned away, finding it hard to ignore the argument at the end of the hall. She walked to a point where she could actually see Quinn and Elijah, frustrated and angry with each other. Somewhere else, Zander was under and Jasper was by his side to help, like Zander had helped all of them at some point.

This is what the mission had done to the team. This is what she and Vincent had done to them. This was their plan, thanks to Missy, and this was a mess they had to clean up. This wasn't Axel's fault. Axel got out, and he played the game, but all of this was on her and Vincent. Axel went after Charlie because he needed something to distract her, since they had pushed so hard against him so quickly.

"Ma'am, why don't you go have a seat?" a nurse asked her softly.

"I will, thank you," she replied, nodding. She went back into the room where they would wheel Zander after surgery. Another hospital room. She was so tired of them. She could get why Zander wanted out of the IMPO. They were always in fucking hospital rooms.

"No news?" Vincent asked softly.

"None." She sat down next to him and they waited together. By the look on his face, she figured he was in the same place she was.

This was their fault.

Then Vincent's phone started to ring. She knew it was going to be more bad news. She just knew it.

21

ZANDER

Zander woke up to the beeping of the equipment he knew he was strapped to. Daylight came through the window, and he felt perfectly normal. He moved to sit up, realizing he wasn't perfectly normal, but there wasn't any pain either. Sluggish. He normally woke up easier than this, used to it after years of a regimented schedule and early mornings.

He looked around the room, seeing everyone sleeping, waiting on him. Except one.

"Hey," Sawyer whispered, jumping up from her spot and moving to his side. "How are you?"

"Good. What's the official word?"

"They got everything. Like Vincent's injury a few weeks ago, you'll be up and moving as soon as you want to be, with some bruising. They said you healed a lot of it on your own, and they didn't have to do much to pull the bullet out and finish the job." She smiled at him and he felt like it was just another good day. Hell, even a great day.

"Jasper?" he asked.

"Still asleep. He gave you blood last night."

"Of course he did," Zander said, chuckling. He carefully began to pull IVs from his elbow and wrist. Thankfully, most Magi were never down long enough to need anything more invasive, like a catheter. "What's the plan?"

"You have a lot of questions. We don't have one right now. We don't know how you ended up hurt, so we're going to address that first. Also, Axel was in New York while we were in the Congo and blew up the gym. No one was hurt, thankfully, but it..."

"It rattled you. What did you do, Sawyer?" He could see the pain and guilt there. The way her shoulders seemed to be weighed down.

"Elijah had to stop us from going to the third raid tomorrow night. Another team is taking our place."

"You were considering..." He thought about that. "You were going to keep going without me, or maybe even Jasper?"

"Yeah, but it's okay. We're not going to. It'll be fine. Another team is going to go in and do it and report back to us."

"And Axel blew the gym up?" Zander felt like he couldn't breathe for a moment. He liked the gym. He had so much fun there. He'd even considered asking Charlie for a job when he was out of the IMPO. That's how much he had loved it. The kids were crazy and too good, thanks to her, but he had loved it. "But Charlie and everyone...they're okay."

"They're fine. One of Charlie's protection detail didn't make it, but there's evidence that he was taken out by Axel so Axel wouldn't be stopped. And that's not everything that happened last night."

"Could the night get any worse?" He wasn't really sure how there could be more.

"There was a riot and several hits carried out in the prison. Missy is dead. So is Talyn. Anyone who might have had a connection to the Ghosts before all of this, gone. Luckily, we've been keeping the ones we've captured recently under lock and key in different locations." Sawyer groaned, rubbing her face. "Alfie and the rest of them are still secure. For how long, I don't know, but it's a shit show, Zander."

"Sounds like it. I mean, he was going to strike back. We knew that, right?"

"I didn't think he would hit us like this...not this fast, anyway." She looked away from him and sighed. "It's fine. This is just how the game is played. So yeah, Elijah stopped me and Vincent from doing anything stupid like leaving for the raid without you. He even argued with Quinn all night over it."

He reached out for her, taking her hand and squeezing. "We all have moments where someone else needs to knock us around to pull our heads out of our asses." He knew from experience.

And it got the reaction he wanted. She began to laugh, soft and weak, but a laugh nonetheless. She looked at him again, snorted and began to laugh harder. "Yeah. So, how did you get shot? You can shield, you dumbass."

"Well, I was shielded, but it was a madhouse. Quinn knocked out the power and everything went dark. I had no idea my shield was cracking from a couple of hits. Debris, mostly. He really tore that place up. Someone got a couple of lucky shots. I took the guy down, but one got in. I threw out a call for help to the first person I could think of before going down."

"Jasper."

"Yeah. He was at my side in an instant. We got cover and

we tried to just let me work on it. We had to be careful, though, since we didn't want to give ourselves away and get pinned down. It happens. This shit just happens. We weren't going to make it good every time. I'll be up by the end of the day and we're back to it."

"I'd prefer if we went back to New York. It would give you and Jasper a couple of days to heal more, regain your energy, and I need to check on Charlie. I have to."

"Of course. I'm not saying we're doing the raid. I'm not crazy." He raised an eyebrow at her accusingly and she looked down to avoid him.

It was a strange time if he was having to put Sawyer in her place. This was going to come back and bite him later, he could feel it.

"So, back to New York tonight, then." She nodded. "I'm glad you like the plan. Zander?"

"Yeah, babe?" he smiled leaning closer to her.

"Don't get shot again." She smiled back at him. "And has anyone talked to Jasper about..."

"No..." Zander sighed. If the important stuff was done, then it was time to talk about the relationship. Also important, he knew that, but it wasn't pressing, not with everything going on. "He's avoided me since we woke up yesterday. Not like that mattered when I needed him, but I'd like to talk to him."

"Me too. He was...different the other day."

"I bet he was," Zander said lightly, looking over to see his sleeping best friend.

"Did you...enjoy it?" she asked, sounding so insanely insecure. He coughed, wondering what she was thinking.

"Enjoy it? When can we sign up to do it again?" Zander laughed. "That was fucking great. Are you serious?"

"Until Elijah and Quinn, group sex was never my thing, but..." Sawyer shrugged. "None of this is normal."

"It's called polyamory, loving multiple people, a group relationship. Jasper and I talked a lot about it as teenagers." He wasn't an idiot. When he and Jasper spoke a long time ago on the idea of sharing her, they looked it all up. Jasper had researched and talked it all out with him. "And it's not socially normal, but I love you. And he loves you. You love both of us. And them." He nodded to the variety of sleeping men around the room. "When we're not out dealing with the world, do you even think of it?"

"No. At home, even at the gym...this all feels right." Sawyer chuckled, crossing her arms over her chest, as if she were hugging herself. "You know me. I'm not one to question good things too much. Just enjoy them while I have them."

"Well, I love seeing you with any of them. I loved being with you and Jasper in bed, even though I'm not into him like Elijah and Quinn are a thing. I'm not questioning it, either. The only person you have to worry about is you."

"And Jasper."

"Yeah, I'll talk to him," Zander promised. "You feel uncomfortable liking it, don't you?"

"A little." She looked like she had a secret and he waited, desperately trying to be patient for her to just say it. "Axel called me a whore."

That had him coughing in shock, as he tried to process that entire comment. "Axel said what? How? When?" Did it matter? He was pissed, but he didn't want to show her how mad he was. She wouldn't appreciate the indignation he felt on her behalf.

"He called Leonard. I picked up."

"Well, fuck him. You aren't a whore and you know it."

"Yeah, I know. It's just another thing he said to rattle me. Threesomes, though? That's stuff people see in pornos." She shrugged again. "I'm confident about a lot of things, as we both know, but maybe this is a little out of my comfort zone right now."

"Then we won't have another until you're feeling less..." He searched for the right word. "Exposed. Or we'll never have one again. We don't need group sex just because we're in a group relationship." He wanted it. He had *loved* it. Watching her come undone with Jasper taking her there. Jasper, who seemed so much darker and passionate. It was a side of his best friend he nearly never saw. That depth of emotion. Jasper normally didn't lose control like that.

It had been hot.

"This is weird to talk about," she finally muttered. "Make sure he's okay?" She nodded to Jasper again and Zander nodded, swinging his legs off of the bed. Just sitting in bed and talking had helped some of the sluggishness.

"Any way to find any food here? And where are we?"

"Paris, and I'll go find a nurse for you."

"Thanks." He grinned as she backed away from him and then left the room.

"She's worried," Jasper murmured. "Isn't she?"

"Oh, you are awake. I knew you should have been up before me. She's worried you're freaked out. For good reason."

"I'm in the same boat as her. I'm uncomfortable with how much I liked it." Jasper groaned. "I've never felt so..."

"You don't need to explain." Zander held up a hand. He could well understand what Jasper was thinking after nearly two decades of friendship. "Just...make sure she knows you're okay?"

"Yeah. And, uh...maybe one day we could do that again." Jasper gave him a guilty smile.

Zander could only laugh. Their lives were such a shit show.

$\sim$

TRAVIS MADE them a portal the moment the team realized Jasper and Zander were up and walking around. Zander breathed easier the moment he touched ground in New York. For the first time in his life, he was happy to see the city.

"So, what's the plan?" he asked Vincent, who was pulling out his phone to make a call. They were standing in the middle of a portal room in the IMPO headquarters, an odd place for Vincent to make an immediate phone call.

"Elijah, Jasper, and I are going to check in with our replacement team, then touch base with the teams holding our current prisoners. We're going to look into the prison situation as well. It's pretty apparent Axel got people, or word, in there to make the hit and cause problems. We just want to get through it all."

"Sawyer, Quinn, and me?"

"Going to see Charlie." Vincent smiled at him. "Sawyer's his family. The gym was her home for years. You and Quinn are better with the kids than the rest of us, including Elijah. I need him with me, anyway."

"All right," Zander nodded, realizing the entire team was now around them, listening in. "Sawyer?"

"I need to find out what arrangements have been made for him." She sighed. "They didn't just put him up in a hotel, right?"

"No. Actually, he's staying at our place. Thompson drove

him up there personally. It's secure. The best place for him. So really, you three are going home for a moment. Sawyer, I'm sure there's case stuff you can work on while you're there. If you want."

"Yeah, I can keep busy."

"Thanks, Vincent." Zander clapped him on the shoulder and got moving. He was ready to see their place again. They didn't even get close to enough time in it after they finally moved in.

"He's different today," Quinn mumbled as they all got onto the elevator together.

"He didn't like Elijah's tongue-lashing any more than I did," she replied, leaning on the back wall.

"Maybe you three shouldn't have needed the tongue-lashing by thinking for two minutes," Zander mumbled.

"Says the one who generally needs to get kicked around to learn anything," Quinn snapped.

Zander stopped before he hit the button on the elevator door. Did Quinn really just say that? Really? He hit the shut off button and it forced the elevator to a stop, making sure no one could interrupt them.

"Excuse me?" Zander asked, turning to look back at the feral Magi. The wolves began to shift uncomfortably. "Really? I've been trying to make myself a better man. I'm learning to accept when I can and can't do something. When it's time to stop or time to push. When it's time to fight or retreat. I'm trying my best, and here you two are, making every mistake you ever kicked me around for. And I'm the one suddenly in trouble?"

"I didn't say anything," Sawyer mumbled, shifting away from Quinn. Zander could feel it too. The feral anger, the meanness. Quinn wasn't in the right place. He quickly hit the buttons he needed on the elevator, so Quinn couldn't take them down on accident. "Quinn? Are you okay?"

"No. I'm going into the woods when we get home." Quinn shut down after that, without a single shred of emotion on his face. There was no emotion at all except the angry feel of his magic in the air around them. Zander and Sawyer stared at him, then locked eyes, wondering what they had just experienced.

They loaded up quickly and started the long drive home, ignoring the feral rage in the back seat. Zander was glad they were going home for a moment. Really glad. It would give Quinn a chance to reconnect to land he could consider his and get away from the rest of the world. It had been too long since they let their pack of wolves recharge on safe land.

The moment he pulled in the driveway and parked by the front door, Quinn launched out of the back, shifted into a wolf and tore into the woods, his boys following him.

"I hope he's okay," Sawyer whispered, watching him go.

Zander nodded, unable to find an explanation - until he remembered what she had told him. "You said he and Elijah argued?"

"Yeah." She sighed, getting out of his Range Rover. He followed and they found Charlie the moment they walked through the door. Everything changed in an instant, from the strange sadness and confusion over Quinn's behavior to complete elation with the sight of the older, hefty black man. "Charlie!"

"Hey, kiddo." Charlie dropped what he was holding on a small entryway table and held his arms open.

Zander chuckled as she practically jumped on him. The hug looked like it was bone-crushing, and it took several long moments for them to detach.

"Charlie, I was so scared. I didn't want anything to happen to you. I knew something could since you went public for me-"

"It's just a building, and it's not even that bad. The IMPO and WMC are already working on a payout to have it rebuilt, even better than ever. A month, and everything will be fine and back to normal."

"Tell me all about it?" she asked, pulling back from him.

"A fireball flew in through your bedroom window. It grew too fast. The guys on my protection detail were able to contain it while we all were trying to get out, but none of them could put it out. It hit the gas line in the kitchen after we were free of it and it took the entire top floor. Nothing else saw much damage. Some structural repairs up there, but the bottom floor is relatively untouched. It's not bad." Charlie was patting and rubbing her shoulder through the entire thing.

Zander watched, somewhat jealous that she had Charlie. He wanted a Charlie. He'd had James, but now James was gone and they were doing this on their own. He wanted someone looking out for him like that.

"It was Director Thompson's idea to hide me here until the case is over. No longer. When you guys are done, I'm leaving, since I don't want to live with all six of you." Charlie grinned. "And he had agents check up on all the kids, just in case."

Zander watched Sawyer visibly relax. "That's good. That's really good."

"Isn't it? Some other interesting things have been talked about as well." Charlie looked over to him. "Thompson offered to make the gym more official. Said maybe I can get a contract helping train new agents, and that should help me financially. Keep me on my feet after this, since I'm going to be going into the red until repairs are done."

"Really?" Zander raised an eyebrow. That was something. The IMPO didn't generally contract people on a whim. No, this was Thompson pulling some strings, since Charlie was who he was and filled the place he did in Sawyer's life. This wasn't *Director* Thompson. This was him trying to be their handler like James once was.

"It would open me up to hire people, create better business, and not worry over my books when I'm teaching two dozen kids for free." Charlie looked back to Sawyer, who ducked her head and went further into the house. Zander heard the laughter down the hall.

"She's happy to see you're okay," Zander said politely, pointing at where she went.

"Oh, I know. I'm glad to be okay." Charlie looked him over now, head to toe. "You got shot. Looking good for a shooting victim." Before Zander could pull away, Charlie grabbed him. He was able to get Zander's forearm, skin to skin contact. The heat from the hand told him exactly what Charlie was doing. Using his healing ability to check to make sure everything was okay. "They did a good job on you. I take it you stabilized yourself?"

"As best I could." Zander tried to pull away but Charlie was watching him carefully, refusing to let go.

"I'll give you the job," Charlie finally said. "When this is over, you will always have a place at the gym, just like her."

"Why?" Zander frowned.

"Because I see young men getting shot all the time where I am. It's not pleasant. If getting you out of the IMPO is what needs to happen, then I'll have a job for you. You'll be the first person I hire to help train these new agents."

Zander nodded slowly. He didn't know how to feel about

this sudden wealth of care he got from Charlie. "Why?" he asked again.

"Like all her strays, if you mean something to Sawyer, you mean something to me." Charlie let him go, those words hanging in the air. "You understand?"

Zander just kept nodding. Thompson and Charlie were both trying to be what James had once been. Before James had gone, they had talked as a team. What would any of them do when they wanted to get out of the IMPO, and things like that. James had always promised he would set up anything they needed to succeed. He knew Charlie probably didn't know any of that, but as an adult man with a big heart, he was doing it for Zander anyway.

"Thank you," he murmured, looking down. "I want to finish this and maybe then, she won't have nightmares. Maybe then, Vincent will get a full night's sleep. Maybe none of us will go into a hospital again and we'll all live past forty. But I can't do more after this."

"Takes a man to admit when it's time to step away." Charlie patted his shoulder. "Let's go find her. Then I'm going to make sure you two eat. Where's the third one? I was told the wolf boy was coming. Quinn."

"He needs a moment to himself, I think. He's already out in the woods."

"Not injured?" Charlie narrowed his eyes.

"No, no. He's fine physically. I promise."

"Good. Now let's go get something to eat."

22

VINCENT

Vincent tapped a finger on the desk, looking over the pictures of the aftermath. The prison went through hell. Two guards were caught on camera killing Missy. Upon capture, they admitted to being paid, as well as blackmailed.

His brother had set this up well. Neither were a part of Axel's business, not really. Just two guys in debt. Two guys with family that they needed to keep safe. Two guys who were vulnerable and hadn't gone to get help from the right people.

"Vin?" Elijah sat down next to him. "This is all a dead end."

Vin closed his eyes. He had promised to keep her safe. Missy had given them everything they had been working with for the last few days, and she didn't even survive a week.

"I can't let this go unpunished," he whispered, looking at a photo of her body. They had strangled her, then stabbed her for good measure, just to make sure she stayed dead. "I promised her, Elijah."

He was so mad, which is why he had Elijah with him. Elijah would keep him in check so he didn't do anything without thinking it through. That's what this had come to. Vincent was thinking about how to keep everyone on the team thinking clearly and on task without going mad.

He had to separate Quinn and Elijah for their own good. Quinn needed to go home and get some peace in the woods, reconnect to what made him so special and not a monster. Sawyer and Vincent just couldn't be in the same room anymore. He didn't think so, anyway. He wanted to pick her brain and keep her busy. He wanted them to go hunting together and find his brother and end this.

So he split them up. Elijah could keep him in check and Zander could keep her at home. For just a moment. Just long enough for them to get over being shaken by what happened while they were in the Congo.

"I know you did." Elijah stayed seated next to him, watching him with clear hazel eyes. "Vincent, it was a long shot."

"He even killed Talyn, who had stepped out and stayed neutral," Vincent muttered bitterly. "Talyn wasn't an innocent man, but damned Axel, he can't let anything go!" He slammed a hand on the desk. Talyn had been poisoned by one of the researchers he'd been working with. That researcher was now in custody. Similar story. Blackmailed. Axel didn't use a single person close to him to pull this off. "And where the fuck was he hiding this entire time? Right under our damned noses!" Vincent swiped a hand over the desk and sent papers everywhere. People were staring at him, other agents wandering around to do their own business. He glared at a couple, who backed away. No one attempted to clean up the papers.

"He stole that trick from Sawyer. There's no way we could have known, Vincent."

Well, that was a comfort. Vincent snorted.

"But there is," Jasper cut in. Vincent looked over to the blond, wondering what he was saying. "We could have started facial recognition programs just around the jail, to see if he'd been spotted near the prison, but the problem was always that we don't know the exact timeline. Or exactly what he looks like. We would have gotten tons of false positives, since this is New York with millions of people in it...and who knows, he might have had enough changes to his look that we wouldn't even get a real one of him. It was too unreliable to consider attempting." Jasper stood up from his desk in the large room and walked over, sitting on Vincent's desk. He grabbed an image still on the desk. Vincent watched him carefully as he folded the image and slid it into his pocket. "But I've had an idea."

"Get on with it," Vincent snapped.

"We know what Missy looked like after Axel escaped. We know what form she took. Sawyer said it herself, the woman was scarred pretty badly, but only the neck scar remained between forms. Can she alter forms or did she copy her last mental image of Axel?"

"He would have gotten any scars repaired as best he could, though!" Vincent didn't see where this was going.

"It's a non-Magi technique, and something we don't use very often, but we can hire someone to make a new version of that face. Something with the scars treated with magic or plastic surgery. There's a chance." Jasper sighed. "I'm grasping at straws. I like the plan of taking down his men and this could take more time, but it's an idea."

"We already use their facial recognition software. Why not hire an artist to make a few new versions of Axel's face?"

Elijah frowned. "The only problem would be if all of those are wrong. He could have very well remade his face the moment he was free. Hardcore plastic surgery. If I were him, I'd do it."

Vincent pointed at Elijah. Exactly. If anyone of them could think of a way to throw them off the scent, Axel would have already done it.

"It was just an idea. There's no harm in trying," Jasper said simply.

"Other than wasting our time," Vincent mumbled, shaking his head.

"Then I'm doing it and all of you can be asses about it." Those words were said with enough of a bite that Vincent snapped his head back up to stare at Jasper. Jasper got off the desk and stormed off without another comment.

"Vin-"

"He's smarter than that! Axel is smarter than letting us get pictures of him like that. Not after everything that's happened. It's how we tied Sawyer to him and caught her. How we've regained small steps over the years. He's not going to be that arrogant. I think he's playing the smarter game right now."

"Vincent-"

"And I don't know how to beat him!" Vincent leaned over, resting on his shaking hands. "I don't know, Elijah, and Charlie was nearly killed. The gym is gone. That's her family and her home and they're gone."

"Charlie is still alive," Elijah whispered. "Vincent, Charlie is okay and the gym can be repaired. It's not the end of the world."

"And Missy!" Vincent felt like he was falling apart. Every little thing was piling up. Angry, frustrated tears pricked at the back of his eyes uncomfortably. He'd never felt so much like a failure. "I promised her I would keep her alive! He broke her. He drove her so mad she tried to kill herself, and it was luck that she didn't succeed. It was all we had." He continued to lean over until he could wrap his arms over his head. "I can't beat him. And even if I do, she has to kill him. She's the only one who can, and I can't..."

He was falling apart again. He wasn't good enough, smart enough. He should have known Axel would retaliate that quickly. He should have known it would be bad.

"I'm failing. I can't even protect-"

"We did everything we could to protect them." Elijah growled, shaking Vincent by his shoulder. "Everything. Protection details, secure locations. We couldn't change the outcome, Vin. It sucks, I know, but we did everything we could. At least some survived the night."

"AND IT WASN'T GOOD ENOUGH!" Vincent jumped away, roaring. "It's never good enough, damn it."

He turned away and walked out of the meeting room, ignoring the agents staring. He didn't care about any of them. They were running paperwork for the team's case and everything they had done so far. They weren't important.

No, the important people were either hiding or dead. He was hiding, sitting at the IMPO headquarters, away from Sawyer and half the team so they could all take a day to do whatever would bring them to sanity.

He hadn't realized Elijah followed him out onto a balcony where smokers would sneak off to until the cowboy touched his back gently. He lit a cigarette and took a long, deep drag on it. He held it out to the cowboy, in case he wanted a puff. Elijah only shook his head.

"What was that about Sawyer?" he asked.

"She has to kill him," Vincent murmured. "She knows how to fight him better than any of us and-"

"No, she doesn't." Elijah tugged, forcing him to turn around and face hazel eyes. "It doesn't need to be her, Vin."

"The WMC-"

"The WMC doesn't have to know. At the end of the day, the WMC never has to know." Elijah leaned forward. "You don't want her to, do you?"

"No," Vincent whispered. "I don't."

He had never said the words, not out loud. Sure, deep in his chest, he wanted his brother dead, and she was the best choice. And to everyone, even to himself sometimes, that meant the same thing.

But deep down, he'd made a promise to her. Anything. He would do anything to keep his brother or anyone else from hurting her again. Every time she killed someone, he saw the new pain she would carry. Or the new scars she would have, either physical or emotional. Most of the time, both. She could cover it up, claiming she was doing it to protect people and therefore, it was okay. She could hide behind the shield of pretending this was just what she needed to do to protect everyone.

But he knew it hurt her.

And he didn't want his brother to hurt her anymore.

"Then we'll do something else. We'll figure this out. Because you're right, Vin. She shouldn't have to do this. This isn't what we ever wanted for her. Not this. We thought we could make her a solid agent and we could all work together and we'd be great." Elijah sighed.

"Nothing went as planned," Vincent agreed softly. They didn't need to tell the WMC. They never had to know. "I built this team to defeat him."

"Yeah, and we've done it before." Elijah smiled. "You coming back to me, Vin?"

"I've been distracted by my own feelings," he admitted. "Elijah, I still don't know if I can catch him."

"We have things set in place. Sawyer is going to be spending the next couple of days looking over the Dark Web, I bet you. Jasper is setting up facial recognition. Vincent, we don't need to catch him tomorrow. Stop rushing this. Focus." Elijah snapped his fingers, as if he were trying to think of something. "Play the game. Slow down and play the fucking game. Like you and Sawyer always say."

"He hit back hard because we hit him hard," Vincent murmured, nodding. "It was an eye for an eye."

"Exactly. But what did he do before we pushed so hard?"

"Nothing..." Vincent looked away from Elijah. "He did nothing since he was ten steps ahead."

"Come on, man. I'm not this smart, not as smart as you two. I know you can see what I see."

"If we regain the steps without him noticing, he won't come back and hit us." Vincent continued to nod. "So we play quietly."

"Exactly. You and Sawyer got wrapped up in this idea that you could take everything from him. But he's just going to do it right back and we have more to lose." The cowboy groaned. "You even got Quinn..."

"Elijah?" He frowned.

"Quinn was *good* once, Vin. He's never been a killer like that. Until this. He sees you and Sawyer hurting. He sees the team hurting and he's retaliating in his own way. The only way he really can, and that's being as powerful as he is. We taught him to hold back. Remember? Because killing dozens of people isn't how you fix anything. He can get people hurt on our side, and it sucks to admit that, but it's the truth."

"Should I talk to him?" He would. This felt like it was his fault. Quinn was protective of all of them, and Vincent was the one pushing for more. For them to be more vicious, to destroy his brother.

"He wants to kill your brother to protect you and Sawyer. To protect all of us, just like Sawyer. Just like you. No, you talking to him isn't a good idea. I...think him not in the IMPO is the only thing I can do for him right now. Him not on the team."

"Excuse me?" Vincent leaned against the railing, holding off taking another drag from his cigarette.

"Once, he killed a bunch of people because he thought he was defending himself from them. He was. Now he's killing people for human reasons, and with all the passion of a rabid animal. This isn't healthy for him. Not constantly like this." Elijah looked away this time, down to his boots. "I want to take Quinn out of the IMPO when this is over. Jasper and Zander are right. If we don't finish this and then move on, we're all going to die before we're forty or become the monsters we hate. Jasper has a point. What's the difference between the WMC and your brother right now?"

"Uh..."

"We gave the WMC the right to do everything we condemn Axel for. But either way, it's the *same thing*. Using people to do things, a lot of times awful things, to achieve personal goals of power." Elijah shook his head, looking back up. "And Quinn's goodness is being shattered under the weight of it. So is Jasper's, and he knows it. Vincent, in another decade, will we have the right to call ourselves the good guys? Do we still have that right after all of this?"

Vincent shook his head, but he didn't know which question he was answering. Maybe he was trying to deny it. He came to the IMPO because these were the people on the right side of the law. They would give him everything he needed to defeat his brother and put an end to one of the most powerful crime families that the Magi ever had.

But he couldn't deny the obvious.

"Okay. When this is over...I'll let you all leave." He wasn't going to force them to stay if they were unhappy. He didn't know what he would do, but he wouldn't force them to stay.

"There's no letting us do anything. We're going." Elijah said the words like it was for a funeral.

Vincent could see it already. The team was broken. There was no fixing this. This was over. When his brother was defeated, he had no idea if he would have any family left. He could hope they all stuck around, just to be with him, live in the same house as him, but he couldn't force them.

And after everything, why would they want to?

"But we're going to stop your brother, Vin." Elijah's voice was stronger now, full of conviction. "I'm not going anywhere until the team makes it through this storm."

"Why does this matter to you?" he asked, hoping for honesty. "You could leave right now and not risk being hurt from all of this. Especially after that car accident. No one would blame you."

"Because when we met, I saw a lonely man who needed a friend. A man who only had his conviction to catch his brother and *nothing* else. And I wanted to give him something else. Anything really, but mostly a friend, someone he could rely on. Together, we built a team. Together we fell in love with a spitfire of a fucking woman. Together we've made a *family*. Somewhere along the way, I realized you gave a lot to me, too. All of those things. We made them *together*." Elijah swallowed. "A really fucked-up family, no doubt, but you've been my brother for years now. And I don't abandon my brothers to their nightmares, to the things that haunt them. And I *never* will, because you'll always be my brother. I'm *never* letting you go back to being that lonely man, Vincent." Elijah reached out and grabbed his shoulder. "So we're going to see this through. And even when we're out of the IMPO, I'm going to live in the house and I'm going to trash the bathroom to make you mad and hope you loosen up."

"I hate you," Vincent said, a smile breaking out on his face. A second later, he was chuckling as Elijah laughed. "I hate you so much."

"Yeah, I know." Elijah grinned. "Finish your smoke and meet me back in there. I'm going to check on Jasper."

"Wait," Vincent said quickly, stopping the cowboy. When Elijah looked back at him again, halfway in the door, Vincent let him go again. "Thank you."

"For?"

"For teaching me what real brotherhood is. And for helping me find the brothers we have now."

"It's not hard," Elijah whispered. "Brothers would do anything for each other, and you already knew that. You just needed to find the brothers who returned that."

Vincent swallowed on that. Was that right? Had he always known that brothers should stick together and do anything they could for each other?

Yes. He had. He knew. It's why he'd killed his father. Because brothers would do anything for each other.

It had just never been returned, and now it was.

And slowly, Vincent let go of Axel in his heart. He'd resisted and he'd lied about it, saying he was over his brother, but he'd never been honest. Somewhere, he was always just holding onto a little shred of love, hoping.

"Vin?" Elijah didn't keep moving inside, just waiting there for more.

"I'm fine, you can go," Vincent murmured, waving him along. "I might have another." He waved his cigarette around before taking another drag. "I think I'll quit after this."

"Okay." Elijah finally went inside, the door closing firmly so Vincent was alone again.

"It's over, Axel," he whispered, looking back out into the city. He felt that stupid need to say it out loud. "Every day, these guys have reminded me time and time again why you aren't my family, but they are. It's time I finally believe, since everything you've ever said to me has been a lie."

All the promises. All the small things from his childhood he was constantly holding on to. Sawyer had said it once. He loved a boy, a brother that no longer existed. Axel Castello was not his brother. Antonio was, and Antonio was long gone.

"I'm coming for you. I'm going to catch you." Vincent took a deep breath, leaning on the rail, talking to the wind as if his brother would hear the words. Kaar landed on the rail, bumping his head to Vincent's arm. A rare wave of encouragement and support came from the raven. "And *I'm* going to kill you."

23

SAWYER

Night was approaching and Sawyer began to worry. Quinn still wasn't back from the woods. The wolves had come back hours before, curling up in Vincent's office with her and Sombra.

But no sign of Quinn, and the wolves weren't giving up anything. They barely even moved. When she put down dinner for the wolves, they had eaten but not moved. They didn't go looking for their Magi at all.

"Sawyer?" Elijah called in. She had heard the other guys come home, but hadn't moved to go see them, captivated and stuck with the sad wolves.

"What's up?" she called back.

Elijah walked in after that, still wearing his thick winter coat. She didn't know why he waited, since it was his office too. "He's still out there, isn't he?"

She could only nod, pointing down to the wolves. Sombra was staying with them, physically comforting the animals, who seemed forlorn and lost.

"Want to come get him with me?" Elijah held the door open wider, an invitation.

"Yeah, let's go. It's time." She grabbed her jacket, swinging it on as she walked to Elijah and left the office. Sombra stayed behind to keep the wolves company.

"How long has he been out there?"

"The moment we got home, he took off. The wolves came back shortly before dinner. That was four hours ago, and they've been like that since. Elijah, what's wrong?" She hadn't wanted to ask about their argument, but if Elijah did anything to hurt Quinn, she didn't know how she would deal with that.

"He and I argued about a lot of things," Elijah explained softly as they walked through the new home. "I don't like how he behaved on the last raid. I really didn't like how he behaved in the hospital."

"He's an adult and you aren't his father." She felt insulted for Quinn.

"He's feral," Elijah murmured, turning to her. "Never forget, Sawyer, that Quinn mentally is an animal first, just because of how he was raised. He will always be feral. We've tamed and trained him, but he'll always be feral."

"What are you trying to say? That he can't grow up and change? Become more human?" She felt more insulted. Did he think Quinn was stupid? No, not Elijah. She never would have thought he would behave this way.

"No, that's not..." Elijah groaned as they walked out the back door. "His first instinct in any situation will be to act the way he had for his entire life before meeting the team. I didn't like his behavior in the hospital and on the raid because he didn't remember anything the team taught him."

She stopped before stepping off the porch as Elijah kept walking. "What did I miss on the raid?" She had never thought to ask what really went down.

"He killed a lot of people, without even giving them a

chance," Elijah answered. "And not because they were enemies, but because he could. He could have as easily captured them all. Hell, Vincent finally reined him in and convinced him to do that instead. No, he lashed out and killed people...like he used to."

She was beginning to see. Now she was understanding. "You think it's...our fault? That he did that?"

"Yes and no." Elijah held out a hand. She took it slowly. Not just her fault. Not just his. Not only Quinn's. But everyone's.

"Keep explaining," she ordered, without any strength.

"I think the IMPO and the job we do is slowly twisting him. And that's why I'm having you on this walk with me. The argument between Quinn and I ended with one thing. I'm leaving the IMPO and I'm taking him with me. He finds it a betrayal to the organization that gave him a place in our world. I told him that the IMPO, the WMC, the IMAS...they have already betrayed him. He knows it, but the IMPO gives him the ability to use his power without real repercussions."

"He's thinking like a human," she realized softly. "Power. The ability to hurt people, to do as he pleases...for what he wants."

"In his case, to protect us and others. And no, the IMPO will never stop him doing what he did the other night. But then again, they don't have a moral high ground to stand on, even if they wanted to. Neither does the WMC."

"And you yelled at him because you're worried about him."

"I'm worried about what this world could be like if it continues to twist Quinn from a strange and wonderful man who happens to be powerful into...a vicious, rabid man with all those human faults who uses his power to get what he wants."

"He's not evil," she bit out, refusing to think Quinn would ever take that path.

"Neither are you, but you'll still use that human power to do what you feel is needed. Sawyer, the difference is that you're on our league, our level. If you fell, then others can stop you."

"But even with good intentions, Quinn could do serious damage and no one could stop him."

"Exactly. So I'm taking him out of the IMPO, whether he likes it or not. He's not happy, Sawyer. He deserves to be happy and have the time to live in this world without being consumed by it. And what if someone tries to use him one day? What if someone threatens us and tries to blackmail him? Look at what happened to those guards who killed Missy. They were good men, and look what happened to them and what they did for the people they love."

"What would he do?"

"I don't care, as long as it's not this. As long as he's not constantly exposed to this evil and being used. As long as he remains...good." Elijah shook his head sadly. "I shouldn't have a right in this, but I can't not protect him from himself. I care too much to see him go down such a dark path thanks to the world we live in."

"I understand and I'll help you," she promised. Now she really understood. She didn't like it, but she understood. "We'll make sure he's always happy, Elijah."

"I knew you would understand."

"So this means I've lost four of you from the team, huh?"

"Yeah, but that's all you'll lose us from." He lifted her hand and kissed the back of it. "Thank you for backing me up, little lady."

"Let's go get our wolf," she murmured, pulling him close to kiss him properly.

Together, they made the first step into the woods. They didn't know these new woods well yet, but she knew Quinn wouldn't let her and Elijah get lost in them. They kept going deeper in, knowing only the general direction of where Quinn had decided to set up camp. Since it was after sunset, she couldn't find the landmarks she had begun to use during the day. There were no worn trails yet on their new property, so it was harder to navigate.

"There he is," Elijah whispered. She looked around, trying to see what he did. Elijah grabbed her jaw and pointed her gaze.

And there he was. Quinn in his wolf form, staring at them from the top of a large rock. The scene morphed into Quinn just sitting on the rock, wary and confused. "Why did you two come out?" he asked. "I wanted to be alone."

"We've been worried," Elijah answered. "Talk to us?"

"Okay." Quinn jumped up and walked away.

Sawyer and Elijah hurried after him and two hundred yards away, they finally got to Quinn's new camp. Quinn threw some logs onto a lit fire and Elijah obviously pushed some magic into the flame, making it catch better and grow bigger. Next, several rocks rose from the earth, big enough for people to sit on. Sawyer just took her own seat, waiting on the two guys to stop dancing around each other. They worked well in tandem. Elijah was always so comfortable in Quinn's space where no one else was.

Finally, they settled and she was in the middle.

"What do you two want?" he asked, rubbing his hands close to the fire.

"You haven't come inside yet," she reminded him. "What's wrong?"

"Been thinking about what you said," he said, directing it around her to Elijah. "I spent the day out here to remind myself what makes me really happy, so I could remember the feeling of it again."

"And you haven't been happy?" She felt wounded. She'd thought he was happy with them.

"I'm never happy in human cities. I'm comfortable around people I know and care for, but I'm not truly happy. This place, while it's not the land I had a month ago, makes me happy already. It feels like a place I am meant to be." Quinn stood up again, pacing. "Elijah, you're right. Every case has eaten me up a little bit. Every single one. I'm beginning to think like them. I'm more powerful than them. I could just kill them and no one could ever stop me." A vicious growl erupted and shook Sawyer to her bones. "And that feels so wrong. Like the bitch in the Amazon. Like Axel. But out here, I feel normal again, and I'm happy, and I don't...hurt people. I never wanted to really hurt people like this before...The job doesn't make me happy. It never has. It was just something I could do, and it gave me a place that I would have never had otherwise in this world I know so little about."

She didn't know what else to do except jump up and pull him into a hug. She just held him as she realized the job had been rotting everyone on the team. Jasper, Zander, Quinn. She knew Vincent was a mess. She looked down at Elijah as she held Quinn. He wasn't like the rest of them. He knew what needed to be done.

"It's okay," she whispered to her wolf. "It's okay. You aren't like them. You never have to be like them. You can stay out here forever. You're better than all of them. You're so much better." She knew why Elijah didn't want to see Quinn torn apart by the modern world he wasn't raised in. He was so wonderful exactly the way he was, and he would lose all of it if he stayed in the mess. He was too good for all of it.

"I just want to protect you all," he murmured, his head buried into her shoulder. "I can do that-"

"But at what cost, love?" she asked softly. "At what cost?"

Not a cost she was willing to let him bear, certainly. One she would bear. One she already carried. She could do it one more time, she was sure of it. Just one more time. For Quinn, for Zander and Jasper. For Vincent.

For the teary-eyed Elijah, who waited silently.

When she released Quinn, he went to the cowboy and the two big men embraced. She heard Quinn whisper an apology. Elijah offered one back. And she knew those two would be okay.

The emotions were running so high on the team, she knew these moments were bound to happen. She knew they were all shaken by their own experiences and issues. The case with Axel kept bringing it all to a head and she was tired.

She was so tired.

"What's next?" Quinn asked. "I know Vincent sent me here to think, to get right again, but what's the team's next move?"

"Are you sure you want to keep going?" she asked, needing to know he would be okay.

"I won't make the same mistakes," he promised. "I lost control. Of my magic, of myself. While I was out here, I remembered all the reasons Elijah and Vincent wanted me to control everything, to hold back. Like Jasper in Atlanta. He wouldn't have lost his leg if I hadn't brought the building down." She winced. She had asked him to do it. "I'm not going to risk any of you, and I'm not going to become them." He pointed away, out into the world. "There's better ways. I just have to always remember that. I needed today to remember that."

He wasn't going to become the monsters they kept running into and battling against.

"Tomorrow night is the third raid," Elijah explained. "A replacement team is going. We're going to review everything we know. Let's hope we can find where he's hiding and finish this."

Sawyer nodded. That was all they had. It wasn't much, but it was better than nothing. She knew Vincent was back in the house, probably pouring over things she didn't know yet. She knew Jasper was digging around photos of Axel lookalikes, hoping for one to be him. Zander was keeping Charlie occupied and safe in their home.

And now she and Elijah knew Quinn would be okay, and it was his final mission. Elijah's too.

"I think we should have a team meeting," she declared. "So everyone can talk and clear their heads." She was seeing her wonderful guys break apart and she couldn't allow that. Anything but that. Was she hurt when they announced they were leaving the IMPO? Of course, but she couldn't let them lose each other. This argument between Elijah and Quinn had proven her point. This could have broken them.

"That's a great idea." Elijah ruffled Quinn's hair as he spoke, causing Quinn to try and push Elijah away. "Everyone's still up. We can do it right now."

"I think that's for the best. Right now, I think we're all over the place, and it's not working." She was glad her cowboy agreed with her. She had plans, ones her men might not like, ones they might leave her for, but she wouldn't be responsible for them falling apart. They were a team before her and they should always have each other, IMPO or not.

"Let's do it." Elijah kept an arm wrapped tight around Quinn, not letting the feral Magi get away. "You too."

"I figured," Quinn growled. "I wasn't planning on avoiding it."

"Sure." Elijah was teasing now. Sawyer felt glad that everything seemed more relaxed between them. That meant they were moving on past the argument.

On the way back, she and Elijah made sure to put Quinn in the middle. They found Vincent sitting in the new dining room and he looked up from his papers with a sigh. Kaar bounced around on the table, eating seeds from Vincent's free left hand.

"Why are all of you up so late?" he asked. He eyed her the most, almost accusingly.

"We want to call a team meeting," she explained. "Care to call down those two?"

"Why?" He was suspicious now.

"For everything. Anything. We have the night free. Let's do it." So she could make sure they would survive this mission, emotionally and physically. She had already fucked up and Zander got shot. She had already messed up and Missy was killed, something Vincent, and in turn, her, had promised wouldn't happen to the doppelganger.

Vincent's eyes went unfocused for just a split second. "They'll be down soon."

She slid into a seat as Zander and Jasper entered. Elijah found a seat as well, as Quinn went to get the wolves and Sombra out of the office. She noticed that the wolves were already in a better mood. That was good. Sombra sat next to her, leaning against her thigh so she could have her head scratched. Sawyer obliged, unable to resist the physical connection with her bond.

"So, a team meeting," Vincent declared. "Who wants to start?"

The   deafening   silence   made   Sawyer   more uncomfortable than anything else she had ever encountered. She had never really known a time when these guys seemed like they couldn't really talk to each other, but tonight it seemed like everyone was having a hard time.

So she started.

"I'm worried about all of you," she admitted. "That this case might be taking a deeper, more painful toll than it should. That maybe I should have forced all of you to rest more after James died instead of jumping to chase Missy's information into the raids."

"I hate that you wear the mask," Jasper mumbled, looking across the table at her. "I hate it, Sawyer. I don't want you to."

She'd figured that was coming.

"The mask doesn't bother me," Zander said, shrugging to prove how much he didn't give a shit. "I'm more wondering how we're all not going to die."

"Reasonable for the team healer, especially one who was just shot," Vincent conceded. "But we've done dangerous before."

"Yeah...that's the point," Zander said with more heat than she had expected. "Vincent, one day our bosses are going to push us into something stupid, and it's going to end with more gravestones. They've tried before, actively tried. There were no accidents when it came to the Amazon mission with the IMAS."

"The team wasn't supposed to go on that," Quinn reminded him.

"So?" she snapped. "We weren't going to leave you out there to die for their idiocy."

"So we all hate our bosses, except maybe Thompson, who is genuinely trying. The only problem is that he's overruled by the WMC a lot. They make the real decisions." Elijah groaned.

"I think we can all agree that the WMC sucks and we just need to make it through the case." She threw her hands up. "And yeah, it sucks that a bunch of you don't want to stay on the team and do more after this, but I also get it. In the end, it's safer, healthier. It's just a better idea to get out while you can."

"So, there's no reason to drag all that up?" Jasper watched her carefully. "You'll be okay?"

"She will be when she figures out what she's going to do with her life," Elijah commented, nearly grinning as he called her out on the one thing she hadn't yet wanted to talk about. She brought this on herself.

"I'm okay. Vincent?"

"The team's health and happiness is more important than our bosses. Fact. There's a lot of other things I can do with the IMPO that don't involve big cases."

"You would stay in?" Zander exclaimed incredulously. "Really?"

Well, this was interesting. She knew a team meeting would drag some things up. She had silently hoped this was one of them. Would it just be her and Vincent looking for justice now?

"I know all the faults and problems everyone has with them, but none of them change the fact that for me, there's only two options. Working for the government, trying to be the good guy, living by and upholding the law, or...Well, my other option would be people wondering if I'm always going to walk in my brother's footsteps. I know that." Vincent pushed his papers away, reached into a baggy and fed Kaar more seeds. The raven made some weirdly affectionate noise. "Sawyer? Me and you?"

"Yeah, I haven't thought that far ahead." She looked away from them.

"Of course you haven't," Elijah muttered. "Sawyer Matthews, everyone. Mission oriented to the nth degree."

"I have to be focused. Fuck, I need all of you focused. Getting this out right now, we can all work to achieve our own goals. If taking down Axel is the only thing between you guys and careers that would make you happy, then work for that. For Vincent and I..."

"He's the last thing holding us back from burying the past," Vincent finished. "Can't have a future until you can let go of the past, not completely."

"That." She agreed with every word. There was no future for her and Vincent until this was over. Not even a small possibility of one. Axel would always be a shadow over their lives, their hearts. He fucked them over more than anyone else on the team.

"Yeah, but you two are taking this way too far-" Zander, trying to be the voice of reason. What a strange time the team was in if that was the advice. Zander telling people they were taking it too far.

"There's no such thing with Axel." Surprisingly, it was Quinn who said it. Her eyebrows went up. "But you're right. We can't become him while we're trying to beat him. We would fail."

"He plays his game better than us, that's certain. He's got wealth, power, followers so loyal that they would die for him like that." She snapped her fingers. "You're right. We can't beat him at his own game. It's not working."

"Elijah said something to me earlier today. About playing a quieter game." Vincent hummed, motioning at all the papers in front of him. "About trying to regain ground on him without exposing what we're doing. I think he's right."

"And there goes the team meeting, back to the Axel situation," Zander mumbled, rolling his eyes.

"Forgive me." Vincent sighed. "It's hard taking a break."

"We know," Zander teased. She was so glad to see the teasing was light. "How about we watch a movie? Why don't we...really relax? Charlie is still puttering around with nothing to do. Does that old man sleep? We'll drag him along."

"No, he doesn't." She chuckled. "When was the last time we had a real movie night?"

"After James' funeral," Vincent murmured, looking away from them.

"Before that...Georgia, at home. Weeks ago. Shit, maybe back in November?" Jasper stood up. "I like the idea of a movie. And you know, this needs to be said. Sawyer, Vincent, we're all planning on leaving the IMPO, but don't worry. Stop worrying even while you tell us you aren't. We're committed to this case. For you both. For justice. We're going to bring Axel down."

Zander began to clap, Elijah quickly following him. One even hooted as the wolves began to make short howls. Sawyer clapped slowly, watching Jasper's stormy eyes.

"I was rattled for a moment," Jasper continued. "And I don't like the organization we work for, not anymore. Maybe never again. But we're going to see this through."

"Finish it," Zander pressed.

"Because this is the mission this team was made to do." Jasper smiled.

"Thank you," Vincent whispered from his seat. "Does this mean I can keep working and not be dragged into a movie night?"

"No. We're taking the night off," Zander ordered, reaching out to grab Vincent. "Because I don't get to fuck with you as much as I used to, and this is a great night for it."

Sawyer laughed as Vincent was yanked from his chair by the redhead and pulled. He tried to protest and walk himself out, but Zander didn't let him go. She eyed the papers left behind, wondering what Vincent was looking over. She didn't have the chance to grab one and see. Elijah wrapped an arm around her waist and lifted her as he stood up.

"Elijah!" she laughed out his name. She didn't fight, though. Jasper and Quinn were grinning at each other as they walked out behind her and the cowboy. She saw Charlie grinning down the hall. "Save me!" she called out.

"No," Charlie answered back.

She was glad he didn't. The team was a fucking disaster, but at least they still could have moments like this and smile. They needed tonight.

Tomorrow she would do something they would hate, but tonight they could reaffirm the bonds of family and team, and everything would be okay.

24

SAWYER

"Hey Vincent?" she said brightly as she walked into his office. "I wanted to run something by you, then head out to do it."

"Okay, let's hear it." Vincent pushed back the papers he was looking over. It was early and she was positive they were the only two awake, which suited her. He wouldn't give her a hard time for wanting to go.

"I'm thinking about a trip to the prison. Take a look at what happened there while you deal with paperwork here." She said it innocently enough, but she had no intention of dealing with the things going down there. She had another objective.

"Let's have breakfast and talk about what everyone wants to do today. We're all going to be anxious with the last raid tonight, especially since we won't be there." Vincent stood up and began to do that thing where someone organizes because they have nothing else to do. "Jasper and I are going through financials. I'm going to place Zander on looking at pictures of Axel lookalikes all day, which is going to drive him mad, but it's busy work. Quinn has free time.

I'm hoping he enjoys the woods more. Elijah might go with you."

She didn't like the sound of any of that. She eyed him. "I can go alone. I'm not going to do anything stupid, Vincent."

"No, but you yelled at me for going by myself, so you don't get to."

"You didn't tell anyone where you were going. And you're probably a high value target for Axel."

"And you aren't?"

He had her there. She raised her hands in defeat. Fine. She would see how things played out at breakfast and go to the prison with Elijah if she had too.

After breakfast, she realized she should have known better. She really should have known better. Sawyer walked into the prison with the team instead of just alone or with Elijah. They all wanted to *see* the damage that had been done by the staged riot. It could possibly give them some clues, but really, they wanted something to do until the raid.

Sawyer was the only person in the building with an agenda. She just needed to shake the team for a moment. When she had mentioned making the trip, she hadn't expected all of them to come with her with this excuse.

"What did you want to do?" Vincent asked her causally.

"Exactly what everyone else wanted to do, but maybe alone." She raised an eyebrow at him. "You know I like working without all the distraction. Not that having everyone here is a bad thing, but I might wander off, see what I can see."

"Be safe," he murmured, kissing her cheek. She smiled at him as he waved her away.

"Thanks," she told him as she backed away from the group while the rest of them were too busy talking to guards about what happened. Only Vincent was paying attention to her.

It was sweet, completely appropriate, and worrisome. He would be the one to figure out she had a plan that she wasn't telling them. She was thankful he was letting her lie for the moment. Or maybe he just trusted her enough at this point.

She wasn't doing anything incredibly stupid. It wasn't about something dangerous. They would be mad at her about this for principle. Though, as she walked to Naseem's cell, she knew they hadn't figured out she'd visited him once before. She didn't bother having the assassin brought to an interrogation room this time.

And as she walked closer, she grew angrier.

Leonard had known she was coming and his words had thrown her off. He'd been ready. Axel would be as well. He wasn't going to let her within a hundred feet of him.

And Naseem could tell her how to fix it. She needed to know. Now it was imperative, and she knew the guys wouldn't like it. It was just another skill for a trade she needed to get out of. But she couldn't get out of the trade until she was the absolute best, until nothing and no one would see her coming. She knew it, but explaining that to the guys? No, she was going to do this alone, like she had tried once before.

She was feeling bloodthirsty as she made it to his door.

"Guard!" she called. "I need to speak to this one."

"Coming, ma'am." The guard walked quickly, punching in the code for the hour. The codes for individual cells changed every hour. A random thing she knew from times when going to prison was her number one concern.

She walked in without announcing herself. Naseem was lying on his bed, reading a book. He moved the book and curiously stared at her.

"I don't know anything about the riot. I've been locked in here since that happened with my meals brought to me. I didn't participate." He smiled. "So this must be about something else, since you would have been told if I was involved."

"Teach me," she demanded.

"No." He lifted his book and began to read again.

"Damn it, Naseem. Teach me." She snarled, grabbing the book and yanking it away from him.

"I'm not going to teach the person who defeated me the one thing I have that she doesn't." Naseem sat up. She tossed the book across the room. The temper, the anger she was always hiding strained her control. "And something has obviously upset you."

She grabbed his jumpsuit and dragged him up, forcing him to stand. "Naseem, I need to know."

"So you can kill him, because he'll obviously be on his guard. I'm not stupid." He tried to pull away, but she had the upper hand and anything she did in the cell would be forgiven.

And she strongly considered testing that, so she shoved him back.

"I was noticed by my last target," she explained. "I refuse to get noticed before I have him. I need to know how you do it. I'm willing to make a deal."

"Parole? Commuting my sentence?"

She bared her teeth. She couldn't do either of those, not for any reason.

"Thought so," Naseem snapped. "There's nothing you can give me that is going to convince me to teach you."

She glared at him, trying to resist crossing the line. She was already toeing it.

"And if you fail to kill him, oh well. It's really not my

place or problem. I'm not getting involved between you and your old sugar daddy."

The callous comment snapped something. She roared, grabbing him again and forcing him to the bed. Before she could even think about what she was doing, she swung downwards, slamming her fist into his face.

It was like every comment about her being Axel's whore came back. It was like every moment someone disregarded her, not knowing what she could do, who she was.

And once Axel was dead, it would all be behind her. She was nobody's whore. She didn't need a sugar daddy. She didn't need anything except the one skill to help her bury all of it.

"Teach me!" she demanded, a roar of pain and anger.

"Fuck you," he growled, trying to shove her off. She was so enraged that he didn't have much of a chance. She slammed another fist down, busting his nose open, blood pouring everywhere.

"FIGHT!" someone screamed beyond the door.

"SAWYER! Someone get this fucking door open!"

"Teach me!" She had to know and she didn't honestly give a fuck about Naseem anymore. Not that she ever really had, but she didn't know how to stop now. He had no right to say anything like that. No right.

Someone grabbed her and she sublimated out of the hold when she was ripped off Naseem. She reformed to tackle the beaten-up assassin back on to his bed, since he was trying to get up.

More hands grabbed her, yanking and trying to pull. They were screaming something but she was only focused on the man her hands were on. Finally, something snapped on one of her wrists and when she was pulled away from her target, she couldn't sublimate.

Naseem began to laugh. "And even if I wanted to teach you, you're a lost cause. This just proves it."

"FUCK YOU!" she roared, fighting against the large hands dragging her from the room.

Her back slammed into the far wall and the door to Naseem's cell shut with a resounding thud. Flaming red hair blocked her view.

"What the fuck!" Zander roared. "What are you doing?"

She tried to breathe and quickly realized what had just happened. Looking down at her hands, she felt lost for a moment. She hadn't just crossed a line, she had blown through it like it never existed. "I'm sorry," she whispered. "I'm so sorry."

"Sorry? You're sorry? You just beat a defenseless man!" It was Jasper yelling now. "What the hell were you even doing here?"

"I..." Oh shit. She knew they would find out. She would have had to tell them eventually, but she hadn't thought it would be like this. There must have been something strange about the way she looked, because when she looked at Jasper, he stepped back. "I'm sorry."

"Why. Were. You. Here?" Elijah enunciated every word. "A guard let us know you came by this way. We didn't like it, but we didn't expect a fight when we arrived. Sawyer, what's going on?"

"I...wanted him to teach me," she admitted, pulling her hands to her chest. Her right knuckles were covered in Naseem's blood. She hadn't hit more than a few times, she was certain of it. She had still done damage, enough damage.

Too much damage.

"Teach..." Zander backed away from her now. "Sawyer..."

"I asked him when I came...to see Missy, after the funeral." She looked away from all of them, unable to handle it. "He can do one thing I can't. Disappear. I melt into the night, but I'm still a Magi. I can still be sensed. Leonard caught me before I made it into his office. It made the fight so much worse than it needed to be. And Axel? Axel is never going to let me within a hundred feet of him. I can't..." She turned so her shoulder would be on the wall. Wrapping her arms around herself, she continued. "Naseem made a comment and...something snapped."

"We're leaving," Elijah declared. "Let's go. You're not coming back here. We're going to have a talk about this at home."

"I've got her," Vincent said from the back of the group. "I'll drive her home."

For some reason, everyone seemed uneasy about that. She nodded. She would go with Vincent. He would understand, she hoped. She knew the guys would be mad, she knew it. That wasn't what she was upset about.

She had lost control. She had just beaten a prisoner who had no one protecting him. She had known she could legally get away with it. No one would arrest her. The handcuff was only on her wrist, a dangling reminder, because they had to inhibit her magic to make her stop.

She hadn't lost control like that in a very long time.

"Come on, Sawyer." Vincent gently grabbed her elbow and pulled her out of the center of the group. Her hands were shaking now, so she just held herself tighter.

"I don't-"

"I know what happened. We'll talk about it in the car." He kept leading her. Out of the hallway, past the front desks, out into the parking lot. He had brought his own car for the trip and opened the passenger's side door for her. He helped her in and waited for her to have her seat belt on before he went to the other side. When he was in, he turned the car on before fishing in his pocket. "Those are Elijah's. Here." He pointed out a specific key on a small keyring. "This one."

She took it and undid the cuff on her wrist as he put his seatbelt on. She held onto all of it as he pulled them out of the parking spot and left the prison behind them.

"We all knew you were dealing with some anger issues after we discovered Axel was free. I thought you were focused and dealing with it better. What happened?"

"You know, Vincent. He made a comment. There's been so much. I need to know what he can do. I need to know how. I can't keep failing. I can't fail again, not this mission, not now." She shook her head. "I figured I would talk to him today. He would tell me or he wouldn't, then I would tell you guys that I already tried any leads through him. I never thought..."

"So, last night, you were just pretending everything was okay?" He sounded hurt.

"Like you don't do the same," she snarled. "Like you don't just keep focused on the case like nothing else is wrong. Like you don't hide it all."

He had no response to that. She knew he wouldn't. They were both hiding all of it, thinking of everything else. As long as the case was moving, they were fine. But the case wasn't moving anymore, and after twenty-four hours, she knew they were both itchy and angry. She knew that since the rest of the team was fine, they had nothing to worry about for a second. At least the team having problems kept their minds off Axel and how they had to get him.

"We can't do this, you and I," he finally said, a heavy sigh at the end. "So we're going to have a talk. Just me and you."

"We've had a few of those," she reminded him.

"Not since the funeral," he fired back. "And everything else we've talked about has been the case. So we're going to talk now. About this. You told me that day to take it one step at a time and that day, it mattered."

"And we've been doing that. I don't see how that matters now."

"I'm just saying, we had that discussion then. You taught me some good lessons about grief that day. You then forced me to step back and process things better. It wasn't easy. None of this is easy. Now we're going to have another talk, and hopefully we'll both feel better for it."

She nodded. Fine, she would talk to him.

"First, you want to defeat Axel for every reason I do. It's our past, and it keeps coming back. He's done terrible things to us, terrible things to people we care about. He'll never stop. We both know that. The entire team knows that. It's why they're seeing this through to the end." Vincent glanced at her for a split second before refocusing on the road. "But I think we both need to let go of the rage."

"For what?" she demanded. "What else could I feel when it comes to him? And when you figure out how to get over it, let me know."

"I think we need to remain as impartial as we can. I think it's the only thing that's going to keep us from doing things that could ruin us. Like today, Sawyer. We just got done telling Quinn that he can't go too far. That we can't become monsters-"

"I'm already a monster!" she roared, slamming a fist into the door. "I'm already one. No, I would never let Quinn become one. Or Jasper, Zander, and Elijah. None of them. Not even you. But I'm already one. I do this."

"And it eats you alive every time you say it!" he snapped. "Every time you say it, you are angry, and guilty for it. You are not a monster, Sawyer Cambrie Matthews. You are a viciously protective woman who is willing to do anything to protect the people you love, and yes, that is admirable. It's something I love about you, but this...Sawyer, beating Naseem is going to make you a monster. A man who is already doing his time, caught and defeated. He hasn't put up any fight since you captured him, since you stopped him from killing Thompson. He knows his fate. Beating him is going to make you the monster, Sawyer, and for what? The ability to do what the Triad could? That's not a skill to protect. That's a skill to kill."

"Kill the other guy first," she mumbled.

"No."

"Vin-"

"No, Sawyer. I'm not letting you go that far. Not anymore. You...you've been taught better. You told me not to let Axel destroy me, and we've come close a couple of times. Trying to rush into the third raid without Zander, pushing as hard as we have. But our team cares, and they keep pulling us all back. Because Axel doesn't deserve it. He doesn't deserve to win by letting us fall apart on our own."

Tears filled her eyes as she leaned over to put her head down nearly to her knees. She hated how her words were thrown back at her. She hated she could give the lesson but not follow it.

"He doesn't deserve you doing this to yourself anymore. We're going to do this as a team. You aren't alone anymore. Stop trying to be the solo fighter. Stop trying to think you can take everything on yourself. You don't deserve to carry all this weight anymore. It's breaking you too. This is the team's job, with you as a member of the team. You don't need to keep hurting yourself anymore. We're strong enough to carry this with you."

"I'm sorry." She had nothing else to say. She knew he was right. Everything, this team, how much she loved them. That made her want to keep them forever, not just together as their team but with her. Her hate for Axel, her terror of him coming back and hurting them...that drove her to work alone, to take it all on herself. "I love you. I'm so sorry."

"Let's get home and just take the day to ourselves," he whispered gently.

She reached out to his dash and turned the music on. Italian opera, his favorite. As she listened to it, she realized he'd done the right thing before the mission to deal with the Druid. Now, when she heard those beautiful words, she thought of Vincent. She thought of them when they went to the Met right before getting pulled down to the Amazon. She thought of countless times they laughed over something or just danced privately in his office. Private moments. Vincent and she were much more private about their love than the other guys tended to be.

"I always did really like this song," she said, turning it up a little more.

"It's a lovely piece," he agreed. "You can change it-"

"No, this is our song," she explained. "You told me not to let him take everything I love from me, not even the smallest parts. This is ours now."

"And so is this case. It's ours."

She leaned back from the dash, stopping her distraction of fiddling with the volume. "Yeah, it's ours," she agreed. "Me and you. The team. This is ours."

She didn't say the exact words, but it was a promise to let the team help her carry the load.

He pulled them into the garage when they made it back home. She had figured the rest of the team would have followed, but she didn't see them. When she inquired with Vincent about it, he smiled.

"I asked them to keep...investigating at the prison for another couple of hours before coming home. I wanted to make sure you and I had some time together."

"Oh..." she grabbed his hand. "And what are we going to do?"

"Honestly? I think it's been too long since I've touched you." He pulled her closer. "And I think we need to find that closeness again. We've been too distant. I'll admit, it's mostly my fault. I would have seen today coming if I wasn't so... concerned about how you and I can be, how we have been on this case. I thought distance would make sure the team could deal with us better."

"You would be with a woman who did what I just did?" She let him pull her into the house.

His response to her question? Laughter. "If I was going to not be with you, it should have been the first time, when I learned about everything else. Sorry, but I'm much too deep in this to let something like that stop me." He yanked her closer as they passed the kitchen, kissing her hard. "I love you. And we all make mistakes. I've made plenty, and yet you're still with me, knowing who I am. Knowing I'm just another Castello."

He slipped into Italian at some point and she continued in it, knowing the language was his first. He slipped into it when he was emotional and vulnerable. "You are so much more than *just* another Castello," she whispered, touching his face. "You always have faith in me. Even today. I'm going to let all of them yell at me later. I'm going to beg their forgiveness, but you...You just took me out of there and talked to me."

"Well, we all have our own ways of dealing with things. I

knew the moment it was happening what had caused it. I knew, Sawyer, and I pulled you out because I should have seen it coming. They'll understand. They're not going to yell at you when they get back, I promise."

She trusted him, but teasingly, she still asked. "Oh? Why are you so sure of that?"

"Because they love you and they know you've been under an immense amount of stress. Zander will heal Naseem, then tell him to get over it. Jasper and Elijah will clear things up with the prison. Quinn will play muscle so no one questions it. They're allowed to be mad at you. I'm allowed, but we're not going to let anyone else do what only we should."

"Thank you," she murmured, kissing him again.

"Come with me. Let's have the rest of the day to ourselves."

"It's been too long since I've touched you," she said, referring back to what he had said. And further back to something weighing on her mind. They hadn't touched, loved, since before James' death. Since before this endless night had dropped on top of them when Naseem showed up at their home to kill her.

Together, they walked to her new room, kissing. She undid his shirt, messed up his hair, and unbuckled the belt of his slacks with a smile.

He chuckled as he pulled her hair out of its ponytail. "Slow down," he ordered. She wanted to scoff at him. "Let me enjoy this. It's been awhile."

With a teasing sigh, she pulled her hands off him.

He kissed her neck, wrapping an arm around her waist, holding her close to his body. "I love you," he repeated. "Through all of this. I'm sorry I haven't been saying it enough. I'm sorry I've tried to keep my distance through this."

Her playful mood melted away as she listened to him. "I'm sorry for hiding my problems."

"Come here," he crooned, kissing her lips again. "We'll make it through this. All of us."

Hearing him say it with so much conviction, she really believed it.

Slowly, he undressed her. Her coat fell first. She kicked off her boots as he undid her jeans. She untucked his shirts while he slid his hands under hers, touching her skin softly.

The shirts were discarded. Then everything else was. He kissed her all the way to the bed. Vincent had a unique way of making her feel beautiful with every touch. She knew he would always be this way, savoring and enjoying. It was purely him, how he enjoyed the world around him.

She climbed onto her new bed first. He followed, rolling her over onto her back as she reached the pillows. She knew he liked having her in the middle of the bed and in the position she was; she was sure it was a view. He was on his knees between her legs, gazing at her like there was nothing more wonderful, nothing more beautiful.

When he leaned down, he kissed her, their bodies sliding against each other like they were meant to be there, tangled up in sheets together.

There wasn't much more foreplay needed. Every kiss he gave her, every graze of his fingertips had gotten her ready. He slid in, making her gasp as a groan escaped from his throat.

"I love you," he murmured again, letting them sit there for a moment. "Through all of it, do you understand me?"

"I love you too," she promised back, meaning every word.

"I promised you I would do anything. Loving you is the most important thing."

Another kiss rocked her to her core as he began to thrust, excruciatingly slow. Her body sang with pleasure as she found that physical piece of Vincent she had been missing. This, the slow, steady way he was with her. The way he was able to turn the rest of the world off. The way they found solace together.

She loved all of them, every little piece of them, for hundreds of different reasons, and this was what Vincent gave her.

It was a quiet event full of emotions. A homecoming that she had needed deep in her soul. Together. They would do this together. Together, they would face the world, full of its miracles, its unknowns, and even its horrors.

Together, they would heal.

When her orgasm rolled through her, it took him with her. They clung to each other, peaceful.

"We can't stay here all day," he said quietly, running a hand over her ribs. "But I think we can until they all get home."

"We could stay here after that, too," she reminded him. "We both know they won't mind if we take the afternoon off too." They shouldn't, but she was willing to indulge the fantasy of it.

"Hm, they'll all want to join now. Thanks to you. I blame you for that." He kissed her so she couldn't make a response to his teasing comment. When he pulled away, he put a finger over her lips. "No, I'm not going to ever share this bed when I'm in it. So if you have any fantasies about that, I'm not interested."

She pushed his hand away, smiling. "I wasn't going to ask. I know better than to ask for that. You're a private man,

Vincent. You all give me so much love in your own ways. There's no reason for you to be overtly loud and passionate like Zander or free with it like Elijah and Quinn. You give me a quietness and a peace while they make their goals to give me anything but. I'm not going to ask you to do anything but be you for me."

"You'll never leave any of us, right?" he asked, kissing her cheek and down her jawline. Then he moved to her neck. "This isn't normal, but it's ours."

"It's ours," she repeated. "It's our family."

She should have trusted them to help shoulder her weight earlier, knowing they could take it. Because they weren't just lovers and a team. They were her family, like Charlie and Liam.

So she made a new goal.

She was going to make it through this case, bury Axel and her past, and she was going to have all of them with her at the end. She refused to imagine a life without them. She refused to sacrifice her love for them and theirs for her in pursuit of Axel.

"He doesn't deserve it," she said quietly.

"No, he doesn't," Vincent agreed.

25

SAWYER

"Look at these love birds. I think this is the best sleep they've gotten since Georgia."

Sawyer groaned, looking up from her pillow to find Zander standing at the end of the bed, grinning. Elijah was next to him.

They looked like they were up to trouble today.

"Well, the little lady is now awake. How was your nap?" The cowboy wiggled his eyebrows in that dumb suggestive way that made her want to laugh. "We got home and you two were out, so we decided you needed the rest. We've been doing the work, no worries."

"You could have gotten us," she told him, sitting up slowly.

"I'm going to say no," Zander replied, chuckling. "I mean, we've woken you up, but Vincent is still out. That says something. That man doesn't sleep very deeply, but he's unconscious still. It's good. You've both needed a rest."

At that, she looked at the body next to her. His face buried into one of her pillows, one of his arms thrown casually over her waist. It was a sight. She ran her fingers through his hair, knowing that might wake him up.

Sure enough, she was right.

"What?" he asked, a mumbling groan of a man half asleep.

"We've apparently fallen down for a nap. What time is it, guys?"

"Dinner. Raid in Turkey begins soon." Elijah leaned down and hit Vincent's foot, causing the Italian to kick out. "Come on, fearless leaders."

"Get out so I can put my clothes on," Vincent retorted.

"We've all seen Sawyer naked. What's you to add to it?" Zander was now snickering. She waved them away, shooing. "Fine!"

"We'll be down soon," she promised. She watched the two troublemakers leave then went back under her covers, pushing against Vincent's warm body. "You were right."

"I know," he mumbled.

"They didn't yell at me."

"I know," he repeated. "You think I don't know them just as well as I know you?" His dark, olive-green eyes opened.

"I think you know me in a very different way." They both smiled. He pulled her closer with the arm he had over her. As he began to kiss her neck again, she tried to push him away, but half-heartedly. "We need to get up."

"They would have given us enough time to do this," he murmured.

"Oh, I know, but I bet those two are outside the door, waiting to burst in and give us a hard time." She knew they were. She could feel them there. They hadn't gone far, literally standing on the other side of the door. Probably silently snickering to each other.

He lifted his head and narrowed his eyes on the door.

"How did you know?" Zander called inside. "Damn! Ruining all our fun!"

"There," he said, turning back to her. "None of that anymore."

"Oh no. We're getting up. We've slept the day away," she reminded him. "Come on. They've been working all day. I have a feeling they've set everything on fire."

Vincent groaned in exasperation. "Why do we never get a good morning after?"

"Considering it's evening, that might be why." She pulled away and slid out of the bed, feeling lighter than she had early in the morning. Something about breaking and letting Vincent pull her back together made her feel better. "And you know, I'm ready to see this case through."

"Really?" he asked, following her every move with his eyes as she began to walk around her bedroom, finding clean clothes to take to her bathroom.

"I'm ready to see what's after it," she explained, smiling. "He has my past. He doesn't deserve my future."

Vincent's answering expression was like a breath of fresh air. It was beautiful and full of emotion as he left her bed. She didn't move as he came closer and kissed her deeply.

"Can I shower with you?" he asked, pulling back for a moment. "I don't want to see what Elijah has done to our bathroom."

"Doesn't he share one with Quinn downstairs now?" She frowned.

"Oh, yeah, but he told me he wasn't going to stop messing up my bathroom, just so I know he's always thinking of me, or something ridiculous like that."

"Oh, you poor man. Yes, you can come with me. Don't try anything."

She was still laughing as she got out of the shower,

dressed, and went downstairs. Especially since Vincent didn't think to get anything to wear before the shower, so he had to walk in a towel to his own room to find clothing.

She found the rest of the team before Vincent made it down. There was a sudden awkwardness as she walked into the dining room to find them putting out dinner for everyone. Charlie was nowhere to be seen, probably hiding until the meal was called.

"Hey guys."

"There she is," Zander exclaimed, grinning. "Come on, sit down and we'll do this now."

She collapsed into a seat.

"So, you talked to Vincent? You aired all that out?" Elijah sat closest to her. "You going to be okay?"

"I'm going to be okay," she promised. His hazel eyes didn't leave her face. He was waiting to see if she broke. "I'm sorry. I should have told all of you how I was feeling, I really should have. It would have stopped what I did to Naseem."

"Yeah," Jasper agreed.

"But I healed him and told him to get over it, so it should be fine."

She snorted at Zander's comment. Vincent did know them well, and she should have really believed it. This was Zander they were talking about.

"In the heat of the moment, we were mad at you, but really? We should have been watching out for you better. You took on everything after James died. We knew this case would be hard on you and we missed it. For that, we're sorry." Jasper reached out to her, taking one of her hands. "We've been a mess for the last few weeks. I've been worried about me so much that I forgot you. I'm sorry."

"It's okay," she mumbled, squeezing his hand. "We'll be okay."

"Yup, we all made our mistakes and we're not going to make anymore." Elijah clapped his hands together. "Quinn?"

"Packs sometimes have problems. We will prevail. We're strong survivors." Quinn looked between them. "As long as we remember what makes us better than them. As long as we remember what makes us stronger than them."

"You said it yourself, Sawyer." Vincent walked in at that moment. "The difference between us and Axel's people? We stand by each other. We don't leave each other out in the cold. We're not competing against each other. We're a team, a unit, and we care. They don't."

She nodded. "So, what's next?"

"Next? We're going to eat dinner, once someone finds Charlie-" Elijah was trying to explain.

"He's on his way," Zander announced. "I already sent him a quick message."

"Perfect." Vincent sat down on the other side of the table from her.

Charlie walked in a minute later, looked around at all of them, then his eyes fell on her. "Did you forget I was here earlier today?" he asked politely. "We used to have a rule-"

"Oh shit, Charlie, I'm sorry!" She began to laugh. "I'm so sorry! No hanky-panky when anyone else was home, I know. My bad!"

Charlie just glared at her. She couldn't stop laughing.

"After dinner, we're going to bunker down and talk the case while we wait on word about the last raids. Jasper, Elijah, and I will all be hooked up to the communications, each listening to our own team to get a live idea of what's going on." Vincent dished up his own food as he spoke. Sawyer realized she was going to need to get some herself if she wanted to eat tonight. Everyone looked like they were starving. "That way, we can know our next move as soon as possible. Sawyer, any ideas on what we'll find tonight?"

"I don't think this will be like the last couple of nights." She sighed, dropping her plate in front of her. None of the food flew off, which she was thankful for. She hadn't wanted to be asked about this just yet, though she was only stating the obvious. "I think after his play here in New York, he's going to call his people to him and hide, let it blow over."

"He's going to try and get ahead of us again," Jasper commented. "Fits his MO."

"Exactly." She nodded, sitting back down.

"Is this really what he does? He makes a big hit, shows himself, then disappears while everyone scrambles to try and find out where he went?" Charlie took a bite of food when he was done talking, looking between everyone on the team. "Coward." His mouth was full.

"It is. He's not the type to do too much publicly unless it's very personal, which is normally when he gets very sloppy. He's also not one to ignore the actual threat, but I would say he's absolutely avoiding the team right now. He hit you, Charlie. He hit the prison." Vincent looked at her again, waiting for her to continue.

"But he hasn't come for us," she finished. "Normally, when someone is a big enough threat, he hits them directly. Whether it's by assassin or his own skills, he deals with them. But..."

"But he always fails to kill little miss, which probably means he would rather distract you and just keep you off the trail." Elijah pushed his food around with his fork.

"Which is only a deterrent." Jasper groaned. "He knows it's going to stop working one day. One day, we're going to catch him."

"Which we know as well," she agreed. "Which means this game is different."

"He's laying a trap, you think?" Vincent frowned at her.

"Yeah, but I want to see what we find from the raids first. Just to make sure I'm not wrong." It only made sense. "He's got everything he wants on the criminal front. We can take out his underlings as much as we want, but if we don't catch him soon enough after that, he just replaces them and it's business as usual. He doesn't want to keep losing good people. He knows we're never going to stop."

"We could wait it out for another four and a half years," Zander suggested.

She shook her head. "No. The world isn't big enough anymore for me and him to both exist in it. And I don't think he'll ever leave us alone, even if we leave him alone. We can't do that, Zander."

"I know. I just wanted to make sure. You can't deny this mission sucks." Zander shrugged, letting his wayward idea fall again. This wasn't the first time someone had brought that consideration up. Legally, the WMC owed her a pardon in a set time period, regardless of anything else. She wouldn't be able to take it in good conscience if Axel was still out there.

"Why don't you kids talk about something lighter? I know a bunch of you are planning on leaving the IMPO. What's next? Where you going to go?" Charlie leaned back in his seat, throwing his hands up. "Wait for after dinner to get back to work, seriously. You all never stop, I think."

"Well, I'm coming to work for you," Zander reminded him. "Remember?"

"Really?" Sawyer's head snapped up. "Really?"

"Yeah, I'm going to hire him to help me train some damned IMPO agents for Thompson."

"You're letting him into our gym permanently?" She faked a face of dismay, but really, she thought it was a good fit for Zander. He would enjoy it and it would give him the physical activity he always craved. And a little bit of power and responsibility he normally didn't have on the team.

"My gym, yes." Charlie grinned at her. "Jealous? You can come too. I think I'm going to have you up my ass until the day I die."

"You think correctly." She grinned. "That's good, though. I like that. It means there's going to be one more person I trust there. Help with the kids too," she ordered her redhead.

"Of course! So what about everyone else? Jasper, have you put any thought into it?"

"Not really? I mean, I could go back to college."

"For what? The only things you're missing at this point are a law degree and a medical license," Elijah teased.

"Well..." Jasper shrugged. "I was thinking law. Becoming a lawyer, you know. At least then I'll actually have the law on my side. I can help people that way and change things." She watched the blush begin on his cheeks. "It's a really small idea. Seriously."

"You can be the good guy," she said. "You can be change."

"Yeah..." Jasper nodded. "It's not-"

"Do it," Vincent cut in. "I think if anyone can handle the nuance of law and not become soulless in the process, it's you."

"Well, Magi law is even more difficult than non-Magi. And we don't give a lot of rights to people, which means most of the time, we're dishing out punishment and putting people into bad positions like...like what the WMC has done to you, Sawyer."

"This is the best I was ever going to get," she reminded him softly. "We all know that."

"That doesn't mean it's good enough. Yeah, so I think I'm going to go into Magi law and become a lawyer the WMC hates. Fuck them. I'm going to bring change. Leaving the IMPO is the first step, but that's step two. Fixing the problem."

"Amen," Elijah declared, lifting his glass. "Yeah, I like that."

"And what about you?" Jasper asked quickly. "What are you thinking?"

"I love blacksmithing and Magi still use weapons. Probably something with that, something I can do from home. I'm tired of all the travel, really. I like the idea of settling."

"What about your art?" Quinn asked. "You could do that."

Elijah began to cough, shaking his head, refusing to say anything else as they all prodded him. She would love to see him expand his artwork, but when this case was over, they would have decades to keep trying. It didn't all need to happen right now.

She was excited for it.

"Fine, Quinn, what about you?" Elijah demanded, glaring at the feral Magi.

"I'll take care of home, no matter what," he answered, shrugging. "This is going to be our place. I'll protect it and find something to pass the time with."

"I think that's the best we can expect from him," Vincent added, directing it to the cowboy.

"Yeah, probably," Elijah muttered. She could see he was trying to hide a grin.

"See, look at these lives you've all got ahead of you.

You're all too damned young to be where you are in the world. This is good." Charlie nodded around at them. "And what about the last of you two? Vincent? Sawyer?"

"I don't know yet," Vincent admitted. "I never thought past the IMPO. I might stay in for life, I think. If I don't have the team, I can take a different role within the organization. It won't be a problem. Maybe I can work with Thompson or something."

Sawyer didn't answer until they were all staring at her. "I don't think that far ahead. We'll get to it when it comes to it." None of them accepted that, still staring at her, now with some displeasure. "Guys, I've never considered anything more than what I have. When I got out of Axel's rule the first time, I stumbled on Charlie. I got lucky. Then I spent four years living in a holding pattern, grateful for what I had and never asking for more. Then you all happened. I just don't know. I never had a dream job. I never thought about what I really wanted to go to college for." She brought up the final problem. "And who would hire me in some off-the-wall, strange profession? Every Magi knows who I am and any non-Magi that doesn't would find out quickly enough. Any job I get will be headline news."

"Fair points," Vincent conceded. "You can stay in the IMPO with me."

"It's an idea," she said noncommittally. She didn't really care for that idea either, but it was the most valid option, and the IMPO knew how to use a woman of her specific skill set.

"We'll figure it out," Zander promised, whispering it to Charlie. "Don't worry."

"You can come back to the gym, full time," the older man offered her.

"No..." She sighed, shaking her head. "I think the time

when I haunted that building every day is over. People like Liam need to take it over, Charlie. He's one of them, and I'm fine leaving it with him and just visiting on occasion. Because once I go back to that gym, I go back to prowling for strays and that led to me getting back into some very illegal things."

"True." Charlie patted her hand resting on the table. "Well, you always have a place, anyway. Visit often."

"Always," she promised. "Enough about the future, though, please. I think I really do want to get back to work." Work was safe ground. The future was full of unknowns. She would have her guys in it, that was certain, but nothing else was. She just had no idea what she was doing.

They finished eating and Charlie wandered off to watch TV in their new living room. The team didn't move, though, setting up work right in the dining room. Headsets were plugged into computers and boxes, communications issues being worked out before it all started.

She stayed out of the way, watching it all unfold. She didn't play with the electronics.

They all settled back into their spots, Zander throwing a ton of snacks on the table. Sawyer was given a phone and frowned.

"What am I doing?" she asked politely, looking up to Vincent.

"Keeping a line open to Thompson. You like him, right? That shouldn't be so bad."

She spun the cellphone on the table and nodded. She called him without complaining, and waited only one ring before he answered.

"Director Thompson speaking."

"Hey."

"Oh. Well, that's tonight. I'm set up, so-"

"Vincent asked me to keep a line open," she explained. "So, what's going on with you? Have we been causing you enough mayhem?"

"I have several city-based IMPO agents calling me every day, demanding we take some of the riff-raff off their hands. I've got high priority targets in hiding, so we can try them once you catch Axel. You know, so they don't get murdered before the end of the case. Three more raids tonight, which means more of this, or just a lot of paperwork. Yeah, you know, I think you've been causing me enough mayhem. No wonder James looked like he never fucking slept."

Everyone in the dining room began to laugh.

"And you have me on speaker phone. Of course. I also got an incredibly angry phone call from the prison today. Don't worry, no one is going to get in trouble for that incident. Everything okay with you guys? You don't call me and you've been bouncing around the world, it seems. To think, it hasn't even been a week since Missy flipped sides, and I feel like I'm a decade older."

"We're all fine. Zander's recovering exceptionally well. It's like the idiot was never shot to begin with. Bad guys should work harder, I think." She teasingly grinned Zander's way, who glared at her.

"I'll get you for that later."

"Try me," she mouthed, then continued to talk to the Director. "All in all, we're figuring it out. We've had some rough patches, but I think we could all expect those."

"Just let me know if you need anything. Now, let's go dark if everything is ready. I've got three green lights in front of me. They're ready to go."

"I'm seeing the same," Vincent called. "Send them in."

"Mission go," Thompson said, sounding distant on the other end.

Then things went silent. Sawyer shifted in her chair. This could take hours. They were in for the long haul as the teams moved in and went after the last of the targets Missy had given them.

She knew there would be nothing and no one to catch, but they still had to try. Maybe they could get their hands on documents that would help them in the future. Maybe some lower-ranking guy forgot something or was left behind to deal with a problem.

She just had to wait.

Sawyer could be patient.

With the team around her, she could be patient and comfortable. She knew whatever was found, they would make it work together.

26

JASPER

Jasper waited along with the rest of the team, just hoping they got *anything* from this last night of raiding on Axel's Ghosts.

He also tried not to think about the massive blunder he'd made at dinner. He shouldn't have said anything. It was such a tiny idea that he hadn't truly even considered it. When Elijah mentioned law school, it was the first thing he could think to say when he knew he needed to give them a better explanation, something to shake them.

But really, he had no idea what he wanted to do with his life other than get the fuck out of the IMPO. Get away from the WMC, at least for a few years, to get his mind right again. He was really glad the team was okay with that and he was even more glad that most of them were going to do the same.

He just didn't really have an idea or a real plan. He just threw that out like an idiot and now he knew they would all wait and watch him. He couldn't go back to college unless it was for that, something Elijah had gotten right. He couldn't just keep collecting degrees until he was old, and scientific research wasn't his thing. Getting a job in education, tenure? Not something that appealed him. It was too inactive, too withdrawn from the world.

A lawyer would be active, at least. Sort of. Not physically active like he was used to, but at least a missing leg wouldn't be held against him in that profession.

As they waited for any sort of status update, his mind continued down this path. Considering his options, finding reasons to toss them aside. Medicine wasn't his thing, but it would put him in college for several years. Then he would need to see patients, though, and he would be constantly listening to Zander explain things he honestly didn't enjoy. The human body did somewhat gross him out in a way that it didn't for Zander. It was probably Zander's healing.

He wasn't interested in work concerning dream-walking, and his other abilities didn't lend themselves to any prospective jobs, not ones that suited him.

He just had no idea what he was going to do.

"Team B is in," Elijah announced, making all of them jump. "Location is empty. They're going to tread carefully, then collect anything they can from it."

"Damn it," Vincent mumbled. "Waiting on Team A, still."

"Team C as well. No word," Jasper added. He should have been focusing.

"Thompson?" Sawyer tapped the cellphone in front of her on the table. "You awake?"

"We could be here for a bit longer, but yeah, I'm still awake. My assistant made a fresh pot of coffee for me before we got started. I'm used to late nights."

"Of course you are." Jasper watched her half-roll her eyes. He thought those two were odd. Thompson and Sawyer were the last people he figured would get along for any length of time, but since James' death, she was the one who spoke the most to their new 'handler.' "Tell me, since we have time…how secure is this place we're in?"

"He won't find you there unless he specifically catches and convinces me to give you up. I'm the Director of the IMPO because I've never slipped and James turned it down. I haven't even told the WMC where you are, something they are beginning to give me heat for. They don't like their most troublesome and important team being off the grid. Not my fault they're too stupid to remember that place exists."

"They're stupid," she agreed, grinning up at the team. "Well, they can stay in the dark for a lot longer. I'd like to keep this place safe. I don't want to wake up anytime soon to see a Ghost over me."

"Exactly, and they can't deny there are too many leaks from their offices. They trust a guy in their office, who trusts a couple more, and eventually, everything gets out. So for now, I'm the only person who knows where you are. At least the only one who hasn't had his memory wiped."

"Can you two focus?" Vincent asked, frowning at Sawyer.

Jasper resisted the urge to snort like Sawyer always did. They were focused, just on problems and possibilities the rest of them weren't, but it wasn't what Vincent wanted them to be focused on. Surely their leader had thought about it, but then, he wasn't the one who woke up with an assassin over him like she had. Jasper could understand her worry over their home security. Even with Quinn and the animals, Sombra had barely gotten Sawyer awake in time that night to save her life. Jasper had thrown words into all their dreams and had pulled the entire team awake at the same time.

What a night that had been.

It had begun the longest, darkest period of their lives. They weren't done yet either.

Jasper couldn't wait to see the case through and leave it. It didn't honestly matter to him what was next, just as long as they got through this now. He felt selfish that he wanted out for himself, to save himself, but he knew the team understood now, all of them.

And Zander? He had no idea the man had been talking to Charlie about a job. That was good. Hell, it was great.

"Special Agent Williams. Team C reporting. We've arrived at the location. Two bodies, shot execution-style, but nothing else. We're going to collect what we can, then pull out."

Jasper jumped at the words and relayed them quickly, confirming with the team on the ground. "Roger that."

"Two prisoners or two people who they thought weren't loyal?" Sawyer asked, almost to herself, looking away from them. "I want them to bring those bodies home. We'll find out who they are and get them to their families."

"Who they are might lead us to a break, as well," Vin added.

Jasper relayed that as well, Thompson quickly agreeing through his own line into the teams' communications.

An hour later, both teams B and C were leaving, with backup coming in to finish cleaning up the mess. Those raids were over, and now it would shift to investigations.

"How's team A?" Zander asked. "Still nothing?"

"Nothing." Vincent was beginning to pace. Team A had taken their role for the night. They were the ones Jasper worried about. If it had been leaked that the team was going after someone, Axel could have laid a trap that another team was walking into.

Another hour ticked by and it was midnight. In Turkey,

it was well past dawn. Vincent pulled his headset off and changed some of the cords, so that anything Team A reported, they would all know.

It was twenty minutes after that when something came through.

"We had a hard fight," the leader said. "We've captured the target and several others. They knew someone was coming for them and hunkered down. We've secured them, with a couple of injuries that had to be addressed." There was a moment of silence. "We're going to get out of here and let the Ankara office take over the smaller shit. Where do you want Balian?"

Balian, the high value target, the Ghost.

"That son of a bitch," Sawyer mumbled from her spot. She continued louder, so the mic would pick her up. "I want that one here in New York as quickly as possible. I think I know his game."

"What are you thinking?" Vincent asked immediately as Team A confirmed and said he would be in New York by dawn in the city. It left them a few hours to talk and collect their nerves to see what mess awaited them from the night.

"Balian is a super-aggro piece of shit. He probably got the call to clear out and wanted to prove he could handle it. I don't know who leaked that was our place or if that had anything to do with it, but he's the type who would rather go to war with the government than run from it." She grinned. "I plan on finding out exactly what he intended personally. You're welcome to join me."

"You're not going to do to him what you did to Naseem, right?" Jasper was incredulous, hoping she wasn't serious.

"No. Just a chat. He's lucky it wasn't me tonight, though." She snorted. "Get all of them home. Thompson, I'm going to be down there in a few hours to meet him on arrival."

"Oh joy," Thompson mumbled, hanging up the phone.

Sawyer began to chuckle as she walked out of the room.

"I'm going with her to look over any documents they secured. Now that all of the raids are done, I might be able to put some of the pieces together." Jasper waited for anyone to tell him otherwise or confirm it. "Guys?"

"Yes, of course," Vincent said, looking up from whatever he was staring at. "I'll go with you. Elijah and Zander, stay with Sawyer. Quinn, hold down home with Charlie in it?"

"Of course," Quinn agreed immediately.

"New York," Elijah began to sing softly.

"We spend a lot of time there now," Zander commented. "Think that will change when we get out of the IMPO? I don't really like that city."

"Not for you, since Charlie's gym is smack-dab in the middle of the Bronx." Elijah laughed, which made Vincent glare, and Jasper raised his hands, leaving the room. The night could have gone worse, which he knew was why the guys were in a good mood. The night could have gone much worse. He was fine with everyone joking around and he knew Vincent would be too in a few moments.

That didn't mean Jasper wanted to get wrapped up in the mess, so he retreated and didn't stop until he made it to his room to get in a nap before dawn. He could pull off a few hours of sleep and a shower.

JASPER DIDN'T ALLOW himself to keep thinking about the future as he sat down in front of the stacks of papers. This was his job for the day. Vincent was with him, and they were going to dig through all of it, every piece of paper taken from every single office over the last week. Jasper was good at finding and organizing data, Vincent was good at finding the pattern. Together, they were hoping to come up with something.

He didn't think about Sawyer, Elijah, and Zander. Those three were off to make trouble for Balian that he wanted no part in, even if it was just a talk. He would rather deal with paperwork any day.

"Where do we even start?" He groaned, waving a hand around to point out all the crap in front of them. "Should we pull someone else in, some admin? The extra pair of hands would be nice."

"They could also be a leak," Vincent reminded him softly, looking over the top sheet of one pile. "This is going to be a nightmare, but I have some advice. Locations. We want to know where business is done and where money goes, even goods. Shipment records and the like. Those are probably the most helpful."

"Of course, but we've looked through all this sort of stuff before."

"Never from this many sources." Vincent leaned back, watching him. "Jasper, this is the closest we've ever gotten to having the complete picture of Axel's organization, documents included. Before this, we've been lucky to take half of this sort of information from a location, and then we could never put it together."

"Because we didn't have enough of the pieces." He figured that's where Vincent was going.

"Exactly. So, while you look through, do two different stacks at once."

"Compare and contrast. Find similarities, not differences." Jasper nodded. That could possibly expedite the process. "Not bad. Still, this is going to take us hours."

"We have the hours to spend. We have nothing but time

on this." Vincent sat down, pointing to a chair across the large boardroom table from him. "Let's get started."

Without anything else to say, Jasper took a seat. Vincent was right. This was all they had, all they would ever have. They weren't taking another case and letting this one slip away, not with so much riding on it. The future came when they put it all together, and they had time.

Jasper dove into Alfie's paperwork, comparing it to another set from a raid the team hadn't done. It was one of the ones they did the same night, though, which meant none of the Ghosts had even known they were coming. If that meant anything, it was that those would hold the most sensitive information, since they didn't have a chance to hide any of it.

Shipments and payments. Addresses from around the world, to others in the organization, and even some that he was genuinely concerned with. He didn't like payments going to an address right next to the San Diego office. He would mark that for someone else to deal with. It was obviously a sign of some corruption in that office.

And it pissed him off. Just the idea of it made him nearly want to stay in the IMPO to flush it out. He was tired, really fucking tired, of hearing of IMPO agents, IMAS soldiers, and the WMC aides and staff being paid off. And so blatantly. He'd always known it existed, but it seemed so systematic and accepted. It infuriated him. The WMC would be the place to solve the problem, if they opened up and allowed others to truly investigate their offices, but since they didn't want to have that happen, none of the agencies were going to be that bold.

The Magi world followed the tone and pattern set by their leaders. He hated them.

Shoving the thought aside, he continued to pull pieces

of paper off his stacks, looking between them, and highlighting anything of interest.

It took an hour for him to begin to hate it, to truly hate it. Another piece of evidence that some non-Magi government was being bought out by Axel to do his business. Non-Magi governments were supposed to work with the WMC, but this one was openly hostile to Magi.

They would take Axel's money, though.

He ground his teeth in frustration, continuing to highlight.

These people. He hated all of them. If he could, he'd see them arrested and put behind bars for a very long time.

And his mind wandered back to that idea he'd accidentally said during dinner the night before.

A lawyer would be able to do it without always being in danger. He could help define the fluid and incomprehensible Magi law that no one really understood. The laws that gave the WMC so many rights, but none to the actual Magi. He could protect those who spoke out against their government and those abused by it, while also dealing with the members of their society who abused it to their advantage and broke the laws when it was convenient. Including the WMC.

"I'm going to do it," he announced, looking at Vincent. Vin just looked confused. "I'm going to become a Magi lawyer."

"Then you'll join the ranks of fifty-three active Magi lawyers in the world, not including the fifteen that sit on the WMC. Of those fifty-three, only twenty aren't prior Councilmembers or aspiring Councilmembers." Vincent shrugged. "It would suit you."

"I didn't...know that." Jasper frowned, letting that in. "How did you?"

"Because my father was one, once. A long time ago. He thought an education in law was the best way to get around it." Vincent smiled. "Magi law is also one of the hardest things to get an education in. They are *very* selective. Do you understand?"

"Meaning...?" He figured he would just apply to a college.

"One hundred applicants a year. They must be a Magi, so any non-Magi is immediately disqualified. From there, those with the best education. From there, who has the most money. Magi law is taught by a school run by the WMC. Only a few people apply every year, nowhere near the one hundred allowed. Fewer can afford it. Even fewer succeed. I considered it, growing up, but then my life exploded." Vincent sighed. "Also, the WMC is the board that confirms or denies someone their license. If they don't like you, they'll find a reason to deny it. That's happened quite a lot. If you work against them, they pull your credentials."

"Why didn't you say any of this last night?" he demanded.

"Do you still want the job?" he asked.

Not at all. It was just as deep in the corruption as everything else. Thanks to his silence, he gave Vincent the answer he hadn't wanted to voice.

"This is why I didn't tell you last night, with the entire team listening in." Vincent pushed away his papers, a sign to Jasper that the discussion was far from over. "But I still think you should take it."

"Why? If I can't change-"

"But you can," Vincent pressed. "Of everyone on this planet, you are the best person for it, I think. Let me tell you the game I see before it even begins. We're going to catch my brother. Me, you, Sawyer, all of us. We're going to do it and end one of the most violent periods in the history of the Magi caused by another Magi. We haven't had anyone ascend like Axel has since the time of the Romans, where, before Christianity took over, Magi were pretending to be *gods*. And Axel? He's the closest thing to that since, especially with his abilities."

"That doesn't-"

"You will be a hero, Jasper. If the WMC works against you trying to become a Magi lawyer, they will earn a bad rap and they have a serious image problem right now. Money isn't an issue and they won't be able to find one aside from that without looking bad."

"They'll let me through to protect themselves."

Vincent grinned. "They'll have to, even if you proclaim every day that you're going to go after them with the education they're going to provide you. And the people will love you for it, don't forget that. I could never do it. Not with my family history. No matter how much I show the world I'm the good guy, I'm still a Castello. I would be turning a powerful criminal family into a powerful legal one."

"How did your dad do it?" he asked.

"A lot of money and a good portion of blackmail on the part of my grandfather and great-grandfather. They couldn't deny him unless they wanted to lose everything they had." Vincent chuckled. "But you? A disabled hero of the IMPO? Why stop at becoming a lawyer in Magi law, Jasper? Why not go straight to the top and be the change you want to see?"

"Are you mad?" Jasper sputtered. "Run for the WMC? I hate it, but we all know those fifteen seats have been filled by the same families for the last...thousand years. An upstart like me..."

"Has the best chance at changing the game than anyone

else." Vincent shrugged. "Just a spur of the moment idea on my part. You know how my mind is. I like to look out and see all the possibilities. Or you can just be a lawyer and help people on small-time cases and try for bigger fish as your reputation grows. Your choice."

"Let's get back to this," Jasper said suddenly, hoping the conversation could drop. He wasn't even ready to think about any of that.

But Vincent had some solid points, like always. Jasper knew all of them would weigh on his mind for a long time.

They went back to toiling over the paperwork, looking for connections and patterns. Piece by piece, Jasper highlighted and sorted by importance, or rather, what he thought would be important.

Some locations kept popping up. San Diego was obvious and apparent for Alfie's, along with other major cities on the west coast.

But even fewer locations showed up on both. They each did business with other Ghosts, so those places popped up. Then there was the last one.

Italy. Somewhere in Italy.

Never an address. Just the Villa. They were going to visit the Villa. They had to send word to the Villa. They sent money and samples of every good to the place. The Villa in fucking Italy.

"He's not stupid," Jasper said softly. "Axel. He's insanely intelligent. I'm not wrong about that, right?"

"He's also immensely arrogant," Vincent replied. "Why?"

"Has he really kept his base of operations in Italy after all this time?" Jasper turned his papers towards Vin, pointing at his highlights. "Nothing more than some villa in Italy?"

Vincent took the papers, pulling them closer. "These aren't shipment reports."

Jasper winced. He hadn't realized he was working so fast that he was off on the wrong stack of papers now. "No, they're emails, I think. Notes, correspondence. I never saw Italy mentioned in any of the real reports."

"No, they would have destroyed anything with an address, but they would need a way to talk to each other about the main hub."

"They never thought we would know they all spoke about the same place."

Vincent shook his head. "One of them on my side doesn't say the Villa." Vincent dropped Jasper's papers and looked through his own. "Here. The vineyard. Italy. I figured it was somewhere they bought his favorite wine from or something. He loves things from home."

"Any other mentions of Italy?" Jasper began shuffling through papers. Another email mentioning Rome. There was even a mention of a small olive grove, though it didn't seem small based on the acreage mentioned.

"I can't believe him." Vincent pushed away from the table, running a hand through his hair.

"Do you think?" Jasper couldn't believe it. "I mean..."

"He loves home," Vincent said softly. "And he could be hiding anywhere in it, since we don't have an address. But yeah, if he thought he could get away with it, he would go back. Hell, he would never leave. Sometimes I wonder if he's somehow more Italian than me."

"You are pretty Italian." Jasper snorted, shaking his head. "So what? We focus on Italy?"

"Yeah. We're going to focus on Italy. God damn him. I should have known."

"Think Sawyer will have any insight?" Jasper was still

mentally fumbling. Axel wouldn't be that arrogant, right? Sure, they had never caught him working there, never caught him living there. They only knew of the few locations in Italy they did because of Sawyer.

"I think she will. We'll keep going here and hope to uncover something. Anything to do with Italy, we mark and keep." Vincent sat back down. "She's probably still with Balian."

"Most likely," Jasper agreed, going back to his papers.

Italy.

Sawyer burst into the room five minutes later, pale. Jasper jumped up. He had a feeling he knew where this was going.

27

SAWYER

Sawyer walked towards the interrogation room with her two shadows on her heels. Elijah and Zander weren't going to give her even a second alone with Balian, and she was thankful for it. She didn't need it, but she was thankful. After yesterday, she knew they were going to watch her carefully - and she couldn't blame them.

She had no intention of hurting the Ghost. Just chat. She didn't know Balian well, but she did know of him well enough to know how to play him.

"Sawyer, before you go in, can we talk about this?" Zander's question made her stop.

"It'll be okay. Nothing is going to happen," she promised, smiling back at him as she reached out to the door. "This isn't yesterday. Balian will break. He stuck around to get into trouble for a reason. I think I know what it is."

"Okay," Elijah agreed, shrugging. "You'll play the lead. We'll just support."

"Thanks." She schooled her face and walked into the interrogation room first. Balian was sitting like she had seen so many others sit now. A steel table, steel chairs designed to be uncomfortable for those who had to stay in them for a long period of time, and a bare room meant to feel lonely and dark. Oppressive. Classic interrogation room.

"I didn't know I was important enough to get a visit from you, Shadow!" Balian threw up his hands in excitement, grinning. "You didn't show up last night. I thought you would."

"I could have been at any of the raids last night." She raised an eyebrow, sitting down across from him. Zander stayed out of the room, but Elijah leaned on the wall behind Balian. It was a good move. "Sounds like you were expecting me."

"I was! Axel..." Balian snorted, a look of distaste appearing on his face. His posture shifted to something more aggressive. He leaned forward to get closer to her. "I never knew he was a coward, but he seems to have run away. Little school boy decided to go home. He asked me and I said no. I was going to fight for what is mine."

"You know if he ever learns you called him a coward, he'll have you killed, right?" This was why she decided to talk to Balian. He was macho, arrogant, and not the brightest bulb in the box. He was loyal to Axel, sort of. He judged people harshly and once someone didn't live up to his standards, he saw no reason to follow them. Somehow, he'd survived quite a long time in Axel's employment, maybe because of his attitude. He was a good judge of strength and loyalty.

"Coward," the Ghost spit out. "I bet he won't do it himself."

"Not wrong there," she agreed. "So, you got yourself captured because you didn't want to follow orders."

"No. I got captured because I decided to stand up and fight for what was mine against a tyrannical government and their dogs. I disobeyed Axel as a sign I was leaving his organization because he's a coward. I will not pay a coward portions of my money. I will not work for one." Balian grinned. "Not when he's just running from a little girl."

"Be careful who you call little," she warned. Only one man was allowed to and he was standing behind the criminal. "He's running scared because I scare him, and for good reason. But it's interesting that you wouldn't try to protect your future by going with him. He commands loyalty to the fullest extent."

"Well, I'll admit to some ulterior motives." The Turkish man shrugged. "If I could kill you, I would be a hero. He would treat me with more respect."

She tried not to laugh at that, or give away how ridiculous the concept of it was. Balian didn't have the training, abilities, or raw power to defeat her. There was no competition.

"And yet here you are, and Axel has run off...home. You are much braver than him, I'll give you that." She smiled kindly. "Balian, do you want to make a deal?"

"No. I know what happened to Missy." The Magi shifted uncomfortably in his chair.

"I thought you said you weren't going to work for him. Balian...you're already a dead man."

The room shifted as Balian slowly realized what he'd done to himself. Disobeying a direct order was already a death sentence. By failing to win his little battle against the IMPO, Axel would see him as a failure and his actions would be seen as betrayal.

Sawyer had some sympathy. Balian wasn't smart. He was overconfident and ridiculous. He was more action and less thought in a world of people who had the tendency to think too much. Working for Axel, he was considered just muscle, constantly hiring thugs and sending them where they needed to be.

"But it's okay. I don't need you to make a deal with me." She stood slowly, nodding to Elijah. The cowboy moved around to her side of the table. "You gave me one thing I didn't know, but should have."

"And what was that?" Balian's eyes went wide in some mix of shock and fear.

"You told me he went home," she murmured sweetly. It had been an offhand comment and she knew it. 'Little school boy decided to go home.'

Balian had been part of the Castello operation long before Axel took over and turned everything on its head. That had been a shocker to Sawyer and Vincent, but it was something she could use.

"Ah, yes!" Balian nodded. "I'll tell you more if you protect me!"

She raised an eyebrow. "I'll think about that." She had no intention of making a deal without discussing it with the entire team. All of this had been a play to get Balian to slip, and if they needed him for more, he would be ready and willing to talk.

She turned on her heel and left the room, Elijah following her.

"Well played, little lady." Elijah's compliment made her feel good.

"Either of you could have done it. I could just do it faster," she said, chuckling. "He's not the sharpest tool in the box."

"I'll stay here and make sure no one goes after him. Can never be too careful."

"Thanks, Zander. I'm going to get Vincent and Jasper. Maybe they've come up with something." Or maybe even confirmed what she now had nagging in the back of her mind.

"Before you go, want to talk about what he said in there?" Elijah leaned on the wall, watching her carefully.

"Home. Axel only has one place he considers home." She turned away from them before anything more could be said. The answer was obvious.

Italy.

Something about the idea of it made her heart race and her palms get sweaty as she walked down the hall towards the elevator. Once inside, she crossed her arms, trying to stop whatever strange adrenaline rush was making them shake.

Italy.

She hadn't gone back in five years. After Henry died, she left and never went back.

When the elevator dinged for the floor she needed, she rushed off, ignoring the other passengers. She knew what she probably looked like. Anxious, and making the space around her just a little too cold for comfort. It only took her another hundred steps to find the room she wanted and barge in.

"Italy," she said at the exact same time they did. The shock of that hit her first, then a steady realization they were right. That monster had gone *home*.

"The papers point to some place in Italy. We know. How did you get it from Balian?"

"He said...he said Axel ran home. Only one place fits that. Axel doesn't consider any place a home except Italy." She was breathing harder than she should have been. "Do you have any addresses? We could get this done right now, guys. If we know where he is...We could go tonight."

"It all seems a bit obvious..." Vincent sighed. "I mean, he should know we'd find him there, arrogant or not."

Sawyer felt like pieces fell into place. "This is the trap," she whispered. "This is his trap."

"Excuse me?" Vincent frowned.

"I've been considering an idea that he'll try to trap us eventually. Pull us into a situation we can't win. This is it."

"We think we've treed the game so we rush in." Jasper nodded. "I like that. Vin?"

"Fuck," Vincent snapped. "Balian, he involved?"

"No, he's just stupid. Axel probably left us all the clues we needed to find him on purpose, and Balian is just going to expedite the process because he's a moron." She grinned. "If we go in knowing it's a trap, there's a chance we don't get caught in it."

"Don't get arrogant. He's setting us up, obviously, and he's probably got more tricks up his sleeves." Vincent pointed a finger at her, pinning her with the point he made. "Remember, don't rush."

She held her hands up. "Not rushing. Just pointing out that we can prepare. We can be ready for anything he throws at us. We can win here."

"We're both in check, then." Vincent hummed to himself. Sawyer waited as patiently as she could, trying not to pace and get antsy. "I wonder why he's doing it now..."

"Does it matter?" Jasper asked.

"Yes. My brother does nothing without thinking it through. He always has multiple levels of reasoning."

Sawyer considered that, closing the door behind her finally. She should have done that earlier, but caught in the moment, she might have exposed a lot of their plans. It would be something they just had to live with now.

"Vincent, do you think it might be a long-term thing?"

She walked closer and sat down at the table. "Do you think maybe he's tired of playing the game?"

"He loves the game...but I think you're right. You have a point, at least. We'll never stop. This is the last case we'll ever do and the only one. We're not quitting until it's over. We wrecked major areas of his business in the span of a week, pushing him to deal with problems himself and try to distract us by attacking back. It was never something he had to do before." Vincent sat next to her. "Sounds like him. He's never been on the losing team, and yet..."

"He's losing," she murmured. "We've cornered him, so he's going to use it to his advantage, or try."

"He wants to end this because when we're gone, everyone else has to start from square one." Jasper motioned to all the papers on the table. "The next guys will get all of this and it'll be defunct. Worthless. We hit fast enough and hard enough because of a lucky break that now no one else has. Missy is dead. If another team takes over, they're ten steps behind."

"While we're only two. He doesn't like how close we are."

"This is his favorite move," she reminded Vincent. "Pretend to be vulnerable, leave an opening, then attack the force you send into the gap. This is his move."

"He's never been driven to do it off the chess board." Vincent considered her. "Can you get an address from Balian?"

"I think I can. He stuck around since he thought Axel running home was cowardly, so he disobeyed the orders. By doing that, he's already a dead man. He might have also been trying to kill me and become a hero? That I'm not one hundred percent sure of; it might just be something he can say to Axel if they ever see each other. An attempt to get back in good graces. Doesn't matter. He was asking me about a deal when I left. I told him I would think on it."

"Let's do it. If he can give us the place, we can start the final act." Vincent stood back up and held out a hand. She accepted and noticed he didn't let her go. He held her hand as they walked out of the room, Jasper on her other side. People stared at the PDA, but no one said anything. Others in the elevator, as she boarded with her lovers, moved away from them, and hushed work conversations quieted.

Feeling bold, she held Vincent's hand tighter and leaned into Jasper, who slid an arm around her waist.

The elevator was empty by the time they reached the floor with the interrogation room. Zander and Elijah were still waiting patiently at the door.

"Well?" Elijah noticed them first.

"Let's find out where my brother is hiding." Vincent didn't stop walking. He went straight into the interrogation room, letting the entire team follow him. They flooded the room and Sawyer watched Balian sit up straighter, trying for some dignity, she guessed. "I want an address or you get nothing."

"Only an address?" Balian sounded surprised. "You don't care who will probably be there? What might be waiting for you?"

"We know it's a trap. I know my brother. It has to be a trap, if he made it this easy after staying off the grid as well as he has. So I can imagine there's going to be trouble there. Just give me the address so we can go and do this."

"I need a pen and paper. What do I get?"

"Parole," she said before anyone else could offer something. "Serve some time and then parole out. You might get back into crime, sure, but I wouldn't recommend it."

"Ah, that works. How much time would I serve?"

"Ten years," Vincent answered this time. "Agreeable?"

"Yes, I agree."

Jasper laid out a pen and a piece of paper for Balian. The Ghost wrote quickly and Jasper snatched it back the moment he was done then rushed out of the room.

"He's going to check on the validity. Make sure the address is real and get satellite imaging started on it," Vincent said in her head. Based on the small nod from Elijah behind their prisoner, he had said it to everyone.

They waited in dead silence. Sawyer checked her phone for the time when she began to start feeling the pain. Her feet were beginning to hurt. An hour had already passed.

Then another hour.

"What are we waiting on?" Balian demanded. "My ass hurts."

"For you to be telling the truth," Zander retorted.

It was ten minutes after that when Jasper walked back in.

"We're good. I told Thompson of the deal with Balian as well and he's working on making sure the paperwork is in order."

The team nearly ran out of the room, everyone trying to talk at once until Vincent snapped.

"Quiet!" he demanded. Sawyer stopped trying to say whatever she'd been intending to him. "First - Elijah, tell Quinn. We'll get a portal to the house to pick him up, then portal into Italy. Second - Jasper, I want to see exactly where that address is. Third, we need to prepare all day. We're in for a long night." He said that last bit to her, eyeing her.

She nodded. They were in for a long night. The final night. Beat Axel at his own game and...

She still didn't know what came next, but if everything went well, tomorrow she would know.

"Sawyer, where did you live with him? It was near Rome, wasn't it?" Vincent looked up at her after he reviewed the documents and photos Jasper has given him.

"Yeah, it was," she answered.

"His new place? It's only twenty minutes away from that property." Vincent took a deep breath. "It's only an hour from the old Castello summer home."

"He went...home," she repeated. "Literally."

"It seems he did." Vincent handed the papers to her. "Jasper..."

"I did run the satellite over to see surrounding landmarks and properties. I ran it against other known addresses we had that he once used. It was something I felt you both should know."

Sawyer saw the simple picture the satellite took of the target and then went to the next picture. It was that damned mansion. Her hands began to shake. "Thank you." She handed all of it back to Vincent, practically shoving it into his arms. "This might seem inappropriate, but-"

"We'll make the side stop. If you want to see it one more time, we can make the side stop before hitting Axel." Vincent was kind and gentle as he said it, encouraging. "We can go."

"Good, because this is the last trip to Italy I'm ever taking." She stepped around him and began to walk away. She didn't move quickly, letting the team keep step. With them at her back, she felt ready to see the place where all her darkest nightmares came from.

28

AXEL

"Sir, maybe this isn't-"

"If you tell me this is a bad idea like the two who walked in here before you, I'm going to kill you and not particularly care," Axel snapped. "The plan is set. They're coming. It could take them a day or it could take them weeks, it doesn't matter, but we're not doing anything until I get them out of our way."

He turned from his view over his vineyard, right next to his large olive operation, to glare at the Ghost. He didn't even bother learning her name. He'd only promoted her in the last week, thanks to his brother and that stupid...He took a deep breath. Now wasn't the time to get enraged over her.

The Ghost was shaking, obviously fearful of him. Good. He needed to instill more fear in them, it seemed. Sawyer had destroyed the best of his inner circle. These replacements were driving him insane. He needed the time to find who the best fit was, but he didn't have that anymore.

Time.

That's why Axel was doing this. He couldn't have them

running through his ranks, constantly taking out his most trusted generals, his confidants, and most loyal Magi. It left him constantly wasting resources to rebuild. If he didn't do this now, early, while he still had some substantial power, then he knew he would be doing it in five years, and from a much weaker position.

He'd never expected his brother and Shadow to hunt so well. And it was Shadow coming for him. He'd heard the black mask he'd given her was making a reappearance, haunting those whose paths she crossed.

He refused to admit the feeling in his stomach was fear. Sawyer had always been an emotional girl - too easy to fall for someone and trust them. Shadow was all of that put away and deadly. He'd made the best assassin in the world by chaining Sawyer with her own emotions and then unleashing her cold rage on everything else. It was the only way he'd given her power, her kills. They would be the focus of all the pain he inflicted on her.

"Get out," he demanded. The Ghost turned and hurried away. "Felix!"

His favorite Magi ran in, glaring at the Ghost as she left. He stopped in front of Axel, looking somewhat concerned. "Yes sir?"

"Are you ready for this?" he asked. "If anything happens, I'm relying on you."

"I ran in Atlanta so that I could continue doing this duty for you, Axel. I won't abandon you now."

"Why couldn't she ever be as loyal as you?" Axel didn't know why he was asking, but if there was anyone who might have an answer, it was Felix. A bit cowardly, but loyal to the bitter end. He didn't care if his master was dead, he would work and weasel his way to do his job without putting himself in danger. He also knew how to figure out other people.

"Sir...if I may be so bold to answer that honestly?"

Axel raised an eyebrow. "Of course." He valued the honesty from Felix, his last original Ghost.

"You never gave her what she needed. Well, you did in the beginning, but something changed in you, which changed something in her. In the end, that ruined everything."

"You mean I should have continued to indulge her, made her feel loved and secure."

"If you had kept her as a thief, I think none of this would have happened."

"But I needed an assassin," Axel reminded him. "And she was perfect."

Perfect.

If there was one thing he was willing to admit, she was perfection. Deadly and beautiful, a Magi meant to kill. It was why he had pushed her so hard, not realizing how close he was taking her to the breaking point. And himself.

"And yet, you had to do a lot to make her stay in line. You expect obedience, as you should. Once you made her your assassin, she didn't give you that. She fought you in private, where none of us knew she was such a troublemaker. You had to blackmail her, you had to put her in her place, remind her where she belonged, and it ate away at your control. Until one day you snapped."

Axel looked away after that. Snapped. Yes. It took years and a short time in prison to realize his own mistakes, his own lack of control over that entire situation. He had shoved both of them past ever repairing the situation. Then, while he was trying to regroup and figure it out so he could keep her in the end, she had already taken steps to betray him.

The mess he had to make to resolve that had been disastrous and gave others a chance to step in. His own brother and that little bastard misfit team of his.

If she had just been obedient, none of it would have happened.

"I lost my heir because of her." He was still enraged. He wasn't a good father by any means, but Henry had been a chance for the next generation. He would have given that boy an empire to rule. A legacy that would have been unmatched. His son would have been great. Even better than him or his brother or anyone else in his family.

And there she had been, believing he would actually hurt the boy. Something about that always made him upset as well, even though he had used it against her.

"Sir, I'm still sorry that-"

"No, it's not you, Felix. I should have kept you closer." Axel didn't blame his necromancer Magi. He'd put the man with Colt in Africa. Axel'd had to portal into the right country, then hunt his men down while they were doing a deal. By the time he'd gotten Henry to Felix, it was too late for the magic to work properly. Reviving Henry at that point would have made him a decaying vegetable, too long dead. "That wasn't your fault."

Axel had never considered he would lash out while angry at Sawyer and hurt his son. That had never been something he planned for. It was her fault. If she had just been obedient and followed orders. If only she hadn't had such a damned moral compass telling her everything he wanted was wrong. If only she could crave power like he did.

He would have made her a queen, and yet, in the end, she was only his nightmare. She could have been, and for a short period was, the best he had, the strongest, the deadliest. He could always rely on her ability to kill, and he enjoyed her in bed more than other women.

And yet she just couldn't fall in line.

Then he lost the only leash he had, the last leash.

"I should have never killed the damned cat," he said to himself. "That was a bad move on my part. It left me with only Henry to control her, thinking nothing would ever happen to him. The cat was just taking up space, or so I thought."

"Yes sir," Felix agreed. "And now she's coming for you again."

"Which is why we're here. She's never going to stop, Felix. Even if I try to reason with her, let her live her own life and live my own, she's never going to stop."

"You should have let it lie when we discovered she was active and alive earlier this year, but hindsight is twenty-twenty. We had no idea or reason to believe we would fail."

He nearly smiled at Felix's ability to reason and understand where his head was at. No, there had been no reason to believe they would fail trying to kill her not once, not twice, but three times.

"I warned Naseem and Councilman Suarez that she refuses to die. They should have listened more carefully." Axel began to chuckle, remembering how easy it was to bend the Councilman just enough to cause a mess in New York. Axel hadn't particularly cared what the outcome would be, just that it was big enough for him to quietly rebuild with no one paying attention. It had done just that, only helped by some vengeful IMPO agent outing her to the world. None of them had even considered there was anything else going on until Vincent's team got involved.

For a moment, he was proud of his brother, and even a

bit jealous. Vinny commanded the loyalty from her that Axel never could. In the end, she was on a Castello's leash.

"She's resilient, that's for sure, sir." Felix walked closer and pointed to a table. Axel looked over to see his father's chess set, a game half played on it. It was set up exactly as it had been the night Vincent killed their father and then realized Axel had been using him. Mistakes. Axel was very good at manipulating people, but when they were those closest to him, he always made small mistakes that ruined it in the end. He was beginning to see his own weaknesses. "Shall we finish the game, sir?"

"No, I never finish that game," Axel answered. "White is in check and Black will get checkmate in two turns. There's no hope. I leave it there to remind myself that I can never fall so far behind."

"And?"

"And the only people who have a chance of taking me to that are coming here for me. We either win or we lose, but I have to do this now. I have no other options." He didn't say it out loud. He was doing this now so he was never at the point where he had no other option but to lose. At least if he dictated the field, forced their hands, he would have the advantage. "Give me a run down on my brother's team again."

"Sir?"

"I underestimated them for years. We've spent the last month making sure we know everything we can about them. Run me through it again." He wanted to make sure everything was perfect.

"Well, you know your brother, so I'll skip him. His second in command officially is Elijah Grant."

Axel just listened after that. Elijah Grant, Zander Wade, Jasper Williams, and Quinn Judge. His brother's little friends, who were playing games they probably didn't understand. Their abilities, who they were. Young men, like his brother, all thinking they could take on the world.

"There's only one I think you should worry about," Felix added as he finished.

"Which?"

"This...Quinn Judge."

"Oh yes, I remember that one." Axel sighed. "The most powerful Magi in North America, and probably the world. I've had those rumors brought back to me. And I remember how his magic felt in Atlanta. You're right. He's the only one on that little team more powerful than me. He's target number one. We need to take him out first. He has two animal bonds, wolves. Impressive, but..." He knew what to do to Magi with animals bonds. They were easily crippled.

And with that, Axel collected himself and walked out of his suite with Felix. They had final preparations to make. With no idea when the enemy would show, they had to be prepared at all times.

He couldn't lose this time. He was throwing everything he had at them. He would come out on top, and then no one would be smart enough to stop him and there would be no team made for the job.

29

SAWYER

"Is everyone ready?" Sawyer called out, looking over the team. Travis stood next to her, uncomfortably shifting around. He was about to do a very long range portal and she knew it was making him nervous. Anything could go wrong, but she trusted him with this. Even when he'd been high, he could take her across the continental United States without a problem. He could get them to Italy. She wasn't worried.

"Yes," Quinn answered, standing behind the entire team. They had gotten Travis and Thompson, then come home immediately. If they moved fast enough, they could slam Axel before he had any idea it was coming. The longer they waited, the more prepared the man would get.

"Thompson, are you sure you can stay here with Charlie for the evening?" Zander asked, and she waited patiently for the same answer Thompson had given for the last hour.

"I can stay."

"I'll be fine, young man. You go do this. End this." Charlie crossed his arms, turning his gaze off Zander and onto her. "Finish this, Sawyer."

"I will," she promised softly. Vincent coughed right after that, stepping forward. She let him take her place in front of the team.

There really wasn't much else for them to do. They had packed up everything they needed for a raid and an hour and a half long, very quiet walk. They weren't going in with too many people. The IMPO office in Rome would meet them once they reached the edge of Axel's current property. That office had no idea they were even on their way yet. They would get a call from Thompson when the team felt it was safe to let the world know what was about to happen. If the office had a leak, there wouldn't be enough time for Axel to get the information that the team was there.

"Travis, make the portal," he ordered.

Sawyer swallowed. This was the final mission. It was noon in New York. Sawyer considered the time. It would already be six in the evening in Italy and after sunset, which would have come much earlier thanks to it being the dead of winter. She pulled up her phone just to make sure, checking. Sure enough, the sun had set for Axel an hour before.

Dawn in Italy would mark a new day for her, and it was so close. She would either be dead, and so would everyone on the team, or Axel would be.

Less than twenty-four hours to go, and she found herself thinking about the wrong thing. What would come after this?

The portal drew her attention and she took a deep breath, bracing for the sensation of crossing through it, holding Sombra's leash to make sure she didn't lose the cat in the dark.

She went in before Vincent, first of the team. She had no idea what she would see on the other side. They had picked this location because no one had lived in it or checked on it in five years.

She closed her eyes as she went through and exited the other side to smells and sounds that haunted her. She stepped further away from the portal, Sombra walking pressed to her thigh. As she opened her eyes, she found herself in a place she never thought she would see again. A living room where she once had experienced the happiest and worst memories of her life.

And she couldn't help but think about what would come next. As she stood in the very place where another chapter of her life ended, she couldn't help but think.

She took the leash off Sombra and let the feline roam, checking the other rooms and hallways to make sure they were alone. Sawyer already knew they were, but the cat needed the reassurance.

Sawyer wandered into the kitchen. The house had been cleaned and repaired since her last memories of it. She found the wall. No longer was there cracked plaster. No longer was there a puddle of blood on the floor where he'd been.

It was like it had never happened.

And standing there, she considered a future, and something worse. Now, in this place, she realized the worst thing she could have.

She knew the team was through the portal. She could feel the disappearance of Travis' magic, meaning the portal was gone as well. But she kept staring at the wall.

"Sawyer?" Vincent called out softly.

She looked over her shoulder at him. "Right here," she whispered. "I lost him right here."

He only nodded, walking closer. None of the team had followed him. She could feel them waiting in the next room.

"Vincent...what are we doing tomorrow?" she asked softly. "When this is all said and done?"

"I...I was thinking I would talk to Thompson..." She could hear the unsure way he said the words.

"As I stand here, I can only think one thing," she admitted. "How much I don't want to do this."

The look on his face was what she'd expected. Shocked, confused. She could relate and knew the next question coming.

"What do you mean?"

"Henry wouldn't have wanted me to have to do this," she answered. "He thought I was so good."

"You are."

"Then why am I here to kill someone?" She knew the answer. She was just leading Vincent through her thoughts. "I'm here because the WMC ordered me to be. They could have sent us to recapture him. They could have had us lead another team to do it. They could have done anything, but they sent me here to kill a man."

"He's already sentenced to death," Vincent reminded her.

"He is, but they would have held a real execution, allowing him one of two options. To fall on his own sword or to be beheaded. Honorable...it would have been honorable. This is dirty. We both know it. I knew the WMC would ask me one day to be an assassin, and I'm so good at it. But I don't like the job." She took a deep breath. It was easier away from this place to cover it all up and pretend she could shoulder the task of killing time and time again. For the greater good, they would always probably say. The Druid was mad. Axel was a danger.

But it was still the only thing they would ever use her for.

And standing there, she wanted more. She wanted to be something else. She wanted to be something Henry looked up to. She wanted to be the Sawyer he saw.

"Are you having cold feet?" he asked softly.

"I'm thinking maybe I don't want to work for people who ask me to kill people for them. And I don't care if it's for personal gain or the concept of the greater good. Because in the end, it's still just killing people, isn't it?" She couldn't stand there, where Henry died, and say she could do it. She couldn't say she could kill another person. It all felt wrong suddenly. How was she supposed to move forward? When was it time to stop? When did the ends stop justifying the means?

Her hands were shaking as she braced them on the wall, tears in her eyes. Here, she could no longer lie to herself and say this was simple. That she had to do this to protect everyone.

No, the only thing she found in this place was suffering and regret.

Because no amount of violence and pain, no amount of killing was ever good enough. Not for Axel. Not for the WMC. All it ever did was weigh on her soul and break her. All it did was add another scar that she had to live with.

Because no amount of killing was ever enough, and in the end, it didn't help her truly protect anyone. In the end, she still lost this boy. In the end, she still lost Midnight.

In the end, it could still break her and lose the team.

"I can't do this," she admitted.

"Then I will."

The words shocked her enough to push off the wall. She spun to see the darker version of Axel's eyes. Vincent...

"Why?" she asked.

"Because I was never going to let you take this on

yourself," he explained. "I just want you to make it through this. He's mine to deal with. Not yours."

She couldn't open her mouth to explain how much that meant to her. She also couldn't open her mouth to explain how much she disagreed with his logic. A man should never kill his own brother.

"No," Elijah's clear tone rang out. "I knew there was something going on with you, Vin. Now I know. You aren't doing this either. Neither of you are killing him." The cowboy walked into the room, the team following.

She caught a glimpse of her jaguar in the shadows beyond the room, watching with bright gold eyes. Something akin to acceptance flowed through the bond. They would hunt, they would capture, and they would let others take the kill.

"Then who will?" Vincent demanded, turning to glare at Elijah.

"We'll give him the choice. Sawyer, you just said it. If this was done right, he would have been taken in front of the WMC. He would have been given a sword, while another waited on the side. He would either fall on his sword or the impartial Magi would behead him. The executioner would just finish the task, but it would give the Magi a chance to do it himself. We'll give Axel his." Elijah took a deep breath. "There's no way to avoid killing him tonight. We'll either succeed or we'll die trying, but we can make sure it's done in a way that doesn't...make us feel less than ourselves at the end. We can do this together."

"Who would be the one beheading him?" she asked softly.

"Me." Elijah said it with a confidence that rocked her a little. "I have the strongest swing. It doesn't have to be gruesome. It'll be quick and it'll be over."

"I don't want any of you-"

"Let us help carry the weight," Zander cut in. "Please, just this once."

She swallowed, leaning back on the wall. "You have," she whispered.

"So now we have a plan. The Rome office will capture and detain everyone they can. Our objective is to corner and secure Axel, then go through with an execution. The right way. The honorable way. Let's show everyone that this never had to be a knife in the dark." Elijah looked between them. "And it doesn't need to make you hate yourselves in the end."

"Why?" Vincent demanded. "Why does he deserve to have this choice anyway?" She heard a dangerous anger in those words.

"He deserves it because we're good men who will offer it to him. Because we're better than him and the WMC." Jasper's words rang clear. "And we'll always be better than them."

She covered her face. In this place, they were deciding how to avenge Henry and so many others. And they were going to give him the option to fall on his own sword.

Vincent leaned on the wall next to her.

"I'm leaving the IMPO," she finally said. "When this is over, I'm not going to work for people who ask me to kill for them."

"What will you do?" he asked. "What will I do?" She knew her decision was leaving him alone with people none of them could tolerate anymore.

"I don't know. There was a time when I helped people. In New York, those kids in that gym. Maybe I could find a way to do it legally." Something about that rang so good and true to her in that place. Help people before they found themselves in her place, or Henry's. Help people find their loved ones, like Zander and Jasper had searched for her for years.

Just helping people.

That sounded good. She had liked that part of the IMPO. Texas and those kids. She had helped them. She could keep doing that, but not as long as the WMC had their way. If she worked for them, she would never help anyone, just kill off the enemies of her government.

"Can I help?"

She looked up at him and nodded. "Yeah. I think that would be good for us."

"Me too," he agreed. "Because you're right. You're all right. The WMC is just another group that lives like Axel, but they lie to themselves and everyone else about it. He at least admits he does everything for personal power. And they're not good for us. Not even for me."

"Why did you want to stay after all of this to begin with?" Zander asked, obviously confused by the internal battle going on in their leader.

"I like the game," he murmured. "I genuinely like the game. I like finding a puzzle of a case and trying to work it out. The IMPO turned into my dream job, and even though it hurt all of you, I thought it would continue to work for me. That I could survive it like I survived growing up in the Castello family."

"Maybe tomorrow," she said, a small smile breaking out. "We can start some...private investigation firm. How does that sound? All the leg work, all the investigatory work. We could be great, you and I."

"We could be," he agreed softly. "Tomorrow, we'll talk about it."

"Tomorrow. I'll hold you to that." She elbowed him.

Here, where Henry died, they talked about their future, and for a moment, with a fight looming on them, she felt like it was right.

"Let's get moving," Elijah said, breaking them out of it. "It's time."

She nodded. Touching the wall one more time, she silently told Henry goodbye and began to walk away. She stopped, realizing one more thing needed to happen.

"Wait," she ordered them as they also began to leave. She reached into her bag and found the one thing she never wanted to see again. Her mask.

What had those boys said? One day she might need it? She wondered if they were right or wrong. What if their skill wasn't accurate?

Now, standing in this place, she had one more goodbye to say.

"What are you doing?" Quinn asked. They were all watching her.

She gripped both sides of it.

"Saying goodbye," she explained. Then, with all the strength she could muster, she snapped the mask in half, unleashing a wave of magic. Broken enchantments, releasing whatever magic that had been stored in the object to make it the perfect mask to hide one's identity.

She handed one half of the mask to Quinn. "Destroy that."

He took it and nodded. "Once we get outside," he promised.

She slid the other half in her bag.

Whether she needed it or not, she would no longer be Shadow. She was leaving that persona to rest just like Henry. Tonight, Axel only had one woman to fear. Her.

Finally, she began to walk back out of the home where

her entire heart had been shattered. Thanks to the men around her, thanks to Charlie, and Liam, and those kids in New York, those pieces had been put back together.

So while she walked, she didn't feel haunted.

She felt hopeful.

30

QUINN

uinn sent his boys out to get the lay of the land as they walked. They were in for a trek, the team. The twenty minute drive on country roads? They had talked it out, realizing it would be an hour and a half walk. He was fine with it, understanding the team wanted to come in without anyone knowing, but he was also concerned about them being tired on arrival. Or something finding them before they wanted to be found.

So he sent the wolves out, to stop that from happening to them.

"This is going to take forever," Zander complained, obviously trying to lighten the mood by not taking the mission seriously.

"Yeah," Sawyer agreed, not really taking the bait.

Quinn half-smiled. He was happy that she'd decided to leave the IMPO with the team, and convinced Vincent in the process. She seemed clearer than she had in a long time. Focused, but not a victim of tunnel-vision, rage, or sadness. There was a confidence in her stride that he felt like had been missing for too long, buried under the weight she always carried.

Something in that house had shifted something in her. Something tangible. It changed the entire mood of the team. They all felt focused and ready. Zander's joking complaints only proved that.

"We'll be fine," Elijah told both of them. "Forty-five minutes out, we drop a call to the Rome office, then keep moving. They'll end up there at the same time as us. We just need to keep moving."

"Elijah's right," Vincent confirmed. "We can handle this. We dealt with a worse walk before."

"Yeah, the Amazon was way worse than this. Let's never do that again." Elijah grinned back at the team. He and Vincent were in the front. Jasper and Sawyer were in the middle, and Quinn was in the back with Zander. They had wanted to stay close, even if it meant they were a group that could be hit at once. They would at least have each other.

"Agreed." Quinn never wanted to go back to the Amazon either, unless he was visiting a very specific waterfall with a very specific person. At the thought, he reached out and grabbed Sawyer's hand, moving up to walk beside her. Jasper looked across her at him, curious but not possessive. "Would you like to go back?" he asked her softly. "To the Amazon?"

"To see a specific waterfall, sure." She smiled in the night. He grinned, kissing her cheek. "I guess you were thinking the same thing?"

"I was," he answered. "Maybe one day. We'll talk about it tomorrow?"

"Yeah, absolutely," she promised, squeezing his hand. He didn't let go when the conversation dropped. He kept holding her hand as they continued closer to their final goal.

He liked the promise of tomorrow. They just had to finish tonight. That was it. It seemed so simple. Tomorrow, he could live a life that suited him. He could work to be a normal Magi without the added pressure of the IMPO, who expected him to use his strength to hurt people. He hadn't liked what he'd done, and he was glad Elijah called him on it. It reminded him of the good he had. He wasn't a monster. He didn't have to be a monster, not for anyone. His pack only wanted him to be himself. They didn't want his power without him. They wanted *him*. He could just be Quinn, and that made him deeply happy.

They just needed to all make it through the night.

Growing up, he'd only had his wolves to truly rely on. That was it. Two brothers that followed him everywhere and trusted him implicitly. But now, he had a real pack, one that only wanted his happiness.

"Do you think he knows we're going to hit tonight?" Jasper asked softly.

"No. I think he knows we're coming eventually. Tonight might seem too fast." Vincent sounded unsure of that.

"He could have accounted for Balian giving him up and does know," Sawyer offered, shrugging next to him.

Quinn nodded. That sounded right.

"He wouldn't expect us to jump into a raid the night after other raids," Elijah tried to reason. "But even if he does expect it, he probably doesn't expect we're bringing in the Rome IMPO office for this. Thompson is even getting people on standby who will portal into that office and flood it right before we call. We're coming in with triple the numbers that he could ever expect."

"We're going to outnumber him by a long shot. He's

probably got his ten best men and a few guards there. He doesn't like big groups. It would have given him away too easily. Plus, there were only a few men on satellite." Sawyer shrugged again. "There's no reason to think he's got an army hiding in the Villa with the vineyard and olives."

"To think he ran home," Zander scoffed. "Baby."

"He loves home, and if there's going to be a place he meets us, it'll be ground he knows better than us. It'll be home. We're knowingly walking into this trap. We should be prepared for anything." Vincent was no-nonsense and straight to the point. "He's a smart man, but I think Elijah is right. He might not have prepared for the sheer numbers we're going to bring down on his head."

"He might think we don't trust the rest of the IMPO to handle this with us. Or he's got a contingency plan." Sawyer was also straight to the point. "We need to stay focused."

"We have at least another thirty minutes before really getting worried," Zander reminded her. "We're in for a long walk before we even call in the reinforcements."

"Then let's drop it and keep walking," she fired back.

So the team did. They had gone over this plan a dozen times while preparing to leave. Quinn made a promise to Elijah he would do what he needed to do for survival's sake and nothing more. He would capture and detain, but not mindlessly slaughter their enemies.

Because they were better men than their enemies.

Quinn had never thought of himself as a good *man*, only a strong male. He'd always been out of place, out of time. But Elijah wanted him to be a good man and he would be that. It seemed like an amazing thing to be. It seemed like it was the thing they had really been trying to teach him. How to go from male to man and yet stay good.

The slow walk continued. They were in no rush. He

checked in with Shade, entering his wolf's eyes. His hand holding Sawyer's kept him grounded and moving forward as he ran with his wolf, showing him the world through new eyes. They were already at the halfway point, waiting and patrolling. There was nothing yet for them to be concerned about. Quinn gave each of his wolves a mental pat on their heads, promising a bone when they got home. When he pulled out of Shade's mind, he turned to Sawyer.

"Check with Sombra," he ordered, knowing she hadn't yet. The jaguar had bounded off, and there was a trust and independence between Magi and feline. She wouldn't have felt the need to check on her cat. "Vincent, check with Kaar."

"Okay," they answered at the same time.

Both of them had to stop for the process. He watched Sawyer's eyes go unfocused for a long time. Vincent was back in his own mind before her.

"Kaar is flying over the wolves. He seems to think they haven't noticed him." Vincent's tone was filled with humor.

"They haven't." Quinn shook his head, pushing that to his boys. The raven, above them. "They will soon. Do you want to send him closer to Axel?"

"No. Axel will take him out of the sky. He never liked Kaar. He's one of the reasons Kaar didn't have a name until you named him." Vincent shrugged. "Not that my bird ever really cared, but I had to keep him away from Axel or he could have gotten hurt. It was a sore spot. Axel thinks animal bonds are useless and weaknesses."

Sawyer bared her teeth, but Quinn knew she was still with her jaguar. It took another two minutes for her to come back as well.

"Of course he finds them useless and weaknesses. That man doesn't know a good thing even if it cut him open and left him to bleed out." She was snappy now. "Sombra is fine. She's ahead of the wolves. I've told her to pull back. I don't want to risk her being seen too soon."

"Good. I figured since I checked on the wolves, getting a read on those two would be useful."

"No, thank you. She's been sending me...weirdness through the bond. Well, after this, she and I will have tons of time to work it all out." Sawyer tried for a smile, but ended up only looking annoyed. "She's such a diva, guys."

"Oh, we know," Elijah muttered. Quinn began to chuckle.

"Kaar's in love with her," Vincent mentioned mildly.

"She wants to eat him." She snorted, rolling her eyes.

"Sounds like their Magi," Zander commented, coughing when he was finished, in a fake attempt to hide it.

"All right," Vincent snapped, now annoyed. "Let's keep moving."

They were all snickering as they walked further on. Vincent kept mumbling about the importance of the mission. Sawyer leaned over to him and whispered something about how they needed to take their last chances to smile for the night and Vincent understood. He was just blustering.

Quinn knew. He hadn't needed the explanation.

Finally, Vincent raised a hand as animals poured out of the night and to the group. Kaar landed on Vincent's shoulder, nuzzling his Magi's head. Quinn's own wolves trotted to him and lay at his feet, waiting for their next order. Sombra didn't come closer, prowling around the team, reminding him so much of Sawyer and how she tended to stalk around.

"We're here. Let's make this call. Elijah?" Vincent looked pointedly at his second.

"Got it." Elijah pulled out a cell phone set up with a secure line just for this mission. First, a call to Thompson, just to verify that men were on their way to Rome through a portal. Then a call to the Rome office with a single address and a name. Instructions. "Thompson, we're good?"

Quinn couldn't hear the response, but the cowboy's smile gave them all the answer they needed. The phone was hung up quickly.

"We're clear on that front. Vincent, you might want to make this second call."

"I will, thank you." Vincent took the phone and dialed. "Did you all know that when I joined the IMPO, I first went to the Rome office and they turned me away? It's still run by the same guy. He's never liked me. This feels good."

"Good." Sawyer was smiling as well. "This is it."

"This is it," Vincent agreed softly. Then his face changed, concentrating. "Assistant Director Romano, this is Special Agent Vincent Castello. My team and I are in a quiet area outside of Rome. Now listen very carefully. Do exactly as I say, and tonight we're going to capture Axel Castello and his closest inner circle. Before the end of the night, Axel Castello will be executed. Do you want to be a part of that? If your answer is no, hand this to your second in command and I promise you, he'll say okay."

Zander began to clap slowly. Elijah joined him. Soon the entire team was clapping, as softly as they could as Vincent nailed the man to a wall and got them the agents they needed to finish this.

"Now, my team will meet you there. See you on the other side, Assistant Director." Vincent hung up. "He's in. Full office. Thompson began flooding him during the phone call and even showed up, taking command. We're going in with a dozen more men than planned. Thompson was able to put two other teams on the task."

"Let's keep moving then!" Elijah clapped Vincent on the back and started walking. Quinn sent his wolves back out, ordering them to maintain a tight circle around the team, looking for enemies. Now was the time to focus. Sombra disappeared into the night as Kaar launched into the air.

Quinn was smiling as they moved forward. They could do this. They had the entire strength of the IMPO behind them. They were a team with resources and trust, and they were better people than Axel and his men.

They had each other.

And tomorrow, they would have new lives.

Thirty minutes later, they were within viewing distance of the Villa. A fifteen minute walk between them and their target. A shorter run, if they wanted to go in fast. They could hear the vehicles on the road now. An entire caravan of IMPO agents about to flood the property.

"Move out," Vincent ordered.

31

ZANDER

"**R**emember the game plan!" Elijah called out as they began to jog towards the compound. "We're going to work through who we need to, focused only on our objective! Let the small fry deal with the small fry!"

"Roger that!" Zander called back, hauling ahead of most of them. The first thing he did was reach out with his magic and begin bursting pipes inside the Villa, probably scaring everyone inside. He pulled the water to him, hard, making holes in the walls. He rarely did magic on that level, knowing he needed reserves to heal, but tonight seemed like a good time to go to his fullest. Quinn ran next to him, the earth beginning to rumble. A wall Zander had already wrecked crumbled away, opening the side of the building completely for the team and revealing several shocked members of the Ghosts.

There was no secrecy now in this mission. That was the idea. They wouldn't know they were being hit hard until it was too late for them to prepare for the force of the strike.

"Sawyer, let's go!" Vincent commanded. Zander glanced

back at them to see both sublimate and fly through the vegetation of the vineyard towards the house. He knew they would find and corner Axel before the rest of the team.

"Vincent, don't do anything stupid," he sent telepathically to their leader.

"It'll be okay," Vincent replied.

Zander let it drop, turning his attention back to the criminals running out to meet the team. He and Quinn would hit them first, which was fine. Zander reached out and tried to shove water at one to knock her down, but she grinned as fire erupted next to her. He would have felt bad, but he knew Elijah would take care of it.

And it didn't take long. Zander saw the exact moment when the woman lost control over the fire and Elijah gained it. With a booming, superior laugh, the cowboy behind him took the flames up higher and forced the Ghosts closer to the team and further from their backup.

"IMPO is here!" Jasper yelled out. Zander glanced over, and sure enough, there was a massive line-up of SUVs, all shielded, rolling up to the front door. The gates on the front drive were blasted apart and suddenly, the enemy realized they were going to be overrun.

Quinn raised the earth and captured the Magi in front of the team. Zander patted his shoulder as they slowed down. "Good job!" he praised.

The feral Magi only nodded.

They moved around the captured Magi, Zander checked them for any serious injuries. He didn't want any of them dying while they were handling the rest. Quinn had done amazing work. He'd engulfed them with dirt, packed tightly up to their shoulders. He'd then used dirt, slowly, to cover their eyes, to stop them from focusing on where to aim their magic. They were perfectly detained.

But then Quinn staggered.

He dropped, his eyes wide, his hands shaking as if the most intense pain he'd ever experienced took him over.

"Buddy?" Elijah stopped concerned, grabbing Quinn by his shoulders, going down to his level. "Quinn, what's wrong?"

"Scout," he gasped out. "He's under attack. I have to- I have-"

"Go!" Elijah ordered. "Go save your wolf!"

Quinn nodded but seemed incapable of moving. Zander swallowed, reaching out to touch Quinn. The bond forced pain from animal to Magi. He might be able to understand what happened to Scout if he could read Quinn. He'd never done it before, but now was the time to try.

"Damn it, Zander, throw a shield over us!" Jasper roared, ducking a fireball.

Zander cursed and did as he was asked, then grabbed Quinn hard, yanking him up. He felt for the pain, mental, but there had to be a source to it, there had to be. Mental pain where?

Legs. Which leg? A snap. Intense, bleeding.

"Quinn," he snarled. "His leg is broken. Something might have hit him. Go protect your boy and get him out of combat." He shoved Quinn, hoping it would jolt him out of feeling his wolf's problems. Zander didn't have an animal bond, but he'd heard how debilitating that pain could be. It was like it was happening directly to the Magi.

His shove was exactly what the Magi needed, and he shifted into a wolf and took off, howling. A black streak of a cat met him and followed, running hard.

Zander hadn't realized that Sawyer had left Sombra outside for support. Then again, Sombra did pretty much whatever she wanted on a normal day.

Then he felt his shield beginning to crack under the onslaught of three Ghosts. He turned back to them, seeing earth and fire getting tossed against the shield. He pulled from the busted pipes in the house and drenched the fire user, letting Elijah snap his fingers and send fire towards the two using earth.

"Let's meet the IMPO team," Elijah ordered. "With them, we can easily put everyone down and meet back up with Sawyer and Vincent. They'll hold Axel down until it's safe to deal with him."

"Roger that!" Zander pushed forward, reaching into his pockets for a set of brass knuckles. He wasn't a blade user like Elijah or Jasper. These would work for him, since it seemed like they were about to fight it out with the three Ghosts in front of them.

He approached a fire user, grinning. The Magi pulled his sword as Zander raised his fists to protect his face.

He let the other Magi attack first and dodged right of the blade, throwing a strong punch at the man's jaw, hearing a definitive crack. Then a shield appeared around the other Magi so Zander made his own. The next time the short sword swung, it tried to bury itself into his abdomen, only to bounce off his shield. Zander delivered two more quick punches then a solid kick with his steel-toed boot.

It didn't break the Magi's shield, but it did send him to the ground. While he was there, Zander kicked his sword away and jumped on top of him, slamming a fist into the shield wrapped around the Magi until it cracked and shattered. He had to be sure. Then he pulled a set of handcuffs, one of three he carried for the night, and snapped them on the Magi's wrist. Before he could stop Zander, the Magi was rolled over and both of his hands were held in place by the enchanted cuffs.

Zander didn't need to worry about this one anymore, so he got up and dove for more action, tackling the female Magi Jasper was fighting against.

Between him, Jasper, and Elijah, they secured all three, cuffed and inhibited, with no magic at their disposal and no way to fight back.

Without saying anything, they kept moving to the IMPO unit, where it seemed there was utter mayhem. No one was stopping them as they rolled up and saw one thing they weren't expecting.

One of the SUVs exploded.

Right after that? Zander witnessed an IMPO agent turn and stab another and leave him bleeding on the dirt drive.

They had dirty agents on the mission.

"Stop that man!" Jasper roared, running forward. Zander could only follow as they saw more and more agents turn on their brothers to protect Axel's people.

32

SAWYER

It took Sawyer two minutes to make the last portion of their journey to Axel's Villa as the world began to explode into drama around her. Vincent was sublimated next to her, in her, around her. It was like that first time they truly trained together. They hadn't done this since, but it felt good now, not uncomfortable. She could practically judge how he was going to move before he did and vice versa. They were one entity, directing and pushing each other to their goal.

They went into the first window they could find and reformed, jumping the two people they found there as water flew out of the walls. She knew Zander had planned on doing a lot of damage, and Quinn's earthquake hadn't helped, but she hadn't expected all of this. Then again, with so many Magi in a fight, everything was fair game. The building probably wouldn't be standing by the end of it.

Sawyer spared no time in knocking the guard unconscious without ever giving him a chance to fight back. Looking over, she saw Vincent had done the same.

"Good job," she told him, nodding in appreciation. "We

need to deal with Felix first. Axel is going to keep him very close, thinking I'll focus and kill him but leave Felix again."

"Of course. We've gone over this." Vincent straightened up, leaving the guard crumpled and sleeping on the floor. She followed him out of the room, silent and ready. There was so much magic in the air, she had the nagging suspicion that while she couldn't feel Axel exactly, he couldn't feel her either.

Maybe there was a chance she never needed Naseem. She would have to send him a gift basket or something full of contraband as an apology.

They found three more guards and Sawyer used a hand gesture to tell Vincent to hide. He stepped behind an open door, pressed against the wall. She cloaked and continued to sneak closer. She hit the first one right to the temple, not hard enough to kill, but enough to drop him without any resistance. She had to judge the strength of that perfectly. She hoped she had, not wanting to disappoint Charlie if she failed.

The next two looked around wildly, trying to pinpoint her. She kneed one in the balls when he turned towards her without realizing, sending him to the floor in agony. The third she grabbed by the shirt and slammed into the wall.

Vincent was by her side right after that and they kept moving like it never happened. Simple enough. They were both Magi who were born for this sort of infiltration work. She hoped Vincent's petrification came in handy during this as well.

Deeper into the large Villa they went. They could hear utter destruction outside and the earth shook dangerously, proving Quinn was up to something, and probably upset.

"Vincent?" Worry ran through her.

"I don't know. Let's hope he's maintaining control," her

lover answered. "I'm worried about him too. Elijah is the best for him, though."

"I know," she murmured, nodding. Elijah would know how to keep their wolf from going too far. Keeping Quinn from crossing that line, since he was so powerful, was so important.

They had to move quickly. The IMPO teams were there now, making a ruckus and being a major distraction to allow Vincent and Sawyer to sneak in. Sawyer continued to keep her mind focused on finding Axel's magical signature. The calm, coolness of it. She had grown cold in response. So long ago, he would make her a little chilled, but when everything went to hell, she realized being cold was so much easier than being hot. It was easier to shut down.

But not tonight. Tonight, she didn't want to be cold and controlled. She wanted to feel everything.

So she held nothing back, letting her magic leak and leave her, filling the halls. It wasn't as chilled as normal. She was going after a man who had made it chilled. Maybe one day, it would be warm like the sun.

"Sawyer?" Vincent frowned at her, obviously curious about what her magic was doing. She needed to come up with an excuse to and found one.

"Your magic has always been very subtle. Maybe I can mask it with my own. He'll only think it's me."

Vincent nodded. The reasoning she offered was accepted. Honestly, she was glad she figured that out as quickly as she had - and it was solid. If she kept Axel focused on her, Vincent would be an unknown, able to sneak around her and detain him.

Finally, she found Axel and another Magi, realizing it must have been Felix. They were moving quickly around a room, almost frantic and scattered. She paused in front of the door she felt them behind and held up a hand for Vincent to stop. He followed the order without question.

She pushed the door open, sparing not even a second to slow and blinked forward, elbowing Felix in the jaw and sending him flying back into a chair. Within another second, earth tried to grab her leg, breaking up from the floor beneath her. She blinked away from it and turned to find Axel on the other side of the room, his eyes wide, then turning angry. She blinked for him and tried to slam a fist into his face as she felt the subtle magic of Vincent come into the room as well.

Her fist met a shield, crunching hard against the unbreakable force. She bit back a yelp of pain and tried again as Axel swung an untrained fist for her as well.

Now she had training, though, and threw up her left arm to stop the hit. She didn't know how to get through his shield, and until she did, handcuffs would be ineffective, unable to touch skin.

"So you've come for me!" he taunted, shoving her back while she tried to judge how to deal with him. "I would say I'm surprised, but I'm not."

"You set this up," she reminded him. "You made this easy."

"I did." He smiled as more of his guards came into the room. She counted five, but there was a chance more were on the way. "And I knew you were bringing in the IMPO, but good try. You think most of them would help you? I own Rome."

She kept his focus as Vincent slowly moved behind him in sublimated form. Then the smoke stopped and began to slowly come apart.

"*SAWYER!*" Vincent's roar of pain screamed and echoed in her head.

"No!" she gasped. "Axel, stop, you'll kill him. He's your brother." She had to stop that. Maybe trying to reason with him. She didn't think it would work, but it was the first thing that came to mind.

"Maybe he shouldn't have been fucking you, then," Axel snapped, a vicious, angry look on his face. It was heartless and bloodthirsty.

And she wouldn't tolerate another Castello dying to this man. They were all doing good except for him.

She roared, ignoring the guards coming for her, and jumped for Axel. She connected hard enough to slam him into the wall and she felt it. The shield cracked.

Every ounce of rage she felt in every nightmare consumed her as she beat into his shield at his chest, cracking it further and further, while Vincent reformed, gasping for his life. She knew the feeling.

A guard, maybe two, grabbed her and threw, sending her to the floor. She jumped up quickly and felt the shield slam around her and the guards that were turned to her. She blocked punches and threw her own. She dodged swords, pulling her daggers to match steel with steel. She fought hard. Suddenly, Vincent was at her back, kicking one away from her.

"He's shielded us in here with them! We need to take them out, then break the shield if we want to follow him and Felix!"

Sawyer growled, this time burying a dagger into the side of a man. They were out to kill her and she needed to keep alive in the pit of death Axel had made. This was pure fighting now. She tried to keep the injuries to a minimum, but in the end, it was her or them.

She wanted it to be her. Her and the guys. She wanted a fucking tomorrow.

Axel knew just how to fuck with her, that was for sure.

Finally, the last one dropped and she leaned on Vincent, looking down at them.

"None of them are dead. I can feel IMPO agents, and maybe some of the team, coming our way. We need to break this shield and run after him. Kaar is keeping over him, watching where he's going."

"He won't have gotten too far, I think." She had a feeling this was about to be a hunt in the dark of the olive trees. They just needed to get the fuck out of the shielded bubble they were in.

33

JASPER

Fury raged in Jasper as he took down the first traitor he saw. The one who stabbed another and was going for the kill. He pulled his gun and fired quickly into the man's abdomen, with no sympathy.

Without missing a beat, he jumped up and kicked down at the man's head with his fake foot, knowing the impact would either knock him out or kill him.

Jasper had wanted to do this nicely, but he didn't have it in him to spare traitors. Not today. Not when his teams' freedom from this shitshow of an organization and world was nearly in their grasp. He wasn't going to let these people stop them from having a tomorrow.

It solidified his need to fix this. To make these people see justice before they could kill their allies, the other men and women who relied on them. One day, he was going to lead the damned charge against people like them.

"Who else? What other fucking agents want to get dirty?" he demanded, looking around at the chaos. First it was Jon, who betrayed them to Axel hoping he could get the glory of catching the criminal. Then it was the WMC, sending the team to the Amazon. Then an agent who Jasper only wanted to forget. That one who was helping Suarez. The one who caused the accident that nearly killed Elijah and stabbed Vincent.

"I got you, boy," someone growled. Jasper spun to see an angry, grinning man come for him.

"Why?" he asked, narrowing his eyes on the other man.

"He pays better."

Such a callous, awful answer. There wasn't even a higher motive. Just money. Just an opportunity.

Jasper charged him, calling up the wind to help him knock the other man to the ground, who quickly shielded to protect himself from the impact. Somewhere in the background, another vehicle went up in flames.

They fell together, rolling in the dirt and punches were thrown. Jasper was able to get the upper hand and threw a punch down on the opposing agent. He was kneed and thrown off. Suddenly there was more than one opponent. A boot connected against his ribs and sent him down before he could completely regain his feet. Another boot slammed against his head and he pulled it. He called the wind again, whipping it up like a tornado and pulled it over him, shoving them back, hopefully sending them flying.

He stood up slowly and sent the tornado at the first, the one who admitted that money was the reason. He sent it crashing into the man and it threw the traitor nearly twenty yards from him. Next, Jasper pulled on his magic and created an illusion, one that would only affect certain people. He marked those he could see for everyone else, making their black uniforms look red.

And he grinned at the shock they had when they were caught sabotaging their allies.

He was stopped by a hit to the back, someone tackling

him down. He struggled, looking for his sidearm and finding it gone. So was his sword. With his fake leg, he kicked at his attacker, causing a scream as bone broke underneath his steel reinforced and magically enhanced leg.

Then there was a rumble in the earth that continued to grow. A howl broke through the sounds of everything else.

"No." he gasped, hoping it didn't mean what it possibly could. Quinn had run off since Scout got hurt.

The earth cracked open in places, swallowing entire groups of people and pulling them under, including the one Jasper was trying to get away from.

And a howl continued through it.

"No!" Jasper screamed, scrambling to stand up and run for the rest of his team. He could barely see through the smoke billowing off the wreckage. He saw people struggling to not get swallowed by the earth. He stopped to pull an ally out, patting the man on the shoulder once before continuing his hunt for his team.

He found Elijah first, still and pale as he also must have realized what possibly happened. Behind the cowboy was an agent, blade drawn and raised.

Jasper didn't have time for that. He sent another blast of wind at the man, causing him to fly back into an SUV ten feet away. Something then forced Jasper to the ground, probably another another Magi with air manipulation. He didn't even care, only forcing himself up and ignoring the assault. He needed to get to Elijah, who was trying to get up himself, knocked down from the side of Jasper's attack.

"Elijah! Where is he?" Jasper called. The cowboy turned, looking relieved to see him, but the paleness didn't leave.

"I don't know! I have no idea if that was about Scout. I

think that's Shade's howl, since Quinn can't use his other abilities in wolf form."

"If we find Zander, we might be able to help him!" Jasper couldn't believe one of the wolves was gone. Not yet. There had to be a chance. Quinn would break without one of his boys. The team couldn't tolerate that sort of loss.

Jasper didn't know anything was coming until a massive black blur flew by and slammed into a screaming man behind him. He turned, almost in slow motion to find Sombra snarling and tearing into a man, looking feral and uncontrollable. She even snarled up at Jasper when he held a hand out.

"Where's Quinn?" Elijah asked the feline.

Sombra tilted her head and turned, taking off.

Jasper cursed. They needed Zander. "ZANDER!" he screamed out.

"HERE!"

Jasper tried to locate the sound and finally found a peek of flaming red hair in the smoke. He took off for the healer and grabbed him once he was close, pulling him away from an agent with minor injuries.

"Stop healing him, we need you!"

"Who?"

"I think it's Scout."

He watched something dawn on Zander's face, putting the pieces together. "Fuck. Let's go."

Together, they both hauled ass, Jasper leading the way, locked onto Elijah's Source, hoping to follow the hot trail of magic the cowboy left.

They found Quinn holding Scout close, fifty yards from the rest of the fight. Elijah staggered as he stopped, shocked still by the sight.

Jasper didn't stop though, unable to. He and Zander

passed the heart-broken and worried cowboy and went straight for the feral Magi, who snarled viciously at them.

"We're here to help," Jasper said calmly. "Quinn, let us help."

"I can heal him," Zander promised. "Please, Quinn, let me heal him."

"He's going to lose the leg," Quinn finally said, his voice rough and broken. "And he's so hurt. Some cunt tried to crush him. She tried to kill him. She laughed."

"Where is she?" Elijah asked, his voice full of retribution and pain.

"Dead. I stopped her magic to save him, but he's so hurt. He's so hurt. It's bad. It's so bad. I...I felt all of it." Quinn's eyes looked lost and confused. Jasper had a feeling he was swimming in pain. "He...he shut the bond down."

"What?" Jasper didn't know what that meant. The animals could do that?

"Let me heal him, Quinn," Zander murmured, kneeling next to the man and his brother, a wolf who had been with him for so long. Jasper looked back to Elijah, who raised a ring of fire around them. Jasper built it up, sending sweeping gusts of oxygen to it. No one would interrupt them fixing a family member. He knew Sawyer and Vincent would understand if they were late. He just hoped they would be able to control themselves until the team caught up.

Jasper reached out and ran a hand over Quinn's head, letting his fingers go through his hair. "Talk to me. Talk to me while Zander works." He needed to comfort his friend, and the best way to do that was distract him. Especially since Zander pulled out a long knife that Elijah was working to heat up, causing it to turn a little orange.

"I can't lose him," Quinn mumbled. "He's alive. I can feel

that, but he won't give me anything else. I didn't know he could do this. I didn't know. I would have let them stay home. To keep them safe, if I thought they would get hurt. I can't put them in danger like this. I can't-"

"Sh..." Jasper wrapped his arm over the feral Magi's shoulder as Scout yelped, cried, and whined, trying to move away thanks to the swift and hard blow Zander gave him.

In one swift, awful moment, Jasper suddenly wasn't the only family member with a missing limb. Scout was going to be a tripod if he lived through this.

Once it was done, Elijah was there, carefully cauterizing the wound as Zander began to pour magic into the small wolf.

34

ELIJAH

E lijah's heart broke in an instant when he saw Quinn over Scout's body, not realizing the wolf was alive. It broke again when Zander did the deed and removed the shattered and ruined leg before it could cause the wolf more problems.

His heart broke a third time as he heard Scout whimper and cry out as he helped Zander do what he could. Elijah figured if he could stop the bleeding with some heat and close the wound that way, Zander could repair internal damage. It was a gambit, a long shot, but he couldn't let his favorite man lose his wolf. No one on the team would ever forgive themselves if they lost Scout. None of them.

He didn't even stop his work when Sombra suddenly appeared next to him, smelling like smoke. He wondered if she jumped through the fire. He also wondered why she was with them and not her Magi. Sawyer had truly left her feline to fight battles and help them, a silent protector.

When he was done and it was all up to Zander, he sat back, letting the big cat press up against him. He rubbed her back, leaning into her as well, knowing she would send this back to Sawyer. That was a comfort unto itself. He hoped her hunt was going well. He hoped they were done and had Axel in custody for what would come.

Finally, Zander leaned back, revealing his face to them again. Elijah didn't like how washed out he was, the dark circles already forming under his eyes. Zander's magic wasn't deep. He couldn't do so much of it, which was why he pushed so far past it all the time. He would need a month to rest.

If they survived the night and succeeded, the healer would have it.

"Is he..." Quinn continued to hold his boy, rocking slowly.

"He'll live. He'll need more attention from an actual veterinarian, but he'll live through the night and more. I promise. Tonight, you aren't losing a wolf. He's just in for a long road to recovery. You'll need to carry him for the rest of the night, just to keep him off his feet."

Quinn nodded, shifting to readjust the wolf's weight. He stood up, Shade dancing around him, and held Scout with the utmost care.

"Elijah, pull the fire down," Jasper ordered, serious. "I think the tides shifted while we've been in here."

Elijah stood up quickly, vanquishing his flames with practically the snap of a finger. Sure enough, things looked calmer back at the Villa. Dozens of people were in handcuffs, lined up and seated, while agents walked around them.

"It's time to find Sawyer, then," he realized. "And Vincent. It's time to go end this, huh?"

"It's time," Jasper agreed.

"I can't use my telepathy to Vincent. I have nothing,"

Zander admitted. "I think even that will have me on the ground."

Elijah looked down at Sombra, who began to pull away from the group, always looking back. Of course she would know where her Magi was.

"Let's go," he murmured, nodding to the big cat. Sombra didn't seem like she was in a hurry, so they just followed, wondering what they would find. He reached out to Quinn after only twenty yards. "Let me, Quinn. Let me."

Quinn took a moment to consider the offer before gingerly handing the wolf to him. Scout was small, but he was still a wolf. Elijah held onto him, realizing just how heavy the load was. If he was having a hard time, he knew Quinn wouldn't have been able to keep it up.

Elijah just held on. He would carry the precious cargo. He would do the deed with Axel. He could shoulder this weight for the team. Always.

35

VINCENT

The earth rumbling violently told Vincent something was very wrong. Quinn. It had to be Quinn.

"Oh fuck," Sawyer mumbled, looking up.

"He's going to bring this place down on us!" Vincent yelled as the rumbling became cracks in the walls, floors, and ceiling. The Villa couldn't withstand the sheer might of his power. There was no way.

She grabbed him and they held onto each other. They had only been stuck by themselves in the shield for a minute, max, before this happened. They hadn't been ready for this to happen.

Sawyer gasped next to him. "Scout," she said, something awful to the name. "Oh no, Scout was really hurt, Vincent. Sombra just sent it to me."

"Fuck." Guilt ate at his heart for a moment. They had all come into this with clear heads, ready to win, ready to have tomorrow. He would never let it go if one of them, even one of the animals, didn't make it.

Pieces of the ceiling started to come down, slamming into the top of the shield, causing cracks.

"Sawyer, it's about to break - then we need to move before everything comes down."

"We're going to have to leave them," she told him, nodding down to the men on the floor, bleeding and weak. There were way too many of them for her to sublimate on her own and he didn't have the sheer power to make that happen.

"We won't tell him," Vincent whispered. "Do you understand me? He can't know."

"I understand. I don't want these guys to haunt him."

He was glad she understood where he was going with that order. He didn't want Quinn to think they were his fault. They weren't, not if Scout was hurt. He knew how deep that soul bond went. Even the thought of losing Kaar brought him pain, an unrecognizable loneliness he didn't want to consider.

No, he would never hold this against the feral Magi he loved like a brother.

Finally, the shield shattered over them. They both went into their smoke forms in a second and flew out of the back of the building as it came crumbling down. He reformed outside, coughing.

"Sawyer, you make the decision. Do we go after Axel or check on Quinn?"

He watched her eyes go unfocused. Her mouth opened, but it took another couple of moments for her to say anything. "Sombra is getting the guys. Scout is alive. She's going to make sure he gets healed by Zander. They've got it. She wants me to go hunting."

"Then let's go." He was ready for this. He had always wondered what it was like to do things the way she did.

Something about that drove him to help her find Axel when she was better suited to it.

And he still wanted to get his hands on his brother. He needed it. For everything. For everyone. His brother deserved to go down.

He touched the bond with Kaar, grinning as the bird showed him the direction to go. He took off running, knowing Sawyer would follow him. She kept pace easily, going through the trees like they didn't threaten to trip her up like they did for him. Vincent was beginning to fall behind, actually. She moved with ease, sublimating, phasing, and blinking through obstacles. He felt like a floundering youth compared to her.

He knew she was capable. He loved seeing her in action. He just felt a little put in his place. He had thought he could keep up. Now he wondered if she was being slowed down by him.

Probably.

Kaar sent him an image of a helicopter ahead of Axel. He ground his teeth, pushing to go faster. "He's trying to run!"

"He always was a coward!" she retorted, blinking even further ahead. He just followed as best he could, scared to use his sublimation to speed up. He hadn't enjoyed the pain Axel had put him through inside. He didn't want to take the risk.

He knew Sawyer saw his brother first, as a roar of rage and power came from her. He hauled ass, hoping to help her before she got hurt.

He arrived right on time to see her blinking behind Axel and delivering a swift kick to his back, sending him into the dirt. Vincent stopped himself from going after his brother, though. His eyes searched the dark and found another target, one who could come back to haunt them, and had before.

Felix.

Vincent sublimated now, knowing his brother was too busy with Sawyer. He flew after Felix, reforming to tackle the little man to the ground. He held one hand to the small Magi as he searched for a set of cuffs. He had Felix handcuffed before he could even put up a fight.

"Not this time," Vincent said to him, hauling him up. "You're going to sit and watch this."

"She can't beat him. She'll never really beat him. He'll win this in the end." Felix continued to throw out praise of Axel Castello as Vincent forced him to sit down. He turned to find Sawyer flying through two trees and slamming into a third.

"Sawyer!" he called.

"Little brother, I'm tired of this." Axel walked out of the dark. Vincent raised his chin in the same defiant way she always did. "Oh, you spend way too much time with her."

"Of course I do. She's everything to me."

"She's a slut. She's banging your friends too."

"Brothers," he corrected boldly. "She's in love with my brothers. And they love her back."

The look of disgust that his brother gave him showed him all the differences Vincent had needed to truly see. Every difference between good men and an evil one. Every difference between the men he chose and the one he thought was the last.

Vincent had family that never looked at him like that, or Sawyer, or each other.

"Brothers? Those...boys you keep with you? Your little precious fucking team? I'm your brother!" Axel was furious, insulted. "Family, Vincent! Family first!"

"You've never proven to be a good member of the family." Vincent shook his head. "No, I found a family. They're good men...and her." He glanced at Sawyer as she stood up, her face dark with emotions he could only try to understand. He understood better than most, but the depth of her feelings concerning Axel was something not even Vincent could truly comprehend.

"Children. You're all children playing house. Playing cop. You don't know, you've never known what's important in this world. None of you." Axel used his hands to collect and shape the air and earth together. Next water was added and the earth began to reform. A spike. "And I'm done playing games with children."

He flashed it with fire, hardening it in a second and launched it. Vincent dove, focusing on it with his telekinesis as he moved out of its way. He couldn't take full control over it, not being as powerful as his brother, but he was able to send it into a tree, shattering into a million pieces.

He righted himself, and ran for Axel, jumping a crack opening in the earth as his brother tried to trip him up.

He watched Sawyer dive in for him, slamming Axel to the ground, cracking the shield he had around himself. Vincent was amazed she was able to keep going. With both fists, she roared and slammed them down on the shielded man. Vincent watched her be lifted and get thrown back.

He took her place, taking Axel into the dirt when he tried to rise up. His brother had made a mistake in not making a bigger shield. Axel was never one for open combat; it had always been Vincent's favorite thing to do. To learn to use his body and his magic in tandem to achieve a physical goal.

No, Axel had always thought he had better things to do than that. His magic would always save him.

They rolled in the dirt together. Axel was still in peak physical condition. Vincent had the training, though. They hit a tree and Vincent was over his brother, who smartly forced him into the tree, slamming his head. Dazed for a moment, he slid off Axel, able to feel the warm, red blood dripping down the side of his face.

Axel connected a boot to his back as he tried to crawl away and get his bearings. Sawyer was back in the action right at that moment, lunging and stopping him from delivering more abuse.

Vincent stood up slowly, dizzy. He watched as this time, she didn't let go. She grabbed onto the shield around him at his wrists and blinked, tossing him into a tree.

The shield shattered, and the air left Vincent's lungs as he watched Axel throw up a wall of fire and force Sawyer away from him.

"He's going to burn out soon," she yelled to him. "He's not as deep as either of us."

"I know!" He needed a plan. "Sawyer!"

"What?"

"Get angry." He hoped she understood his meaning, and she did. She turned back to the man they had to defeat and everything near her became frosted in the cold Italian night. It flooded his sense of everything. He could feel the cold, and only the cold.

And he sublimated, gently shifting into the form even as his rational mind told him it was a gamble. Vincent didn't like gambles.

This one just made sense.

Sawyer continued to try and attack his brother head on, daggers drawn and ready for war.

"Why didn't you wear your mask, Sawyer? You were always better at being a shadow than a real person."

"Because you get to be afraid of *me* tonight," she answered from beyond flames before blinking back in. It was quickly becoming a battle of how many times she could throw herself. Vincent crept closer.

"Where's my brother? He's hiding around you, isn't he? Using your magic as a distraction?"

Vincent mentally began to curse; he was within only a few feet of Axel. The flames had been no obstacle. Now he just needed to make it the remaining distance. He reformed right behind his brother, reaching for his spare cuffs. They had all carried multiple pairs for this night, just in case.

Axel spun, eyes wide. Sawyer wrapped her arms around his, holding him there, in place.

"You sneaky piece of shit," Axel growled. "And what now? Are you going to stab me while this fucking whore holds me for you?" He tried struggling, but Vincent knew his magic was depleted, or close to it. He formed a shield and Sawyer broke it by slamming him into another tree with a quick blink, then blinked back with a dazed and panting Axel.

Vincent said nothing as he reached for one of his brother's wrists and snapped the handcuff on.

His brother sneered. "Really? I'll get out again - you know that, right? I was nice this time and let you all play. Next time, I'll just have you killed as quickly as I can."

"No," Vincent answered. He resisted the need to take one of her daggers and sink it deep in Axel's chest. He wouldn't do that. Not tonight. Better men. They were better men than Axel and would always work for that. Killing him now would weigh on them for the rest of their lives.

He deserved some honor, because the team was willing to give it to him.

Vincent pulled away and Sawyer tossed Axel to the

ground. They sat in the ring of fire, hoping it would die soon. It was fueled mostly by magic, but already a few of the olive trees were catching.

Sawyer's eyes were unfocused when he looked at her.

"The team," Sawyer said, panting. "The guys are on their way. Sombra is leading them, though she's taking her time."

"That's good," he murmured, reaching out to her. They leaned together, their foreheads touching. Once the team was here, they were going to end this together. He ignored Axel. He wasn't going anywhere. Not this time.

36

SAWYER

The fire was gone first, engulfed by the earth, along with the half a dozen trees it had jumped to. Next, she saw them. Sombra led her men to her and Vincent. Her family.

"Isn't it funny how the past keeps coming back?" she asked Axel as she knelt and began to scratch her beautiful cat under her jaw. "Unescapable, really. You bury the hatchet and leave the handle sticking out. A Southern American saying."

"Shut up," he demanded.

"No," she whispered.

"So, this is it." Jasper looked at her sadly. "It's time."

"It is," she murmured, leaning into her jaguar. It was time. For Midnight. For Henry. For James. For everyone she never knew or met that had been destroyed by Axel. For families wrecked and left to bleed out from their losses. For the loss of innocence and goodness in the world.

It was time.

"Turn me over. Let's get this over with." Axel scoffed. She knew it was an act. One look at him and she saw fear in his eyes. He was playing this off like he'd been arrested again, but everyone knew better. He knew tonight he was going to die and there was nothing else.

"Antonio, tonight you have a choice," Vincent said as Zander hauled Axel to his feet and moved him to a clearer area.

She stood up slowly and saw Elijah carrying poor, sleeping Scout. Jasper and Quinn didn't move far from the cowboy either, as if they were each ready to help carry the load. Shade stayed pressed against Quinn's leg, as if it was the only way to make sure his brother was okay. Kaar swooped down and landed on Vincent's shoulder, a scene she'd seen now a hundred times. It was practiced and easy, in a quietly impressive way. She had wondered how Vincent got used to it, since the raven wasn't small.

They watched Zander push Axel back to his knees.

"And what is that choice?" Axel finally asked. She walked closer and stayed on her feet, even though she suddenly felt tired. Elijah gingerly laid Scout next to her, walking closer. It left her with Quinn and Jasper, both hovering over the wolf. Sawyer pushed a suggestion through the bond for Sombra to go comfort them, but the jaguar denied it. She would stay with her Magi now. Images of a little black house cat.

This was personal for her too, in a very strange, far off way.

"Elijah will hold a sword. You will have your own. You have two options. Fall on yours or fall to Elijah's."

"That's honorable of you," Axel bit out. "Really? Not even the WMC made me that offer. They just wanted to behead me. Not that I blame them."

"We're better people than the WMC," Elijah answered, pulling the longsword from the sheath on his back and over his shoulder. It sang a beautiful haunting note of steel and death.

"Are you?" Axel snidely retorted. "Yet you'll still kill a man on his knees."

"I'm sorry," Elijah answered calmly. "But I won't let you hurt anyone else by forcing them to fight you and kill you in cold blood. There's no need for assassins. There's no reason for brothers to kill brothers."

Sawyer swallowed a lump of emotion in her throat, holding back tears at those words. Vincent looked at her across the clearing. He mouthed one word.

Anything.

They would all do anything for each other. If that meant Elijah would bear the sword that would cut off Axel's head, then so be it. No one would ever hold it against him.

In the end, it was Axel's decision after all. It was all Axel's.

Vincent pulled his short sword and tossed it on the earth in front of Axel. Now, only Elijah was within range to be attacked.

Sawyer knew the cowboy would win. Axel wasn't good with a blade. He'd always found them beneath him.

"I'll give you to the count of twenty," Elijah told him as he picked up the sword and put it into position. He angled it before Axel so that all he had to do was fall forward, letting it slide into his heart. It was sharp enough that it would go easily.

"Now?" Axel asked softly. She heard the moment of defeat. She knew in that moment that even he knew it was absolutely over. If he tried to run, he would die. If he tried to fight, he would die.

There was no reason for a blaze of glory. The last stand of Axel Castello was already over.

She heard Felix, further away, calling out for them to stop. He would pay them anything to not kill Axel Castello. He loved the man. She nodded to Jasper. He walked away to get Felix and drag him closer. He could have a better view of everything at the end and know there was nothing he could do about it.

"Tell me where Henry is?" Vincent asked softly. "If you want to go out on one good note, tell me where he is."

Axel looked up but said nothing. Sawyer nodded at Elijah this time.

"Twenty."

Axel was breathing deeply. Felix was sobbing.

"Nineteen."

She counted the seconds mentally now, ignoring Elijah's words. She could keep a twenty second count.

Axel wasn't moving. He was staring at Vincent, considering the question.

"We were never good to each other, not after Mom died," Vincent said in Italian. "I never got to know him. I want to at least say good bye. If you do this, I'll bury you next to him, if that's something you want."

Sixteen.

Sawyer's throat threatened to close at the touching offer Vincent just made to a monster. One last plea for humanity.

Fourteen.

The silence was deafening. He said nothing, only turned his gaze on her.

Ten.

Vincent didn't try to ask again. The clarity of Axel's eyes in those last seconds was terrifying. She was locked in olive green, wondering if he had finally found something while facing down his own death. Some important piece of the puzzle he was always missing.

Five.

"He's buried in the Castello Mausoleum without a name."

Sawyer's heart stopped.

He didn't say it to Vincent.

He said it to *her*.

Three.

She would never know the answer to her question, her private wonder about what was going on in his mind.

Axel closed his eyes.

He fell forward.

She couldn't believe her own.

One.

He was already dead when Elijah's sword came down and made sure nothing could ever bring him back.

She fell to her knees, staring at the head that rolled away. That was it.

They stood in the grove of olive trees on the cold winter night without saying a word. Felix was loud and awful, whimpering and crying out for his master. He could put Axel back together, if they just let him go. He would give them anything.

None of the team moved. Sawyer stopped looking at Axel's body after a while. Someone sat down next to her.

"We should take his body back to the other teams," Zander whispered calmly.

"Not yet," she murmured. "We should burn his body before leaving, too."

"Why?" Jasper asked that time. Quinn fell to the earth next to her. She reached out and gently petted Scout.

"I want to watch the sunrise," she answered.

Vincent and Elijah joined last, finishing setting up the

funeral pyre. Her cowboy went to her back while Vincent lay in front of her. They all faced east.

It was hours later when others found them, took Felix away and left them alone with Axel's burning body again.

And slowly, steadily, they watched the sun rise again.

"Tomorrow," she whispered for them. "It's finally tomorrow."

It wasn't over yet. Sawyer straightened her outfit. The team around her all still smelled like smoke and fighting, but none of them were letting this get pushed off. They had done it, and it was time for the WMC to follow through with their promise. The only two missing? Scout was with a Magi vet, making sure there was nothing that would cause him permanent problems except the leg, and Kaar, who refused to come into the building.

She thought she would feel elated, but she didn't. She wasn't sad either. There was a contented feeling in her chest. A feeling of readiness that had settled it. It was over. There was just one more thing to do.

They had driven to Rome before leaving Italy. Sawyer had written Henry's name on his place and Quinn used his magic to make sure it was cut into the marble. Forever, Henry's place would be there.

And forever, her place would be with the men who helped her find him and put him to rest. Who helped her get to this day, this moment.

They walked into the Council Chamber again. Only a few rough weeks since the last time they entered. This time, there was no heavy feeling in the room. If they tried to betray her, she would go public with everything that had happened and walk away from their employment anyway.

No, they owed her this.

"Miss Matthews, it's an honor to see you on this day," Councilwoman D'Angelo greeted her. "And I understand that...it's time."

"It is," she agreed. They had Thompson pass along that message. He said none of the WMC disagreed.

"And his body?"

"Cremated and the ashes left in the Castello Mausoleum next to his son's tomb." It was Vincent who answered, since it was his idea. It was the best they could do. Elijah had burned him hot and they had refused to leave until they had something to take to Rome. It had made them very late getting to New York, but she didn't care.

"Of course." Dina nodded quickly, then looked around to the other Council members. They were still down those who had been killed, but elections were going to begin for emergency fills any day now. They had been working on that while the team went after Axel. "We're all in agreement. Sawyer Cambrie Matthews, this is the official record of your crimes." Dina motioned to a table set in the center of the room. "Next to it is the official declaration of your pardon. You will keep the original. All you need to do is sign it, and an enchanted copy will be stored here for as long as the WMC reigns."

She didn't wait. She walked evenly across the room, grabbed the pen they had waiting and signed her name to the document. Next to it wasn't just the record of her crimes, but also the deal she had made with the IMPO. It lit up in flames and disintegrated, leaving her with only her pardon. The deal fulfilled at last.

Looking back for a moment, her mind wandering, it

hadn't really been that long. Caught in July, the deal was made in August. Or did she go all the way back to the original? That if she helped defeat Axel she would be free...

It didn't matter. With this piece of paper, she was redeemed. Oddly, it struck her that maybe she never really needed it, except to those who didn't matter. The ones she always wanted with her loved her with or without it.

She lifted the piece of paper and held it out. Waiting patiently, she watched Vincent walk forward and take it. He was the guy who kept all this stuff for everyone. She trusted him with it far more than carrying it around for herself.

Thompson began to clap and so did everyone else in the room, including her men, the only ones she had eyes for. Everyone else could fade away, but their pride and happiness mattered most. She wished they'd had time to get Charlie and Liam before the small event. It wasn't even public. Quietly, later in the day, the WMC would release a press statement that Sawyer 'Shadow' Matthews was pardoned and left to her own life. What she would do was her decision.

She already knew. Only the team knew their plans.

"Special Agent Matthews," Dina murmured kindly. "It's been a pleasure to know you. I hope we continue to have a working relationship."

"Actually, we won't," Sawyer answered, smiling politely. She reached into her back pocket to get the wallet she had grown accustomed to carrying around. Inside was her official IMPO ID and the badge. She held it out. "I'm not interested in the IMPO. I'm not sorry about it, either. You all can find someone else. There's a ton of great agents, once you weed out the corruption."

People gasped. Thompson began to sputter as Dina took

her badge slowly. Sawyer looked back at the guys, grinning like a fool.

Together they pulled their own badges out, and dropped them in front of Thompson, who looked like he would have a heart attack.

"We quit," Zander told him, smiling as well. "It's been fun. Not really. We're retired as of today. We expect to see our pensions for years of good service in the coming months."

"Of-of course," Thompson agreed quickly, looking between them.

Sawyer didn't say anything else. She reached down and felt the thick black fur of her jaguar. Together, they walked out of the Council Chamber, her team surrounding her.

They were going to go find tomorrows together. Tomorrows without the strain of the IMPO. Tomorrows without the possibility of Axel.

Just tomorrows.

37

SAWYER

Fifteen Years Later

"I THINK our time is up, Sawyer."

Sawyer groaned. "Why? This is the best hour of my week. You know that."

Her doctor chuckled. "Yes, well, we've discussed several times how you shot yourself in the foot by ending up in a long-term relationship with five men. What were you thinking?"

"For a man, you are always surprisingly perceptive about your own sex." She eyed him.

"For a woman who's been with five men for over fifteen years, I figured you would have figured us out by now."

She started to laugh. *Fifteen years.* "Oh fuck, they lost their minds when I turned forty, Doc."

"I know. I remember you stomping in, mad and needing to rant. Still that scared of being forty?"

"No, I've gotten used to it. The body slowing down and

such. It was bound to come eventually, after everything I've put it through." She didn't try to move. She knew Doctor Larson had no one after her. He never did. He always left extra time in case she wanted to wait around and refused to leave.

"You didn't have much to talk to me about today," he noted. "Are you sure there's nothing? I can spare a moment to hear it."

"No, not this week. Be proud of me. I haven't had a nightmare in a year. I bet one will pop up eventually, but it's my new high score."

"And how's the rest of it?"

"Well, to be honest, I'm wasting my time with you because I don't want to get home during homework time. Plus Zander needs a ride home from work. You know, the holidays are over and everyone is getting back to their regularly scheduled busy lives."

"It happens to everyone," he reminded her.

Sighing, she nodded. Yeah. It was a normal thing, a normal life.

She loved it.

"I'll leave you then, if my company is so awful." She said it playfully, teasing the older gentleman.

"If I thought your company was bad, I would have denied you as a patient fifteen years ago," he retorted, closing his notebook. Solid point. "Tell them all hello from me."

"Always," she promised, grabbing her bag.

She strolled out of his office, and then out of the building. She was in her car in record time, knowing she was behind schedule. She was done with Doctor Larson thirty minutes before, and that had been the third time he'd tried to get her out the door. Zander was probably freezing outside the gym now, wondering if she forgot about him.

She could never forget, though. She had tried once or twice. Somewhat sadly, Zander Wade was a permanently attached tumor on her heart that she couldn't get rid of. Not like she had ever tried very hard, but she had made a token effort.

She didn't find Zander outside the gym, tucked in the center of the Bronx. She frowned, parking as she considered where he could possibly be. No one had told her through a text that they had picked him up.

She saw what was going on when she walked into the gym. He was chatting with some youths, all in their early twenties, probably fresh out of Academy. IMPO agents.

She didn't say anything as she leaned on the door of the training room. One of them tried to start a play fight with Zander, causing him to react. She grinned as Zander, while very good, was outdone, landing on his back in a painful slam.

Age was making all of them a little slow. Seeing this every so often made her remember that.

"Don't hurt my man," she ordered loudly from her place. They all turned to her and she saw Zander's pained expression turn into a grin.

"We were just having some fun before closing it out for the day."

"And here I thought I was late," she replied, raising an eyebrow. In his forties, she expected some maturity from Zander. Not all the time, just some. He was better than he had been in their wild youth, the same ages as the agents he now trained, but this was still Zander Wade. If he could make something a good time without anyone getting hurt, he would.

"Well, guys. I need to head out. The lady calls."

"Wait, is this your girl? The..." One of the agents studied her.

"My name is Sawyer," she told him softly. "And anything else you've heard...well, read the old news and draw your own conclusions."

"Yes ma'am." He nodded, looking away. "Well, sir, same time tomorrow?"

"Of course." Zander wrapped an arm around her but she didn't try to move with him, letting him finish his work. "Same time, and bring pads. We're going to work on some things you all might enjoy."

With that, she turned him to leave. She caught a glimpse of Charlie and Liam, waving. She was due in the gym the next day as well and would catch up with them then. They seemed to have their hands full with nearly a dozen young boys and girls, probably all between the ages of seven and ten. She felt a pang of sympathy, but not a big one. Tomorrow she was dealing with the teenagers because those two said they couldn't keep up like she could. They had abandoned her with the passionate youths with smart mouths and half brains. She loved them, but they annoyed the shit out of her sometimes.

On the drive back to their home, she heard Zander groan and looked at him with concern.

"You shouldn't let them throw you around like that anymore. You're taking a beating."

"They like to test me and see what kind of man once helped Shadow gain her pardon. You're still a legend, Sawyer, and nothing is ever going to change that. So I put up with them. It's not like their teams will ever be as good as ours." Zander gave her a tired smile. "Think we'll make it home *after* homework time?"

"No, but I keep hoping," she answered, beginning to laugh. She wasn't going to touch the other topic with a ten-foot pole. Every new group Zander trained was the same. Who was this guy with the retired, once-famous assassin as a lover? They had never gotten married, but the relationship was clear. She had never married any of them, but it changed nothing. They were her men, her family, and the world knew that. It was once an argument, where she tried to fight the reputation, tried to fight that it would be used for and against all of them.

At forty, she was done caring about it. One day she would be old, and she could admit she would still be a legend. She would be a legend among the Magi long after she died, she bet.

"I hope Elijah handled that. He's good at it."

"He is, isn't he? Too bad Quinn is the worst influence ever," she reminded him. That made him laugh too. "Do you think Jasper can pick you up tomorrow? Or maybe you can pick him up? Force him to get home earlier than dark o'clock?"

"I can try," he promised. "You know how he is about his job. He loves it."

"He does," she agreed, humming an agreeing note as well. "But you know, just because the holidays are over doesn't mean we don't have family dinners together at least once a week."

"Let's be real. You want him home earlier because he's the best at homework time."

They were inside the house and they knew immediately that homework time was absolutely not over.

"JAMES HENRY MATTHEWS! You will finish your homework before your mother gets home!" Elijah roared, obviously out of patience with whatever her son was doing today. She winced.

"But Uncle Elijah! She's going to be home soon, and I want to go play with the wolves before it gets dark!"

"You would already be done and playing with the wolves if you focused and did what I asked you."

"It's boring! I know all of this already!"

Oh, he was really going for every excuse he could. She and Zander walked towards the dining room gingerly, knowing Elijah's fatherly temper would explode if they caught James' attention before he let them. Sure, James Henry was her son, adopted by her at birth, and raised by her, but that didn't stop the men she loved from becoming his fathers. He called them uncle for the world, but they all knew he meant dad. The world just wouldn't understand, and her men? They never took it personally. They loved him to pieces.

So interrupting homework time would only spell a worse day for Elijah and James. It was the only time any of them had to get on to him. He hated homework. He was a grade ahead in school already, only nine years old, and he still seemed smarter than everyone else in his class. Hell, half the time she wondered if her boy was smarter than her.

She peeked into the dining room, smiling. She waved at Elijah, who groaned.

"James, go say hi to your mother." He sounded so defeated, his head falling down to the dining table with a thump.

"Mom!" James jumped up, looking her way like it was the first time he'd ever seen her. Her heart swelled like it did every day she came home to him.

He leapt for her and she caught him, realizing quickly

he was getting too big for the action. She spun them in a quick circle before putting him down and cursing old age.

"Why isn't your homework done?" she asked him immediately, knowing Elijah would get onto her for being too soft if she never brought it up. She was a soft mom, no doubt; it's why she hated homework time. She also just didn't care about homework. She thought it was a pointless endeavor meant to drive kids insane. Her son was evidence to the fact.

"Uh..."

"Yeah, now the excuses end," Elijah muttered, making Zander behind her laugh harder than she would have liked.

"Uncle Zander!" James purposefully diverted, leaving her to hug Zander without really giving her an answer.

"Sounds like Jasper is going to need to give you a talking-to when he gets home, isn't he?" Zander was chiding and yet also sweet. He lifted her boy and walked him back into the dining room. "Tell you what. If you get all your homework done, you can play with me on the game, how's that? It's too cold outside to play with the wolves anyway."

"Okay..."

"I heard my name?" She jumped and turned to see her lawyer. Jasper was looking between them. "I just walked in. I was able to pull out early, but I had to practically run or I'm sure they would have found some way to keep me for another three hours."

"Ah, is my Councilman upset with his schedule?" she asked, leaning over to him. He chuckled, kissing her like she wanted. "I was just saying to Zander earlier that I wanted you to make sure you got off early enough for dinner."

"I'm sorry. The holidays being over, me being the junior Councilman...The WMC likes to keep me busy."

"I hope it's a good busy," she said, running her fingers

over the front of his perfect suit. The campaign hadn't been a good busy. She had a young, very young boy. James had been six and didn't understand why the other kids looked at him funny and people were always taking pictures of them. He didn't understand that Jasper was running for the WMC to make it better, so that nothing bad could ever happen to someone. So no one had to go down the same path his mother did to have a good life.

She had always loved Jasper, but the day he publicly got on worldwide television and told the world that he loved her, and they had a family...Her heart had been so full. They had tried to use the team against him in a smear campaign. So they all sat down and told their story one more time. In the end, Jasper became one of the Councilmen representing North America on the World Magi Council.

It was the perfect job for him, and he was making all the changes she knew *his* parents would love if they had lived to see their son's work.

"It's a good busy," he promised, kissing her again. "Is it still homework time?"

"It is. Please? I think Elijah is going to have a heart attack. He needs your help."

Jasper nodded, walking to the dining room. She ducked out, leaving those three to get James back on track. She needed to say hello to her last two men before getting on with starting something for dinner. She wondered which she would pull in to help with the task, even though it was her day on the schedule. One of them always did help. She was guessing Quinn today.

She went out the back of the house and whistled. Sombra tore out of the woods first, coming straight for her.

"Hey girl! Thanks for staying home today." She went

down to kiss the top of the jaguar's head. "Keeping them out of trouble for me, right?"

Sawyer didn't get a clear answer and then found herself in a pile of animals. Shade was on her before Scout, who was the most excited but a bit slower than he used to be. They licked her face like dogs, something Quinn had taught them. When she'd asked him why, he said boys deserve dogs.

He wanted them to be a part of James' life, to help make it more normal, but still a brand of unique that only the team could offer him.

"Get off of her!" Quinn called out. "Boys!"

The wolves retreated and she reached out blindly, Quinn grabbing her hand to help her up.

"Hey!" she greeted him brightly. He just took her cheeks and pulled her in for a slow, delicious kiss.

"Need help with dinner?" he asked softly.

"How did you know?"

"James isn't done with homework time. I'm only allowed back in the house if you needed me. I was hoping." He gave her a small, guilty smile.

"So you're the reason he's not done." She really should have known.

"He wants to play," Quinn tried to explain.

She just shook her head. "He needs to learn that doing his homework, doing the small tedious work is just as important as doing the big work."

"Not like you reinforce that."

"That why I left Elijah, Zander, and Jasper with him. Where's Vin?"

"He's been in the office all day," Quinn told her. "Will you bring him out?"

She kissed his cheek as they walked back into the house. "I always do."

She left Quinn in the kitchen to get dinner started. She had to go find her last lover and her business partner.

They had done it. Now, the home office didn't say Vincent and Elijah on the outside of the door; it said The Castello-Matthews Private Investigation Firm. It was their shared office, where they worked to find missing children, sometimes assisting the IMPO on select, very select, cases. They helped build cases against abusive spouses and found homes for orphans, and they made no distinction between Magi and non-Magi. They did a lot of work for free, just wanting to help out.

It helped they both loved the mental work and it was rewarding.

But sometimes, Vincent would go too deep. Sometimes she did. They made a promise to always pull each other out when it happened. This wasn't the game with Axel. There were none of those anymore, not for them. And if they both went too deep? They had a loving, large family to save them from themselves.

"Vincent?" she called softly, opening the door.

"Oh." He jumped at her sudden appearance, his feet falling from his desk. "Sawyer. How was your day?"

"Good," she commented lightly, taking him in. His hair was messy. Like everyone else, he was beginning to get those laugh lines, the wrinkles that showed he lived a good life. This scene took her back though, back to the beginning. "You weren't in here..." She looked down at his crotch, smiling.

He laughed, shaking his head. "I was trying to nap my way through homework time," he conceded, spreading his arms in defeat. "Can you blame me?"

"Most of the time? No. Sometimes? Yes." She met him in the middle of the room after he turned on some music.

"Welcome home," he said softly. "Dinner?"

"Quinn's on it," she told him.

Slowly they danced until Elijah stomped in and stole her, claiming he needed to give her a proper hello since James was now secure with Jasper and Zander helping him. Vincent let her get stolen and she didn't fight the cowboy as he held her tight. Later, they would have a large meal with the people they loved. She would tuck James Henry into bed, then find one or more of them waiting in her room.

And tomorrow it would be the same.

And the day after.

And the day after that.

It was a good life, where the sun's warmth was only matched by one thing.

The warmth of the love she had filled it with.

DEAR READER,

Goodbye, Sawyer.

This series was my dark love letter to strength, to overcoming the darkest parts of ourselves and the world around us. Now that's it's over, it's left a hole in my life. Sawyer was always a treasure to write, through her successes and her mistakes. Through her worst times and her best. I hope, I truly hope, that you have loved the experience as much as I have. There will be no more full length books. There are no plans for follow up novellas. So again I say, goodbye Sawyer. Goodbye Vincent, Elijah, Quinn, Zander, and Jasper.

Thank you all for reading this series.

Reviews are always welcome, whether you loved or hated the book. Please consider taking a few moments to leave one and know I appreciate every second of your time and I'm thankful.

And if I still have you... Sign up for my newsletter for exclusive content and information on my upcoming works! I send it out monthly. Newsletter Signup!

Or you can come join me in being a little bit crazy in The Banet Pride, my facebook reader's group.

ABOUT THE AUTHOR

KristenBanetAuthor.com
Kristen Banet has a Diet Coke problem, smokes too much, and cusses like a sailor. She loves to read, and before finally sitting to try her hand at writing, she had your normal kind of work history. From tattoo parlors, to the U.S. Navy, and freelance illustration, she's stumbled through her adult years and somehow, is still kicking.

She loves to read books that make people cry and tries to write them. She's a firm believer that nothing and no one in this world is perfect, and she enjoys exploring those imperfections—trying to make the characters seem real on the page and not just in her head.

facebook.com/kristenbanetauthor

twitter.com/KristenBanet

instagram.com/Kbanetauthor

bookbub.com/profile/kristen-banet

amazon.com/author/kristenbanet

ALSO BY KRISTEN BANET

Witch of the Wild West

Bounty Hunters and Black Magic

Age of the Andinna

The Gladiator's Downfall

The Mercenary's Bounty

Complete Series

The Redemption Saga

A Life of Shadows

A Heart of Shame

A Nature of Conflict

An Echo of Darkness

A Night of Redemption

Wild Junction

The Kingson Pride Series

Wild Pride

Wild Fire

Wild Souls

Wild Love

The Wolves of Wild Junction Duet

Prey to the Heart

Heart of the Pack

ABILITIES

Note:

It's important to remember that every Magi is unique. Two Magi could have the same ability and use them in different ways due to their personal strength levels.

Legends are the exception. (ex. All Druids are exactly the same in power and abilities.)

Example: Sawyer can walk through a thick wall with Phasing but another Magi may only be able to pass through a thin door and push an arm through a window for a short time.

Ranking Code

Common- C, Uncommon-U, Rare-R, Mythic- M

- Air Manipulation-C- The ability to manipulate the element of air or wind.
- Animal bonds-C- The ability to bond with one to five animals. A person with this ability can feel emotional currents of the animal and use the animal's senses by inserting themselves in the animal.

- Animation-C- The ability to make inanimate objects do tasks for time periods. I.e. Dancing brooms
- Astral Projection-R- The ability to use a non-corpeal form that can be seen by others. Renders physical body unconscious.
- Blinking-U- The ability to teleport short distances (10-20 feet) within eyesight.
- Cloaking-U- The ability to become invisible.
- Dream walking-U- The ability to walk through the dreams of others and go through the person's subconscious to reveal secrets and memories to the person.
- Earth Manipulation-C- The ability to manipulate the element of earth.
- Elemental Control-M- The ability to manipulate all elements and all combinations of them.
- Enchanting-C- The ability to enchant physical objects with specific properties, such as never losing a sharp edge for a blade.
- Fire Manipulation-C- The ability to manipulate the element of fire.
- Healing-C- The ability to heal physical wounds.
- Illusions-U- The ability to alter an individual's perception of reality.
- Magnetic Manipulation-U- The ability to control or generate magnetic fields, normally a very weak ability.
- Mind reading-M- The ability to read another's mind, normally requiring touch.
- Naturalism-C- The ability to control the growth of plant life and identify plants' properties.
- Petrification-R- The ability to freeze a person's

movement without harming them by touching them. Can also be used to harm, by stopping basic life function for a short time.

- Phasing-C- The ability to walk through solid objects with concentration.
- Portals-U- Temporary holes through time and space to travel nearly instantly. (Not time travel)
- Reading-R- The ability to read the abilities of others, requires touching the individual.
- Shape-shifting-U- The ability to take the form of one animal, not chosen by the Magi.
- Shielding-C- The ability to create force fields that block physical interaction.
- Sound Manipulation-U- The ability to manipulate sound waves.
- Sublimation-R- The ability to transform into a gaseous form, normally looks like black smoke.
- Telekinesis-C- The ability to move objects physically with the mind.
- Telepathy-U- The ability to send thoughts to others for silent communication. Cannot invade the thoughts of others. This is a one-way ability, unless the other person also has telepathy.
- Tracking-R- The ability track a single individual by having a item that belongs to said individual.
- Water Manipulation-C- The ability to manipulate the element of water.

IMPO AND IMAS

Both organizations have a rank structure, but the IMPO is more relaxed than the IMAS.

International Magi Police Organization

Officer - Low level law enforcement officer

Detective - Case investigator isolated to the city they are assigned to.

Admin - Paper pushers, secretaries, assistants.

Lawyers - Self-explanatory. Magi lawyers who are experts in Magi law.

Special Agent - Case investigator that travels globally and carries out long-term investigations such as crime lords, internationally known criminals, and serial killers. Report to handlers and always work as a team.

Handlers- Normally retired Special Agents that act as liaisons between the Asst. Director/Director and Special Agents.

Assistant Director - Second in charge of the IMPO.

Director - The head of the IMPO. Reports directly to the WMC.

International Magi Armed Services

Chain of Command: 1 is the lowest rank, 7 is the highest.
Generals report directly to the WMC.

Enlisted

E-1, Private (Pvt)
E-2, Private 1st Class (PFC)
E-3, Lance Corporal (LCpl)
E-4, Corporal (Cpl)
E-5, Sergeant (Sgt)
E-6, Gunnery Sergeant (GySgt)
E-7, Master Sergeant (MSgt)

Officer

O-1, Lieutenant (Lt)
O-2, Captain (Capt)
O-3, Major (Maj)
O-4, Lieutenant Colonel (LtCol)
O-5, Colonel (Col)
O-6, Lieutenant General (LtGen)
O-7, General (Gen)

IMAS Spec Ops

Special operations (or special forces). Teams are named for
gods and goddesses of war. (Ex. Team Ares or Team Mars)
Soldiers of all ranks may apply. Only the best succeed.

Made in the USA
Las Vegas, NV
16 February 2021

18000879R10232